THE SEA HAWK

Praise for *The Sea Hawk*

'The swashbuckling tale of Kanhoji Angrey, the seventeenth-century sea admiral who fought the British and the Dutch with admirable courage and gallantry, has inspired generations. And no one tells it better than master storyteller Manohar Malgonkar. It's wonderful to see this classic revived sixty-five years after its original write.'

—Pritish Nandy, poet, journalist and maker of films

'Kanhoji Angrey's is the second most important story, after Chhatrapati Shivaji, that unfolded in the rocky and rough terrains of Maharashtra. Kanhoji, however, isn't as lucky as Chhatrapati Shivaji. The visionary warrior who laid the foundation of India's navy has largely been forgotten. *The Sea Hawk* is the story of the late Maratha fighter narrated by one of the master storytellers of our times, Manohar Malgonkar. This captivating real-life fiction is a must-read for students of history and the common man alike. It's a tribute to one of our unsung heroes.'

—Girish Kuber, author and editor, *Loksatta*

'This lively and well written account of a famous Maratha naval commander ... sweeps the reader along at a rattling pace.'

—*The Times Literary Supplement*, London

'Very readable ... full of historical information.'

—*The Times of India*

'A book of historical biography so skillfully done.'

—All India Radio

'A rare combination of history and literature.'

—*The Hindu*

THE SEA HAWK

Life and Battles of Kanhoji Angrey

With an Introduction by
Shanta Gokhale

MANOHAR MALGONKAR

HarperCollins *Publishers* India

This edition published by HarperCollins *Publishers* 2022

HarperCollins Publishers India, Cyber City, Building 10-A, Gurugram,
Haryana-122002, India

www.harpercollins.co.in

2 4 6 8 10 9 7 5 3 1

P-ISBN: 978-93-5629-082-2
E-ISBN: 978-93-5629-083-9

Typeset in 10.5/14 Adobe Caslon Pro at
Manipal Technologies Limited, Manipal

Printed and bound at
MicroPrints India, New Delhi

FSC MIX Paper FSC™ C218906

This product is made of FSC®-certified and other controlled material.

HarperCollins Publishers, Macken House, 39/40 Mayor Street
Upper, Dublin 1, D01 C9W8, Ireland

Contents

Introduction

In these times of blurred categories when biography sells as fiction, it is important to note how Manohar Malgonkar describes *The Sea Hawk: Life and Battles of Kanhoji Angrey*. In the first line of the preface, he says, 'This is a true story, so far as a re-constructed story can be a true story.' Thus, in a single line, he vouches for the two elements that go to make a good biography. The narrative material must be authentic and the biographer must reconstruct it in such a way that it reads like a story.

Malgonkar's sources for the facts of the story are impeccable. He thanks 'Sardar C.S. Angré, the present head of the Angrey family, who was good enough to discuss the family history with me,' and 'Rear-Admiral B.S. Soman, Flag Officer, Bombay, [who] went through the manuscript and obtained the maps and the charts of the period from the Indian Navy.' Rear-Admiral Soman was soon to be appointed Flag Officer Commanding Indian Fleet before retiring as Chief of Naval Staff. Our reading of the story reveals other sources that include letters preserved in the East India Company archives and several contemporary writings such as James Douglas's *A Book of Bombay (1883)*.[1]

The preface also tells us that the idea of a book on Kanhoji Angrey was suggested to Malgonkar by Peter Jayasinghe, the founder of Asia Publishing House. The book Malgonkar wrote for

1 Douglas, James. *A Book of Bombay* (Bombay Gazette Steam Press, 1883)

him, *Kanhoji Angrey, Maratha Admiral: An Account of his Life and his Battles with the English,* was published in 1959.[2] Twenty-five years later, in 1984, he recast the account as a biography of Kanhoji Angre and published it under its present title. Long out of print, it comes to us now in this fresh edition.

A question that all biographers since Lytton Strachey have had to ask themselves is, how much fiction can I allow myself to use in telling this story. Hard-line biographers disapprove of fictional elements like invented dialogue and imagined insights into the subject's thoughts and feelings. Too much invention is clearly ruled out when the biographer's subject is alive and looking over her shoulder. However, when the subject is a figure from history, who is to challenge a biographer's freedom to invent? The only limit imposed then is by the amount of authentic material available to hang invention on.

One might put Irving Stone at one end of the expansive spectrum that stretches between fact and fiction. *The Agony and the Ecstasy*[3] begins with thirteen-year-old Michelangelo making a crayon sketch of himself and saying, 'My head is out of rule, with the forehead overweighing my mouth and chin. Someone should have used a plumb line.' Such invention was possible because of the prolificity of portraits available to the writer, painted by those for whom Michelangelo had probably sat. At our end of the spectrum, all Manohar Malgonkar had as pictorial references of Kanhoji Angrey, were innumerable approximations of his likeness made by artists who had never set eyes on him. They generally depicted a heavily whiskered man in the robes and turbans of the times, with a curved Maratha sword in one hand and a round Maratha shield in the other,

---

2 Malgonkar, Manohar. *Kanhoji Angrey, Maratha Admiral: An Account of his Life and his Battles with the English* (Asia Publishing House, 1959)

3 Stone, Irving. *The Agony and the Ecstasy: A Biographical Novel of Michelangelo* (Doubleday, 1961)

but otherwise varying in feature and stature from the anodyne to the heroic.

Astute storyteller that he is, Malgonkar, therefore, begins his tale not with a description of Angrey, but of the land for which he was to become the uncontested master. This narrow strip of land known as Konkan stretches along the western coast of India, from Bassein in the north to Karwar in the south. The region had not changed much between Angrey's time and Malgonkar's, allowing the writer to describe it with specificity and vigour: 'A rocky, unfriendly coastline, its few natural harbours guarded by forbidding black fortresses; its soil, a brittle mixture of crumbling rock and red laterite and broken sea-shells, too poor to sustain its abundant population; and yet a landscape miraculously green … A palm-fringed Gauguin seaboard, its green picked out with flamboyant reds and yellows, hibiscus, mohawa, gulmohur, silk-cotton.' The passage evokes in prose what the early twentieth century poet, Govindagraj, evoked in poetry, translated as: 'Rugged land, hardy land, land of rocks and boulders / Delicate land, tender land, land of fruit and flowers.'

Malgonkar then goes on to describe Angrey's times of cut-throat conflict between the Portuguese, the English, the Dutch and the Siddi, with the Marathas and Moghuls hovering threateningly in the background. Where is Kanhoji Angrey in all this, one asks. The answer comes in a single clinching statement that presents him to us, not in body, but as a force: 'If, however, in the first years of the eighteenth century, any of the foreign powers along the coast of Konkan had been asked to nominate a common enemy, none of them would have picked out either the Moghuls or the Marathas. Their answer would have been the same: Kanhoji Angrey!'

This storytelling device is reminiscent of the half curtain that screens the first entry of major characters in Kathakali. Moved up and down in turn, the curtain allows us glimpses of the character's feet and head gear. Soon hands appear above the curtain in mudras reflecting the character. When our breath can be held no longer, the curtain is folded away and the character is revealed in its full glory. So it is with Malgonkar's Kanhoji Angrey. Dimly glimpsed at first through folk tale and legend and early exploits at sea, which eventually lead to his elevation as *Surkhail* (Admiral) of the Maratha navy, Kanhoji Angrey is revealed in his full glory almost halfway through the biography as a mature man of thirty-eight. 'A man of incredible stamina, bold, brave and independent; yet, a man of patience and cool judgment; a man who exuded a hairy-chested maleness, who laughed uproariously and danced and sang with his men, and who never hesitated to fling the same men into assaults against unknown odds; a man with the sternness and mental discipline to punish a spy or a traitor by ordering him to be trampled under an elephant's foot, and yet with the softness of heart to undertake to look after the man's wife and children.' In one stroke, Malgonkar conjures up for us a man of many parts, full of the contradictions and complexities common to human nature. He ends his description with James Douglas's felicitous lines from *A Book of Bombay*, '… born and begotten of the sea, full of its wild and savage energy … rocked to and fro by its waves into hardihood and indomitable pluck.'

And yet, 'The British called him a land-shark who devoured everything on land as well as on water; they called him a robber, pirate, villain, rebel and sent emissaries to wait upon him with instructions to speak to him "civilly" and make a fabulous offer to buy him off. The Portuguese called him even worse names and yet likened him to Barbarossa and sent him expensive presents.'

A contemporary British chronicler named Clement Downing, digs into Angrey's birth story and comes up with what he claims is the original account. '[His] father was an Arabian Cofferey (Zanzibar slave) who... renounced the Mohammedan faith...was discharged from the Moghul service for misdemeanour… joined the Grand Sidey (Siddy) and was of great service to him so that he gave him his own sister to wife.' Having turned a Maratha into a

Zanzibar slave, the gentleman proceeds with: 'The present Correngey Angria is not the true begotten son of his father, but an impostor: this Angria was the son of a Cofferey man and woman that were... (the Siddy's) slaves.'

The reason why Downing felt free to play around with Kanhoji Angrey's birth story is because no authentic account of either his birth or early years exists. Malgonkar fills the lacuna with a legend that has him living with a Brahmin who, having spotted him one day sleeping under a tree, his face protected from the sun by a five-hooded cobra, predicts a great future for him. Malgonkar points out drily when compared with Downing's 'original' account, 'the legend is perhaps less far from the truth—even if we do have to swallow five-headed snakes.'

Personal details, therefore, constitute only a small part of the story. The greater part belongs to the sea battles that Angrey fought to keep his hold on Konkan and the forts that the Maratha king had charged him to guard. Battles could erupt anytime and anywhere in the region save during the four months of the monsoon. Then guns fell silent, sails were furled and ships huddled on beaches under cover. While the rain raged, 'The rulers and the ruled, the invaders and the invaded cowered behind high walls and shivered, and made propitiatory gifts to the rain-god to lift his siege.'

In conversations with friends and critics, Malgonkar always maintained that one's work could be authentic only if one wrote out of first-hand knowledge. Having himself led an adventurous life, he had first-hand knowledge of several spheres of activity. He had been an army officer, a tea garden manager, a miner and a big game hunter. He also had an insider's knowledge of princely life, his grandfather having been the Dewan of the former princely state of Dewas.

The specific knowledge that Malgonkar brings to Kanhoji Angrey's story, comes from his stint in the army. His understanding of military strategy gives him an acute insight into Angrey's tactics, even when they do not involve a battle: 'A year later, he had decided on his course of action. He sailed with seven *gallivat*s and camped at the mouth of the Pane River, close to Bombay: just that and nothing more. No shot was fired, no rude notes exchanged, no ships seized and no villages plundered. His mere presence was now enough to block off Bombay's communication with the mainland. All shipping between Bombay and the mainland was paralysed. Then, after doing sentry-duty at Bombay's door for a week, Kanhoji Angrey withdrew his squadron and sailed off on a cruise. It was a triumph of pure tactics, like a clever move in a game of chess.'

Malgonkar's descriptions of sea battles carry a charge that can only come from a writer who knows intimately what he is talking about. Equally, when he decides to step back from the nitty-gritty of battle, he can give us vivid descriptions of the general setting and the mood: 'Imagine then, a squadron of the Maratha navy, two hundred and fifty years ago; a *ghurab* being towed with incredible speed towards some doomed ship, being brought into position so that its big guns could fire into the rigging at point-blank range; and then the *gallivat*s, twenty oars dipping in unison on each side, their blue and green pennants fluttering in the wind, their enormous trumpets blaring, their tomtoms beating the tattoo of death, and the swordsmen swarming their decks yelling the frightening Maratha war-cry "Har-har Mahadeo"...'

The Sea Hawk: Life and Battles of Kanhoji Angrey is thus both authentic history and rip-roaring tale. Conflict—the soul of drama—is also the soul of this story. The story is constructed in short, sharp chapters, often ending with a hook that compels us to turn the page. It is a story that stands with both feet planted firmly on the ground and no flights of fancy. In our land of legends, folk tales and hagiographies, the balance Malgonkar achieves between his obvious admiration for his subject and his commitment to veracity, makes it both an informative and a refreshing read. His prose, criticized in his time for not being 'Indian', does not hurt our ears today. Indianness was a criterion used seriously to judge art, literature and drama in the first decades after Independence. Today, the field is open to every kind of prose, including Malgonkar's British English, which flows with natural ease and is eminently readable.

Mumbai
May 2022

Shanta Gokhale
Author and translator

Preface

This is a true story, so far as a re-constructed story can be a true story. To those, in particular, who know Kanhoji Angrey as 'Angria the Pirate', I would like to say that I have really tried to describe events exactly as they happened.

It was Peter Jayasinghe's idea. 'Would you like to write a book about Angrey?' he asked me. I am thankful that my somewhat natural initial hesitation did not make him change his mind.

My thanks are due to Sardar C.S. Angré, the present head of the Angrey family, who was good enough to discuss the family history with me, and took an interest in the project right from the start.

Rear-Admiral B.S. Soman, Flag Officer, Bombay, went through the manuscript and obtained the maps and the charts of the period from the Indian Navy. The Navy also gave me its kind permission to make use of these maps. To the Indian Navy and to Bhaskar Soman, my grateful thanks.

Dinkar Kerkar did all the battle-maps reproduced in this book. I would like to take this opportunity of assuring 'Cracker' that if the rest of the book measures up to his work, I shall be more than satisfied. He was helped with the maps by Dr. Shri Nandan Prasad of the Historical Section of the Ministry of Defence. My sincere thanks to both.

My thanks, also, to Mr. Y.G. Naik and Mr. C.H. Gore of the Asiatic Society of Bombay, for letting me keep some of their books longer than I would have dared to ask for; to Professor B.K. Apte of the Deccan College, Poona, for putting me on the right track of the sources of information; and to Mr. K.P. Parakhi, also of Poona, who sells rare books at the most unbusinesslike prices.

—M.M.

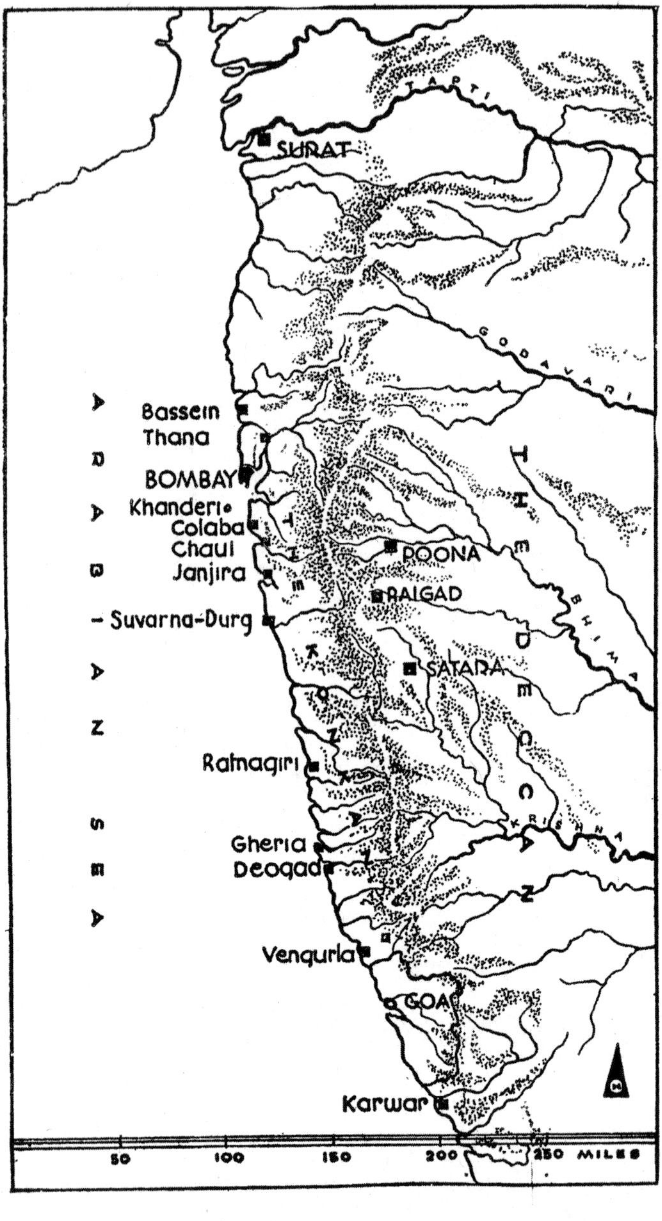
SURAT
TAPTI
GODAVARI
Bassein
Thana
BOMBAY
Khanderi
Colaba
Chaul
Janjira
Suvarna-Durg
POONA
RAIGAD
SATARA
BHIMA
Ratnagiri
Gheria
Deogad
KRISHNA
Vengurla
GOA
Karwar
ARABIAN SEA
KONKAN
THE DECCAN
50
100
150
200
250 MILES

THE KONKAN

1

The Land

Geographically, this story is confined to the Konkan, a thin sliver of the western coast of India, usually painted green on the map to show low-lying coastland, beginning at Bassein in the north and ending at Karwar in the south—a narrow, rugged coastline 400 miles long but seldom more than 40 miles wide, bulging slightly at the throat to take in the city of Bombay, like a snake that has just swallowed an oversized frog.

Geologically, it is of fairly recent origin, having been thrown up, as the scientists explain, from the bottom of the sea by a volcanic upheaval, or, as the Hindu priests pronounce, created by the god Parasurama by pushing back the ocean a hundred *yojanas* when he discovered that having gifted the whole earth to Brahmins, he himself had nowhere to live. Whoever is right, you can see for yourself the twin furrows made on the face of the cliffs by the ebb and tide of the sea where it used to beat in those not so ancient times, high up where the eagles soar.

A rocky, unfriendly coastline, its few natural harbours guarded by forbidding black fortresses; its soil, a brittle mixture of crumbling rock and red laterite and broken sea-shells, too poor to sustain its abundant population; and yet a landscape miraculously green where the cashew-nut and jack-fruit trees grow wild in the hills and the incessant salt breeze helps to produce the best mangoes in the world. A palm-fringed Gauguin seaboard, its green picked out with flamboyant reds and yellows, hibiscus, mohawa, gulmohur, silk-cotton; a land of slender women, graceful as the betel-palms, and wiry, agile, jockey-sized men, fond of wine and music, quick to anger and passion, creatures of the sea and the shore, equally at home on land or water.

To the west lies the Arabian Sea. On the east, the land is cut off just as abruptly by the sheer wall of mountains known as the Western Ghats, or just 'the Ghats'. For a moment, neither the plains nor the mountains give ground, creating in their combat a chain of steep, jagged peaks which successive waves of invaders have caused to be crowned with pickets and watch-towers built in the days when man felt secure only on the tops of mountains.

This land, the Konkan, forms part of the Deccan, which, in those days, was the name given to roughly the western half of the peninsular portion of India. The Deccan is the land of the Marathas.

It was an era of turbulence: warfare was endemic. But in the Konkan, for four months of the year, there could be no war. Early in June, the wind rose to a roar of warning, and a final clap of thunder heralded the south-west monsoon. By this time, the field had been cleared for Varuna, the rain-god—campaigns halted in mid-stride, sieges lifted, and ships pulled up on dry land, their hulks oiled to keep them from rot. By July, the wind and the rain had won total victory, the waves rolling rocks the size of haystacks and the rain whipping the cliffs in merciless clouts, swelling up the thousand rivers of the Konkan into mad, roaring monsters, killing hundreds of animals caught up in the open and destroying the spirits of men. The rulers and the ruled, the invaders and the invaded cowered behind high walls and shivered, and made propitiatory gifts to the rain-god to lift his siege.

2

The Man

Unite the people;
fill their minds with a single thought: Freedom!

—Ramdas

For close on four hundred years, the Deccan had been ruled by Muslim kings, its people content to serve their alien masters. Then a great man called Ramdas had rallied them together in a call for independence, and an even greater man called Shivaji had led them, and had won back for them a large portion of the Deccan from the Sultans of Bijapur, setting up a new kingdom and a new dynasty.

At the time of this story then, the Marathas had, at long last, begun to rule over the greater portion of the Deccan.

In faraway Agra, there were the Moghuls, lords of an empire which was then a fifth portion of the known world, but at no time masters of the Deccan. The reigning Moghul was Aurangzeb, sixth in that great line from the founder, Babar, and also destined to be the last of the Great Moghuls: a scholar; an ascetic in the midst of the most fabulous splendour, a religious fanatic dedicated in the years left to him to the utter destruction of the new power in the Deccan: the Marathas.

The long, bitter war between the Moghuls and the Marathas had already begun; a war with heavy religious undertones, Muslims against Hindus. Aurangzeb had shocked every Hindu mind by destroying their holiest temple: that of Kashi-Vishweswara in

Benares. Submission to him did not merely mean exchanging one Muslim ruler for another. It also involved the renouncing of religion or, as an alternative, the acceptance of the dreaded *Jezea*, the tax imposed on all non-Muslims. As Aurangzeb's campaign sank deeper and deeper into the black cotton loam of the upper Deccan, *Jezea* became a bigger and bigger monster—towards the end, all non-Muslims had to pay ten per cent of their annual incomes in *Jezea*.

The Marathas had tasted freedom and realized that there was no substitute. They rose as one man to defend it. Their virulence stunned the invader, for they were fighting for the preservation of everything they held sacred.

On the sidelines, watching the conflict of giants with hawklike eyes, and at the same time prospering as traders can prosper only in the midst of war, were the European powers: the English, the Portuguese, the Dutch.

The English, still uncertain of themselves, were wholly occupied in maintaining their precarious toe-holds in India; courteous to both the Moghuls and the Marathas, paying tributes and compliments to both with equal facility, playing it safe; playing it safe, and yet being English, also keeping an eye open for the main chance.

More aggressive than the English, more sure of themselves, just as ready to take sides in the conflict as to defy both the Moghuls and the Marathas, were the Portuguese; their penetration into India already two hundred years old, their absolute overlordship of the sea unquestioningly accepted by all the ruling powers in India. The Portuguese were the most powerful European power in India. The Moghuls claimed to rule the land; the Portuguese claimed to rule the sea. If their power was already on the wane, no one knew it yet, least of all the Portuguese themselves.

The Dutch too were there, but the Dutch were on the way out, slowly giving ground under British pressure, concentrating on building an empire elsewhere. They hung on to the bits and pieces of their dwindling estates in India for another hundred years, but their bigger settlements were in another part of India. In the Konkan itself, the Dutch were not much in evidence.

None of the European powers was on friendly terms with the other, and particularly between the British and the Portuguese there was constant tension and bitterness. In their own part of the world, they were perpetually at war with each other, and out in the East, they quarrelled amongst themselves with the heightened intensity of expatriates, each gloating over the discomfiture of the other, bitterly resentful of each other's triumphs.

If, however, in the first years of the eighteenth century, any of the foreign powers along the coast of Konkan had been asked to nominate a common enemy, none of them would have picked out either the Moghuls or the Marathas. Their answer would have been the same: Kanhoji Angrey!

To neutralise the man they chose to call a pirate, the British spent every year a sum equivalent to a million pounds at today's value. They dug a ditch around the town in Bombay as a protection against him, and then they erected a wall behind the ditch. They even joined hands with their bitterest rivals, the Portuguese, in an effort to destroy him.

The Portuguese made friends with him and fought with him in turns, and all the while they secretly intrigued against him and helped his enemies. The Dutch lost an implausible number of men the only time they attacked one of his forts, and then they called up a squadron of warships all the way from Batavia in an effort to bring him to terms. In the meantime, they studiously went out of their way to avoid his waters.

The British called him a land-shark who devoured everything on land as well as on water; they called him robber, pirate, villain, rebel, and sent emissaries to wait upon him with instructions to speak to him 'civilly' and made a fabulous offer to buy him off. The

Portuguese called him even worse names, and yet likened him to Barbarossa and sent him expensive presents.

No ship could pass the Konkan waters singly, and not even warships were safe. They went in convoys, armed to the teeth, and a custom grew among the trading communities to present a purse of five hundred sovereigns to the captains of the escorting warships if they brought their convoys safely to port. The custom lived long after the Angreys were finished.

Whoever ruled the land, whoever lorded it over their trading settlements surrounded by ditches and walls, there were no two opinions as to who ruled the waters of the Konkan coast during the first years of the eighteenth century: Kanhoji Angrey.

3

Cobwebs on a Legend

So little is known about the early years of Kanhoji Angrey that this history must begin with a folk-tale; a folk-tale still current in the Konkan, and, surprisingly enough, preserved in a yellowing roll of paper said to be two centuries old.

It seems that while serving as a cowherd in the house of a Brahmin teacher in the township of Harnai, Kanhoji, then about ten years old, fell asleep under a tree. When the Brahmin went to look for the boy, he saw that a five-headed cobra was shading Kanhoji's face from the midday sun with its hoods. This, the Brahmin was instantly convinced, showed that Kanhoji was destined to become a king. When they returned home, the Brahmin checked up his findings in Kanhoji's horoscope and in the thesaurus. The stars confirmed everything: the boy would become a king. From then onwards, according to this legend, the Brahmin began to give Kanhoji the kind of education that would befit him for his destiny.

The pages of Indian folklore are full of the most horrifying snakes, and the conception of a snake spreading out its hood to shade the eyes of a sleeping person chosen by destiny for greatness, is not an extraordinary one. No Hindu child brought up on a diet of mythological bed-time stories, would be unduly perturbed by the apparition of multi-headed snakes. Why, the puranas are full of serpents with many more heads—the earth itself is said to be resting precariously on the thousand heads of a gigantic sea-serpent!

If the learned Brahmin had left behind a copy of the horoscope of his pupil which he is said to have consulted, particularly since he was convinced that it was the horoscope of a king, it would have helped to fix the date of Kanhoji's birth.

As it is, no such record exists. The best that can be done is to accept the probable date of his birth as surmised by the historians. They say that Kanhoji Angrey was born about the year 1669.

But it is more than likely that Kanhoji was sent off at a young age to the house of a Brahmin in Harnai village for his education. There were no schools, except for the most elementary learning, and it was a common practice for the sons of the well-to-do families of the warrior class to obtain their education from Brahmin gurus. Knowledge had always been a special prerogative of the Brahmin class. To learn from them you had to live with them, doing the humblest chores; and indeed the flow of wisdom often depended on your humility and the degree of devotion to the teacher.

In the days of Kanhoji's boyhood, the Maratha warrior class was, by and large, illiterate. Even Shivaji, many historians insist, could not read or write, though this, as it happens, is not true: many letters written by Shivaji have recently been discovered. The warrior class was, at last, beginning to be interested in learning, the languages and science, if not the scriptures, and it was quite likely that Kanhoji's father, Tukoji, roaming, rootless soldier in the days when warfare was synonymous with the fair season, decided to place his son in the hands of a Brahmin in Harnai village. In war-torn Konkan, Harnai, situated on the mainland near Suvarna-durg, must have been a far safer place than any of the fortresses of Shivaji.

The paper containing the legend of the five-headed cobra goes on to describe how, when the Brahmin became convinced that the boy in his service was destined to become a king, he asked him what he would give his teacher when the prophecy came true:

'Anything you ask,' young Kanhoji told him.

'All I ask for is the field I now cultivate for the landlord; the field and the orchard surrounding it.'

'It shall be yours,' Kanhoji is supposed to have promised.

Even if this conversation never took place, let us hope that when, some twenty years later, he became the maritime commander of the Maratha Kings and the virtual ruler of the Konkan, Kanhoji remembered his old teacher with sufficient affection and regard to bestow upon him the gift of the field and the orchard surrounding it. The legend goes on to say that he did: folklore is always so much more satisfying than history.

For the nameless Brahmin of Harnai did an excellent job. His pupil, the greatest Indian maritime commander of his times, was also a surprisingly learned man, and delighted in quoting Sanskrit extracts from the scriptures and books of philosophy, much as the learned Brahmins do to this day.

The Angreys took their name from Angarwadi, a small village near Poona. The original family name was Sankpal, and all the Angreys before Kanhoji were known as Sankpals.

What family circumstance, what storm, what chance or accident of war, picked up the family from the waterless wastes of up-ghat Deccan and hurled it into the lap of the Arabian Sea, neither folklore nor history explains. The earliest reference to an Angrey at sea is in the year 1640, only they were not called Angreys then. In the naval battle between the Portuguese and the King of Bijapur, which took place in that year near Chaul, Kanhoji's father, Tukoji, son of Sekhoji Sankpal, is said to have shown 'great valour'. The Bijapur squadron was commanded by Shahaji, the father of Shivaji, who later founded the Maratha kingdom. In the battle of Chaul, the Portuguese squadron was defeated, and north Konkan, the coastline between Chaul and Bombay, came under the rule of the Kings of Bijapur.

It seems that Tukoji Sankpal was in the service of Shahaji and yet not in the service of the Bijapur Sultan. This is not altogether surprising. Loyalties, in those days of endemic warfare, did not have to stretch beyond one's own immediate superior. Military service was voluntary, and often wholly mercenary; who was your master, who your enemy, did not matter. Service did not necessarily impose a chain of servility, linking every soldier with his ruler or his highest commander. Tukoji left Shahaji's service soon after the Chaul action. He is not heard of again until twenty years later when he was made a *Sardar* (Commander) of 'twenty-five' by Shivaji, the son of his erstwhile master.

From then on, Tukoji continued in Shivaji's fleet for many years. There is little doubt that he took part in many of the battles in Shivaji's life-long war with the Siddies of Janjira, then the only formidable obstacle to Shivaji's mastery of the Konkan. Tukoji must have also taken a prominent part in Shivaji's naval expedition to Karwar which took place in 1665. At this time he had risen to be a commander of 'two hundred and fifty'. Still later, Tukoji was appointed the *Surnobat*, or Deputy Commander, of the sea-side fortress of Suvarna-durg[4], the Fort of Gold.

Thus was established a tradition which bound future generations of Angreys to ships and to the sea. For the next ninety years—until the ruin of what came to be called the 'Angrey Navy' was accomplished by a powerful combined operation launched jointly by the English, and ironically, the inheritors of the Maratha kingdom—the name Angrey became synonymous with naval might along India's west coast.

Again, nothing is known about the formative years of Kanhoji Angrey's life. Assuming that he was placed with his Brahmin guru

---

4 In England, on Woolwich Common, there stands a conspicuous monument known as the tower of Suvarna-durg, erected to the memory of Commodore William James who captured the fort in the days of descendants.

(preceptor) at the age of eight, the next five or six years are a total blank. In fact, the only reference to his career during these years is contained in the same crumbling roll of paper discovered in Harnai, which describes how Kanhoji was shaded from the sun's rays by a five-headed cobra.

'From then on,' the story goes, 'the Brahmin gave the boy rich clothes and treated him with special consideration. Kanhoji was very fond of weapons and collected swords as a hobby. Seeing this, the Brahmin was more than ever convinced of his pupil's destiny.

'When Kanhoji's education was finished, he became eager to begin his military life. The Brahmin consulted his lexicon for an auspicious moment, and when that moment came, he sent Kanhoji with his blessings to the Commander of the fort of Suvarna-durg. The Commander was impressed by the boy and engaged him on the spot. He soon found that Kanhoji was a clever and hard-working boy, and began to show him special favours. Kanhoji also won the friendship of the other officers and men in the fort and many of them became devoted to him.

'Then, accompanied by a band of his followers, he carried out a raid into the Siddy's territory. The loot gathered was distributed equally amongst those who participated. In a year or two, these raids became quite regular.

'Once, after one of these raids, Kanhoji's party was ambushed by the Siddy's soldiers, and Kanhoji himself was taken prisoner, and put into stocks. On their way to Danda Rajapur, the Siddy's capital, they had to camp near a river, and since it was a cold night, the soldiers made a log-fire and went to sleep round it. Kanhoji, however, managed to keep awake, and when the others were asleep, he set fire to the wooden stocks clamped on his hands and feet and broke free. Then, grabbing a sword from one of the sleeping men, he killed five or ten (*sic*) of them and then dived into the creek. He swam across the creek and reached the village of Harmule, from where, the next evening, he went on to the village of Tadil. The Siddy's soldiers were still in hot pursuit. Hungry and tired, Kanhoji sought shelter in a house in Tadil. The owner of the house, a Muslim merchant called Faki, took him in. Faki's daughter had, a few weeks earlier, delivered a child. Faki had her sent off to a neighbour's house and made Kanhoji sleep in her bed, next to the newborn child.

'The Siddy's soldiers soon came to the house, and although Faki remonstrated, insisted on searching the house. They came in and saw Kanhoji, who was covered with a blanket, sleeping near the baby, so, taking him to be the merchant's daughter, they did not disturb him. The next evening, Kanhoji left Faki's house and reached Suvarnadurg safely. The search for him was still going on ...'

The story goes on, chopping heads and breaking hearts by the dozen, and taking breathless leaps across the facts of history; but from here onward, we have no need to follow it. Now we begin to come across historical guideposts, distressingly few in the beginning, but unmistakable, so that it is no longer necessary to cling to overwritten folk-tales.

But even this folk-tale, obviously written by some court bard to please his audience, cannot be any more absurd or distorted than the account of Kanhoji's birth and early years given by a contemporary British chronicler, Clement Downing, in what purports to be a 'History' of the Wars with 'Angria the Pyrate':

> 'The original account of Kanhoji's birth,' Mr. Downing says, 'is that his father was an Arabian Cofferey (Zanzibar slave) who... renounced the Mohammedan faith...was discharged from the Moghul service for misdemeanour... joined the Grand Sidey (Siddy) and was of great service to him so that he gave him his own sister to wife.'

In one sentence, Downing has hacked away the roots of the proud if humble Maratha heritage of Kanhoji as well as his religious faith, and made him a son of a Zanzibar slave and the sister of the Siddy of Janjira. As has been pointed out even by English historians, there was, until twenty years ago, no such thing as 'conversion' into Hinduism. You had to be born a Hindu, you could not become one.

But wait; there is more to come! Not content with the above version of Kanhoji Angrey's beginnings, Downing goes forward, purposefully swinging the tar brush, not even prepared to concede legitimacy of birth:

> 'The present Correngey Angria is not the true begotten son of his father, but an impostor: this Angria was the son of a Cofferey man and woman that were… (the Siddy's) slaves.'

There is a good deal more in the same strain. Of the two versions, one ostensibly the work of a court flatterer, the other purporting to be 'original', the legend is perhaps less far from the truth—even if we do have to swallow five-headed snakes.

But history has already walked in and stolen the scene from the weavers of legends. It tells us, almost casually, without a single blast of the trumpet or beat of drum, of a friendship that was struck between two boys in or around Harnai: Kanhoji Angrey and Balaji Vishwanath, one a lusty specimen of the up-ghat Maratha warrior clan, the other a pallid bookworm from the class of haughty, narrow-minded Konkan Brahmins. There could be little in common between the swarthy, meat-eating, rough-tongued outdoorsman, Kanhoji, and the chaste, grey-eyed intellectual, Balaji, who must have been a few years older than Kanhoji. Balaji did not know how to hunt or shoot or how to wield the curved Maratha sword and dhal or even ride a horse. Even before Kanhoji left Harnai, Balaji had taken on a job as a clerk in the salt works at Chiplun, run by the Siddy of Janjira. He must have made an excellent clerk; for a time.

Years later, the boyhood friendship between the two was to change the course of Maratha history. Both Kanhoji and Balaji reached the highest positions in their respective spheres, and both together helped to make one of two contending heirs to the Maratha throne into the real king. Both started new dynasties, and two generations later the descendants of one destroyed the descendants of the other.

But even when he became the Chief Minister of the Maratha Kingdom, Kanhoji's boyhood friend, Balaji Viswanath, still could not ride a horse, and required 'a man on each side to hold him on'.

4

Beginnings of the Maratha Navy

Power is his who controls the waters

On 6 June, 1674, at a moment pronounced auspicious by the priests, Shivaji was enthroned at Raigad. For the first time in history, a Maratha was ruling in the land of the Marathas. No one remembered who the last Hindu King was, nor when and where he reigned; neither did they care, on that day. The proclamation made at the coronation described Shivaji's kingdom as 'extending up to the limits of the ocean'.

Among those who came to Raigad for the ceremony was Mr. Henry Oxinden, leading what is described as an 'embassy' sent by the East India Company's President at Surat. Mr. Oxinden brought a dozen shawls and a diamond ring as a gift for Shivaji and stayed on in Raigad three months to conclude a treaty. The Company wanted greater trading facilities: a reduction of customs duty, and the restoration of all their wrecks on the Konkan coast.

'We asked,' says James Douglas, 'what we ourselves had not then the ability to grant in our own kingdoms.' Mr. Oxinden doggedly stayed on at Raigad all through the suffocating premonsoon heat and then the terrible lash of the early rains, his embassy eating so much goat's meat as to have alarmed its Muslim butcher. But he got the concessions he wanted.

The reference in the coronation proclamation to the control over the oceans must have caused Mr. Oxinden considerable distress. None of the other rulers in India had so far shown any interest in the sea. At the same time, Shivaji's claim was not altogether a flight of fancy in the fourteen years that he had taken to carve out his kingdom, he had also built up a formidable fleet. Indeed, they say that the sea was his first love, dating from the time he spent as a youth in Mahad, near Bombay.

The Portuguese, in Goa, had already taken note of the growing power of Shivaji's fleet and signed a treaty of friendship with him. The Viceroy had sent his emissary to Shivaji with gifts and had undertaken to supply him with cannons at a fair price in return for a promise that he would not molest their ships.

At the time of his coronation, Shivaji had 57 major ships of war (excluding smaller craft) with a total fighting strength of over 5,000 men. Five years later, there were 66 major ships. Even his expedition to Karwar and Ankola nine years earlier had been mounted with 85 assorted *gallivats*, each ranging from 30 to 150 tons, and three three-masted *ghurabs*, with a total fighting strength of 4,000 men—a formidable force even by today's standards.

This Karwar expedition is notable for two reasons: it did not fight any battles, and it was the only naval expedition of any size that was personally commanded by Shivaji. It is said that Shivaji's ship was blown off-course by an unseasonable gale which he took to be a warning from the gods. He was also a very bad sailor and is said to have suffered miserably from sea-sickness. The main object of the Karwar expedition was almost certainly not territorial gain or plunder, and it cautiously avoided the Portuguese coast. Shivaji's fleet was barely five years a-building, raised from scratch. It was now being given its trial run; the ships and their commanders and men were being put through their paces much as they do with newly-fitted-out ships to this day.

Once again, in 1670, the fleet went out to 'show the flag', and caused the English at Bombay many anxious moments. They had convinced themselves that Shivaji was mounting a combined operation against Surat. The fleet sailed past Bombay, its every move watched by the English with bated breath, but turned back without firing a shot. It was only then realized that this too was a full-dress rehearsal and a flagshowing voyage of the coast. Shivaji's military genius was far ahead of the tactics understood in those days.

Shivaji was unquestionably the first ruler in India to have realized the need for protecting the coast. His ships gradually began to patrol the coast in increasing numbers, 'defying the Portuguese, the Dutch, the Siddies, and the English and (in all) twenty-seven hostile powers; living on the tributes offered by the people along the coast and collecting for the King, rations ... gold ... and other tribute. In this manner, it soon came to be regarded as a formidable fighting force, a veritable army upon the high seas.'

Side by side with the development of the fleet, Shivaji carried out a systematic campaign to capture the forts along the coast and to build up fortifications at strategic points. He collected around him hand-picked men who might, in today's phraseology, be described as 'technicians': engineers, shipwrights, workers in brass and lead, gunsmiths. There were Muslim workers in his service, as indeed, Portuguese, French, and Dutch.

In all, Shivaji built thirteen new sea-side forts along the Konkan coast, and fortified and improved many others. The hulks are still there, with great gaping holes in their sides. Perhaps the best preserved is Sindhu-durg, built on an island off Malwan, earmarked but never destined to become the headquarters of the Maratha naval force. Thirty-two flags used to wave there over as many bastions; today it stands a sullen sentry in dented armour, forgotten at his post. You can go all around Sindhu-durg and still miss the entrance gate, for it is concealed in many folds of walls which are miraculously preserved, as though the daily prayers chanted by the descendants of the priests originally appointed by Shivaji to ensure that 'the sea should not encroach upon its walls, nor should an enemy prevail,' still retain their efficacy. A footprint of Shivaji, implausibly large, is still worshipped in Sindhu-durg, the Fort of the Ocean.

In 1679, Shivaji took over the island of Khanderi close to Bombay, and had it fortified in the teeth of the strongest opposition by the East India Company. The Company sought the help of the Siddy of Janjira in an effort to oust the Marathas from Khanderi, but the Siddy double-crossed his allies and himself went and occupied the adjoining island of Underi, which is said to have caused the English even more distress than the occupation of Khanderi by Shivaji. For more than a hundred years, Khanderi remained with the Marathas, although the very next year the Siddy sent a raiding force to Khanderi and brought back to Bombay as a peace-offering to the Company basket-loads of human heads to display in the streets. He was only prevented from putting them up on poles in the streets by the horrified protests of the Company's Governor.

Perhaps the last sea-side fort that Shivaji built was on a rocky out-crop off Alibag, twenty miles south of Bombay. Hitherto, this small island had, for many years, contained a minor outpost of the Maratha forces. Now it was to be converted into an impregnable, self-contained, fortress with numerous 'sweet-water' tanks and with its own ship-building yard capable of holding out for long periods without outside help. Since the island was nothing more than a vast, bare rock (*kul*) surrounded by water (*aap*), the new fortress came to be called *Kul-aap*, a name which, even before the fort was completed, was transformed by the people into the much simpler 'Kulaba' or 'Colaba'.

In years to come, the fortress of Colaba became the home and headquarters of successive generations of the hereditary naval chiefs of the Maratha Kings, the Angreys. In later years, the family came to be known as the 'Angreys of Colaba'.

But the Angreys did not have much to do with Colaba until after the turn of the century. Before following up the beginnings of their story, it might be just as well to get some idea of the political background to the career of the first of the Angreys: Kanhoji. In order to get properly oriented, it will be necessary to delve into the history of the Konkan and find answers to the questions that naturally arise. What were the Portuguese doing in the Konkan all those years ago? And the British? Who or what were the Siddies? What were they up to?

5

The 'Terribil' and his Successors

Quinquireme of Nineveh from distant Ophir
Rowing home to heaven in sunny Palestine,
With a cargo of ivory,
And apes and peacocks,
Sandalwood, cedarwood, and sweet white wine.

—John Masefield

The advent of the Portuguese in India is a tale of unbelievable contradictions: of cold, sustained courage and endurance, of amazing feats of pioneering and seamanship, of burning religious zeal; and of treachery, brutality, and blind rapacity. They were giants who performed miracles of navigation only to go raving mad at the end of their odysseys. They came to India to trade, and lived and prospered by open piracy and slavetrading: the single standard of brute force governed all their actions in the early days.

They were the pioneers, the first Western Europeans to come to India by sea. The great sailor, Vasco da Gama, reached Calicut on the Malabar coast on 22 May, 1498. The Raja of Calicut, who was known as the Zamorin, received him hospitably and gave him permission to build a trading post.

But long before the Portuguese came to Calicut, the Konkan ports were familiar to the merchants of the world. From the cold dawn of history, the Persians, the Arabs, the Jews and the Chinese, knew the fabled ports of Ophir (Supara), Kalyan, Seymoul (Chaul) and Sanjan, and thousands of them had settled down in these ports and prospered, living in complete amity and in an atmosphere of religious freedom and tolerance, building their own places of worship; the Parsis had a fire temple in Chaul hundreds of years before their great immigration.

Vasco da Gama was followed by Alphonso Albuquerque, Alphonso the *Terribil*, the conqueror of Goa; his statue stands on the promenade of Panjim, facing the sea. Destruction was his mission in life. 'I took Kurhat[5] and put everyone to the sword,' he writes without passion, and then he gave orders for Kurhat to be 'burned from top to bottom'. (*Goa*: Remy.) Kurhat, incidentally, was subjected to this treatment merely to 'intimidate' nearby Ormuz. Three years later, Ormuz too suffered the same fate.

This, then, was the pattern of Portuguese expansion in the East. After capturing Goa, Albuquerque turned upon the Zamorin who had befriended his compatriots when they first came to India. He killed the Zamorin after a 'great slaughter' of his men, and burnt down his city.

The Portuguese were using cannons and muskets against spears and arrows and swords, bullets and grapeshot against bare flesh: they could not lose.

That terrible invention of war, gunpowder, had been in use for nearly a hundred and fifty years, but its use was not common in India. Some crude forms of mortars were in use in the armies of the Indian rulers, but the arms the Portuguese possessed and the kind of gunpowder they used, gave them an overwhelming advantage. They were more like hunters of animals than soldiers, killing without fear of their fire being returned.

Invincible, Albuquerque and his successors roved all over the East, 'the sword in one hand and the crucifix in the other', taking whatever they fancied and leaving in their wake a trail of

5 Coastal town in the Persian Gulf.

smouldering ruins, and wherever they felt like settling down, they settled down and established their trading posts. In 1507, they took Chaul; in 1508, they took Dabhol. A few years later, they established themselves in Bombay where the 'people, terrified, fled away'. Everyone could not have fled away however; 'our men captured many cows and some blacks who were hiding among the bushes', Caspar Correa writes, 'of whom the good were kept and the rest were killed.' (S.M. Edwardes: *The Rise of Bombay*.)

Thousands of Hindus and Muslims abandoned their homes and ran away in terror from the Portuguese settlements as their conquerors desecrated their homes, temples and mosques. The non-Christians in Goa had to leave the town every evening at sundown. If found practising their own religion, they were instantly put to death.

Goa was the greatest slave-market in Western India. The Portuguese brought slaves from Africa as their personal servants, and they captured and sent thousands of Indians to the markets of Europe; they kept mistresses by the dozen and maintained private whore-houses for their guests; they got punch-drunk every day and fought duels over their friends' wives; they smoked and swore and took what was not theirs and killed wantonly; and amidst the shattering of the Ten Commandments, they held daily prayers to the glory of God, and upon the ruins of the temples and mosques they built the most magnificent churches and cathedrals.

By their religious intolerance, they destroyed for all times the traditional feelings of friendliness and hospitality that the Konkan had shown to all strangers who came to her ports to the Jews and the Parsis and the Greeks and the Chinese and the Malays and the Ceylonese, who had frequented her coast a thousand years before the advent of the *Terribil*.

There is a saying in the Konkan that even if a chameleon makes a great dash, it can never get further than the first hedge. The Portuguese expansion in the Konkan had been halted almost before it had got under way, at the first likelihood of opposition; as soon, in fact, as the Indian rulers had introduced cannons and muskets to their forces. And although the Indian weapons were at no time as good as the weapons of the Portuguese, the Indians were infinitely better soldiers. The Portuguese had become too rich too soon and won their battles too easily; they had become overfed and indolent and dissolute.

'Finding much gold,' one of their Governors writes, 'they laid aside the crucifixes to fill their pockets, and not being able to hold them with one hand—they were grown so heavy—they dropped the sword too, being found in this posture by those who came after them.'

That was the position in which the British found them, stooping with the weight of gold in their pockets, but devoid of either crucifix or sword. By this time, the conquerors had turned into merchants, at last content to carry on with the profits of international trading, fabulous as they were; establishing diplomatic missions at the courts of the Indian rulers and sending presents to their officials.

Long before the beginning of the eighteenth century, the Portuguese had ceased to represent a threat on land. Of all their conquests in the Konkan, only five pockets remained: Goa, Chaul, Bassein, Thana and Bombay. The Viceroy lived in Goa.

But on the sea they were just as powerful as ever. Their ships were faster, heavier, stronger, and above all, better armed than the ships of the Indian rulers. They compelled all indian shipping to acknowledge their authority over the sea: no ship was permitted to use the waters of the Konkan unless it carried a cartaz from the Portuguese Viceroy. 'These seas belonged unto the King of Portugal and none aught to come here without his licence', the first British were told.

The Portuguese were unchallenged masters of the Indian Ocean. Until the arrival on the scene of Kanhoji Angrey, the only ships which could flout the authority of the Portuguese were the ships of the East India Company.

6

The First Hundred Years of John Company

Everything that is worth having in India has been derived from English rule.

—Lord Wolsley

Birds of prey and passage in India.

—Edmund Burke

The first Englishman who came to India was Thomas Stevens, an ardent preacher who asked for nothing more of life than the opportunity of guiding the uninitiated into the path of the true faith. He landed in Goa on 24 October, 1579, and lived there for the next forty years, richly fulfilling his life's chosen task. In course of time, Thomas Stevens became 'Father' Thomas Stevens, and translated the Bible into the Marathi language, calling it the *Christian Purana*[6].

The four Englishmen who followed Father Stevens a few years later, however, had little thought of coming to India: they were brought into the country much against their will. They had set out from Lisbon on a modest, one-ship trading expedition to the Persian Gulf. Through the centuries, the Gulf had become a rich trading mart between the East and the West, the centre of the world of

---

6 A copy of the Christian Purana, printed in Rachole, Goa, in the year 1616, may still be seen in the Chapel of St. Francis in Goa.

commerce. To the Persian Gulf came vessels from Lisbon, the Malay ports, Ceylon and Calicut, Java, Borneo and Timor, and the great Mocha fleets of the Moghul emperors; and its seaboard had become a crossroad for the endless lines of caravans laden with cinnamon and camphor, rubies, cardamom, seed pearls, musk and amber; silk, porcelain and lacquer from China; ivory and muslin from Bengal. Those who wished to trade in the wares of the Orient had no need to go further than the Persian Gulf.

But in the Persian Gulf as in India, the Portuguese were already on the scene. Also, like the British at a much later stage in history, they controlled the more important ports along the route to India.

Inevitably, when the English merchants reached Ormuz, at the mouth of the Persian Gulf, they fell foul of the Portuguese Deputy Governor there—and thereby stepped right into the pages of history. The Deputy Governor made them captives and ordered their merchandise seized. Then, in the manner born of all good *Deputies* he passed on his prisoners, complete with their cargo, to 'higher authority'—the Portuguese Viceroy at Goa.

When, therefore, on 29 November, 1583, John Newberry, John Eldred, William Shales and Ralph Fitch, landed in Goa, it was as prisoners of the Portuguese that they came.

Unlike Thomas Stevens, however, they soon were tired of life in Goa, although admittedly, they were not subjected to any severe hardships by their captors. After a period of confinement and a certain degree of pressure to convert them to the Jesuit faith, they were allowed to move about freely in the town of old Goa. They were even told that they could sell their merchandise through Portuguese middlemen, but only at prices fixed by the Portuguese authorities.

Old Goa, the sprawling capital which is now a silent ruin of crumbling churches and graves, is situated on an island, and it is possible that the Portuguese Viceroy relied upon the Banastari creek, which divides the capital from the mainland, to prevent his prisoners from making a break for freedom: the creek, and the fact that the Englishmen could not speak the local language—that is, if the Englishmen were foolish enough to venture by themselves into the vast, unknown interior of India.

But the Englishmen were foolish. They sold all their goods recklessly, to the delight of the Portuguese middlemen; they sent presents to placate their captors and showed every evidence of settling down in Goa for good, and one day they stole or bought a small bast and rowed themselves across the creek. It was as easy as that.

By the time the alarm was raised they were deep within the sunless jungles of the Western Ghats. The Viceroy ordered a house-to-house search and offered large rewards for their capture, but then as now, the frontiers of Goa were no further than a day's resolute march from the capital. The birds had flown. For many years afterwards, the King of Portugal was to write sharp letters to his Viceroy, Count d'Alvor, telling him how upset he was at the escape of the English prisoners and goading him to greater efforts to capture them again.

Once outside Goa, the English merchants separated. During the next few years, they travelled the length and breadth of the country. One of them managed to get back to Persia, but was never heard of again. Another, unmindful of the fact that there was still a price on his head, returned to Goa and barely escaped with his life. They all saw much in their travels in India: great rivers and mountains; immense waterless deserts and jungles teeming with wild animals; extremes of heat and cold, wealth and poverty; cities bigger than the biggest in Europe, and above all countless articles of merchandise that would fetch good prices in the markets of Europe. After a visit to Agra, which was then the Moghul capital, one of them wrote:

> 'In the Royal store were 1,000 elephants, 30,000 horses, 1,400 tame deer, and such a store of ounces (leopards), tigers, buffles, cocks and hawkes, that is very strange to see.'

It was wonderment such as this, the tales brought home by these first travellers about the wealth of India, the certitude of rich pickings by trading with India, and the fabulous prosperity of the Portuguese, that goaded the founders of the East India Company to seek permission from the Queen to trade in the East.

The founders of the Company are said to have constantly sought the advice of Ralph Fitel, merchant, Portuguese prisoner and intrepid traveller, lately returned from that fabulous country: India.

On the last day of the year 1600, Queen Elizabeth I granted the East India Company the monopoly of trade with the East: 'A privilege for fifteen years, granted by her Majesty to certain adventurers for the discovery of the trade for the East Indies ...'

Another eight years were to pass before Captain Hawkins, the first representative of the East India Company, set out for India bearing a letter from King James I, addressed to the 'Great Moghul'. Hawkins' ship *Hector* reached Surat in 1608. In those days, Surat was a prosperous seaport with a population of over 4,00,000. The Portuguese had a riverside settlement at Surat, consisting of a flourishing factory and residential buildings, surrounded by a massive stone wall. Out in the channel, the Portuguese also had a squadron of warships to protect their shipping.

From Surat, Captain Hawkins went to Agra to present his letter to the Moghul Emperor. The reigning Moghul, Jehangir, received him with courtesy and friendliness, and with true Oriental hospitality proceeded to find him a wife, 'of the same faith'. She was an Armenian lady of great charm.

But what Captain Hawkins wanted from the Emperor was not a wife but trading concessions, and these, for all Jehangir's apparent friendliness, were not readily forthcoming. The reason was not far to seek: the Portuguese were already there, well dug-in in Jehangir's court, by now past-masters in that principal art and occupation of all court circles—intrigue. Imperceptibly, Jehangir's attitude began to stiffen. Certain facilities for trade, earlier conceded, were peremptorily withdrawn, and Captain Hawkins had to return to Surat empty-handed.

The British answer to Portuguese intrigue was, characteristically, a squadron of the Navy. In 1612, came four British warships under the command of Captain Thomas Best. They sought out and attacked the Portuguese ships at Swally, near Surat, and after a brief engagement, succeeded in capturing them. After that, the British troops from the ships went ashore and drove out the Portuguese from their settlement at Surat. From then on it became the English settlement.

This show of force had the desired effect. The very next year, Emperor Jehangir gave the Company permission to establish a factory at Surat. That is where the British opened their first warehouse in India—in the riverside premises captured from the Portuguese.

The Honourable East India Company was in business.

Apparently, there were enormous profits to be made from the sale of such things as nickel, lead, mercury, glass beads and mirrors, to India; and taking away spices, silk, indigo, ivory, muslin, beeswax, ginger and lemon-grass to the markets of Europe. But there were even larger profits to be made from the export of human beings, and the English merchants were not averse to making them. Admittedly, slave-trading never became the East India Company's main business as it did of the Portuguese at one stage, but as late as 1685, the Company's council at Surat were writing to the Karwar factors to 'supply slaves for export ... at Rs. 15 per head'[7] and, with true commercial thrift, cautioning them to try and get them cheaper.

7 This letter goes on to say, 'three pairs of dwarfs (male and female) are to be sent home to His Majesty.' (House of Shivaji: Jadunath Sarkar)

As the years passed, more factories had to be opened to cope with the increasing volume of trade. Of these, Rajapur, Bankote, Karwar and Bombay were in the Konkan.

Bombay was a more direct legacy from the Portuguese than the settlement at Surat, which was taken away from them by force. Bombay, an altogether juicier plum, came as a gift some fifty years later, from the Portuguese to the English King, and from the English King to the East India Company. It was part of the dowry brought by the Portuguese Princess Catherine of Braganza at her marriage to King Charles II. Charles promptly leased it to the Company for an annual rent of £10. Nobody seems to have thought much of Bombay in those days, except of course, the East India Company, anxious to possess a place of its own.

Shivaji often taunted the English delegation which attended his coronation about the manner in which Bombay had been acquired. 'You are fitter to live by trading than by arms', he is said to have remarked to Henry Oxinden.

At the time, Shivaji's observation was based on facts, for in its early days, the Company, totally absorbed in making quick profits, kept itself aloof from the politics and warfare of the Deccan. But it soon gave up this policy for strong-arm methods. In the disturbed state of the country, the Company found that to protect its settlements and merchandise, it had to build fortifications and employ armed guards. Its ships had always carried powerful guns so that they could double as warships whenever the need arose. Gradually, the ships became bigger and more powerfully armed and the settlements grew into forts, fully garrisoned and armed for prolonged defence. By 1667, when Shivaji plundered Surat, the English 'settlement' was already capable of being successfully defended.

The Company's neutrality, however, turned out to be a thin cloak. As soon as it discovered that its own military force had become strong, the Company began to dictate terms for better trading concessions and to play one power against the other. In 1661, this new policy of the Company was given official recognition, when King Charles conferred upon it the right to make peace or war 'with any prince or people, not being Christians'. The next step for the Company was to strike and circulate its own coins.

The society of adventurers was rapidly growing into a new kind of monster—a trading firm with all the earmarks of a ruling power.

But it was too good to last. Barely twenty years later, the East India Company was in serious difficulties, and for the next twenty-five years it was almost touch and go whether it would have to wind up its affairs and leave. It was found that in spite of enjoying the monopoly of the most profitable trading concession of the times, the Company had actually begun to lose money. One of the reasons for this was, of course, the ever-rising military expenditure of the Company: making wars, maintaining large forces, was, then as ever, a costly business. But that is something the Company's directors had made pro vision for. Its profits, after taking into account all risk of 'normal warfare' amounted to more than 100 per cent annually. The Company's financial troubles were mainly due to the growing propensity amongst its servants to give the pagoda tree an extra shake or two and not show the transactions in the company's ledgers.

The kind of pay and prospects offered by the East India Company were such as to deter all but the most needy or the least conscientious. The Company, on its part, had always showed a marked preference for what it termed the 'adventurers' to the gentlemen. This principle of policy was, with somewhat surprising candour, even embodied in an official resolution. Encouraging the gentlemen, the Company's Directors argued, discouraged the adventurers. It was no doubt largely as a result of this policy that the Company had managed to fill up its ranks with many an unscrupulous servant who cheated it at every possible opportunity. When honesty had been tied up with perpetual poverty, it is not surprising that most of the Company's servants sought to make private fortunes by 'irregular and dishonest means'. Discipline had vanished and the Company's authority was openly flouted by its officials.

The climax came in 1683 when the garrison at Bombay, commanded by Captain Keigwin, openly rebelled against the Company's rule. They declared that they held the island for the King and that they would not submit to the Company's authority. Keigwin arrested the Company's Deputy Governor at Bombay, held him captive in the fort, and sent off a letter to the King announcing that he would hold the island for the King, 'till His Majesty's pleasure should be known'. Keigwin was an honest and straightforward officer, too straightforward to fall in line with the Company's standards of administration and trading practices, but it seemed that the King himself was more on the side of the Company than his own soldiery. A year later, as a result of a good deal of pressure exerted through the King and an unqualified promise of a general amnesty, Bombay was restored to the Company.

But the trials of the East India Company were by no means over. All these years, it had drawn much of its power and infuence from Royal patronage, it is said, by paying large sums of money to people around the throne and even to the King himself, in return for favours received. In the last decade of the seventeenth century, the Company's annual budget for bribes was £90,000, or nearly two million pounds at today's value.

One wonders how much King Charles II perennially in need of ready cash, received under the counter for leasing Bombay to the Company for the absurd sum of £10 per year; how much when he conferred upon the Company the right of making war or peace; how much to throw his weight on the Company's side during the Bombay rebellion? Or whether the Duke of Leeds and other powerful interlopers around the King permitted any of these funds to reach Charles at all?

But towards the end of the seventeenth century, the power of the King himself had been on the decline and the flight of King

James threw the Company wide open to the attacks of rival trading interests. The rich pickings made by the East India Company had always caused severe heartburning amongst other merchants wishing to trade with India. They now began a powerful campaign to throw open the trade to all comers. As a result of these efforts, another company came into being and began to trade with India in open rivalry with the original or London Company, as it was called. Two was definitely a crowd. A fierce and undignified rivalry ensued which is said to have caused the 'greatest amusement to the newsmongering natives'. Above all, profits fell drastically.

In the sixteen-eighties, the Company was groggily panting for breath. At this time, the Moghul Emperor seized its factories, withdrew its trading concessions, threw its merchants at Surat into confinement and ordered his maritime commander, the Siddy of Janjira, to drive out the British from Bombay.

The Moghul Emperor, Aurangzeb, knee-deep in his campaigns in the Deccan, had at last been provoked into action: the East India Company had just been asking for trouble. For one thing, an unimaginative Governor called Sir John Childs, had, without the least provocation, given 'confidential' orders to the Company's ships to seize all the Moghul ships at sea. The Company's high-spirited Captains must have enjoyed themselves: it was like shooting down fat, tame ducks, for the Moghul ships of the coastal trade were not equipped for fighting. Within a year, they had rounded up as many as fifty Moghul ships loaded with merchandise, and had brought them as prizes to Surat and Bombay.

In addition to this undeclared war by the Company, the activities of the English pirates had also increased. It will never be possible to determine the extent of participation of the Company's officials in the ventures of what came to be called 'the Malabar pirates' who haunted the Arabian Sea in the late seventeenth and the early eighteenth centuries. 'The prizes gained were so great and the risks so small that the Company could hardly restrain their own men from joining the sea rovers,' says Bidulph. The Moghuls, with good reason, regarded both the pirates and the Company as being one and the same—after all, both flew the English flag.

In the past, provided the English pirates kept their activities within reasonable limits, the Moghuls chose to ignore them. For one thing, the Emperor lived at Agra, a thousand miles away from the sea, and it took a month before the reports of happenings along the coast reached his ears. As to the local Moghul officials, it was easy enough to placate them with suitable bribes. On the rare occasions when Aurangzeb chose to be difficult, his remedy was simple, if not very effective. He would order his Governor at Surat to throw the Company's President and officials into confinement and to seize such of the Company's establishments as he could lay hands on, until the necessary compensation was paid. The Emperor's Subedar, fattening on the Company's bribes, always saw to it that the compensation was what the Company would regard as 'fair'.

But the wholesale seizure of scores of Moghul ships, some of them belonging to Aurangzeb himself, was quite another matter. This time, the Moghul Emperor was not in the far north, but right in the Deccan, surrounded by a vast army. He ordered the Company's officials at Surat into confinement, and ordered his coastal Commander, the Siddy of Janjira, to attack Bombay.

Gleefully, the Siddy invaded Bombay with 25,000 men. Within a few weeks, Mazagaon, Sion and Mahim, today some of the most populous parts of the city, fell into his hands. Only the fort remained with the Company.

The Siddy was prepared to wait, playing cat and mouse at the walls of the fort, his troops perpetrating 'unheard-of excesses' upon the population. He cut off their supplies from the land side and waited, hoping to draw them out for an open fight or to starve them.

The siege of Bombay lasted a whole year. Disease and the Siddy's excesses brought the population close to extinction. If it had not been for the Governor of Surat, Mukhtyar Khan, who was jealous of the Siddy and in the pay of the Company, Bombay would have fallen.

Through Mukhtyar Khan, secret emissaries were sent to Aurangzeb's court, offering enormous bribes and at the same time 'making the humblest submissions' on behalf of the Company. In course of time everything was forgiven, but Sir John Childs, the Governor of Bombay, 'who did the disgrace' was ordered to be 'turned out and expelled'. Aurangzeb ordered the Siddy to lift the siege, but the Siddy took his own time doing so, and before leaving, he set fire to the fort of Mazagaon and left it a heap of burning ruins.

But the internal troubles of the Company were not over. It took another seventeen years for the two rival companies to agree upon a formula for sharing profits instead of competing with each other. In 1707, the two companies were amalgamated to form the United East India Company, and immediately settled down to adjust prices in such a way as to make up for all the losses incurred during the years of rivalry. Once again, all was well with the John Company.

The next 150 years were years of uninterrupted prosperity and expansion; years which saw the absurd phenomenon of a gigantic, populous land being taken over and ruled by a handful of adventurous traders.

But in the Konkan, the first fifty of those years were by no means plain sailing. The East India Company had to contend with the rising power of Kanhoji Angrey and his descendants.

Before leaving the Company in everlasting sunshine, it would be just as well to take a quick look over the shoulder at Surat. Until 1687, the business of the Company was carried on from Surat, where the Governor lived, in uncomfortable proximity to the Moghul Subedar, for whenever he chose to, Aurangzeb could have him thrown into confinement. Bombay was an unhealthy fishing village. Being the only British possession in India, the Company had kept a small garrison there and later built a fort. Around this garrison, the city was growing fast.

By 1680, its population had already grown to 60,000. Surat, on the other hand, was not living up to its earlier promise. The River Tapti was slowly silting up at the mouth and blocking the channel. Surat did not belong to the Company; the English were there in a settlement, just like the other traders, the French and the Dutch. Perhaps a greater drawback of Surat was that being an important Moghul town, it was a favourite target of Maratha raids; Shivaji had raided Surat in 1667 and again in 1670. On the latter occasion, the city was said to have been 'leisurely plundered for three days'.

Surat was obviously no place for the headquarters of a prosperous trading company. In 1687, the East India Company shifted its main office to Bombay. The very next year, the King of England sold the island to the Company.

7

The Siddies of Janjira

The reason for building up the Maratha Navy was the Siddy of Janjira.

—Parasnis

Janjira is an island fortress thirty miles south of Bombay. The word 'Janjira' comes from the Arabic word 'Jezira' meaning 'an island'. The fortress was never conquered by Shivaji or his descendants. Owing, no doubt, to its invincibility, in the Marathi language the word 'Janjira' has come to mean 'an island fortress'.

The rulers of Janjira came from Abyssinia. Originally they came as traders, but trade was obviously not their *metier*, so they became professional sailors and took service under the rulers of the Deccan. It seems they called themselves 'Sedies' because in Africa it was an honourable title. The Marathas, on the other hand, call all Negroes 'Siddies'; they transformed 'Sedy' into 'Siddy'.

How the Siddies came to rule Janjira is not known. The story goes that in the year 1498, an Abyssinian adventurer, disguised as a merchant, obtained permission from the chief of the fortress to land 300 boxes supposed to contain valuable wares. The permission was duly granted. Each box, however, contained an armed soldier. In the middle of the night, the soldiers came out and took possession of the fort.

It is more likely, however, that the Siddies are descendants of the Abyssinian seamen who, in the early part of the seventeenth century,

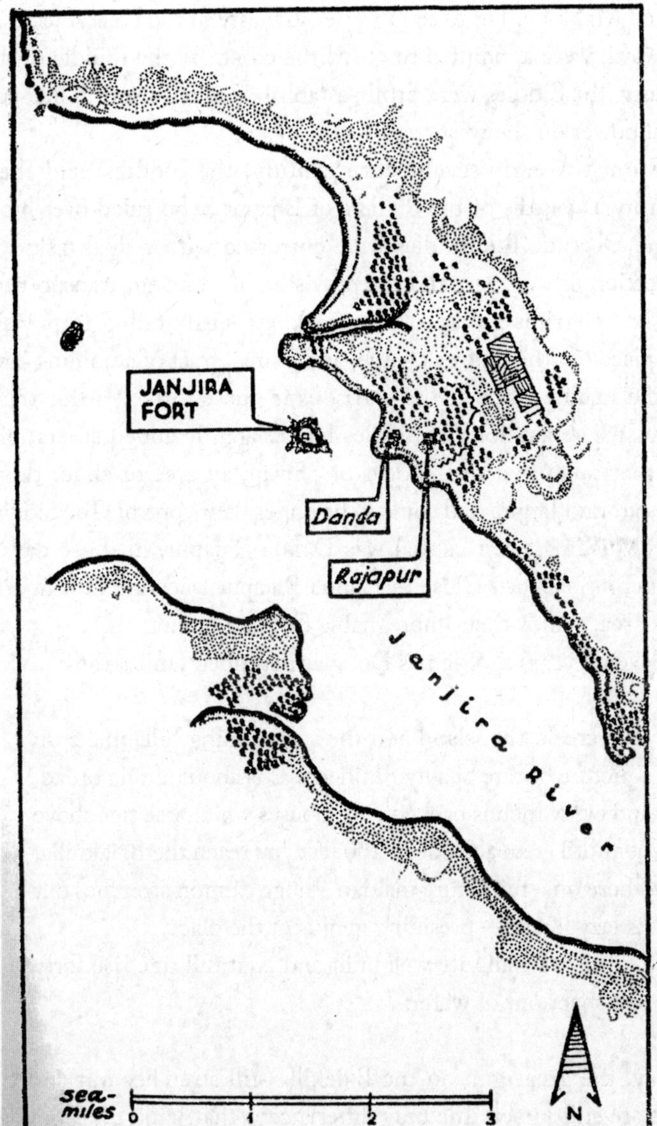

JANJIRA FORT AND SURROUNDINGS

helped Malik Umber to set up a new dynasty in the Deccan, and as a reward, were appointed to guard the coast. By the middle of the century, the Siddies were firmly established as a powerful, if small, naval power on the west coast.

From the early seventeenth century, the Siddies held their territory as vassals of the Sultans of Bijapur, who ruled over most of the Deccan. The Siddies were entrusted with a dual task: the protection of the coast and the provision of sufficient transport for Muslim pilgrims going to Mecca. A few surrounding forts were also placed in the Siddy's charge, and a small tract of adjoining land for the maintenance of the garrisons in these forts. To this tract, successive generations of Siddies had diligently added several bits and pieces, so that in the days of Shivaji, an area of about thirty miles around Janjira had come to be under their control. The Siddies were Muslims, their capital was Danda Rajapur, in those days a prosperous seaport. Close to Danda Rajapur, separated by an arm of the sea, stands their impregnable fortress: Janjira.

Seventy years ago, James Douglas described Janjira thus:

> 'The creek, the island and the surrounding hills make up a picture of rare beauty. Jinjheera ... is about a mile broad, and every inch is packed with houses which rise tier above tier until at an altitude of 200 feet you reach the Balakhilla, where on a miniature maidan a huge cannon stretches out its lazy length—presiding genius of the place.
>
> 'The sea walls are well built and ... at full tide rise forty feet sheer out of water...'

Today, the great gun on the Balekilla still stretches out and the walls are still intact. The only difference is that Janjira has now no guard at the gates standing with naked swords, and you can come and go as you please. Until a few years ago, custom dictated that after sundown the great gates with the stone carving of the mythical

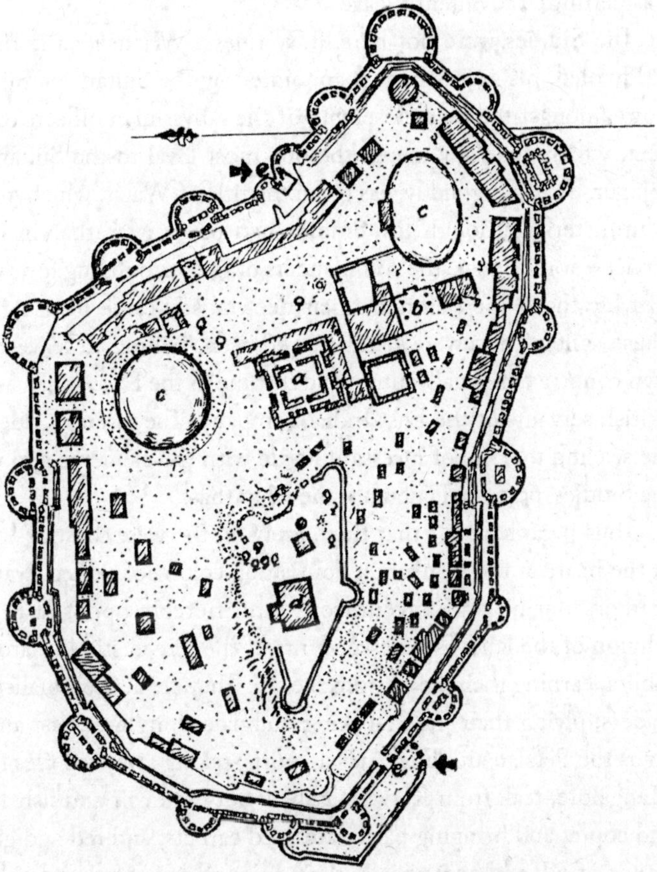

a. The Seddees House
b. The Mosque
c. Two Tanks
d. A large Magazine on the Hill
e. The two Gates

JANJIRA FORT

tiger—each claw holding an elephant—were shut down and no one was permitted to enter or leave.

The Siddies were not hereditary rulers. Whenever the ruling Siddy died, his successor was appointed by the Sultans of Bijapur from amongst the most deserving of the Abyssinian officers of the fleet, which generally meant the one most loyal to the Sultans of Bijapur. The ruling Siddy was given the title of Wazir, which meant a 'minister'. Although the Siddies had many Marathas in their service—for instance, the commanders of the surrounding forts were all Marathas—the sailors in their fleet mostly came from Africa. These sailors then were hand-picked men, willing to leave their own country to seek adventure and fortune in the East, much as the British servants of the East India Company. They were wedded to the sea and to a life of incessant battle with the elements and with the Siddies' perpetual enemies: the Marathas.

Thus it came about that there grew on the west coast of India, in the heart of the Konkan, a flourishing colony of skilled, warlike seamen, daring and adventurous, and fiercely opposed to the religion of the land. The descendants of these men still live around Janjira, earning their living from the sea. They are active, small-time traders, plying their frail, creaking sailboats along the coast and as far as the Persian and East African ports; taking away red tiles from Mangalore, teak from Karwar, cashew nuts and coir and fish-meal and copra; and bringing back dates and carpets, and red and green drums of oil, and occasionally the odd brick of contraband gold or silver or a packet of hashish, much as their ancestors did in the days of the first Siddies.

The Siddies and the Marathas were in a perpetual state of war with each other, a war passed on from generation to generation, like a blood feud. That the Marathas—occupied as they were in resisting mightier opponents—kept the Siddies in check, repeatedly wresting from them whatever new tracts they had managed to add to their domain in their habitual forays into the surrounding country and even forcing new alliances upon them, is to the everlasting credit of the Marathas: that the Siddies managed to survive at all and hold their own, when many mightier powers fell, is to the greater credit of the Siddies.

The clash came early in Shivaji's career. In 1648, Shivaji invaded the Siddy's territory and captured one of his outlying forts. This was the beginning of the long war between the Marathas and the Siddies which went on, with few interruptions, for the next hundred years. From 1659, Shiva sent forces against the Siddy every year. For his thirteenth attempt, in 1670, Shivaji took personal command of the operations and is said to have 'put forth his whole strength' into the attack against Janjira. This was the only time that the Siddy nearly came close to surrendering his fort. But there were others in the Siddy's court who were made of sterner stuff than the ruling Siddy, Fateh Khan. They threw Fateh Khan into confinement and continued to defend the fort with grim determination. With the end of the monsoon, Shivaji lifted the siege and turned his attention upon more pressing and—more profitable —operations.

During these yearly Maratha onslaughts, the Sultans of Bijapur, the overlords of the Siddies, had sent little or no help to them. The officers who, at a critical moment, had risen to the defence of Janjira, now decided to sever their ties with Bijapur. They made overtures to Aurangzeb, offering to hold their territory as vassals of the Moghuls and also offering to transfer the Bijapur fleet to the service of the Moghuls in return for protection against the Marathas. Aurangzeb was more than willing. Those who had assumed control of the affairs of Janjira now deposed Siddy Fateh Khan, who had been prepared to surrender the fort to Shivaji, and elected Siddy Kassam as their new ruler. Aurangzeb sanctioned an annual grant of four lakhs of rupees to be paid to the Siddy for the maintenance of his fleet, and sealed the new alliance by conferring the title of 'Yakoot Khan' upon the Siddy—a more grandiose title than the 'Wazir' conferred by the Sultans of Bijapur.

But the Siddies soon found that as far as military help was concerned, the Moghuls took their obligations of sovereignty no more seriously than did the Sultans of Bijapur. Consequently, by themselves, the Siddies never became a threat to the Maratha power, and although they continued to make occasional forays into the surrounding country, these were, at best, hit-and-run raids. On their part, the Marathas, too, had acquired a healthy respect for the fighting abilities of the Siddies. They came to realize that however powerful they might be on land, unless they could also beat the Siddy in his own element, the sea, they would never succeed in overthrowing his power.

A contemporary Maratha record laments: 'Janjira, surrounded by water, would not yield; was invincible. To capture Janjira was to rule the seas. Shivaji ordered the construction of ... five hundred ships.'

The ships were duly built, but Shivaji did not use them against the Siddy; his hands were more than full, putting his new-found kingdom into running order, and, at the same time, guarding it from Moghul onslaughts. The Siddy could wait, provided he was not allowed to raise his head. Shivaji continued to maintain pressure against the Siddy, but he had learnt from the experience of thirteen failures that the attempt to reduce the Siddy by force of arms would have seriously weakened his strength against the Moghuls. If he could avoid it, Shivaji did not want a major conflict on two fronts.

It was left to Shivaji's son, Sambhaji, when he became the King of the Marathas, to employ the fleet against the Siddy of Janjira. The result was disastrous.

8

In the Reign of Sambhaji

In 1680, Shivaji died at Raigad. 'The infidel went to hell', wrote Khafi Khan, Aurangzeb's official historian. Shivaji's elder son, Sambhaji, became the King of the Marathas.

At this time, Kanhoji Angrey was eleven years old, still a pupil at the house of a Brahmin in Harnai village, fretting against the shortcomings of a Brahmanic way of life—the total absence of meat and spices, the frequency of waterless fasts and the long hours spent in chanting meaningless prayers.

Unfortunately, these years of Kanhoji's boyhood are lost in the chaos of the sorry hash that Sambhaji made of his kingdom. Too much was happening in the Deccan: the Moghuls were at war with both the Marathas and the Bijapur King; the Marathas were at war with the Moghuls, the Siddy and the Portuguese; even the British, busy minding their account books and performing amazing feats of neutrality in the midst of all this warfare, were called upon to defend themselves against the Siddy's attack on Bombay. It is not surprising that little of what Kanhoji Angrey did in those days has found its way into historical records.

Sambhaji, the white hope of the Maratha army if not of Shivaji's statesmen, was destined for tragedy. He was a fearless man, second to none in personal bravery, but he was allegedly a slave to sensual pleasures. His rashness, his temper and his cruelty, completely obscured whatever military gifts he may have possessed, and made impossible demands upon the loyalty of his people. Infrequent flashes of personal bravery were obviously not enough to preserve from ruin a sprawling new kingdom won by the sword and held together by the most efficient system of administration yet devised.

The Moghul Emperor, Aurangzeb, was readying for a last great effort to conquer the Deccan Shivaji, the 'mountain rat' was dead: the time had come to strike the death-blow. The Grand Army was already stirring; soon, the gigantic, unwieldy machine of war, twenty miles long and six miles broad, would begin to roll, devouring everything in its path, impeded only by its very dimensions.

To oppose this threat with all his resources should have been Sambhaji's principal concern, as it had been his father's—what, well over two centuries later, came to be defined as the 'overall strategic objective'.

Instead, Sambhaji chose to fritter away his strength on 'the more humble design' of reducing the Siddy of Janjira. He secretly planted a saboteur in the Siddy's fort to blow up the Siddy's ammunition magazines when the attack began. But this plan was discovered by the Siddy, it is said, through a maid-servant, and the saboteur was promptly put to death.

Here we have the whole pattern of Sambhaji's military campaigns: a total disregard for overall strategic exigency and bold planning, and utter carelessness in the execution of the plans. A tattling maid-servant had foiled his plan. The attack when it came, was a miserable failure. The Siddy's garrison was ready and waiting, its ammunition magazines still intact.

Undaunted by this setback, Sambhaji set in motion another plan to capture Janjira; a plan which, in the boldness of its concept, was the forerunner of such World War II innovations as the pipe-line under the ocean (PLUTO) and mulberry harbours, and even Professor Pyke's great floating platforms of ice and sawdust. Sambhaji's logic was indisputable: what protected the Siddy's stronghold was the channel separating it from the mainland. Why not fill up the channel?

Work on this 'immense mound of earth and stones' was soon begun. To this day, you are shown what are said to be the remains of the earthwork, now overgrown with vegetation. On the spot where you stand, stood the terrible-tempered Sambhaji, tensing his frame against the south-west wind much as you are doing today; waiting with unconcealed impatience, watching the progress of the causeway across the arm of the sea that was to enable his men to march right into the fortress.

While he was thus waiting, news was brought to him of a Moghul column of cavalry that had already penetrated deep into the Deccan, and was now barely fifty miles behind him. To Sambhaji, eager for a battle, the opportunity for a head-on clash with the Moghuls must have come like an answer to a prayer. He deputed Dadoji Raghunath to carry on the siege of Janjira, and himself turned to deal with the Moghul cavalry.

Hussain Ali Khan, the Moghul General in command of the column, could never have bargained for a counter-thrust so neatly planned so boldly executed, by a numerically inferior force. By a series of major raids, Sambhaji brought the column to a halt. Then he stopped their supplies from all sides. When the Moghul troops had been short of food and fodder for some days, he attacked.

This was the one brief and important moment of respite in a dismal round of failures. The Moghul column was routed, and it was all Hussain Ali Khan could do to withdraw the major portion of his troops before the rains began.

But to return to Janjira. Owing to the division of the forces, the work on the causeway had to be abandoned. Then the rains began. Dadoji Raghunath, encamped on the mainland across the channel, was not prepared to abandon the siege. Nor was be prepared to wait until the rains were fully over. He chose August, the month of the heaviest rains, to launch his attack against the fort with its forty-foot-high walls. The charge of the Light Brigade could not have been a more insane blunder or a more costly failure. The slippery rocks and the beating of the surf killed half the assailants, and the Siddy's men killed the rest. They must have enjoyed themselves shooting the helpless Marathas from behind the fort walls. At long last, the siege was given up, and Dadoji Raghunath withdrew whatever was left of his beaten forces.

It is unlikely that Kanhoji Angrey, then only twelve years old, participated in this first action of Sambhaji against the Siddy. But it seems probable that he joined Sambhaji's forces soon afterwards in a fairly humble capacity. Thirteen always seems to have been a favourite age for adventurous boys to run away to the sea.

There is a reference, unfortunately not very reliable, to Kanhoji Angrey 'manoeuvering Sambhaji's sea-going squadron' when he was sixteen years old. How many years did you have to put in before the mast before you were given command of a ship, or permitted to 'handle' a squadron—even if you began as the son of the *Surnobat* and Deputy Commander of Suvarna-durg? If we make it three years, it just seems possible that Kanhoji took part in the next expedition against the Siddy, particularly since this was mainly a naval venture.

The most reasonable assumption seems to be that as a boy of thirteen, Kanhoji Angrey joined Sambhaji's fleet. He was posted at Suvarna-durg, where his father, Tukoji was, or had been until a few years earlier, the Deputy Commander of the fort. It is unlikely that Tukoji was still around when Kanhoji began his military life. Even if he was alive, he must have been in his sixties, and unlikely to be still in service.

After hurling back the Marathas from the walls of Janjira, the Siddy added insult to injury by making an audacious raid after the retreating Marathas deep into the hinterland and capturing and carrying away the wife of Dadoji Raghunath, who it will be recalled, had been the commander of the Maratha forces which had attacked Janjira. Another expedition to teach the Siddy a lesson now became imperative. In the meantime, the Moghul army could be left to rampage freely, gobbling up the Deccan in large chunks.

In October, 1682, thirty Maratha vessels set out to find and destroy the Siddy's fleet. The Siddy had barely half the number of ships at his disposal, but the sea was his natural element. Kassam Yakoot Khan himself led his squadron. He carefully chose his position and waited for the Maratha fleet to appear, like a hunter waiting at a game-track. The two fleets came to grips at the mouth of the Thana River. Sambhaji's ships went charging in, carrying every inch of sail, as though in a thundering cavalry charge of the sea. It was a pathetic example of suicide warfare. The battle was short and decisive. The Maratha fleet was soundly defeated. Four of their ships, including the flagship, were captured by the Siddy, and many others sunk. Only some half a dozen ships got away. It is interesting to take note of the fact that the Maratha fleet was also led by a Siddy, the Siddy Misry, who had deserted to the Marathas. Siddy Misry was mortally wounded and died in captivity.

If young Kanhoji Angrey received his baptism of fire in this ill-fated naval battle, he learnt a lot from it: he had learnt how not to go into battle. He had learnt what the majority of the Maratha commanders lacked: the necessity of calculating risks, of 'thinking out' a battle before going into it. In modern military parlance, he had learnt to 'appreciate situations'.

We now have a glimpse of Kanhoji Angrey as a young man, age fourteen to sixteen; a likeness composed from a jumble of impressions; a half-remembered form seen in a quick flash; like a diver plummeting down or a thoroughbred taking a fence.

He is of middle height, with the darkness of skin given to a brown man by the sea and the sun, with arrogant, piercing black eyes in a heavy-set face, and flashing, even teeth; a creature of the sea and the sun and the earth, but representing the turbulence and storm of the sea and the scorching summer heat of the sun, not their peace and serenity, and the unyielding hardness of earth. He is strong as an ox, with a deep chest, knotted arms and work-hardened hands; an amazingly powerful swimmer, an excellent swordsman and skilled horseman; an earnest young man with a simplified philosophy crowded with war and religion—in that order—who loved to show off his knowledge and skills and daring and strength, and who found in warfare a complete, exultant fulfilment of life; simple in his tastes in clothes and food, and content with the companionship of his comrades-in-arms; a man of action surprisingly fond of reading and with a rare sensitiveness for the richness and poverty of words; direct in his manner but subtle and biting in his language.

There he was, the boy who had collected swords as a hobby and now used them with devastating skill, with no thought beyond the present; impulsive, easily swayed by emotion, loyal to a fault, convinced that warfare was an end in itself, not the means to an end. A mixture of boy and man, of sweat and toil and down-to-earth living, with latent powers of intellect and discernment; a mixture, also, of soldier and sailor and pandit, and of courage and caution: the raw material of which all heroes are made.

9

The Lion and the Lizard

At this stage, it is necessary to make a brief excursion to Bijapur, where tourists go to see the famous Boli-gumbaz, the Whispering Dome. It is almost, but not quite, too late to bring Bijapur into this story: the kingdom is already in the last throes of its death agony.

The Sultans of Bijapur, known as the Adil-Shahas, had been the undisputed rulers of the Deccan for close on two hundred years. It was from the domain of the Kings of Bijapur that Shivaji had carved out the Maratha kingdom. Before Shivaji, all chieftains and other land-owning noblemen in the Deccan, both Muslims and Hindus, had unquestioningly accepted the overlordship of the Bijapur Sultans. The Siddy of Janjira began as a vassal of Bijapur. Even Shivaji's father, Shahaji, was a chieftain under the Bijapur Kings and took part in a number of military actions as a commander of the Bijapur forces. With the rise of Shivaji, the power of the Sultans of Bijapur had been steadily on the decline. A large tract of territory had already been lost to the Marathas, and the many efforts of the Bijapur Kings to win back the territory had been defeated by the Marathas. Even when Shivaji was enthroned, the Bijapur King had done little to show his displeasure.

But this does not mean that the Sultans of Bijapur had resigned themselves to the existence of the new Maratha kingdom. Their war against the Marathas was only suspended for the time being in the face of a greater threat: Aurangzeb.

The Bijapur Sultans were independent sovereigns, established in India long before the Moghuls came. Although they were Muslims by religion, they had little in common with the Moghuls. By now they had acquired many of the manners and customs of the Deccany Hindus, and had even intermarried with them. They observed many of the Hindu festivals like *Holi* and *Dassara* and even offered prayers to some of the Hindu deities. After many generations of living in the Deccan without contact with the outside Muslim world, such identification with the people of the land was almost inevitable.

For one thing, the Muslims were, at all times, in an almost insignificant minority in the Deccan, said to be numbering less than 100,000; and without the co-operation of the Hindus, the Sultans of Bijapur could never have carried on the business of government. Many Hindus enjoyed positions of eminence in the Bijapur Court. If anything, the Bijapur Sultans detested the Moghuls far more than they detested the rising power of the Marathas.

In his avowed conquest of the Deccan, therefore, Aurangzeb had two enemies to contend with: the Marathas and the Sultans of Bijapur. For reasons best known to himself, Aurangzeb decided to concentrate first on Bijapur. Perhaps he felt that with Shivaji's death the Marathas were as good as finished. Judging by the way Sambhaji was carrying on, the old Emperor was not far wrong.

But there was still a lot of life left in Bijapur. After a series of rearguard actions and scorching the earth behind them, the small Bijapur army led by a valiant, teen-age king, Sikandar, fell back to the walled capital city, and there held on grimly for a whole year. Then, overwhelmed by starvation and sheer weight of numbers, Bijapur fell, but not without a desperate, last-ditch battle at the city walls. Aurangzeb is said to have wept when he saw the ruins of Bijapur, which did not prevent him, however, from making a prisoner of its boy-king, Sikandar Adil Shaha, barely nineteen years old.[8]

So ended the dynasty known as 'the Adil-Shahi'. Their fabled garden city, watered by a great underground aqueduct, is now a collection of ruins, silent and doleful, surrounded by a waterless moat and massive walls of hewn stone, six miles in circumference. The surrounding country, which was once a mass of greenery studded with the villas of the rich, is now a land of eternal famine. Because of an inadequate railway system, Bijapur is not even popular with tourists. But it is always worth a visit. They show you an enormous cannon called the *Zamzama*, and offer to have you photographed sitting inside the barrel. You pay a fleeting visit to Ibrahim Roza's tomb which was, for some time, used as a travellers' bungalow, and you marvel at its grace and gaze at the roof which is hung on incredibly slender supports. It took 37 years to build and cost seventy lakhs of rupees.

Bijapur is a haunted city, a city of tombs; tombs which a thrifty government has converted into government offices and other buildings of utility. By day, the city is tawdry and discordant; schoolboys on bicycles hurry by, clanging their bells and raising clouds of dust, and gramophones blare the latest film hits in tin-shed tea-shops. But at night, the schoolboys go to bed and the tin-sheds disappear into the gloom. The monuments come to life and stand out by themselves, and the ghosts of the Adil-Shahas walk the streets.

Before you leave, you must visit the Boli-gumbaz, another tomb, the biggest and the most imposing, where the mortal remains of Mohammad Adil Shah lie buried. It is a stark, austere, chalk-white monument of terrifying dignity, said to possess the second largest

---

8 Three years later, Sikandar, the defender of Bijapur, died in Aurangzeb's camp under mysterious circumstances, almost certainly poisoned by Aurangzeb.

dome in the world, and so perfect in its acoustics, that the merest whisper within its walls echoes and re-echoes seven times, dying out in ghostly sibilants; and a clock held against the surface of the wall can be heard distinctly across the width of the dome, 130 feet away.

But it is now getting dark and the bats have begun to flit amongst the cupolas and minarets. You are anxious to get away: few people would care to spend the night in the Boli-gumbaz.

10

The Choice of the Turtle

This was the high point of Aurangzeb's long reign. The Empire was bigger than ever: it is said that a caravan could not have crossed it in two years. Except for some portions of the south, the entire map of India was dyed a vivid green.

Bijapur was finished. Even in Maratha country, organized resistance had ceased: Aurangzeb's columns could roam about at will. Only the forts remained intact, still wholly Maratha possessions, flickering like lamps in the wilderness. They said there were 365 forts in the Deccan, one for every day of the year. But unlike the days of Shivaji, each fort was now on its own, isolated, with no hope of assistance from outside; each one an outpost abandoned to its own resources.

There was a new surge of activity amongst the Moghuls, an unaccustomed liveliness brought about by the smell of success. Aurangzeb now directed his full attention upon the Deccan forts. He selected two commanders for the task: Yettikad Khan for the highland region, and the Siddy of Janjira, Kassam Yakoot Khan, for the Konkan. Everyone in the Moghul camp must have felt that the new campaign was almost a mopping-up operation; that it was only a matter of time before all the forts would be winkled out in ones and twos. Even before Aurangzeb's, commanders set out on their missions, his secret emissaries were already in contact with the Subedars of the forts, offering large rewards for a quiet surrender, threatening dire punishments in case of resistance.

The forts began to fall, like mud houses collapsing in a flood, without visible signs of damage. Many of them gave up without resistance. Tattora fell, and the whole chain of supporting forts from Tattora to Panhala. In the Konkan itself, Sagargad, Rajkot and Pali were surrendered to the Siddy by their respective commanders, without a fight.

There are vague references to Kanhoji Angrey having taken part in naval engagements against the Siddy in the defence of Rajkot and Pali and having shown conspicuous daring and skill. But again, there is no reliable record, and since, in any case, Siddy Kassam succeeded in capturing the forts, Kanhoji's personal contribution did not obviously make much difference to the issue of battle. The damage done by the worm boring from within could not be offset by odd flashes of military skill and daring.

The Siddy, too, was at the height of his power and glory. His next objective was Suvarna-durg, the Golden Fort. The year, as nearly as it can be ascertained, was 1688.

Suvarna-durg, about a hundred miles south of Bombay, is an island fort surrounded on all sides by water. Its fifty-feet high walls enclose an area of eight acres and the fort used to contain three fresh-water wells, including one in which you could reach the water level by going down a flight of steps. Carved in stone upon the arch of the main entrance gate is the figure of a turtle which is said to be the guardian deity of the fort. Suvarna-durg was commanded by Achloji Mohitay.

Also in the fort was Kanhoji Angrey, perhaps no more than a 'sardar of twenty-five'; not yet twenty years old, with many a skirmish, both on land and at sea, to his credit; known amongst his comrades and his enemies for his daring and skill, his courage and his amazing strength—already a bit of a hero.

The Moghuls never considered a siege adequate unless they could surround their objective with troops, and the siege of Suvarna-durg fitted neatly into this tactical pattern. On three sides stood the

Siddy's fleet, cutting off escape and stopping supplies. On the land side, waiting with bared teeth across the width of the arm of the sea, was a strong detachment of the Siddy's troops.

And in the fort itself, was the ever-present fifth column of the Moghuls, hacking away at the roots, concentrating on the key men; distributing largesse, promising rewards, threatening reprisals ...

Having blocked up all exits, the Siddy was willing to wait, pinning his faith on a proved method of conquest: negotiated surrender. It was so much easier to take a fort by working from within.

The 'negotiations' were soon completed. Achloji Mohitay, the Commander of Suvarna-durg, agreed to hand over the fort to the Siddy.

It was a dream situation for an ambitious young officer and all it needed was the spark: the hour had struck, it needed the man. For Kanhoji Angrey, it was the moment of cataclysm; his whole life would depend on how he reacted to the situation; whether it was in him to rise to the occasion.

They say he sent a secret message to the King at Raigad, informing him of the Commander's defection and offering to save the fort if he was given command. They say that the King gave full authority to Kanhoji to take whatever steps he chose for the continued defence of Suvarna-durg. It all sounds nice and proper, but that is not how revolutions are made. It was also unlike Kanhoji Angrey, a man of fierce pride and passion, quick in thought and action, with too much agility and suppleness to be deterred by the dictates of procedure from doing what he was convinced was right. For one thing, it would have taken at least three days for a messenger to reach Raigad and return with the King's authority, even presuming that he was permitted an immediate audience with Sambhaji, which is unlikely.

Of necessity, the change-over must have been too swift for any such formalities, but it had to be smooth and sure, for failure would have meant instant death. As such, its detail must have been carefully worked out well in advance. At least two men outside the besieged fort were in the know of the secret. One was Balaji Vishwanath, a clerk in the Siddy's salt works at Chiplun. He had been doubling up as a spy, sending information about the Siddy's troop movements to Kanhoji Angrey, and, it is almost certain, goading him to action. The other was a holy man called Brahmendra-swami, who lived in anonymity in the hills near Chiplun, and of whom we shall hear more as this story progresses. The Swami is said to have sent his blessings to Kanhoji Angrey's plan. There is little doubt that a few others within the fort itself must have been in the secret, for the seizing of power overnight cannot be accomplished without the help of active partners.

There was then an overnight coup. Kanhoji and his associates placed Achloji Mohitay under arrest and took over command of the fort. They announced to the garrison that the fort would be defended to the last; that surrender was not to be thought of.

Then, after the first shrinking experiment in self-assertion, Kanhoji Angrey did a very thoughtless thing. He launched a cross-channel attack against the Siddy's troops.

The attack was a failure. Too late, Kanhoji must have realized that it took more than bravery and leadership to be a successful commander; that the tactics of an audacious commander would not serve to defend the fort. Most of his storming party were neatly picked out by the Siddy's waiting soldiers, and Kanhoji himself was taken prisoner.

But he did not remain a prisoner for long. He may have bribed his guards to let him slip away, or he may have made a dash for it. In either case, he had to swim the mile-wide channel, and his captors must have laughed at his foolhardiness because they knew that the waves would dash him into pulp against the rocks. Incredibly, within a few hours, he was back in the fort, battered and weary, but once again its commander.

Again, failure had taught him an unforgettable lesson. When you were strongly entrenched, it was more profitable to defend. You could not attack from within unless you were assured of outside help. What was needed in a siege was dogged resistance; conserving food, sparing ammunition, and keeping constant watch. It would be a long wait, for the Siddy was not likely to relax his siege until the arrival of the monsoon: only King Rain would send his feet scuttling away to some safe anchorage.

Suvarna-durg took a lesson from its guardian deity, the turtle: it drew in its limbs and head behind its strong shell and prepared itself for a long wait.

The Siddy did not even wait for the monsoon. The Marathas were now doing exactly what he had done time and time again. His carefully-laid plans had failed. Now there was no question of taking the fort without a prolonged siege and a costly attack.

After a few weeks of waiting, he quietly withdrew his fleet and went off to seek more rewarding objectives.

The hour had come and gone; the man had withstood its challenge; Kanhoji Angrey had quaffed the first heady glass of the wine of success. He had gambled and won, and he had stemmed the tide of defeat. A grateful monarch saluted his courage and initiative by investing him with the robes of a Commander and giving him formal command of the fort of Suvarna-durg, the Golden Fort, where he had spent his boyhood. Barely a dozen years earlier, his father, Tukoji, had been the Deputy Commander in the same fort.

Here again we have a brief but clear glimpse of that man of destiny, Balaji Vishwanath—like a ship in the night seen in a vivid flash of lightning—although there is nothing to connect him yet with future greatness. But he is not in the shadows any longer. He is a man on the run with a price on his head. The fact that the innocent-looking clerk in the salt works at Chiplun had been a Maratha spy—that he was in regular communication with Kanhoji Angrey, sending him information about every move of the Siddy's fleet and troops—has been discovered, and Siddy Kassam Yakoot Khan has sworn to make an example of him.

But Balaji Vishwanath was not a spy for nothing. He was tipped off by a friend in good time. He fled.

Deprived of his man, the Siddy wreaked his vengeance upon Balaji's brother, Janoji. He had him seized, sewn up in a sack and drowned in the sea alive!

Instinct, or the advice of his spiritual guru, Brahmendra-swami, guided Balaji's footsteps unerringly to Poona which was going to be the centre of Aurangzeb's activities during the next ten years. Poona, a growing military headquarters, had plenty of openings for a bright young man who could read and write and keep accounts. In 1689, Balaji Vishwanath became a clerk in the revenue office of the Maratha Subedar of Poona. By 1695, he had reached the position of the Assistant Subedar, and as such, became responsible for whatever passed for administration in the chaos of war. His chief duty was to arrange for the supplies of fodder and stores required by the armies camped around Poona. It seems that although he was a Maratha official, he was just as efficient in organizing the supplies for the armies of Aurangzeb whenever the Moghuls happened to be camping at Poona. It was a tribute to the special genius of Balaji Vishwanath that the commanders of both the warring sides were equally grateful to him for his assistance.

The man who was a clerk in the salt works at Chiplun is on the way up. But he has barely scratched the surface of the rewards in store for him. 'You will reach the highest position in the land', Brahmendra-swami had told him, and Balaji Vishwanath had implicit faith in the Swami's words.

11

'In Defeat: Defiance!'

In the year 1942, the British Commander-in-Chief in the Middle East, General Auchinleck, sent out a commando party to kill or capture the opposing German Commander, Erwin Rommel. The party, under Major Geoffrey Keys, was landed by submarine at a place called Beda-Littoria in Libya, where Rommel lived. Major Keys and his commandos got into Rommel's house and shot up a number of its inmates, but Rommel himself was away.

In much the same manner, in the year 1689, the Moghul General, Taqrib Khan, organized and led a commando raid sixty miles into the heart of the Maratha country through some of the most difficult terrain, to capture or kill the Maratha King Sambhaji. The planning and staff-work that must have gone into this expedition is worthy of a military staff-study. 'Having procured correct intelligence, and guides well-acquainted with the passes through the ghats and the intricate windings of the route, he chose a few active infantry and a small party of horse', and set out for Sambhaji's riverside pleasure-palace near Sangameshwar.

Unlike Rommel, Sambhaji was where he was expected to be. The rest was easy. He was captured and taken to the Moghul camp at Tulapur.[9] There, under Aurangzeb's orders, he was publicly exhibited, bound upon a camel. Then Aurangzeb ordered a red-hot iron rod to be thrust into his eyes and his tongue to be cut off. Only after these orders had been duly executed, was the head cut off, and his body badly hacked into pieces and thrown to the dogs.

The nature of Aurangzeb's vengeance shook every Maratha to the core. All the damage that Sambhaji might have done while he lived, was wiped out by the death he suffered: in a flash, his cruelties, his temper were forgiven and forgotten. What Aurangzeb had intended to serve as an example to terrorize the Marathas into submission, had a directly opposite effect upon them: it gave rise to the most terrible vows of vengeance.

Drawn together in a moment of shock, the Maratha chieftains, who during Sambhaji's reign had cut themselves off from the King and had begun to operate on their own, suddenly awoke to a new sense of responsibility. The fragmented components of Shivaji's carefully built-up military hierarchy were once again swept together.

Unfortunately, their unity lasted only as long as the crisis lasted.

Of their own accord, the Maratha chieftains gathered together at Raigad to decide their future course of action. Sambhaji's son, Shivaji (later to become King as Shahu), was six years old. Until he came of age, they decided to appoint Sambhaji's step-brother, Rajaram, as Regent. Calmly, 'they calculated their means of resistance, and saw with dismay a public treasury exhausted, the laxity of all discipline, the unprovided state of their forts, and even the probability of their being reduced.'

---

9 Tulapur means 'weighing-town'. Forty years earlier, Sambhaji's grandfather, Shahaji, to settle a bet that he could weigh an elephant, did so by putting the animal on a barge in the river. After taking off the elephant, he had the barge filled with stones until it submerged to the exact level of water while carrying the elephant. He then had the stones weighed. On account of this incident, the place had come to be known as Tula-pur.

This was the legacy inherited by Rajaram, Shivaji's second son. But amongst those gathered at Raigad to take stock of the situation, there was no panic or desperation, only grim resolution. They realized that their primary concern was the protection of the new Regent, Rajaram. To keep the people together, to keep alive the idea of a Maratha kingdom, it was essential to provide a focus for the aspirations and loyalties of the people. Emboldened by their success in capturing Sambhaji, other Moghul commanders were bound to attempt similar raids to capture Rajaram. To guard against this, they decided that Rajaram should have no fixed abode but that he should move about from fort to fort, keeping his movements secret; and if the forts were in danger of falling, then, as a last resort, shift his camp to Jinji, a small Maratha pocket on the east coast of India a thousand miles away, leaving his chieftains to carry on the war against the Moghuls as best as they could.

It was a wise decision. For even as the new Maratha Regent and his councillors were making their plans for the future, the Emperor's General, Yettikad Khan, was marching towards Raigad at the head of a powerful column.

The siege of Raigad began at the end of the rains. But there was no question of Raigad falling easily. It was one of the strongest forts, with a plentiful store of food and ammunition.

The attacking force, commanded by Yettikad Khan and assisted by the Siddy Kassam Yakoot Khan of Janjira, battered at the walls of Raigad well into the spring of 1690 without making the slightest dent in its defences. A new stubbornness amongst the Maratha soldiers was already apparent. Besides, Raigad was consecrated ground, with a special symbolic significance to every Maratha; it was the capital, the centre of the Maratha power; it was at Raigad that Shivaji had been enthroned, married, died and cremated.

Above all, although Rajaram had left Raigad long before the attack began, Sambhaji's wife Yesubai, and the young heir to the throne, Shivaji, were still at Raigad.

In the end, it was treachery that won the fort for the Moghuls. A man called Suryaji Pisal undertook to lead a party of his own soldiers into the fort and to throw open the gates to the Moghuls. His price was the grant of a large tract of land to be given to him in perpetuity.

In the middle of 1690, Raigad fell into the hands of the Moghuls, and with it the future king of the Marathas and his mother. Both of them were taken away to Aurangzeb's camp, and the Emperor is said to have treated them with unusual consideration. Perhaps Aurangzeb was already lamenting the results of his barbarity to Sambhaji.

Sensitive Marathas still hang their heads in shame at the mention of Suryaji Pisal's name—the man who betrayed their young Prince and sold their capital to the Moghuls.

But even the fall of Raigad and the capture of the heir to the throne were not enough to shatter the new spirit amongst the Marathas. Even now, as the Emperor's victorious columns were fanning out into the plains of the Deccan, there was no sign of defeatism. Two more forts, Miraj and Panhala, were surrounded by the Moghuls, but the Maratha chieftains had already begun to retaliate; they were planning, not panicking; they had begun to form themselves into independent groups and to carry out lightning raids into the Moghul columns.

Rajaram was now ready to make a dash for Jinji, leaving the Deccan to the Moghuls and to his chieftains. But before leaving, the formalities incumbent upon a new ruler had to be completed. He appointed a skeleton cabinet and gave them the widest powers; he also announced various new military commands and nominated the commanders. His government and his commanders were not unlike the exiled 'free' governments and generals of the last war. Many of his chieftains found themselves appointed to the command of forts which were in Moghul hands. But all the same, Rajaram saw to it that there was a cabinet of ministers even if it was a shadow cabinet, and that there were commanders of forts even though they had no forts to command: the form had been maintained, which was vastly preferable to leaving a total vacuum in the Deccan or to the chaos of Sambhaji's reign.

Among the new appointments was the name of Siddoji Gujjar, placed in command of the Maratha fleet and given the overall responsibility of defending the coast from both land and sea. Siddoji Gujjar was granted the altogether new rank of *Surkhail* or Grand Admiral. By a curious coincidence, it was about the same time that the British Navy, which until then had designated its flag officers as 'generals-at-sea', began to call them 'Admirals'.

The Deputy Commanders of Siddoji Gujjar were also named. There were two of them. One of them was Bhawanji Mohitay; the other, a young man of twenty who had recently soared into the limelight. His name was Kanhoji Angrey.

12

Northern Command

Among the senior military commanders who accompanied Rajaram to Jinji, was Siddoji Gujjar, the newly-appointed Chief of the Maratha navy. The fleet and the command of the coast fell to the two Deputy Commanders: Kanhoji Angrey and Bhawanji Mohitay. The Northern Command, with the remnants of the fleet at Suvarna-durg and Gheria, came to Kanhoji Angrey as an independent command.

Shivaji, when he died, is said to have left a fleet of 'four to five hundred ships'. This figure is on the high side and almost certainly includes Shivaji's mercantile fleet. However, most historians agreed that Shivaji had built up a fleet of at least two hundred fighting ships of various sizes.

Of the magnificent fleet, now, barely ten years after Shivaji's death, only a shrivelled stump remained. According to Conde de Ericiera, the Portuguese Viceroy, the fleet that came to Kanhoji's lot 'consisted of no more than eight or ten vessels'.

They seem to have had a bewildering variety of sea-craft in those days, ranging from flimsy dug-out tonies to stately three-masted *ghurabs*. One writer gives a list of as many as fifty-one different kinds of vessels. Of these, only five were exclusively used as fighting ships: the *ghurab*, the *gallivat*, the *manchwa*, the *shibar* and the *pal*.

The *manchwa* was no more than a tony or fishing boat, only suitable for coastal use and carried no more than fifteen men; and the *gallivat* was a row-boat with sails. The *pals*, the *shibars*, and the *ghurabs* were sea-going vessels equipped with two or three masts and carrying sails.

The biggest naval ships were the *ghurabs*, usually with two and occasionally with three masts. They ranged from 150 to 300 tons and there were always one or two *ghurabs* of about 400 tons. The *ghurab* can be compared to the British and Portuguese frigates of those days, bearing in mind that neither the *ghurab* nor any of the other Maratha naval ships were anywhere near as seaworthy as their European counterparts. The *ghurabs* were squat, broad-beamed vessels, riding high in the water, their prows, long and thin like blades of swords, almost touching the water, and they were subject to violent pitching and rolling in the open seas. They say that Shivaji's reluctance to undertaking personal command of naval operations was due to his experience in a *ghurab* in the Karwar expedition, when he is said to have suffered continuously from seasickness.

As their main armaments, the *ghurabs* carried two big guns firing forward through portholes cut in the bulkhead. These were from nine to twelve-pounder guns. There were also twelve to sixteen other guns, from six to eight on each side; which fired shots of from six to nine pounds. Each *ghurab* carried from 100 to 150 fighting men in addition to the crew.

But, like the cruisers and battleships of the navies between the two world wars, the *ghurabs* seldom went into action by themselves. They were almost invariably accompanied by a screen of *gallivat*s, which were faster and more manoeuverable than the *ghurabs*. The *gallivat*s hardly ever exceeded seventy tons. If they were bigger than that, they were placed in the category of *ghurabs*, since there was little difference in their basic design. In fact, many European writers have referred to the smaller *ghurabs* as *gallivat*s and the larger *gallivat*s as *ghurabs*.

The *gallivat*s, which were the real backbone of the fleet, were fast row-boats with sails. They had two masts of which the mizzen mast was 'very slight' and the main mast 'triangular and large'.

The *gallivats* were built more for speed and easier handling than for strength or endurance, and often armament was sacrificed for lightness. The decking was mostly always of split bamboos and incapable of sustaining the weight of cannons. Some of the larger *gallivats*, however, used to have wooden decking and carried six to eight two-pounder or four-pounder guns, but these heavier *gallivats* were not very popular.

You can see the *gallivats* to this day in the Konkan almost exactly as they were in the days of Kanhoji Angrey, bucking with each slap of the waves, and, if you are venturesome, you can take a ride in one and experience all the thrills and trials of eighteenth century sailors; they are like graceful Arab ponies riding with the ungainly gait of camels.

The *gallivats* carried forty to fifty oars and could be rowed at four miles an hour. They were versatile little craft, like the cavalry of the navy—and almost equally expendable against a resolute defence—and, at the same time, also rather like the transport corps, because the *gallivats* were often employed to tow the *ghurabs* into action.

The *ghurabs* and the *gallivats* were the two main types of fighting ships. The others, the pals and the *shibars*, were hybrid vessels, smaller than *ghurabs* but bigger than *gallivats*. We are not likely to encounter many of these odd craft in the pages of this book.

Firearms were at a premium. In fact, besides the guns fitted in the ships, there were no other firearms. The chief weapon was the curved, one-handed Maratha sword and the round shield (*dhal*). But the sword was necessarily a close-quarter weapon, mainly used by boarding parties. The other weapons were bows and arrows and spears and stones—each ship was stocked with piles of stones to be hurled into other ships just before getting to grips.

These were the weapons. The guns, bows and arrows and spears, and lastly slingshots and stones, were what might be termed 'long-range' weapons. The ship's guns mostly always fired at point-blank range; gunnery was in its infancy and anything beyond three hundred yards away was considered an almost impossible range. The bows and arrows and spears were used at amazingly long distances, however, and a hundred yards was almost normal range for their employment.

The ship itself was under charge of the *Nakhoda*, the Captain. He had one or two assistants known as *tandales*. The *tandales* were men-of-all-work combining several duties connected with the rowing of the ships, the handling of the sails, keeping stocks of food and water, and even acting as 'cheer leaders'.

Of the fighting strength of the ships, the most pampered were the gunners. There was a perpetual shortage of trained gunners, and since the Portuguese and the British were believed to owe their success in battle entirely to their superior gunnery, European gunners were always in great demand. In fact, almost any European could get a well-paid job with an Indian ruler by merely pretending that he was an expert gunner, and many did. The Marathas and the other rulers in India were always on the look-out for European gunners, and they often paid exorbitantly for the services of so-called expert European gunners. The gun-teams formed nearly half the fighting strength of a vessel, the others belonged to the boarding parties.

All the ships flew pennants and flags of assorted colours somewhat indiscriminately. They also carried ten-foot long brass trumpets and large tomtoms and made 'an amazing noise'. Neither the men nor their officers wore uniforms.

They preferred to stick close to the coast, putting themselves between the coast and the enemy ships, keeping under the protection of their own coastal guns, and, as far as possible, tried to avoid the open sea in heavy weather. Indeed the weather conditions they liked best were a dead calm, since their rowing boats could then easily overtake sailing ships.

Before Kanhoji Angrey, the senior officers of the Maratha fleet and in command of the coastal forts were mostly always Muslims. Many of them were deserters from the Siddy's navy and their loyalty was never above suspicion. In Sambhaji's fleet even the highest naval officer was a Siddy, the Siddy Misri, who was a close relative of Siddy Kassam Yakoot Khan. The seamen themselves were, however, mostly Hindus, recruited or drafted from the fishermen clans of the Konkan.

During the four months of the monsoon, the entire fleet had to be moth-balled. Most of the *gallivats* and other smaller vessels were actually hauled up and kept on dry land in some safe cove, and a boom erected across the entrance to the cove. The roofs of all vessels were covered with palm thatching, and their hulks painted with coconut grease. It was only after the end of August, after the Coconut Day, which is said to signify the end of the monsoon, that the first little tony ventured out into the water, and after that, within a few weeks, the whole fleet was fitted out and cleaned up and put out to sea. Both for the sailors and soldiers, the rainy months were months of compulsory rest from warfare, and most of them, as many as ninety per cent, were sent away on leave.

Imagine then, a squadron of the Maratha navy, two hundred and fifty years ago; a *ghurab* being towed with incredible speed towards some doomed ship, being brought into position so that its big guns could fire into the rigging at point-blank range; and then the *gallivats*, twenty oars dipping in unison on each side, their blue and green pennants fluttering in the wind, their enormous trumpets blaring, their tomtoms beating the tattoo of death, and the swordsmen swarming their decks yelling the frightening Maratha war-cry 'Har-har Mahadeo'; getting closer and closer with each stroke of the oars ...

But we are getting ahead of the story. The picture of a well-turned-out Maratha squadron in full war-cry belongs to a later date. The eight or ten ships that Kanhoji Angrey inherited could not have been anything more than a hotch-potch of patched-up *gallivats* and lesser vessels. It is possible that he may have had a battered old *ghurab* or two. But whatever he had was certainly not enough to take on the Siddy, who had at least ten times as many fighting ships. In his attack on Bombay, to drive out the British from there, the Siddy had employed 'eleven ships and seventy *gallivats*'.

After the first flush of assumption of his new command had receded, the future must have seemed bleak to young Kanhoji Angrey. He, Kanhoji, was by royal command in independent charge of a hundred-and-fifty miles of wide-open coastline. His fighting force was this collection of battered old ships and the ragged garrison of half-a-dozen coastal forts. Some three thousand men had to be fed regularly, even if they could not be paid regularly. By royal command too, the money for all this was supposed to come from the land dependant on the numerous inland forts of the Marathas. In actual fact, of course, these forts were either in Moghul hands or dominated by their forces. The morale of his men—if commanders thought in terms of morale in those days—must have indeed touched bottom.

13

The Rise of Bombay

Again there is a thick fog upon the next seven or eight years. The limelight had swung all the way to the east coast. There, in the hill fort of Jinji, the Maratha Regent, Rajaram, held his court in exile, much as Chiang Kai-shek did in Chungking during the Japanese invasion of China. There too, at the foot of the fort of Jinji, lay the main bulk of the Moghul army in a siege that was to last for eight years. What happened in the Konkan, a backwater a thousand miles away from the main current of history, was hardly worthy of notice.

All the same, much was happening along the western coast of India.

The English, to all appearances, were being knocked about from all sides, but at the same time digging feverishly to entrench themselves in the soil of the Konkan. This was the time when there were two English trading companies in India, each vying with the other in a campaign of intrigue and slander. Sir Nicholas Waite, the Governor of the new Company, had vowed that he 'would spend Rs 20,000, but that he would have the (old Company's) flag struck at Surat'. He almost succeeded. His opposite number, the Governor of the old Company, Sir John Child, countered by sending a *banya* to Surat to poison one of Sir Nicholas's council.

These were also the days of piracy on a grand scale. The Malabar pirates had become the terror of the merchants of Surat. Everyone, including the Moghul Emperor, was convinced that the pirates were backed by the Company and that many of the Company's servants actually assisted them. The fact that William Kidd looted some of the Company's own ships by a daring attack near Rajapur, was obviously not sufficient proof of the Company's innocence.

In 1695, the looting of Aurangzeb's largest ship, *Ganj-Sawai* (Great Treasure), by that acknowledged nabob of the Malabar pirates, Henry Every, brought matters to a head. *Ganj-Sawai* carried a number of Muslim ladies from Aurangzeb's court who had just finished their pilgrimage to Mecca. What was perhaps even more important, she also carried gold and silver worth fifty-four lakhs of rupees. The English merchants swore themselves blue in the face denying all responsibility for the outrage, but Aurangzeb paid no heed. He resorted to his usual remedy-by-squeeze; he threw the Company's officials at Surat into confinement and when the Governor of Bombay, Sir John Gayer, went to Surat to protest, he had him also thrown into prison.

Servants of the old Company were sure that the Emperor's action was instigated by the rival Company: Sir Nicholas Waite was putting his Rs. 20,000 to good use. He had sent word to the Emperor that the officials of the old Company were 'thieves and confederates with the pyrates'.

But the merchants soon wriggled out of that one. By now they had discovered that the best antidote to Imperial displeasure was bribery: everything, including the molesting of high-born ladies of the court, had a price, and they had also learnt that the price varied inversely according to the liberality of palm-greasing at lower levels.

As further proof of their *bona fides* the English even offered to take on the duties of escorting the Emperor's Mecca-bound ships. But they found that the field was already overcrowded by other aspirants for the job. Similar offers were also made by both the Dutch and the Portuguese. Aurangzeb flatly turned down all offers. He had no trust in any of the foreign traders and he was secretly convinced that they were all in league with the pirates. In any case, accepting any of these offers would have meant putting the Siddy out of business.

Since his attack on Bombay, in which the British had been driven to take shelter behind the fort walls, the Siddy too had been getting more and more demanding. He used the Mazagaon creek within a mile of the Bombay fort as his monsoon base, and the Company's officials did not dare to dispute his right to do so. He had expanded his domain considerably by ousting the Marathas from many of their coastal forts, and his ships made increasingly audacious and long-range raids upon the coastal towns. He had taken and fortified the island of Underi, close to Bombay, without paying any heed to the strongest British protests. The East India Company had to do a lot of tricky tight-rope walking between what they described as the 'predatory Marathas' and the 'semi-barbarous African'. But if the English were beaten, they did not know it. On the one hand, they were barely managing to keep going in the face of overwhelming odds, and on the other, they had embarked upon an ambitious plan to 'render Bombay, come what might, rich and populous'.

They paid a cruel price.

Most of Bombay, in those days, was a tide-washed bog, giving off the most 'unveryhealthful vapours'. The seven islands which constitute Bombay had not quite joined up. The early settlers died like flies. Of the twenty-four passengers that came to Bombay with John Ovington towards the end of the seventeenth century, twenty died before the end of the first rainy season. It was the monsoon that seemed to overwhelm them, and 'two monsoons were the age of man' was almost literally true. In particular, the European children had an alarmingly high death-rate: not one in twenty reached maturity.

But Bombay was being developed, 'come what might', heedless of the death stalking its muddy streets. A post office and a cotton press were established, and even the building of a church was begun. Unfortunately, the funds raised for the church were embezzled by the then Governor, Sir John Child, and the building could not be completed for another eighteen years. Parsis, Hindus and Christians were invited to settle in Bombay and told to 'occupy what land they pleased'. By the turn of the century, the population, depleted by the Siddy's attack and the disease left behind by his troops, had once again passed the 60,000 mark. Silk weavers were encouraged to come and settle down, and houses were provided for them. Advances were made to cultivators and fishermen, jobs were reserved only for those who lived in Bombay. 'Persuade all you can from the main to go over and settle at Bombay upon terms of having constant work', was the slogan provided by the Directors of the Company.

Bombay grew, against all the laws of nature; a boom town, tawdry and noisy, rose out of the oozy bed around the seven islands, and with it grew the honourable East India Company.

The Marathas, struggling to preserve their land from the Moghul invasion, barely had enough time to raise their heads and take notice of what was happening around them. Beyond making periodic protests to the Company about its permitting the Siddy's ships to 'winter' in Mazagaon, they did not concern themselves with the activities of the Company. Whenever the Marathas protested, the English made meaningless submission to the Siddy. The Siddy took little notice of the British protests and continued to use the waters around Bombay as his own. The English thereupon sent glowing assurances of neutrality to the Marathas, and everything went on just as before.

It was not until the end of 1698 that the first slight tiff between the Company and the Marathas took place. Two ships laden with salt from Bombay were seized by the Commander of Padm-durg. The seizure of these boats must have come as something of a jolt to those who had begun to think that as far as the coastline around Bombay was concerned, the Marathas were finished; that it was the Siddy who now ruled the coast.

But the Commander of Padm-durg obviously meant business. He imprisoned the merchants from the salt-boats and is said to have 'most miserably beat them, saying they cared not for the English or anyone else'. A few days later, all but two of these merchants were released on their agreeing to pay a ransom of Rs 20,000, and they were sent to Bombay under an escort of the Commander's soldiers. The two merchants kept behind were kept as hostages for the proper performance of the agreement made by their shipmates.

The English, however, could always show a trick or two to the Marathas when it came to a matter of hostages and ransom. They promptly put the Padm-durg escort into confinement and demanded the release of the hostages held in Padm-durg.

But no one bothered about people being held as hostages those days, unless the hostages were very important people; and they did not bother much about important people either. For instance, Sir John Gayer, the English Governor of Bombay, who had been thrown into confinement by Aurangzeb after the capture of his ship *Ganj-Sawai* by the pirates, was still languishing in prison—he was there for seven years. There is little doubt that the hostages now kept by both sides would have been forgotten and left to their fate had not the Company decided to back up its action with sterner measures. It placed an embargo on all the ships belonging to Bombay, forbidding them to carry salt to any place along the coast, 'until full assurance from the several Subedars, that the like abuses should not be done to our people in the future'.

On the west coast, salt is manufactured mainly around Bombay, by evaporating sea water captured in salt-pans. The whole of the Deccan depends upon this salt. The English had pounced upon a vital weakness. Within a matter of weeks, they had won their point.

> 'The Subedar of Conagy Angra having wrote the Deputy Governor for leave for the salt boats to come to his country, promising that he would get the two men that were imprisoned by Padamdrooke releast, and that for the future

> none of our inhabitants should be abused, we permitted the salt vessell to goe.'

This is the first reference to Kanhoji Angrey in the records of the East India Company.

14

On a White Charger

On his way to Jinji, Rajaram had many a hair-breadth escape. Aurangzeb seemed to know all about his plans, and every Moghul Subedar, every Moghul detachment in the Deccan had been alerted to keep on the lookout for the runaway Maratha king, and large rewards were offered for his capture.

Rajaram's party was attacked by a Moghul patrol on, of all places, a minute island in the Tungabhadra River. He barely escaped with his life, sacrificing half his escort and all his horses. From then on, they travelled on foot, disguised as holy monks. In Bangalore, they had another narrow escape. As they were cooking a meal in the precincts of a temple, someone noticed that one of the monks was having his feet bathed by another. This led to whisperings which one of Rajaram's men was lucky to overhear: it turned out that their whole party was going to be arrested. Within a few minutes, Rajaram was spirited away by his bodyguard, while the rest of the party went on cooking their meals as though nothing had happened. After a little while, the Moghul soldiers came and surrounded the camp. Rajaram's followers were imprisoned and subjected to severe beatings to obtain confessions from them. They all resolutely confessed to the same thing: they were religious mendicants! After a few days of confinement and third degree, they were released.

Of the three hundred horsemen that had originally left the fort of Panhala, only the battered remains reached Jinji late in the year 1689, a bedraggled party of five Brahmins in the last stages of exhaustion. They had covered nearly a thousand miles in just over a month, most of it on foot, through country infested with Moghul troops and informers greedy for the prize money.

Their appearance at the fort gates must have confronted the commander of Jinji with a sore test of loyalty. Offering shelter to this runaway prince whom he had never seen before, he must have known, was only inviting disaster. It would have been so much simpler to turn away the band of scruffy refugees.

But, inexplicably, the bonds of loyalty held. Shivaji's influence still proved their magic. Jinji welcomed Rajaram with open arms and offered him everything it had. On his part, Rajaram took everything that Jinji had, including the hoarded treasure of centuries, as though it were his by right.

At Jinji again, the pathetic formality of announcing a full cabinet and other officials was gone through with due ceremony. Gold bangles and other presents were sent to all the prominent men in the Deccan, announcing the accession of Rajaram as Regent. How the gold was come by is not important: gold is the same colour irrespective of how it was obtained. What is important is that the Maratha noblemen were once again made aware that they had a Regent and a Cabinet; the Regent a son of the great Shivaji, and the Ministers of the Cabinet charged with specific duties after the pattern of Shivaji's Cabinet. Rajaram also announced magnanimous grants of lands to Maratha noblemen who had rendered service since the death of Shivaji.

The awkward fact that none of this land was now in the possession of the Marathas did not seem to matter at this stage. On Rajaram's side, the gifting away of this land was merely an expression of his resolve to drive out the Moghuls and return to the Deccan as its ruler. On the part of the recipients, it was something to live for and look forward to, a paper to be stored away and presented for encashment only after the Moghuls had been driven out. How exactly they were going to drive out the Moghuls, neither the Regent nor his people had the faintest idea.

Then, having meticulously fulfilled his obligations of a Regent in exile, Rajaram got down with equal earnestness to enjoying the pleasures and pastimes of oriental royalty. He married 'three or four women during the first two or three months of his arrival, (and) dancing girls were brought to the court in many troops.'

Aurangzeb had ordered his best General, Zulfikhar, to reduce Jinji. Zulfikhar has already made a brief appearance in this story when he had attacked Raigad; only, he was called Yettikad Khan then. The title of *Zulfikhar* was bestowed upon him as a mark of appreciation for his capture of Raigad. He came and camped at the foot of Jinji fort but made no attempt to attack the fort itself. His flabby, dispirited army lay squirming ineffectually in the baking wastes of Coromandel for eight years, making occasional forays into the surrounding country to collect tributes and supplies and breaking up a few Hindu temples as and when the mood seized them. Periodically, Dawood Khan, one of Zulfikhar's deputies, ordered a charge against the fort in moments of drunkenness. Maratha columns also helped to relieve the monotony when they came thundering down the slopes in lightning raids and played as much havoc as they could before the Moghuls 'got down to saddling their horses'.

Zulfikhar had no intention of attacking Jinji. He had a secret understanding with Rajaram that he would not do so unless compelled by the Emperor, and he sent him advance information of all his plans. It is said that Zulfikhar was only waiting for Aurangzeb to die before declaring himself an independent ruler of the Deccan and wanted Rajaram's help to strengthen his rule. In the meantime, he was willing to let things slide. But Aurangzeb went on living, surprisingly vigorous for his eighty odd years. He began to lose patience and made it clear to Zulfikhar that unless he launched an attack against the fort of Jinji, he would remove him from command. It was not until 1698 that Zulfikhar pressed home the attack against Jinji and captured the fort, only, however, after making sure that his plans were known to Rajaram well in advance, and giving him ample time to get away. A few days after the capture of the fort, he even permitted Rajaram's wives and family to leave the fort. Then, as though to make up this excessive chivalry, Zulfikhar ordered all the prominent leaders in the fort put to death, and plundered everything that the fort contained.

This was the price Jinji paid for giving refuge to its ruler.

Meanwhile, Aurangzeb, still encamped in the Deccan with an enormous army on his hands, was trying hard to find fresh tasks for his troops. For a while he toyed with the idea of attacking the Portuguese settlements. But the Portuguese, wise to Moghul ways, knew all the answers. Hardly had Aurangzeb's men burnt down the first few villages in the Portuguese territory near Daman, before their emissaries were at his doorstep with suitably imposing bribes. Almost overnight, Aurangzeb's advisers found it expedient to impress upon him the wisdom of maintaining friendly relations with the Portuguese on the grounds that they could be relied upon to supply the Moghuls the guns necessary for reducing the Maratha forts. The logic was irrefutable. To Aurangzeb, anyone who would help in destroying the Maratha power was an ally. The operations against the Portuguese settlements werc called off by an Imperial decree, almost before they had begun.

The Emperor then decided to do something himself about capturing the Maratha forts. Before setting out, he addressed letters to the more important Maratha commanders; letters of the 'look-and-be-afraid-for-I-am-the-*Naag*' kind. This is what he wrote to Baurikar, the overall Commander of the Deccan forts:

> 'My army is now marching to conquer the forts in the possession of the miserable (Rajaram) and to extirpate him

> ... all the places and forts belonging to that wretch will be conquered and annexed to the Imperial dominions. The luckless Rajaram, like his brother now in hell, (Sambhaji), will be captured by the warriors of Islam and put to death.
>
> 'If you ... be led by good fortune to yield the forts to my servants, you will be exalted with the gift of high rank and favours, otherwise ... you will see what you will see: you will be imprisoned and executed along with all your women and children and all the members of your family, old and young.'

But Aurangzeb's threats and promises had already begun to ring hollow. He did not win many forts by his letters. The Maratha commanders had begun to prefer the 'salt and bread' of their own exiled ruler to the 'high rank and favours' promised by the Great Moghul.

During the years of Rajaram's exile, something had happened to the Deccan which, if it were not a cold fact of history, could only be regarded as a miracle. All unnoticed by anyone, the wheel had begun its upswing; the Marathas now had a powerful army. Admittedly it was not a single, unified army but only a collection of numerous guerilla bands which harried the Moghul armies and plundered the countryside. Two of these bands had developed into muscular armies under the two most daring and skilled commanders of the time, Santaji Ghorpade and Dhanaji Jadhav. When, driven away from his last hideout at Jinji, his life spared by the grace of his foe, Rajaram returned to his country, it was not as a fugitive that he returned, but at the head of a formidable military force seasoned in warfare. In fact, Rajaram now had an army capable of opposing the Moghuls openly, and right enough, soon after his return, he personally undertook an expedition into Moghul-dominated territory to claim his tribute, at the head of a force which, in size, was greater than Shivaji ever commanded.

The transformation amongst the Marathas was no more than a momentary phase, however, and to provide a reasoned explanation for it would not be possible. It was a fortuitous combination of many predominant traits of Maratha character both good and bad: their excessive loyalty, their pathetic veneration of the cow and the Brahmins, their love of plunder, their dislike for sustained work, their hatred of the Moghuls, their fear of the *Jezea*, their hardihood, their blind devotion to the land of their villages; all these and a hundred more, tempered by the harsh needs of the times, had produced this result.

The unity was not to last long. The very next year dissensions had already crippled the strength of the Marathas, but now, at the time of Rajaram's return, they were able to take the field in large numbers, and think in terms of driving out the Moghuls by force of arms.

Here was Rajaram, forced to flee his capital and his homeland, dressed as a beggar, begging for shelter, beaten by the Moghuls at every stage and even flushed out of his last hideout, returning as in some fairy tale, riding upon a prancing white charger and leading an army, which at last looked capable of driving out the invaders from the Deccan. Somewhere along the line, Rajaram had also dropped being the 'Regent'; he now called himself 'the King of the Marathas'.

15

In Which They Served

A few months before Rajaram returned to his homeland to assume the reins of his kingdom, his maritime Commander-in-Chief, Siddoji Gujjar, had died. Everyone knew who the next Naval Chief was going to be: the effective command of the fleet as well as the larger portion of the Konkan had already passed into the hands of Kanhoji Angrey. There could be no other choice.

In the maritime sphere, Kanhoji Angrey had performed miracle of even greater proportions than the transformation of the Maratha army. In the nine years since the Command of the northern fleet had devolved upon him, he had built it up into a compact, powerful striking force of forty assorted vessels, already spoken of with awe and treated with respect along the coast.

During those years, Kanhoji had shown tactical wisdom beyond his years and experience. He had scrupulously avoided a major showdown with a major enemy. Commanders in the field can seldom choose their enemies, but they can often choose their objectives, bearing in mind that a thorough appreciation of the limitations of your own troops is just as important as a thorough knowledge of their capabilities. Hitherto, the Marathas had shown an inclination to rashness, a readiness to take on all comers. They had little or no knowledge of naval tactics and regarded all naval battles as though they were cavalry charges. Kanhoji Angrey seemed to have learnt to look at warfare with far more detachment; realized that success in battle was not merely a matter of blind courage, that a scrupulous avoidance of unnecessary risks was just as important as any requirement of tactics.

Conscious of his limitations, he chose his tasks with care. The English, he left severely alone; the misdemeanours of the English could wait until his fleet acquired its muscles and its teeth. In the meantime, there was a lot that he could learn from the Europeans: their gunnery was superb, their ships were first-class. When a clash with the English became inevitable, as in the case of the two salt ships seized by the Commander of Padm-durg, he had given in with good grace.

With the Siddy too, he had avoided a head-on clash. The Siddy's fleet was still the most powerful single naval force along the coast. He had carefully preserved a state of armed neutrality between himself and the Siddy which, in effect, amounted to a tacit understanding and acknowledgement of the spheres of each other's activities: the Siddy operated his squadrons in the northern Konkan, between Surat and Janjira; Kanhoji was content to stick to the southern regions. This in itself must have created a separate crop of problems, since by right south Konkan was the responsibility of Bhawanji Mohitay, who, it will be recalled, was the other Deputy Commander appointed by Rajaram. Luckily for Kanhoji Angrey, Bhawanji Mohitay seems to have been the sort of man who was content to sit back in the impregnable fortress of Sindhu-durg and tend his coconut palms and mango trees. If someone else was fighting his battles for him, he, Bhawanji Mohitay, was not the one to raise petty objections about spheres of responsibility.

The relatively peaceful waters of the south Konkan coast must have provided an ideal training ground for Kanhoji's navy, if his collection of odd ships could be called a navy. The Siddy and the English confined their activities to northern Konkan; the Portuguese in Chaul and Goa never went looking for trouble; the Rajas of Kudal and Wadi were small-time chieftains; the British at Karwar were only a paper imitation of the British at Bombay. The wide open coast of south Konkan was just made to order for a fleet finding its sea-legs; the further south you went, the pickings became easier and easier.

He began cautiously, employing his ships not as a naval force but as a sort of coastal police, pouncing upon ships that did not carry Maratha papers and forcing them to pay ransoms. There was no such thing in those days as the freedom of the seas. Any ship that did not belong to a friendly power was fair game. The objective, somewhat over-ambitious at this stage, seems to have been to enforce all ships to acknowledge the Maratha domination of the waters of the Konkan. 'Vessels of all nations were attacked,' writes Grant Duff, 'repeated descents were made along the coast, and few of the defenceless mercantile towns from Travancore to Bombay, escaped a visit.'

On land too, Kanhoji had managed to take back from their commanders some of the Konkan forts that were supposed to be only nominally under his command, and indeed, a few forts which were not even nominally under his command, since, if they came under the Maratha rule at all, they were placed under Bhawanji Mohitay.

In 1695, when he was twenty-six years old, Kanhoji Angrey seems to have been sufficiently confident of his power and position to have gone off on a religious pilgrimage to Nasik, accompanied by his wife, Mathura. A few months later, he was back in the Konkan, attacking the fort of Sagar-gad which was taken by the Moghuls the year before Sambhaji's death. He captured Sagar-gad without much difficulty. In the same year, he shifted his headquarters from Suvarna-durg to Colaba. This was a move of major significance, for it brought him squarely in the midst of the two major powers along the west coast, the Siddy at Janjira and the English at Bombay. It also announced that he no longer bothered about keeping clear of the Siddy's sphere of activity. Indeed, the Siddy was quick to take notice of this encroachment on his sphere of activity and gave instant orders to his ships to seek out and destroy Kanhoji's ships, but the only result of the Siddy's wrath was a few inconclusive skirmishes. In the same year, Kanhoji is also said to have fought an action against Portuguese ships, but this too must have been a minor affair.

Kanhoji's having shifted his fleet from south Konkan to the vicinity of Bombay, must have come as something of a blow to his good friend, the Raja of Kudal. The Raja had been attacked by the Sawant of Wadi, another warlike prince of the south Konkan, and had appealed to Kanhoji Angrey to send him supplies and a column of troops: 'Come to my rescue,' said the Raja of Kudal's letter, 'kill the Sawant, and take for ever a portion of my entire revenue as though you were a brother.'

It was a tricky situation. The Sawant of Wadi, although a completely independent operator in the hills and jungles around Vengurla, had accepted a vague sort of allegiance to the Maratha Kings from the days of Shivaji. Sending any active help against the Raja of Wadi would have meant opposing a Maratha vassal. Kanhoji sent his friend the Raja of Kudal a shipload of rice and other supplies, but pleaded that he was 'too busy with higher affairs of state' to send any active help.

The fact that an independent ruler should seek Kanhoji Angrey's help against another ruler was further testimony to the power and influence now wielded by him. His ships were already beginning to be known as units of 'Angria's Navy'; hitherto, all Maratha ships were called 'Sevagee's navy' or 'Ramraja's navy'. His agents collected revenue in his name as 'the Lord of the Konkan'. He flew his own red standard wherever he lived. The overlordship of the Maratha King, never very effective in the Konkan, must have gradually receded into the background. Kanhoji Angrey was the man on the spot: to the people of the Konkan, he represented the ultimate in power and authority. The King, ruling from a distant hideout, was merely a clay figurehead. The transformation of the fleet and the systematic reconquest of a large part of the Konkan had been achieved by one man, and God knows he had received little enough help from Rajaram except possibly a glowing announcement at the time of the coronation ceremony at Jinji, and the gift of a gold bangle made up from a widow's hoard.

The bonds of Maratha overlordship over the Konkan could not have been stronger than the dimming memory of the days of Shivaji or the fraying threads of loyalty to a lost cause and a runaway King. The people and the noblemen of the Konkan recognized no other master than Kanhoji Angrey.

But Kanhoji Angrey himself recognized no other master than the King of the Marathas, and now he waited for Rajaram's return, ready to offer him a large part of the Konkan re-conquered during the King's exile, unswerving in his loyalty, untouched by the thought of renouncing the suzerainty of the house of Shivaji.

As an ambitious and brilliantly-successful military commander of twenty-nine, Kanhoji Angrey may be forgiven if his anxiety for Rajaram's return was not altogether without thought of personal advancement: as soon as the King returned he was certain to promote Kanhoji Angrey to the post of the Naval Commander-in-Chief, now left vacant by Siddoji Gujjar's death. As a special recognition of his services to the kingdom, Rajaram might also announce the grant to Kanhoji Angrey of the *Jari-Patka*, the honour of flying the golden standard which had been awarded to the two chief Army Commanders: Santaji Ghorpade and Dhanaji Jadhav.

The 'higher affairs of state' which provided Kanhoji Angrey with a ready-made excuse for declining to help the Raja of Kudal with anything more than a shipload of rice, was the imminent arrival of Rajaram in the Deccan; for we have already reached that moment in time: the summer of 1698.

But Kanhoji was destined for bitter disappointment. Rajaram was not anxious to fill up the appointment of the overall commander of the fleet and of the Konkan. Instead, he promoted both his Deputy Chiefs to be independent Commanders in their own respective spheres: Kanhoji Angrey in the north and Bhawanji Mohitay in the south. It is possible that Kanhoji outranked Bhawanji Mohitay, since he alone was given Siddoji's rank of *Surkhail* or Grand Admiral.

One wonders how much Rajaram's decision was influenced by the shipload of grain sent by Kanhoji Angrey to the Raja of Kudal, whose enemy the Sawant of Wadi was a Maratha vassal. The Sawant of Wadi had routed the Raja of Kudal's forces and taken his territory, and now, upon Rajaram's return, was one of the first to reiterate his allegiance to the house of Shivaji. It is almost certain that as in all senior promotions, there must have been 'some kind of politics' involved which deprived Angrey of his rightful promotion. Although there can be no exact analogy for this sort of thing in modern history, it is as though Mr. Churchill had broken up General Auchinleck's command in the Middle East before appointing Montgomery in his place.

The return of Rajaram, his assumption of power and his pointed reiteration of the overlordship of the Konkan and 'unto the limits of the ocean' must have come as a sharp tug at the reins to someone who had been accustomed to nine years of unfettered freedom—and even the rank of *Surkhail*, the Grand Admiral of the Fleet, must have seemed a brass imitation of the real thing when divested of half its former power and glory.

This, surely was a moment for decision; if an excuse was needed for a parting of the ways, for renouncing the Maratha overlordship and striking out on his own, this was it. In effect, it would have merely amounted to no more than a continuation of the way he had carried on for the past nine years.

Almost surprisingly, Kanhoji chose to remain within the fold: all that he had won in nine years of incessant strife he now placed at the feet of his master, and he was content to take what was given.

Kanhoji's decision to remain loyal to the house of Shivaji at this stage is the most convincing proof of his credentials—that he was, at all times, a servant of the State, to be promoted or relieved of his duties according to the wishes of his monarch. However powerful his fleet, however effective his rule of the Konkan, however loyal his commanders of the coastal forts, the ships were not his, nor was the Konkan nor its forts: he was merely a custodian of the Konkan, or a part of it, not its master.

It was loyalty such as this, an almost blind devotion to an ideal, multiplied a hundredfold in each of the Maratha chieftains that put their tottering kingdom back on its feet. In the next hundred years, the Marathas went from success to success and held sway from Delhi to Seringapatnam, making them the last 'indigenous empire-builders of India' and the immediate predecessors in conquest of the British.

Unfortunately, their fall was even more rapid and spectacular than their rise. There was no slow decline or disintegration; no lingering, painful wasting away, but a sudden grand collapse—like a ship sinking.

16

Grim Stocktaking

But Kanhoji Angrey had little enough leisure to nurse grievances. Supreme Commander or merely a glorified Deputy Commander, the problems of the Konkan were still his problems. The shifting of his headquarters to Colaba and his feverish strengthening of its defences had been the point of no return. The cold war between himself and the Siddy of Janjira could remain cold no longer. Any moment now, it would flare into a vicious shooting war, and Kanhoji looked forward to it with eagerness: there was nothing like warfare to take away the taste of sawdust from your mouth.

As soon as the rains were over, Siddy Kassam Yakoot Khan came charging into coastal Colaba on an avowed mission of plunder and destruction. But Kanhoji was not going to make it easy for the Siddy this time. He refused to be drawn into a pitched open battle on the Siddy's chosen ground. The Siddy hung on for six months, sending insulting messages to Kanhoji Angrey, and then having 'scorched' as much of the countryside as he could in a final burst of temper, returned to his domain. He is said to have felled 8,000 coconut palms around Colaba. A palm tree takes twenty years to bear fruit.

But at this game of plundering the countryside, two could play just as well as one, and barely had the Siddy turned his back, when Kanhoji Angrey retaliated by making a deep raid into Thal, in the Siddy's domain, and inflicting equally merciless damage.

Open warfare with the Siddy also necessitated a re-orientation of Kanhoji's relations with the other coastal powers. The English, for one, always gave the impression of being hand-in-glove with the Siddy: was well known that they allowed him to take in supplies and water in their ports and played host to him during the rains. In the face of this alliance, it was unlikely that the treaty made with the English at the time of the seizure of the salt-boats by the Subedar of Padm-durg would hold for long. But on his part, Kanhoji was anxious to avoid any acts of hostility against the English. He had publicly declared that he had 'ordered all his masters of vessels that whenever they met any of our ships, not to interrupt them, but quietly to pass and make them a salaam', the Bombay Council records, and goes on to add, 'which, we believe more through fear than any respect or friendship'.

The Portuguese too were getting increasingly hostile. They had always been accustomed to regard the ocean as a private thoroughfare and resented any reminder that the waters of the Konkan were ruled by the Marathas.

But the Portuguese would have to wait, for here was Siddy Kassam Yakoot Khan again, stung by a strong dose of his own medicine, waiting for revenge. The moment the rains stopped, the Siddy's fleet came swooping down from Mazagaon and surrounded the fort of Colaba.

If Siddy Yakoot Khan thought that the siege would starve the garrison into submission, he was mistaken. Indeed if Kanhoji Angrey may be said to have learnt one lesson from Shivaji, it was that none of his forts was ever found to be short of provisions. In fact, most of them were sufficiently stocked to hold out a siege until the ensuing monsoon. Equally so, there was now no question of allowing the fleet to be drawn out into some specially-selected killing ground and having it finished off at one stroke, as had happened when Sambhaji's ships had sought an action with the Siddy:

> 'The Siddis lies before Caulaby and Cundry, though hath grand force yet Marathas find a way to gallbats from one place to other as likewise to go out robbing,' comments the factory record of the East India Company, and, three weeks later: 'The Siddy still continues his siege without doing any great matter … we shall be watchful.'

While the East India Company remained watchful, the Siddy's siege of Colaba continued, and despite the siege Kanhoji Angrey's ships continued to patrol the coast and collect dues from ships and from coastal towns, and his troops actually made another foray into Thal, deep within the Siddy's territory.

In the end, Yakoot Khan gathered his fleet and sailed away, muttering to himself that it was the East India Company that was secretly helping Kanhoji Angrey.

Colaba had not turned a hair, and as for the English helping Kanhoji against the Siddy, it seems that they themselves had begun to sit up and take notice of the growing Maratha fleet. In April 1699, the Governor of Bombay had reason to urge upon his Council the need for 'small vessels for convoys to encourage the trade of these islands … the Sevagees are now growne stronge and impudent so that scarse any boats can pass to and from the islands without convoys.'

Above the ghats, the aged Moghul Emperor had whipped up his army into a last shudder of activity. He had devised yet another master-plan for the destruction of the Marathas: the Moghul Army was to be divided into two columns; one under Zulfikhar, the conqueror of Raigad and Jinji; the other under his own personal command. Zulfikhar was entrusted with seeking out and destroying Rajaram's army in the field; Aurangzeb himself took on the task of reducing the forts. At the time, he was eighty-three years old.

The royal command went forth: whips cracked, and the gigantic town which had been the emperor's camp for twelve years creaked and groaned and began to unroll. Fat, easeloving Moghul commanders, who had built large houses of brick and stone, shifted their belongings with reluctance. People still haunt the camp site near Sholapur looking for trinkets and gold coins.

Aurangzeb's first objective was the fort of Satara, Rajaram had spent a few days after his return. Nothing could save the unfortunate fort now; it had become a question of the Emperor's personal prestige. Threatening letters had already gone forth to its commander, and spies and saboteurs had already begun their underground work. There were also the shining new guns and the barrels of gunpowder supplied complete with trained gunners—by the grateful Portuguese. Above all, there were the explosives, specially conserved for just such a task.

Digging day and night at the foot of the fort walls, it took four months to place the great mines into position. And when they were primed and ready to be fired, the entire Moghul camp turned out as for a ceremonial procession, and brought the defenders crowding up to the walls of the fort from within to see what was happening. The first mine went off beautifully, did a lot of damage to the fort walls and killed a satisfactory number of the defenders. The second, the larger one, burst outwards, killed over 2,000 from among the Moghuls neatly bunched together to watch the spectacle.

The gloom spread over the Moghul camp by, this mishap was, however, almost immediately dispelled; for news came that Rajaram lay dying in the fort of Sinhgad not a hundred miles away, suffering from an attack of what must have been pneumonia. He died in the middle of March. The year was 1700.

Rajaram's death gave rise to a good deal of enforced jubilation in the Moghul camp, but it is unlikely that Aurangzeb himself thought that it would break the Maratha power. He had now seen three Maratha Kings die, all younger than himself; he had captured scores of their forts and killed thousands of their fighting men; he had razed their villages to the ground by the hundred and burnt millions of acres of standing crops. None of this had brought him any nearer to his goal. By now, even Aurangzeb must have seen the writing on the wall: he was not destined to destroy the Maratha power.

As he lay tossing in his bed in the austere white tent in the breathless, pre-monsoon heat of Satara, Aurangzeb must have often wondered to himself when all this was going to end. Three of his wives had died in the Deccan; was he going to die too?

Waiting for Satara to surrender, Aurangzeb may have tried to strike a balance sheet of profit and loss: eighteen years of incessant warfare in the Deccan without once going back to his capital, some five lakhs of his soldiers had already died in those years; to what end? Much of the territory captured by him had already been won back by the Marathas, even while he, Aurangzeb, acknowledged 'King of the World', was still camping in their midst.

At that, in up-ghat Deccan, things were not so bad. His army still held sway, and many of the up-ghat forts were still in the hands of the Moghuls. But even he could have had no doubt about the way things were going in the Konkan. Except for the Siddy's small domain, there was nothing in the Konkan now that belonged to the Moghuls; not the tiniest tongue of land or creek. Even Aurangzeb could hardly have failed to have heard of the new star on the horizon who had wrested the initiative from the Siddy, a naval and land commander called Kanhoji Angrey who was reputed to regard all warfare with the same scientific detachment as that accursed mountain rat now burning in hell, Shivaji.

Even the fall of Satara, a month later, could not have brought much consolation to Aurangzeb and, in his very next venture, the siege of the relatively unimportant fort of Purlee, his great column was caught napping by the monsoon. Within one month, the Moghuls lost more men and material than they had lost during a whole year's campaigning. An outraged rain-god was often far more merciless than either the Moghuls or the Marathas.

17

In a Sailboat Down the Coast

Rajaram had left two sons by two different wives: the older, Shivaji, was ten years old; the younger, Sambhaji, was three. Shivaji was an idiot.

Rajaram's senior wife (and the mother of the elder prince), Tarabai, an ambitious, resourceful and determined woman, hastily rounded up some of the prominent Maratha chieftains, and at one stroke got them to agree to accept her son Shivaji as the heir to the kingdom, with herself as the Regent during Shivaji's minority. Her first action as the Regent was to throw the mother of Rajaram's other son into confinement. Tarabai did not believe in taking chances.

No one could have found much fault with what Tarabai did even though it looked like a barefaced attempt to bypass the direct line of succession. Of the direct line, there was no one around. It will be recalled that Sambhaji's son was taken away by Aurangzeb at the fall of Raigad, and he and his mother had already been Aurangzeb's prisoners for more than ten years. There had been many an ugly rumour about the young prince in captivity: some said he had been circumcised and converted to the Muslim faith; others that Aurangzeb had been regularly dosing him with *pousta*, a slow-acting poison made from opium, which was guaranteed to kill a man's will-power and to affect his brain. But of course, the best argument in favour of bypassing the direct line of succession was that there was absolutely no chance of Sambhaji's son ever being released.

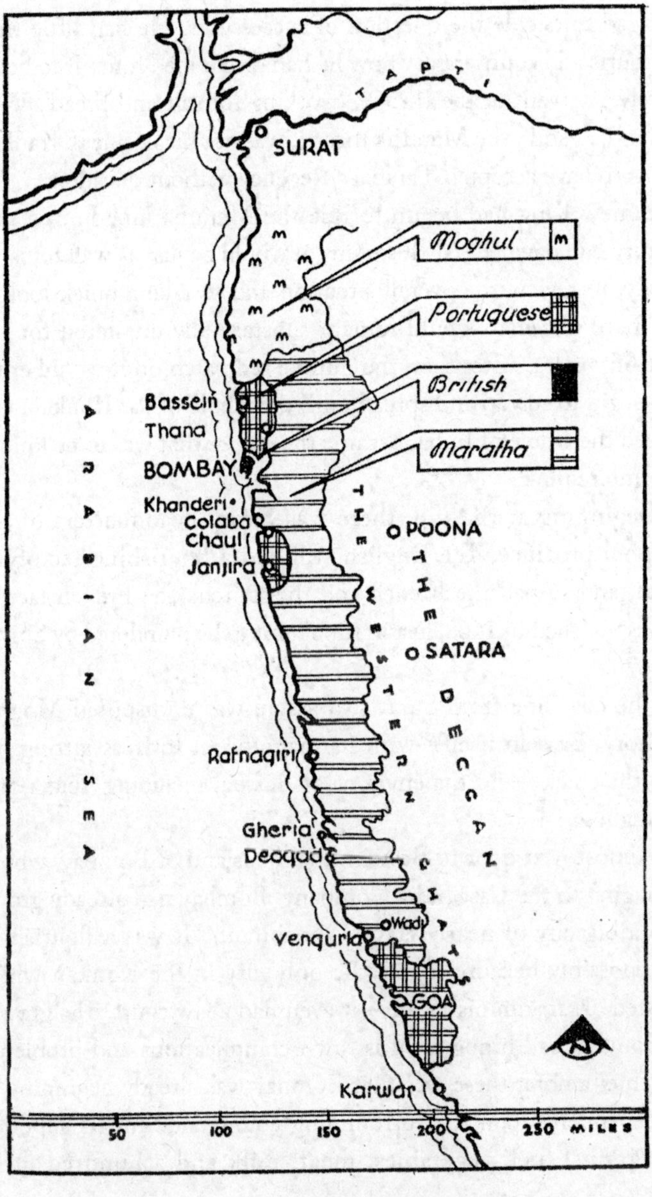

THE KONKAN, 1700

Kanhoji Angrey is not mentioned amongst those who went to Sinhgad to decide the question of successions. He had little time for courts and courtiers. By now he had disciplined himself to being merely a servant of the throne, 'working for salt and bread'. Who sat on the gaddi, the Maratha throne, was not his business. Kanhoji seems to have accepted Tarabai's Regency without question.

A new King had begun to rule the Maratha kingdom, a new century had dawned. At this point, it would be just as well to pause briefly, to review the overall situation and to take a quick look at the map. The map would remain substantially unaltered for the next fifty years. After that, the minute red patch on it would erupt and begin to spread and spread until the whole of the Konkan, and indeed the whole of India, became the colour that was to be known as 'Empire pink'.

Beginning at the top, there was Surat, headquarters of the Moghul province. The English still had a flourishing factory at Surat, and so had the French and the Dutch. The French factory was established in 1668, just in time for it to be plundered by Shivaji in 1670.

The coastline from Surat to Bassein was undisputed Moghul territory. Bassein itself—with its magnificent fortress jutting out into the creek—and the environs of Bassein including Thana, was Portuguese.

Almost next door to Bassein was the island of Bombay, wholly belonging to the East India Company. Bombay had already grown into a big city of nearly 70,000 inhabitants. It was a flourishing city, possibly because it was the only city in the Konkan which boasted of an administration—it even had a law court. The growth of Bombay had brought on its own complications and problems; the chief among these was that Bombay was already beginning to be dependent upon the surrounding countryside for its supplies, foodgrains, fuel, vegetables, meat, milk and a hundred other necessities of a metropolis had to be brought in from outside. Except for a small strip in the north where Bombay adjoined Portuguese Bassein, the surrounding territory was, at least nominally, Maratha territory. If the Marathas could have enforced their rule effectively, Bombay would always be at their mercy for its daily needs.

Ten miles further down, at the entrance of the shipping channel to the harbour of Bombay and dominating the channel, were the twin islands of Khanderi and Underi. Khanderi, it will be recalled, had been fortified by Shivaji in 1679, and during the next few years, it had been successively attacked by the English and the Siddy, both jointly and by, each on his own. But of late, no one seemed to have worried about Khanderi. It was still supposed to belong to the Marathas, but the Marathas did not have a strong garrison there and any of the European powers could have taken it for the asking. Khanderi was soon to come into prominence.

Underi, 'the island of rats,' was said to belong to the Siddy, with even less reason. Again, no one had cared to challenge the Siddy's claim to Underi, made as a result of a short-term occupation in a pet of retaliation against Shivaji's occupation of Khanderi.

Twenty miles further down the coast was the fortress of Colaba, where Kanhoji Angrey had moved his headquarters two years earlier. The country surrounding Colaba was also supposed to be a part of Angrey's command, but apparently, as we have seen, the Siddy could come raiding any time he wanted, devastating the countryside in retaliation for earlier wrongs or even in a burst of sheer high spirits.

Within a day's sail from Colaba was the ancient mercantile port of Chaul or Rewadanda, famous in the forgotten past, long before the days of Vasco da Gama or even Marco Polo. The Greeks came there in the days when the Parthenon was being built; the Parsis came in the tenth century. Now, Chaul was Portuguese.

A few miles below Chaul was the impregnable fortress of Janjira, the home and headquarters of the Siddy Kassam Yakoot Khan. A pocket of nearly twenty miles on all sides of the fort was regarded as the Siddy's domain, but again, in the absence of a strong permanent garrison on the mainland, much of it was open country.

From Janjira to Goa, the coastline was definitely both controlled and administered (which meant little beyond the fact that it was subjected to the taxation of the *chauth* and *sardeshmukhi*) by the Marathas. Round about Vengurla, the new power of the Sawant of Wadi was beginning to make itself felt both at sea and along the coast. Their Chief, KhemSawant, had already acquired a formidable reputation, and the Portuguese had transformed his name into 'Quemar Santo' (the saint burner), on account of the ravages caused by him in their churches. But the Sawant was, and always remained, a highly localized power. At Vengurla itself, the Dutch had a small establishment, but it was neither strongly garrisoned nor fortified.

In Goa, we come to the end of this coastal voyage. Goa was a strongly garrisoned, well-fortified Portuguese enclave; a neat prosperous segment of the Konkan about fifty miles long and thirty miles at its widest. The boundaries of Goa are exactly the same today. The country south of Goa, right up to Mangalore, was also claimed by the Marathas, but this was merely a nominal claim, based on the lightning raid Shivaji had carried out nearly thirty years earlier, and also on the attack Kanhoji Angrey had made in the more recent past.

Of the four major powers who more or less effectively ruled their sections of the five hundred miles of coastline from Surat to Karwar, the English alone had, up to now, tried to stick to a policy of 'business first'. In the process, their consciences may have been made to take many an amazingly high hurdle, but they rarely allowed themselves to forget the fact that they were here for trade and that money mattered above all. 'We don't want an extent of land if we could but obtain pepper cheap and sufficient,' the Directors advised the Governor of Bombay at about this time. As far as possible, they avoided open hostility with the local rulers, and it was only when it became necessary for them to with one party or the other, that they endeavoured to give 'such assistance to the weaker power as would prevent their being too speedily overwhelmed'.

As to exactly when it became necessary to take sides, the English had their own, highly elastic rules. The principle of maintaining a 'balance of power' was followed with mercantile ruthlessness, subjecting their neutrality to the weirdest contortions. What it amounted to in actual practice was the thwarting of the rising power of the Marathas at every opportunity. No one could have blamed the English for taking up arms in self-defence, as they did during Shivaji's sack of Surat, but the English had begun to *play* at politics to further their business interests, and since the only curbs to their hitherto unrestricted business activities along the coast could come from the Marathas, Kanhoji Angrey became a natural enemy of the East India Company.

The Portuguese did not even pretend to have any rules, or, more correctly, they had only one rule: it was that the Indian Ocean was their private thoroughfare and that no one else could use it without their permission. Ships not in possession of the Portuguese papers used the sea at their own risk. The permits, or *cartaz*, were sold at fairly reasonable prices but they imposed the most vexatious restrictions upon the ships that carried them: they were not permitted to carry Christian slaves, and were forbidden to visit any ports belonging to the enemies of the Portuguese; they were also forbidden to trade in the items of merchandise which the Portuguese chose to declare as their monopoly.

Ships found without their *cartaz* could be, and often were, seized by the Portuguese, and made to pay heavy indemnities, or, at times, sunk. The ships of the Indian rulers, including those of the Moghul Emperor, were not exempt from the obligations of carrying the *cartaz*. Admittedly, the Moghuls and the other Indian rulers were issued with as many permits as they required merely for the asking, but the conditions of the *cartaz* themselves were in no way relaxed, and at all times, the Portuguese retained the right of searching all ships: any Portuguese sea captain could accost a passing ship and demand to search it.

Except, of course, the ships of the East India Company. The English ships were strongly armed, their guns were just as modern and their gunnery just as effective as that of the Portuguese, and they had a nasty habit of shooting at Portuguese ships without much provocation. But all other ships, including the ships of the Great Moghul on the way to the Mecca pilgrimage, had to obtain permits from the Portuguese and subject themselves to the humiliating restrictions imposed by the lords of the sea. Oddly enough, even when the Moghuls were said to be at war with the Portuguese, Indian merchants did not dare to set out on their voyages unless they were given their *cartaz* by the Portuguese.

The Siddy of Janjira was a lone wolf, although, in theory, he was the maritime commander of the Moghuls. He swooped down upon anyone that came within his reach that was weak, and anything that was worth taking, he took. But his range was limited to his local waters, to within about forty miles on both sides of Janjira. On the high seas, the Siddy's ships only ventured out with Portuguese passes. But even in his home waters, the Siddy was quite powerless against the Company's ships. His choice was naturally restricted to the ships of the Marathas, and to their territory. The Marathas were, after all, hereditary enemies; their country was the Siddy's natural hunting ground. Fighting came to the Siddy just as naturally as sailing, and destruction of Maratha property was just as rewarding as plunder.

Lastly, the Marathas; the people of the land. They were at last beginning to think that the Konkan and its coastal waters belonged to them and to no one else. The teaching of Ramdas and the example of Shivaji had now become a living creed. They had become aware that the sea was free, that no one had a right to check their ships on the high seas. Surprisingly enough, it was the English who taught them: the English ships did not have to take Portuguese *cartaz* or anyone else's *cartaz*, and no one dared to ask them the reason why.

But the mere realization that the control of the coastal waters had to be wrested back from the foreign powers was not enough. A beginning had to be made to win it back. If the ships plying along the coast had to pay coastal dues, it was up to the Marathas to collect them; if the ships belonging to owners in the Konkan had to carry permits, they should be permits issued by the Marathas and no one else.

The process of thought was not new, but hitherto the steps it imposed were not within the bounds of the capacity of the Maratha navy. As it happens, even when the fleet was first established, forty years earlier, its duties and responsibilities were clearly defined: protection of the coastline, safeguarding of the country's sea trade, and the collection of customs dues from all ships. But until now, the Maratha fleet had been a paper fleet, clumsily handled by land-soldiers, employed without skill. Now it had acquired teeth and claws and powerful muscles. It was ready for its tasks.

Above all, the fleet now had a coldly efficient commander, determined to enforce his authority along the coast in the only way in which the coastal powers understood: by the use of force.

Kanhoji Angrey had already begun to offer all sea-going ships his own permits which were called *dastaks*, at roughly the same prices charged by the Portuguese, and offering roughly the same benefits—protection at sea from pirates and from other coastal powers. Ships not in possession of his *dastaks* were to be seized and held for ransom.

The prudent traders had begun to equip themselves with both the *cartaz* and the *dastaks* and then hoped and prayed that they would not run into any pirates, for the protection offered against the pirates by both the Portuguese and the Marathas was merely nominal, only within sight of the coast.

Two powers, the Portuguese and the Marathas, were now claiming ownership of the waters of the Konkan. A third power, the English, was determined not to stand any interference from either. Trouble was inevitable.

To the English, the rules imposed by the Marathas could not have been strange. The Maratha fleet was now only exercising its rightful functions. England had almost identically the same rules in her own waters and the English fleet enforced them with the strictest rigour. Even the methods employed by the Marathas for enforcing the rules were fully in conformity with the accepted maritime practice of the day.

But what the East India Company resented was that there should be any rules at all. For nearly a hundred years now, they had grown used to the fullest freedom of the coastal waters. To them, the rights and wrongs of the case were of no interest. Their overriding argument was one of usage: English ships had used the coastal waters without restriction for a hundred years, they could not be subjected to any restrictions now.

The Company had little time for the so-called rights of Indian rulers; but, on the other hand, if they had, they would hardly have been able to build an empire which ruled every sixth man in the world.

18

The Company's Men

After the failure of his attempt to take Colaba, the Siddy seems to have lost much of his zest for warfare. Minor skirmishes between the Siddy and the Marathas, however, went on as a matter of course. The most noteworthy of these was a raid carried out by Siddy Kassam Yakoot Khan on the island of Khanderi. Khanderi was neither strongly garrisoned nor fortified, and, at the time of the Siddy's attack, it was not even directly under the command of Kanhoji Angrey. But the attack was easily beaten off. This time, the Siddy did not even have the satisfaction of bringing back a few basketloads of human heads as souvenirs of his excursion.

In defeat, the Siddy turned upon those who had always befriended him: the Company. He charged that it was the Company that had helped 'the Sevagees with ammunition because (if ?) they does not supply them, the Sevagees take all vessels belonging to the island they can master and ... hovering about the island, seem to threaten some mischief to it'.

Admittedly, there had been no open hostility between Kanhoji Angrey and the East India Company since Kanhoji's assurance given in 1698 that the Company's ships would not be molested. But this did not mean that there was any friendliness between the two. On its part, the Company had always been careful to keep a sufficient number of 'cruisers around to oblige him to civility'. Once, in 1701, some of the Company's men had asked ten of Kanhoji's men to dinner, but that had been the limit of their friendliness.

No; the Company's men had certainly not helped the Marathas against the Siddy. On the other hand, they had persistently, and as a matter of policy, supported the Siddy in order to 'use him as a foil to the Angria'.

Within the next three years, however, there was a distinct hardening of the Company's attitude towards Kanhoji Angrey which smouldered for over ten years before it broke into a declaration of war.

What were they like, these early Englishmen in India, the men romanticised by ten generations of British writers? What lies underneath all that calcified grime of centuries besides the thick layers of gilt slapped on by Meadows Taylor and his successors right down to John Masters?

The far-too-familiar picture of the clean-limbed, Empire building Englishman who lived by a code and was just as ready to die for it, was, God knows, largely true to life. But it belonged to a later period of history. The early Englishmen were a race of smaller men, without stature; a collection of greedy ledger-clerks and grocery salesmen; and their code, if they had a code, had no relationship with the playing fields of Eton.

It was not until the late eighteenth century that England began to send out to India some of the men from her ruling classes. A surprisingly large proportion of them ruled well and wisely with a sense of responsibility for the land and its people that was second to none. A few of them even came to love India and the Indians and devoted their lives to the service of the country. When they left, they left behind life-long friends and traditions of service such as future administrators have found it well-nigh impossible to live up to.

But these men of sterling character who managed to combine service to the land with careers under the East India Company and later under the British Crown—and whom future Kiplings turned into stiff, unbending caricatures and London music halls transformed into figures of fun—were as different from the general run of the early servants of the East India Company as the Junkers were from the Nazis.

For England, those were the great days of colonisations: of high-spirited English youths going to distant lands to settle down on vast holdings of land granted to them by the English King and to till the land with enormous gangs of cheap slave labour. They went to America and the West Indies holding in their hands the title-deeds to their lands. India had no land that the King of England could allot in million-acre grants. The only opening in India was trade, and trade with India was the monopoly of the East India Company. If you wanted to go to India, you went either as a servant of the East India Company, or not at all.

And the Company did not offer you much!

Those who who went to seek their fortunes in foreign lands, went to the great virgin countries, to America and to the West Indies; only the humblest, the aspirants for minor clerical jobs came to India: the pioneers seeking adventure or fortunes, the precursors of the little armies of public school 'Old Boys', went West: the clerks and brokers came to India. They were the misfits from the squalid industrial towns of England, willing to sign away their future to become junior 'writers' in the East India Company and earn five pounds a year—for that was the salary of a junior writer in the Company and, it is worth emphasizing, they did not rise to be junior writers until after seven years of what was stipulated as being *satisfactory* service, and then only if they were able to furnish the necessary securities. Until then, they worked as apprentices, without pay.

The common run of the men who served the East India Company, did not come from England's super-men; nor did they belong to the solid, middle-class traders of England, for the outstanding virtue of middle-class traders is their honesty and integrity: the majority of the Company's servants were not renowned for either. That the standards of honesty and integrity they encountered in India, and particularly amongst the Moghul officials were, if anything, lower than their own, is beside the point—the Moghuls made no pretensions to superiority in this respect. The fact remains that the Company's servants were not the paragons of truth and virtue, giants in a land of pygmies, staggering under the white man's burden, that romantic imagination has painted them to be.

These then, were the elite in the Company's service: its councillors, its factors and writers; those who had been given the power of making peace or war and to keep an armed force on land as well as at sea, maintain ambassadors at courts, and speak and trade in the name of the King of England.

Now let us take a look at the Company's soldiers and sailors.

'The Company's policy was to keep its officers and men in a state of degrading subjection,' Bidulph tells us. 'They took into their service, men of low origin, devoid of military training and … who would submit to any treatment … the refuse of the vilest employments in London.'

Whenever there was an 'emergency', the factors and clerks cast aside their pens and ledgers and assumed command of troops. Considering that the majority of the Company's military officers had even less soldierly backgrounds, perhaps the civilians in the Company's staff cannot be blamed for the overnight assumption of military ranks higher than their regular officers: one of the Company's officers in Bombay had been a trumpeter in England, and another a London barber.

The pay of the foot soldier was eight shillings per month, and was always subjected to numerous cuts by the military officers. In practice, the men seldom received more than six shillings in the month, as their officers always kept back at least two shillings per man for their own perquisites. One of the Company's military commanders, Captain Milford, (who was largely responsible for the fiasco of the expedition against the Raja of Karwar, described in a subsequent chapter) when called upon to explain why he had been keeping back a part of the men's salaries, haughtily retorted that 'he took no more profit from the soldiers than what other officers did, all through the island of Bombay', which explanation seems to have satisfied the Council at Bombay. Officers were often worried as to whether their soldiers would withstand 'the recoil at the noise made by their own (fire) arms'.

The Company's councillors and factors certainly did not win any conspicuous diplomatic victories; they made no friends with the people or rulers of India. They came as traders and lived as traders, their supreme object was to make money, to balance the Company's books and show a handsome profit for the Company; but far too many of them consistently doublecrossed the Company.

Nor did the rabble that made up the Company's army in those early days win many conspicuous military victories. In tactics, in close in-fighting, in the use of ground, in the use of the sword and the spear and the bow and arrow, in making improvisations, in their ability to take the field without a mammoth tail of supply and transport, and in their individual toughness, the Company's men and officers were no match for the battle-seasoned Marathas.

What the Company had was guns and firearms; the best guns and the best gunpowder of the times. It was the Company's artillery at land, the Company's powerful guns on their trading ships and warships that won the Company its battles in India. It was like using armour against small-arms. Against these superior weapons the armies of the Indian rulers did not stand a chance. Later, the Company's army won its battles mainly by its superior discipline, but there was little enough discipline in the Company's fighting men in the early eighteenth century.

Admittedly, the Indian rulers too had guns and artillery, but their guns were shoddy, cheap copies of the guns brought or manufactured by the Company, and the powder used in them was of the crudest type. Gunnery, in the Indian armies, was in its infancy, both at sea and on land, and it was, at times, more hazardous to the gunners themselves than to their foes, since a very large proportion of barrels exploded while firing, and at least a third of the charges were misfires or 'topplers'. In fact, for their supplies of guns and gunpowder, the Indian rulers depended almost wholly upon the European powers, and somewhat naturally, the Europeans supplied their insatiable demands only with what was obsolete and of the lowest quality.

But even with the acknowledged superiority of their firepower, the English were not permitted to have their own way in the Konkan for at least another fifty years. They tried hard enough and often enough, and annually spent a sum which in today's values would amount to ten crores of rupees in a ceaseless effort to neutralise the Maratha navy.

Along the Konkan coast, it was a question of better leadership and better tactics against better arms, perhaps even a question of more skilled handling of ships against superior ships. Let not the future successes of the Company's arms detract from the earlier prowess of the Indian units against them!

19

'... Remember His Name'

The chaos of the past twenty years had suited the East India Company rather well: all around them was war, and they could not help prospering. If there was anything the Company looked upon with distaste, it was the likely emergence of peace.

The gradual restoration of order along the coast and the consequent enforcement of normal regulations upon shipping and trade had begun to rankle the Company's councillors. They had got used to the idea that the Indian coast was free to all their shipping. What they had been allowed to enjoy by default for nearly a hundred years, they had come to regard as a matter of right. They contended that even the Moghul Emperors had never claimed any title over the coastal waters, and the attempts of the new Maratha Admiral to enforce his own *dastaks* on all shipping, were regarded by them as hostile acts.

There were other, somewhat indirect, grievances too. The restrictions imposed on coastal trading ships had begun to cut into the Company's profits, and the growing naval power of the Marathas had begun to upset the carefully preserved balance of power along the coast. If the Marathas joined hands with the Portuguese, they would present a formidable threat to the Company's interests. The English had never trusted the Portuguese; and even their life-long friendship with the Siddy had begun to show deep cracks under the pressure of his recent reverses at the hands of the Marathas.

In the year 1701, the Council recorded its resentment at the disturbance of peace of the waters around Bombay caused by Kanhoji Angrey by 'choosing it as the arena for his struggles with the Siddy.' The argument seems to be that the Siddy could take shelter in Bombay waters with impunity, but the Maratha ships could not follow him there; that if the Siddy went raiding anywhere into Maratha territory, it was perhaps just as it should be, but so long as he was in the waters around Bombay, he could not be subjected to retaliation.

After all, the Siddy was a friend, even a secret ally, and the waters around Bombay bore the Company's ownership.

The next year, Kanhoji happened to seize a merchant ship at Calicut which had six Englishmen on board. The vessel was a private trading vessel, and the Englishmen had merely taken passage on it, but the Company always took the view that any ship that had Englishmen on board or carried cargo meant for sale in any of the Company's trading posts, was to be treated as belonging to the Company itself, and thus granted all the facilities and treaty privileges that the Company's own ships might be entitled to. The Council at Bombay wrote a sharp letter to Kanhoji Angrey asking for the immediate release of the ship—not just the six Englishmen on board, but the whole ship. To this, Kanhoji sent back word that he would 'give the English cause to remember his name'. What happened to the seized ship is not known, but it is possible that the captive Englishmen were released after payment of ransom.

In 1703, Kanhoji Angrey seized a Dutch warship of thirty guns. At this time, the Dutch and the English were allies in their war against France, but they had never been friendly in the past, and barely twenty years earlier, Admiral de Ruyter had terrorized England by burning Sheerness and sweeping through the Medway and the Thames, and his guns were heard in London. In any case, there was little friendship between the Dutch and the English in India, and there was a bitter and perpetual feud between their two factories in Anjengo on the Malabar coast. As such, it is difficult to understand why Kanhoji's seizure of the Dutch ship should have angered the East India Company as much as it did: 'The villain has trapped the ship,' the Governor protests. 'The Sevajees have grown very insolent.'

The East India Company was waiting for a chance to teach the Marathas a lesson, and its chance came within the next few months. In September 1703, there came to the shores of Bombay, a ship loaded with cargo from Aden. The ship was registered in Rajapur and carried a *dastak* issued by Kanhoji Angrey. The Bombay Council 'resolved' to detain both the ship and all her passengers and cargo. The resolution does not say upon what conditions, if any, the Company was prepared to release her or her passengers or cargo.

A clue to the way the East India Company's corporate mind worked is provided by the word 'resolved'. So long as there was a resolution, even if it was a matter of three unlettered English merchants sitting at a table and endorsing an absurd whim, it had all the weight and sanctity of a parliamentary decision.

The seizure of the ships and the holding up of their passengers to ransom was no more than an occupational hazard of sea-trading in the eighteenth century, even more so in Europe than in other parts of the world. The East India Company too had freely indulged in this practice just as much as any other coastal powers. Indeed, the Company had gone so far as to capture scores of ships of the Moghul Emperor at a time when they were enjoying the most generous trading concessions from the Moghuls. These were also the days when English sea captains, who attacked Spanish and French ships wherever they could be found, were acclaimed as national heroes, and there was still a great deal of glamour attached to the raiding of African villages and carrying away hundreds of slaves bound hand to hand in mile-long chains, to be crammed into ships like cattle and sold in the American ports. That the East India Company, innured to the activities of European sea captains should be outraged by the capture of a Dutch warship by the Marathas and regard it as an act of 'insolence' to be retaliated against by the seizure of a Maratha ship, is an example of the double standard followed by it in all its dealings with the rulers and people of India.

Kanhoji Angrey allowed this open act of piracy on the part of the English merchants to go unheeded. He did nothing for a whole year; a year in which the Company's councillors noted with mounting self-satisfaction that their pressure-tactics were paying good dividends. The fact that there was a treaty between them and Kanhoji Angrey which was signed five years earlier after the capture of the salt boats by the Subedar of Padm-durg, did not seem to worry the councillors unduly, and Kanhoji, on his part, did not remind the Company of the treaty. It was just as well, for the councillors were in no mood to be reminded of treaty obligations. They had decided amongst themselves that since Sir John Gayer, the Governor who had made the treaty with the Subedar of Padm-durg, was now a prisoner of Aurangzeb, the treaty need not be taken too seriously.

Angrey was still far too busy building up his fleet and strengthening his forts to invite open hostility with the Company. He was perfectly aware that ship for ship, the *ghurabs*, the *gallivat*s, the *pals*, and the *shibars*, of his fleet were no match for the English or Portuguese ships. He must have often gazed with longing at the handsome European ships, riding far out at sea, every sail straining: they were better designed, more strongly built and altogether more sea-worthy; they were more heavily armed and could absorb a terrible lot of punishment. In fact, almost the only way the Marathas could overpower one of their bigger ships was in hand-to-hand fighting, after boarding her—if the European ships kept their distance, the Marathas had little chance against them.

The biggest Maratha *ghurab* was no more than 400 tons, and of these, there were no more than two or three in Kanhoji's fleet. More than a hundred years earlier, at the time of the Spanish Armada, the

English and the Spaniards had both used ships of over 1,000 tons, and each side had dozens of ships of over 400 tons. The Portuguese ships, too, were every bit as good as the English ships. Admittedly, the best fighting ships of England did not come to India, but those that did come were far superior in seaworthiness, armament and armour to the best ships built in India.

In England, ship-building was a well-developed industry, and the designing of ships a fine art. Peter Pett had already lived and gone and had left his stamp upon all English shipping. Compared to them, Kanhoji's ships were clumsy and slow, not half as steady in rough weather, not half as strong.

Kanhoji Angrey's principal aim and occupation in the early years of the eighteenth century was to build bigger and better ships. In India, there had been no improvement in the design of ships since the days of Nearchus. It was almost as though all the ships were built after one standard pattern and the only difference was that some of them were bigger than the others. There had to be a radical change in the whole concept of ship-building.

Kanhoji began by planting enormous tracts with teak; both banks of the Bankote River had been cleared and put under teak plantations. Ironically, the fleet which the teak wood was intended to strengthen was burnt to ashes long before the trees grew up to full size. According to the English records, it was the only natural asset left behind by the Angreys.

At this time, he seems to have gone out of his way to cultivate the friendship of the Portuguese. It was from the Portuguese that he hoped to acquire guns and ammunition for his fleet: 'Kanhoji has little powder and ball in Colaby, but he knew from where they would be supplied; boats were gone for it,' the East India Company's Bombay Council laments. After exchanging presents with the Captain-General of Bassein, he had publicly announced that the Portuguese 'may have free access to any of their (Angrey's) ports and build what houses they then please.'

His chief contact with the Portuguese was a man named Manuel Moraes de Carvalho whom Kanhoji Angrey had employed as an adviser on the design and construction of ships. In fact, he gave employment to a number of foreign technicians: gunners, makers of gun barrels and gunpowder, experts in judging horses and many others, but above all, ship-builders. Besides Manuel Moraes de Carvalho, another Portuguese name also crops up prominently, that of Manuel de Castro, a soldier of fortune who was said to be an expert gunner—or so he said.

All the same, Kanhoji must have realized that his ships would never be as good as those of the Company. Even if he managed to catch up with their seaworthiness and strength, he could never match the guns of the English in size and performance, nor hope to get the kind of gunpowder that the Europeans manufactured. His best chance against the ships of the European powers was to get his sea-captains to show more daring and skill , to depend on their greater familiarity with the coastal waters, to ensure that every one of them knew his job thoroughly, and above all, to evolve the kind of tactics that would nullify to some extent the advantages possessed by the foreign ships.

The ships of the East India Company, although they were primarily meant to be trading vessels, were armed just as powerfully as the ships of the British Navy. Indeed, the Company had already begun to maintain its own private navy, which, oddly enough, bore the same name as does our navy today: it was called 'The Indian Navy'. The Company's fighting ships regularly patrolled the Indian coast.

The tactical system that was finally evolved may well have been the result of an accident. Its requirements were simple. There was no question of engaging in a fleet action with the European ships on the high seas: the waters had to be chosen and the ships had to be isolated. The wind could be of little advantage, since the foreign ships were better sailors. Often enough, Kanhoji's commanders chose to attack from leeward, so that whenever the opposing ship turned upon its pursuers, they could drop away to leeward and sneak off into shallower waters or to the protection of the coastal guns. It was something like the tactical manoeuvre developed later by the French against the English towards the end of the century, the only difference being that Kanhoji Angrey's ships nearly always operated within sight of their own coast, taking care to keep themselves between the coast and the enemy ships.

Bearing in mind the disparity between their respective naval strengths, Kanhoji often went to extremes to avoid the prospect of making new enemies, particularly in his early days. He realized that in case of hostilities, the Siddy would join the English, and Kanhoji was in no position to withstand a naval battle with their combined fleets. He must have pondered deeply over the open hostility shown to him by the Company by seizing a ship bearing his *dastak*, before taking any action.

A year later, he had decided on his course of action. He sailed with seven *gallivat*s and camped at the mouth of the Pane River, close to Bombay: just that and nothing more. No shot was fired, no rude notes exchanged, no ships seized and no villages plundered. His mere presence was now enough to block off Bombay's communication with the mainland. All shipping between Bombay and the mainland was paralysed.

Then, after doing sentry-duty at Bombay's door for a week, Kanhoji Angrey withdrew his squadron and sailed off on cruise.

It was a triumph of pure tactics, like clever move in a game of chess. The Council at Bombay saw it and took in its full meaning: if Kanhoji Angrey chose to be difficult, he could cause a lot of damage to their trade by merely blockading Bombay.

'Angria, a Sevagee pirate independent of that Rajah, came into the bay,' the Governor of Bombay reported to his Directors, and hastened to call a meeting of his Council.

Now the Council felt it expedient to resuscitate the Treaty of 1698 which it had earlier chosen to ignore. This time, they were not concerned so much with the 'insolence' offered by Angrey as with the likelihood of what might happen to coastal trade if the blockade was repeated. They decided to remind Kanhoji Angrey of the Treaty and of the friendliness that had always existed between the Company and the Marathas. They deputed a Mr. William Reynolds to wait upon Angrey 'wherever he might be found ... and acquainting the said chief robber … civilly,' that he could not be permitted to search or molest any shipping around Bombay, 'without breach of that friendship the English nation has always had for the Raja Sevajee and all his Captains in subordination to him'.

Mr. Reynolds was, however, particularly cautioned not by word or gesture, 'to threaten or insinuate any design or hostility against him'.

The Council's resolution needs some comment. Its inconsistencies are apparent: the Company seems to have made up its mind that the 'chief robber' was independent of the Maratha King, and yet it is anxious to remind him of the friendship between Shivaji and the English nation. Anyway, Shivaji had died more than twenty years earlier. The words 'English nation' are a delightful example of the way the Company chose to represent the 'English nation' or 'the English King' whenever it suited its purpose, and, at other times, lapsed into a mere body of merchants.

But Angrey had no patience with the Company's warnings, however civilly administered. He bluntly told Mr. Reynolds that the English had 'never kept their word with him', although he had done many services for them:

> '(The Marathas) had peace with the Portuguese and every one of their portes free to them; was known (that the Marathas) had held out warr with the Mogull forty years, lived now by their sword and seized what boats and other vessell belonging either to the Mogulls, vessells from any of his forts of Mallabart excepting such as had Conagee

> Angras passports; the English being at liberty acting as they please.'

From now on, it was war. Kanhoji had made it clear that he was going to seize all ships that did not carry his *dastaks*, and the English could act 'as they pleased'. The East India Company, on the other hand, had no intention of obtaining passports for their ships from the Maratha *Surkhail*.

20

'Without a Coffin'

Many of the prominent Maratha *mankaries* (chieftains or noblemen) had accepted Tarabai's Regency, at least as a matter of form. But above the ghats, her rule never became effective. For one thing, there was hardly a village or township which was not in the actual zone of warfare, and for another, her government was no more than a shadow government: there was no territory to govern, no law to administer, no revenue to collect. Harried by Moghul columns, Tarabai herself fled from fort to fort with an entourage of faithful followers, looking after her ailing and witless son who had been placed on the *gaddi* and, at the same time, trying to establish some sort of order in the Deccan.

At the same time, however, the military strength of the Maratha people, if not of the Maratha Regent, had become more formidable than ever. This was the heyday of the independent columns: of vast bodies of troops permanently on the prowl, looting to live, savagely destroying everything that came in their way, making little distinction between what belonged to friend or foe, knowing no other profession but warfare.

A new generation had grown to manhood since Aurangzeb's invasion of the Deccan; a generation that had never known peace or stability, convinced that the only occupation for an able-bodied man was the profession of arms. They had become soldiers to keep themselves alive, and now twenty years of incessant warfare had trained them in every twist and turn of guerilla fighting; had wrung out of them all fear of war, toughened them, hardened their system to pity or censure, given them a creed and purpose in life.

They accepted war as an inescapable feature of living, not knowing what it was to be without it; their thoughts never reached out to a time when there had been no war, and even less to a time when there would be no war. The Moghul Army was something that had always been there, inevitable, like the monsoon; beyond control and yet, like the monsoon too, something that provided an occupation and a living; an enormous target to sharpen your swords and try out your lances upon. To harry them, to loot their caravans, cut off their unwieldy supply trains of bullock-wagons, was both a rewarding pastime and a patriotic duty. It was there, the great Moghul Army, like a whale permanently stranded upon the beach, to throw stones at when you were boys, to reminisce about when you were old men …

Aurangzeb, anxious to get it all over and go back to Agra, first offered the Maratha *mankaries*, who led the columns, full pardons and enormous grants of lands if only they would accept his sovereignty and surrender their forts. But by now the *mankaries* had become too clever to fall into such simple traps and warfare had become too profitable a feature of life to be abandoned lightly. With a cunning which matched Aurangzeb's, they sent emissaries to him, acknowledging him to be *Alamgir*, 'the King of the World', and professing everlasting allegiance, but they always managed to stay out of his reach and continued as before.

In any history of the Marathas, these petty chieftains deserve a special page—and a special salute—all to themselves. Left without a leader and without the faintest hope of making a concerted stand to stem the Moghuls, the Ghatgays, the Maneys, the Powars, the Nimbalkars, the Daffleys and others, acted with surprising courage and coolness. Each of these chieftains turned himself into what, a century and more later, came to be glamourised as guerilla leaders. Indeed, the Maratha chieftains went one better: they combined the role of the guerillas with that of the 'underground'. Outwardly, they vied with each other in making declarations of the most undying loyalty to the Moghuls, and at the same time, did everything within their power to harass the Moghul forces. The result was devastating.

What historians have characterized as the 'predatory instinct' of the Marathas, now had the fullest scope. With the years, their guerilla bands had grown up in size. No one was barred, not even such professional highway robbers as the Pindaries. 'Every lawless man, and every disbanded soldier, whether Mohomedan or Mahratta, who could command a horse and a spear, joined the Mahratta parties', says Grant Duff, and as their size grew, so did their range and daring.

Their banner was the saffron flag[10] of the Marathas, their war-cry the same dreaded 'Har-Har Mahadev'; and their reward was plunder; but plunder when committed inside territory controlled by the Moghuls, had all the sanctity of a crusade.

To the Moghuls themselves, there was neither withdrawal nor progress; no prospect of redress from their present stagnation. They had lived the greater part of their lives in the Deccan; the old had died and the young had become old, quietly resigning themselves to the haunting fear of a slow death in the Deccan; no longer driven by a cause or lust for rewards, no longer fanned into enthusiasm by religious zeal or stung by the vituperations of a bent old man, no longer pricked by the thoughts of home; lost in reveries of a past only to be startled out of their dreams by the thunder of hooves; content to go on and on until nothing was left, not even bitterness. Just as much as the Marathas, the Moghuls would not have known how

---

10 Saffron is the colour of renunciation, and holy men in India who have renounced all worldly attachments wear saffron garments. It is said that when Shivaji, after he had established his kingdom invoked the blessings of Ramdas, the saint gave Shivaji a strip of his saffron robe, which Shivaji began to fly as the flag of his kingdom.

to make a living if the war had abruptly ended. They were already a lost generation.

The one man in the entire Moghul camp whose grand ambition still drove him to frenzied efforts was Aurangzeb. His last few years were spent in a laborious campaign, battering savagely at the Deccan forts, throwing away men and money with reckless abandon, only to find that as soon as his back was turned, the forts were reoccupied by the Marathas with surprising ease. By now, even Aurangzeb could not have been unaware that the majority of his commanders were secretly in the pay of his enemies.

If, as Clausewitz tells us, the aim of all wars is to break the enemy's will to resist, there was no hope for Aurangzeb; war held no horrors or privations for those who had taken to it as the most honourable and rewarding of all professions, and would not have known what to do without it.

The Maratha columns were self-contained units: there was no overall direction, no integration and no discipline. The vast force lived on the land and for its pay depended on the plunder it collected. What Tarabai gave them was a focus for loyalty: they fought in her name and they fought as Marathas for a common cause and under a common banner—and against a common enemy.

Somewhat naturally, the havoc they caused collectively was not realized by the Marathas themselves. They did not know that they had already beaten the Moghul Army, that all that was needed was a final concerted push.

In the Konkan, however, things were different. The fleet was not a collection of independent squadrons operating on their own: it was one fleet acting under one commander who was not content merely to carry out periodic raids of destruction and plunder. There was a sustained effort to rule and to govern, to offer protection to those who came under that rule and to punish those who flouted it. Above all, the Konkan was ruled as a part of the Maratha kingdom, and in the name of the Regent, Tarabai.

While, as far as the Moghuls were concerned, they had little to choose between the situation in the Konkan and that above the ghats, the important difference for the Marathas was that the Konkan was being governed, and it was being governed in the name of the Regent. Above the ghats, the collective effect of a hundred independent columns had been to bring the Moghul Army to a standstill, but there was no such thing as a government, merely the abstraction of a Regent.

Six years after Rajaram's death, Aurangzeb must have realized that the fires had cooled off; he was not getting anywhere by taking the Maratha forts one by one after prolonged and costly sieges only to lose them back.

He could plainly see the pattern now, the pattern that his war was acquiring. Tarabai's government would never become a formidable force. At the same time, there was no hope now that the independent columns above the ghats and the Commander of the fleet in the Konkan, could be decisively beaten by his army. If the Marathas themselves had not yet realized that they had beaten the Moghul Army, Aurangzeb saw that the Moghuls had lost the war. It would go on as a gigantic stalemate, with the great bulk of his army slowly bleeding to death of the vicious bites taken by the enemy columns.

There was still a chance to save something from the wreck, however, and to break the pattern before it hardened. And the means to his achieving this was right in his camp: Sambhaji's son, the heir to the Maratha kingdom. If Aurangzeb could make common cause with him, and set him up as a Maratha king, it would divide the people of the Deccan into two camps.

When Raigad fell in 1689, the six-year-old son of Sambhaji had been taken away by Aurangzeb together with his mother. Aurangzeb's daughter, Zeb-un-nisa, had taken the boy under her care and it seems that Aurangzeb himself had, after a fashion, become attached to him. One of the first remarks that Aurangzeb made about the boy whose father he had murdered, was to the effect that for a descendent of robbers, the boy looked surprisingly like a *sao* (not a thief). Whether this was said in bitterness or humour, Aurangzeb gave the prince the name by which he was to be called all his life. Sao later came to be transformed into Shahu.

Shahu, then, was Aurangzeb's last desperate hope of breaking the Marathas, and many of the prominent Moghul commanders, including: Zulfikhar, welcomed the proposal: which was to set up Shahu as the ruler of the Marathas and a vassal of the Moghuls.

Shahu was now nearly twenty years old, and remembered nothing of his past life, having been brought up all his knowing years in the Moghul camp, fussed over by an elderly spinster, almost certainly subjected to brain-washing, and, they say, assiduously dosed with pousta to destroy his will-power. He had grown up like an animal born in captivity, with no idea of what life was outside the foetid enclosure that was the Moghul camp; pampered and petted and encouraged in all the diversions of the idle rich of those days, but deprived of free thought and fresh air.

But, however much he thought about it, it was not in Aurangzeb to release Shahu. Shahu was, after all, his greatest trophy of war: after twenty-five years of campaigning, he had little more to show than a captive prince. He toyed with the idea for a whole year and opened negotiations with the Maratha leaders through intermediaries, but in the end he could not bring himself to go through with it. If he allowed Shahu to go back to rule his people, and the Marathas still refused to be cowed down, or, if they renounced Shahu altogether, it would have killed the old man.

As it was, Aurangzeb did not have long to live. He had passed his ninetieth birthday and he is said to have had a premonition of death. Haunted by an unknown fear, he called Shahu to his bedside and made him swear that he would never take up arms against the Moghuls. A few days later, on a cold February night in 1707, Aurangzeb died in his white tent, pitched exactly in the same spot where he had camped amidst barbaric splendour twenty-one years earlier, when he began his campaign against Bijapur. Austere in death as in life, his last words were:

> 'Carry this creature of dust quickly to the first burial place and consign him to the earth without any useless coffin'.

21

A House Divided

Aurangzeb's death broke the Moghul threat to the Deccan: the mainspring that had kept the rusty machine of war going, had run out. His three surviving sons were quarrelling amongst themselves for his throne even as his frail body was being interred. All three of them had succeeded to the commands of powerful armies in the field, and now each of them hastened to proclaim himself as the Moghul Emperor. It took a whole year and two savage battles before the issue of succession was finally decided in the only way it could be decided—after one of Aurangzeb's sons had defeated the two rival armies and had killed both his brothers.

So the Moghul line continued, but there was no question of beginning where Aurangzeb had left off.

Aurangzeb's death left a great void in the Deccan; the colossus had toppled, and where he stood was emptiness. For a time, the Marathas were too dazed to act, even though Tarabai exhorted them to unite and destroy the remnants of the Moghul Army in the Deccan. But hers was a lone voice in the wilderness: no one else seems to have realized that this was the moment of retaliation, for the last concerted push.

Within a few weeks, however, any concerted action had become out of the question. Even as the Marathas recovered from the sudden shudder of release, they were subjected to new and greater stresses; stresses which tore away the very fabric woven by Ramdas and Shivaji, and split the land into two opposite camps.

For the past twenty-five years, the Marathas had a common enemy and a common loyalty: even when their military strength was disunited, they fought as Marathas and under a common banner. Now the cementing influence of Aurangzeb had gone. The enemy no longer loomed immense, like the Himalayas, blotting out the skies. The blazing passions of a generation had to find new directions. There was a sudden rending split, and the Deccan found itself a house divided. It looked as though by his death Aurangzeb would achieve what he had failed to achieve in his lifetime.

The cause of the split amongst the Marathas was the emergence upon the scene of Shahu, the heir to the throne.

He who had been fated from childhood to drift in the wake of the Moghuls, a bit of shiny flotsam around the Emperor's throne, was tossed by the storm into the main current of history: now he saw his chance, saw it and grabbed it with both hands. As the Moghul Army of the Deccan was marching towards Delhi to fight out the issue of who was going to be the next Emperor, Shahu, accompanied by a few trusted followers, made a bid for freedom.

For some time past, Shahu had been in touch with affairs in the Deccan. Through intermediaries in the Moghul camp and almost certainly with the full knowledge of Aurangzeb, Shahu had established regular contact with a facile young man with sharp grey eyes called Balaji Vishwanath. Balaji Vishwanath was now the secretary to Dhanaji Jadhav, one of the two chief Generals of Tarabai. At the same time, Balaji was on the friendliest terms with a surprisingly large number of Moghul officials. He knew Zulfikhar personally, and even seemed to have influence with Zeb-un-nisa, the Emperor's daughter, upon whom Aurangzeb had grown to lean more and more heavily in his last days.

We have seen Balaji Vishwanath as a youth in Harnai, and later as a clerk in the salt works at Chiplun, from where the fear of the Siddy's vengeance had driven him away to Poona. Now he is the chief administrative assistant of Dhanaji Jadhav, the leading

Maratha General, and as such, a man of considerable influence. A little while ago, he had been the key figure in the background during the abortive negotiations that Aurangzeb had held with some of the Maratha leaders for the release of Shahu when he had established close contact with Shahu and filled his mind with thoughts of returning to the Deccan to rule Shivaji's kingdom. He is a fast-moving, glib tongued man at whose magic touch all doors opened; a man who spoke of high affairs of state with a convincing air, a man of talent and tact, a man to be watched.

Shahu must have been faced with a hard choice. He was renouncing everything he had grown up with and loved, for an opium dream; leaving behind his mother and younger brother to the mercies of the Moghuls; giving up security and safety and a life of luxury for hardship and danger. There were also Shahu's two young wives, bewildered young women who had been tied up with him for life, to be abandoned in their teens, all the appetites of youth still unslaked.

Above all, he was painfully conscious that he would never be free from the dominating influence of the Moghuls. Firstly, there was his death-bed promise given to Aurangzeb that he would never take up arms against the Moghuls. Besides, the Moghuls would have in their possession his mother and his brother, his two wives and an entourage of two hundred followers as hostages. It was impossible to break away wholly from the Moghuls; he would carry the taint of their influence all his life. Would the Marathas accept him with these limitations?

But Shahu acted like a man with a mission, a visionary hardening his heart to worldly values; acted as though all the pettycoat influence, all the brain-washing, all the years of dosing with *pousta* had left him untouched. He was a young man of twenty-five, in full vigour and manhood, answering the ringing voice of duty.

He had no money and no following. His only asset was that he was Shivaji's direct heir. Very few people in the Deccan remembered anything about him: he was a six-year-old boy when he was made captive; now he was nearing his twenty-fifth birthday. He was more a Moghul than a Maratha—he hardly spoke the language properly.

The first thing Shahu did, as soon as he was out of danger, was to send off messengers bearing letters to all the prominent military commanders in the Deccan whose names had been household words even in Aurangzeb's camp, announcing his return and soliciting their support.

There were now two Maratha Kings: one, Shahu; the other, an idiot who had been put on the throne merely to ensure continuity, and only in the belief that Shahu, the real heir, would never return.

It must have been a matter of some comfort to Shahu, as he faced the grim prospect of a King whom no one wanted and no one recognized returning to claim his kingdom, that the man who had encouraged him to return, Balaji Vishwanath, was said to wield great influence with the two most outstanding military commanders in the Deccan: Dhanaji Jadhav and Kanhoji Angrey. Shahu had sent messengers to both, asking for their support.

In the face of the threat to her Regency, Tarabai acted swiftly and decisively. She sent for all the prominent Maratha *mankaries* again, and boldly announced that Shahu was an impostor, a Moghul stooge pretending to be the Maratha heir. The real King was her son, who had been solemnly enthroned. There was now no going back upon what the priests had sanctified and what the gods had ordained.

She gave them a lavish banquet. During the meal, she made them swear, over a plate of milk and rice, that they would never desert her cause.

All the commanders who had gathered at Panhala took the milk-and-rice oath, binding themselves irrevocably to Tarabai's cause. She was a dynamic and resourceful woman, full of hardness and ingenuity. She was perhaps the most strongminded and clear-headed of all those who had ruled the Marathas since Shivaji. But she was fighting against too many odds.

Among those who swore undying allegiance to Tarabai and her son was Dhanaji Jadhav, whom she immediately promoted to the highest military command in her kingdom.

Later, when it was found that Shahu was not an impostor, one of those who had sworn allegiance to Tarabai was so torn between honour and loyalty that he took his own life; some others changed sides after making the necessary penance to obtain release from their oaths. Many others found it expedient to renounce both sides.

Kanhoji Angrey did not go to Panhala, and took no oaths. On his part, he had been unswervingly loyal to Tarabai in the past and would continue to be so, but he was not the man to be influenced by intrigue or pressure; he would not have relished the idea of being made to go through a rite to reiterate his loyalty. Indeed, if the time came and his convictions warranted it, he would not have hesitated to break an oath, however solemn.

As though to make certain of Kanhoji Angrey's loyalty, Tarabai announced at her Panhala conference that she had promoted him to the overall command of the fleet and also to the command of the Konkan, and that she had already sent off the robes of his new office to Colaba.

At last, Kanhoji had achieved the rank and title to which he had always aspired. His new seal of office proclaimed him to be 'Grand Admiral for ever' and 'Viceroy over the Konkan'.

One wonders what that astute and industrious man in the background, Balaji Vishwanath, thought about the two most powerful commanders in the Deccan openly aligning themselves on the side which he had already made up his mind to scuttle. No one could have been more conscious than Balaji that Shahu's success or failure would depend on whether or not he secured the support of these two commanders. But it is unlikely that Balaji worried much about it at the time. In his own mind, he must have been certain of winning over both Kanhoji Angrey and Dhanaji Jadhav to Shahu's side when the time came.

That the time was going to come, Balaji Vishwanath could not have doubted for a moment. He had already caught the scent of blood; he was convinced that he was the man chosen by destiny to put back the Maratha kingdom on its feet, and he was knocking at destiny's door with both fists.

22

Lord of the Konkan

They love a Captain to obey,
Boisterous as March, yet fresh as May.
With open hand and brow as free
Lover of wine and Minstrelsy
Ever the first to scale a tower,
As venturous in a lady's bower …

—Sir Walter Scott

Whoever possessed size, strength, wildness and
fierceness was called the son of a Possiden.

—Norse: Greek and Roman Mythology

He did possess great strength, but neither great size nor fierceness or wildness. He possessed to a great extent all those rare and undefinable attributes that go to make a leader: a philosophy of life that was a combination of Omar Khayyam and Kipling's *If*, with strong overtones of religious discipline.

A man of incredible stamina, bold, brave and independent; yet, a man of patience and cool judgment; a man who exuded a hairy-chested maleness, who laughed uproariously and danced and sang with his men, and who never hesitated to fling the same men into assaults against unknown odds; a man with the sternness and mental discipline to punish a spy or a traitor by ordering him to be trampled under an elephant's foot, and yet with the softness of heart to undertake to look after the man's wife and children.

He repeatedly and publicly acknowledged the overlordship of the Maratha Kings and Regents, and yet flew his own, blood-red standard. He collected revenue in the name of his monarch and yet brooked no interference in the internal or external affairs of the Konkan; a proud, even arrogant, stiff-necked man, 'born and begotten of the sea, full of its wild and savage energy … rocked to and fro by its waves into hardihood and indomitable pluck.'

A sailor and soldier, equally fond of ships and horses, a powerful swimmer and dashing horseman, he paid fabulous prices for the best swords of Toledo and Damascus and the best horses from Arabia. And he also collected guns from England, much as an English squire would collect them, admiring their finish and engravings as much as their performance. In looks, he seems to have borne an astonishing resemblance to his present descendant, Chandroji Angrey. He was, Gorse wrote two hundred years ago, a 'well-set corpulent man rather blacker than commonly the Dekhneys are, full-faced, with a sparkling eye and a full countenance'.

He had three wives and many concubines. The wives were Mathura, Lakshmi and Gahina, and all of them lived in the same house. He was the father of seven legitimate children—a daughter and six sons—and he had almost certainly at least as many more children from his mistresses. There were many women in his life, favourites of the moment, dancing girls and others, ever-changing objects of a sailor's loveless passion.

A man fond of song and dance and drama: he used to maintain a troupe of singers and actors and also a batch of professional dancing girls, for the sole purpose of giving song and dance performances and plays at his court.

Whether Kanhoji Angrey was as fond of wine as he was of women and song will never be known: the Maratha historians, obsessed with the idea that there is something shameful about drinking, usually go to great pains to avoid all reference to it among their heroes; the popular vices of fighting men are scowled upon by those who write about them. And the European historians never came into sufficiently close contact to record whether Kanhoji Angrey was fond of alcohol in any form. It will always remain a mystery.

But his world was certainly not inhabited wholly by women and song and rowdy sailors and soldiers. He was an astute diplomat, clever at presenting his own side: some of the letters he wrote are masterpieces of clarity and forthrightness, and, surprisingly, of abounding sarcasm, and yet, fully in conformity with the polite adornments of the day. They present an agreeable contrast with the often crude and woolly communications of the British and Portuguese representatives. He encouraged learning and respected men of learning: for the pandits, the astronomers, the lawyers, astrologers, medicine-men, reciters of scriptures, artists, cookery-experts, horse-experts and the appraisers of precious stones, he seems to have entertained an outdoorsman's unreasoning reverence for the knowledgeable. He is said to have always treated them with hospitality and almost invariably sent them off with presents.

In surprising contrast to this streak of riotous loving and living, he was an intensely religious man, and he rarely took a holiday except to go on religious pilgrimages. The dancing girls and actors and other performers he maintained were mainly intended for performances at the various religious festivals, and he used to spend every year implausibly large amounts of money for performing religious rights with the proper amount of ceremony. For Dassara alone, which is the festival of harvest and also the beginning of the season of warfare, he is said to have regularly spent a sum which in today's values would amount to nearly two lakhs of rupees, for buying incense, camphor, oil, flowers, sweetmeats for distribution, gold and silk cloth for giving away to the Brahmins, and for feeding the Brahmins.

The feeding of Brahmins is one of the holy deeds of the Hindu religion, said to bring rewards in this world and the next. Many of the religious festivals are not complete unless the stipulated number of Brahmins have been given sumptuous meals. It is not a matter of just food, either, because the feeding is not regarded as complete unless the Brahmins are also given some sort of presents in addition to the meals. The presents are called *dakshina* and they have to be given in the form of pieces of gold, or at least silver coins, as well as coconuts and flowers. Even to this day, surprisingly large sums are earmarked during religious festivals for the feeding of Brahmins.

Kanhoji Angrey is said to have made something of a fetish of feeding Brahmins and giving them presents.

In addition to the large number of gods and goddesses in the Hindu religion, each family usually has its own household deity. Kanhoji's ancestral goddess was Kalimbika, an incarnation of the goddess of destruction, and he had her brought from Suvarna-durg to Colaba and installed her with considerable fanfare in a specially-constructed family temple at Hirakote, which lies across the channel from Colaba.

But more than the family goddess, more than the Brahmins retained in his court and the hundreds of temples in his domain, the greatest spiritual influence in his life was an almost blind veneration for a swami called Brahmendra-swami.

A swami is a holy man, something between a saint and a mendicant: someone who has acquired so much spiritual power that he can do good to his followers, or contrarily, bring down curses upon them for disregarding his wishes.

Brahmendra-swami, a unique complex of a hard driving businessman and religious preceptor, a king-maker and mendicant, usurer and public benefactor, fabulously rich and given to the most outrageous fits of temper, seems to have been the driving force in the life of Kanhoji Angrey: he almost never undertook a new venture unless it had been sanctioned by the semi-naked holy man, Brahmendra-swami.

This, then was Kanhoji Angrey: age 38, the *Surkhail* or the Grand Admiral of the Maratha navy as well as the overall Commander of the Konkan, who had fought the Siddy to a standstill and was now ready to take on the others. He has already made a name for himself. In fact, he has already achieved one of the rarest tributes that a military commander can aspire to: he has impressed his personality upon the Konkan to such an extent that the English and the Portuguese, the Dutch and the French, no longer refer to the Maratha ships as 'Sevajee's grabs' or 'Ramraja's grabs', but have now, in one accord, begun to refer to them as 'Angria's *gallivat*s,' or even 'Angria's navy.'

So can you imagine an Austrian trooper towards the end of the eighteenth century referring to the opposing French force as 'Napoleon's Army'; so can you imagine a 'Desert Rat' of our own Second World War referring to the German African Corps as 'Rommel's Bastards'. But history cannot produce many more examples of this phenomenon in which a military force is identified with the name of its commander. Few sailors or soldiers in war are aware of the names of their own Generals or Admirals; the names of the enemy commanders are almost unknown.

Oddly enough, it was this very phenomenon that had also lent support to the charge that Angrey had broken away from the Marathas: his enemies twisted his rare military distinction into a thing of dishonour and shame. The identification of his name with the navy of the Marathas was the main argument put forward by the English that he was a chieftain on his own, operating without the sanction of the rulers of the land; that the ships under his command had nothing to do with the Maratha Kings.

As it happened, the English were perfectly aware of the exact status and position of Kanhoji Angrey. He was appointed to be the *Surkhail* and the *Wazarat Ma-aab* with a good deal of fanfare, and Angrey himself had repeatedly made it clear to the Company's Council that he was 'the Admiral of the Maratha Empire ... to whom the sovereignty of the seas belonged, and that he was determined to maintain it against all such as refused to acknowledge it or not take his passes.'

But the East India Company's Council had 'resolved': Kanhoji Angrey, Grand Admiral of the Marathas, had nothing to do with the Maratha King. The Council's resolution could not be altered.

23

'His Holiness: Lord of the Universe'

It was that irrepressible man on the run, Balaji Vishwanath, who may be said to have 'discovered' Brahmendra-swami. It is doubtful if the Swami would have ever amounted to much if he had not had Balaji for a devotee; it is even more doubtful if Balaji would have amounted to anything without the constant help of the Swami. They both worked with untiring zeal, firstly for themselves, and secondly for each other. One became the Prime Minister of the Maratha King with almost absolute power and the other became the man-behind-the-scenes in Maratha politics, moving all the pawns at his wish and whim.

He was born in poverty and his original name was Vishnu. He lost both his parents when he was twelve. Soon afterwards, he took to long spells of solitary meditation. At fifteen, he went to Benares to become a fourth-degree Brahmin, which means he renounced all the cares of the world as well as its pleasures and became a holy man—a saint. He also changed his name to Brahmendra-swami, which might be translated as 'His Holiness, Lord of the Universe'. Then he began his grand pilgrimage: a 3,000-mile march from the Himalayas to the southernmost tip of India, taking in all the *tirthas* or holy places, on the way. At the end of the pilgrimage, he came and settled down in a forest on the outskirts of Chiplun.

It was in this forest near Chiplun that he was 'discovered' by Balaji Viswanath: a holy man lost in meditation had found his first disciple, a clerk in the Siddy's salt works.

'You will rise to the highest position,' the swami announced to the young man who prostrated himself at his feet.

The meeting was charged with significance. By themselves, they were nobodies; by their effect upon each other, they became figures of history. Between them, they guided the history of the Deccan, often shaping it to suit their personal ends.

Brahmendra-swami and Balaji Vishwanath must have first come together in the early sixteen-eighties. In 1688, Balaji Vishwanath ran away from Chiplun. But by that time, the holy man and his young disciple had become a powerful combination; each finding a catalyst in the other.

For ten years after Balaji Vishwanath had left Chiplun, the Swami continued to live in solitary meditation. In 1698, he decided to 'reveal himself'. He was already in his fiftieth year.

Kanhoji Angrey, too, had become a follower of the Swami long before he revealed himself publicly. The silent man in the forest lost in meditation and prayers must have made a strong appeal to the religious streak in Kanhoji Angrey. They say that through Balaji Viswanath, Angrey had secured the Swami's blessings for his *coup* before attempting to take over command of Suvarna-durg from Achloji Mohitay. From then on, the contact had strengthened; particularly since Kanhoji ascribed the success of his desperate gamble to the blessings of Brahmendra-swami.

Right from the moment he revealed himself, the Swami began a systematic campaign to extend his following. He shamelessly exploited his supposed spiritual powers—his ability to do good to his followers and to bring down heavenly curses at will. He let it be whispered that he performed miracles. He is said to have sailed across the creek riding upon a banana leaf, only, however, in the middle of the night; that he had second sight which could be used to find out hidden treasure; that he could bring down the rains in times of drought. For forty years he ran what can only be described as a colossal racket. He threatened dire punishments to those who went counter to his wishes, and he shamelessly withheld his blessings until the right price was forthcoming. By the most extraordinary coincidence, those who paid his price and obtained his blessings in their ventures, prospered.

He built some of the biggest temples of his day and spent large sums of money on their consecration and maintenance.

He built tanks, wells, bridges and roads; he laid out gardens and planted vast tracts with forests. He incessantly dabbled in politics, proclaiming himself to be the guardian of the Maratha kingdom, pushing forward the cause of his devotees and ruthlessly suppressing their opponents. A man of hair-trigger emotions, he forced his disciples to go to war with the Siddy for avenging a personal insult; yet he seldom used his undoubtedly great influence to patch up the differences amongst the Marathas themselves. He had devotees amongst the Muslims as well as amongst Hindus, and Siddy Rasool, Kassam's successor as the ruler of Janjira, gave him a generous annual grant for the maintenance of his estates near Chiplun. At one time, the Swami even offered to use his good offices to bring pressure upon the East India Company at Bombay. He never forgave a slight and he never granted a favour without receiving payment in cash or kind. He wrote insulting letters to some of the highest personalities in the Deccan demanding the return of the money he had loaned; and at the same time he appealed to them for extortionate donations, threatening to throw their ancestors into hell if they did not pay up. He had renounced all worldly pleasures, and yet, mile-long caravans of bullocks were regularly employed to bring the special stores needed for his many establishments and the choicest table delicacies were sent to him by his numerous followers. Self-professedly celibate, he had a collection of fourteen personal maids to look after his comforts. Greedy, selfish, ambitious, vindictive, unscrupulous, he never allowed a starving man to go hungry from his doors and he helped thousands of the needy with money and influence.

But man of God or utter charlatan, avaricious moneylender or supporter of the Maratha wars with private loans, miracleworker or fake, the most consistent thing about Brahmendra-swami was that he never backed a wrong man. If he succeeded as he did, when each village and township in India, each street in the larger towns, has its own Swami; men who live and die without acquiring a following or fame, it can only be explained by resorting to the overstrained *cliche* that nothing succeeds like success. Everyone that the Swami blessed shot up in the world; everything that he touched, became gold.

And now, in the year 1707, Brahmendra-swami sent off a special messenger to Shahu, conveying his blessings upon the prince, and welcoming him. As gifts to the Maratha prince, he sent a holy thread and a loin cloth: 'You will overcome all opposition and rule in peace,' the Swami told Shahu.

To Shahu, the bewildered expatriate returning to claim his throne, denounced as an impostor and a Moghul agent, the message from Brahmendra-swami must have come like a clear sign from the sky. Suddenly, he was no longer a friendless stranger, but a man with influential backing. Shahu's gratitude knew no bounds.

If the Swami was not blessed with divine foresight, he must have been taking a desperately long chance. At a time when all the leading Maratha *mankaries*, all the important military commanders, had ranged themselves solidly on Tarabai's side, bound down by the milk-and-rice oath, the man who predicted Shahu's success must have been a lone voice in the wilderness. And yet, knowing that the man was Brahmendra-swami, must have sent a cold shiver down those who had vowed to stand by Tarabai.

Brahmendra-swami's pronouncement came as a particularly nasty shock to Kanhoji Angrey. He had whole-heartedly supported Tarabai and her son: as far as he was concerned, there could be no two views on the question. And now, his acknowledged religious preceptor, the man whose blessings he had always sought before making a major decision, his counsel in difficulties and the man who was prepared to loan large sums of money whenever the need arose, had openly thrown his great weight on the side of the pretender Shahu.

Kanhoji Angrey's rigid code faced its first great challenge. He had sworn to be loyal to the Maratha King. But who was the Maratha King?

The question must have tormented him for a long time, and once again, the thought of breaking away from it all and setting up a dynasty of his own must have haunted his mind.

But in the end, characteristically, he chose to remain loyal to Tarabai. There was no question of changing sides lightheartedly, even if it meant breaking faith with his spiritual adviser. He admired Tarabai as a person, and was not prepared to renounce her for a stranger who had grown up in the Moghul camp, even if he was the real Maratha prince. Besides, it was Tarabai who had made him what he was, the *Surkhail* for ever and the guardian of the coast. He had eaten her salt, and he would not let her down.

Even if it meant civil war!

24

Pirate!

In 1703, Kanhoji Angrey had bluntly told Mr. Reynolds, the East India Company's delegate, that he would seize all ships that did not carry his *dastaks*, and that the English could do what they liked. Almost immediately after this, he seems to have begun to make good his threat. For reasons mentioned in the ensuing paragraphs, there can be no reliable record of all the English ships taken by Kanhoji, but there is little doubt that their number was such as to have caused grave concern to the Company's officials.

The English retaliated with virulence, only to discover that they were not doing much damage: the Marathas did not depend upon sea trade, and the only suitable targets for the Company's fury were small fishing vessels and salt boats. As in the past, the Company also gave considerable help, and much more encouragement, to the Siddy of Janjira to inflict as much damage upon Maratha shipping and Maratha territory. They would have liked to help the Siddy more than they did, but for one thing, it would have looked like taking sides openly, and the Company was still trying to keep up an appearance of neutrality; and for another, they did not trust the Siddy.

At this time, the Siddy had two strong backers: Aurangzeb, the Great Moghul, who gave him an annual subsidy of four lakhs of rupees to maintain his fleet, and his new-found friends from abroad whom he referred to as the 'hat-men', who kept him supplied with the best powder and shot, and who permitted his ships to use their ports freely.

Taunted by Aurangzeb, egged on by the English, the Siddy, Kassam Yakoot Khan, made valiant efforts to break the rising power of Kanhoji Angrey. For two or three years, as soon as the rains were over, he dutifully went and attacked one or the other of Angrey's forts, but every year he found the opposition getting stronger and stronger.

Often, he had to withdraw in haste to ward off a counter-blow at one of his few remaining strongholds. The English, watching his efforts with trembling anticipation, gradually grew resigned to the Siddy's repeated failures.

The Company's concern over Kanhoji's increasing hostility is expressed in a letter the President at Surat wrote to the Directors in 1706:

> 'Your Honours will, I presume, from Bombay have a particular account of the Sevajee Canajee Angra, their ill and near neighbour. (It is astonishing how 26 years after his death, Shivaji's name still crops up in the Company's records). He hath lately taken a ship belonging to Mr. Mildmay and Your Honour's broker at Carwarr, a ship of Mr. Bouchers of about 200 tons, her cargo amounting to 70,000 rupees, the *Diamond* of Madras carrying 12 guns and 26 Europeans, her cargo worth near two lakhs of rupees, and one of the Island's *manchuas*, another ship of about 200 tons, to whose belonging I don't yet hear, and a Dutch Hoigh man'd with about 26 Dutchmen, besides sundry other small vessels.'

It is unlikely that these heavy shipping casualties within a relatively short period of time were all attributable to Kanhoji Angrey. It must be remembered that this was also the heyday of the Malabar pirates who played havoc with the merchant shipping of the Arabian Sea.

The Malabar pirates did not come from Malabar, nor did they confine their activities to the Malabar coast. Surprisingly enough, most of them were Englishmen—Englishmen who had settled down in America. 'In New York, Boston, Jamaica and the Bahamas, ships were fitted out, nominally for slave trade, though it was no secret that they were intended for piracy in the Eastern Seas,' Bidulph tells us. Then he goes on to add: 'Whatever compunction ... (the pirates might) ... have felt at attacking European ships, there was none about plundering Asiatic Merchants where great booty was to be gained with little risk.' Besides, 'plundering and ill-treating Asiatics was a venial offence, and many a seaman after a cruise with the pirates returned to their calling on board an honest merchantman without being thought much the worse for it.'

In the face of this provocation, there would have been little blame attached to an Indian ruler if he had set out to capture or sink all European merchant ships. It is possible that in England, he would have been hailed as a hero, of the same calibre as Hawkins and Grenville if not of Nelson and Drake, but a national hero all the same, and his doings would have been regarded as no more than an act of fitting reprisal. But viewpoints differed in Europe and India, and those who came to India from Europe did not always bring their standards with them.

Admittedly, there were Asian pirates too, in particular the Arabs and the Singhanians. In 1996, the Muscat Arabs had swooped down on Salsette, within twenty miles of Bombay, ravaging the countryside as they pleased, killing the Portuguese priests and carrying off 1400 captives into slavery, and in the early years of the eighteenth century, the Muscat pirates could muster 'one ship of 74 guns, two of 60, one of fifty, eighteen carrying thirty-two to twelve guns each and a host of smaller vessels, carrying never less than four guns.' But these were the lesser fry. The fiercest and the boldest were the Englishmen; Kidd, Every, Teach, Bridgemann, John Hand, and their like. A few years earlier, and, it is worth emphasizing, before the arrival on the scene of Kanhoji Angrey, the losses of the East India Company from the attacks of these pirates are said to have amounted to a million pounds, and as was only to be expected, 'the losses to the native merchants were much more serious.'

But even if Kanhoji Angrey was not responsible for all of the Company's shipping losses, there is little doubt that he accounted for a major portion of them, and in particular to the sinking or seizure of warships. These losses of fighting ships could not, under any circumstances, be ascribed to the Malabar pirates.

There was no war between the East India Company and the Marathas, and yet, there was no peace; both sides were taking a heavy toll of each other's ships.

At one stage, there seems to have been some talk of a truce. There was an exchange of letters between the Company and Kanhoji Angrey in 1706. In his letter, Kanhoji had denied responsibility for some of the losses ascribed to him, and had offered to restore the ships he had actually seized, 'provided articles of friendship are agreed upon with the Rani.'

The negotiations, as it happens, came to nothing, but Kanhoji Angrey's letter quoted in the Company's records offers the clearest proof of his continued loyalty to the Rani, Tarabai. In the year 1706, he had told the Bombay Council in so many words that any treaty made with him would not be effective unless it was ratified by the Maratha Regent.

But Angrey's protestations of loyalty to the Maratha throne fell on deaf ears: four years earlier, the councillors had already made up their mind that he had broken away from the Maratha overlordship, and whether they had much evidence or not, it suited their purpose to go on speaking of him as being independent of the Marathas.

The process of thought could lead only to one convenient conclusion: that Kanhoji Angrey was a pirate. The Company's Council, with many a skeleton to hide away, had found a handy cupboard. The whole thing fitted in beautifully with the circumstances of the times. One pirate more in the impressive galaxy of the Malabar pirates, Beyt pirates, Muscat pirates, the Singhanians, did not matter much provided he helped to write off the numerous financial losses of the Company through sinkings and other misadventures. A pirate of their own was what the Company must have almost longed for, and now that they had acquired one, they were going to play him up for all they were worth.

Kanhoji himself had done nothing to give the impression that he had broken away from the Marathas. On the contrary he had often enough proclaimed his loyalty to them. He lived openly and held court, not in a hide-out like a pirate, and there was nothing shifty about his activities. He signed all his letters '*Surkhail* for ever by the grace of—(the King)—.' He restricted his activities to the Konkan coast, which was his legitimate command, and never went plundering ships on the high seas as did many of England's national heroes of those times; and he never molested a ship which carried his *dastaks*. None of the other powers, the Moghuls, the Portuguese, the Dutch, had yet referred to him as anything but the Maratha naval commander. What he did was fully in conformity with the maritime practice of the day.

But the East India Company had spoken; its councillors had resolved: Kanhoji Angrey, *Surkhail* of the Maratha fleet, doing no more than his duty in the strict confines of his waters, only seizing such ships as refused to carry his clearance papers, which could be purchased for twenty rupees each, was given the label that will be associated with the name of the Angreys for all times: the Pirate!

25

Three Men and a Meal

The year 1707 was a momentous one in the history of the Deccan. It was the year of Aurangzeb's death. It was also the year of the beginning of the Maratha civil war.

Shahu, the heir to the throne, was on his way back to the Deccan. His companions did not include a single capable military leader, but he was lucky to have with him an astute banker and an influential priest. He knew that he had the secret backing of Balaji Vishwanath, who was the secretary to the chief Maratha General, Dhanaji Jadhav, and he also had the open backing of Brahmendra-swami, again, almost engineered by Balaji Viswanath.

With these meagre assets, Shahu began his journey home. On the advice of the banker and the priest, he sent off letters to Tarabai and to all the Maratha chieftains along the way. Tarabai was resolved to oppose him with all her power. A few of the chieftains, however, came to join him, hesitantly, more for personal reasons than out of conviction, but by the time he reached the borders of the Deccan, his following was still slender.

Shahu's was the more forcible claim. After all, Tarabai was merely the Regent, acting for her son Shivaji, an idiot who had been placed on the throne only because Shahu, the real heir, was a prisoner and was not expected to return. Now that he had returned, it seemed only fair that Tarabai and her son should step aside with grace and give Shahu his rightful place.

At the same time, even those who believed that Shahu was the rightful heir, were not enthusiastic about his return. They had already written him off, twenty years earlier, and to take him back now and renounce Tarabai, a colourful and courageous woman who, by sheer force of character combined with her resourcefulness, had won a place for herself in their hearts, would have involved too many drastic readjustments. By emerging from the ranks of the forgotten, the already grieved for Shahu was being an awkward nuisance, an added complication in the disorders of the Deccan.

Above all, was Shahu really Shahu ?

Tarabai had proclaimed him to be an impostor, and no one could be certain whether the frail boy taken away by the Moghuls twenty years earlier was this prematurely balding man who claimed to be Shahu; a man who spoke his own language in a hybrid dialect and had learnt the manners and ways of the Moghuls—a man who looked and behaved most unlike a Maratha.

The Maratha chiefs who were not already committed to Tarabai's party held back for many weeks, refusing to take sides until they were certain of Shahu's real identity; hoping that somehow the decision would not have to be made; that things would sort themselves out in such a way that there would be no civil war.

They half hoped that Shahu would turn out to be an impostor.

Tarabai herself must have been so certain that he was an impostor, that she ordered one of her trusted *mankaries*, Persoji Bhonsley, to go and meet Shahu and pronounce judgment upon him. This, as it turned out, was a move which backfired.

Persoji Bhonsley, accompanied by his brother, set out for Shahu's camp to pronounce judgment upon Shahu's *bona fides*. Persoji belonged to the same family as Shahu (whose surname was also Bhonsley), and, in fact, was distantly related to him. He had been a close associate of Shivaji, and he was also one of the few people who had seen Shahu as a boy.

Amongst the Marathas, and particularly amongst the families of the noblemen, the ritual of who can sit at a meal as equals is governed by the most inflexible rules. People of different castes cannot sit at the same *pankti* (row) to eat, and only people belonging to the same family can eat out of the same *thali* (platter).

Persoji Bhonsley met Shahu on the banks of the Godavari River, beyond the borders of the Deccan, and he seems to have been instantly convinced that Shahu was not an impostor. The very next day, Shahu arranged a public ceremony at which Persoji Bhonsley and his brother sat down to a meal with Shahu, and they all ate out of the same thali, thereby accepting him as their own kith and kin. At the same time, Persoji announced his decision to join Shahu's party. He was soon followed by a number of *mankaries* who had been waiting uncertainly for a cue such as this: there was no doubt left in their minds that Shahu was Shahu.

But Tarabai was determined not to be convinced. She denounced Persoji Bhonsley as a traitor, and sent a letter to Shahu telling him in no uncertain terms that she would never take him to be anything but an impostor and a Moghul agent, and that she would resist his return with all her might.

Shahu was stunned by Tarabai's letter. Although he had anticipated some resistance on the part of his aunt, he had never thought that she would be prepared to go to war to oppose his return. At this time, the rains provided him with an excuse to halt in his tracks. For four months he waited uncertainly, his resources dwindling, his followers getting more and more restive. At the end of the rains, egged on by Persoji Bhonsley and others who may be said to have burned their boats behind them, Shahu resumed his march towards the Deccan, still hoping to arrive at some kind of settlement with Tarabai, still reluctant to commit himself to open warfare.

But the stage had been reached when there was no question of avoiding war. Tarabai was determined to oppose his return. She wanted all or nothing. She ordered her chief military commanders, Dhanaji Jadhav and Parasuram Pant, to attack and destroy Shahu and his followers. In October 1707, news reached Shahu that a strong Maratha army was already marching against him.

Thus we come to the historic battle of Khed: a battle which should have meant the total annihilation of Shahu's modest force and the end of his dream, but was transformed into an easy victory for him.

The two armies faced each other on the opposite banks of the River Bhima: to the north, was Shahu's ragged collection of new-found followers; facing them were two powerful, battle-seasoned Maratha armies under the two most successful Generals of the times—Dhanaji Jadhav and Parasuram Pant, both bound by the milk-and-rice oath to support Tarabai, come what may.

The circle is now full. Dhanaji may have been the 'hero of a hundred battles', but the cleverest statesman of the times, Balaji Vishwanath, was the man behind Dhanaji Jadhav and it was he who was largely responsible for Shahu's decision to return to claim his throne.

Even as the two opposing armies faced each other, Balaji Vishwanath persuaded Dhanaji Jadhav to go with him to a midnight conference with Shahu. By the time they had finished, Dhanaji Jadhav had decided to change sides. The milk-and-rice oath had cracked under the pressure of Balaji's powerful diplomacy.

Just as the battle was about to be joined, Dhanaji, the senior Maratha Commander, declared that he had changed sides and would not take part in the battle. The other Commander, Parasuram Pant, not wishing to take chances against the redoubtable Dhanaji, decided to disengage his forces and fled to Satara.

The battle of Khed was over: the victory was overwhelmingly Shahu's. From the battlefield itself, Shahu announced that he had appointed Dhanaji Jadhav to be the Commander-in-Chief of the Maratha land forces.

Then, with Dhanaji at his side, to say nothing of Dhanaji's secretary, Balaji Vishwanath, Shahu marched in a triumphal procession towards Satara, and was soon installed there as the King of the Marathas. Tarabai, with her few remaining followers, had already retired to Panhala, a fort near Kolhapur. Dhanaji's defection must have come as a great blow to her, but Tarabai was not the woman to give up in despair.

The year 1707 was also the year of the death of Siddy Kassam Yakoot Khan, the man who had ruled Janjira ever since Kanhoji had come of age. The new Siddy, Rasool Yakoot Khan, gave every indication that he would prefer to live in amity with Kanhoji. Some sort of truce seems to have been arrived at, and the measure of accord is reflected in the fact that both sides decided that Sagar-gad, which had formed a constant bone of contention between the two, should be treated as joint property and should fly the flags of both the Siddy and the Marathas.

At least for the time being, the seasonal war with the Siddy showed every indication of having cooled off. Kanhoji could now devote his attention to the strengthening of his coastal forts and to expanding his fleet. From now on, he would also be enabled to devote more attention to the misdeeds of the other powers along the coast: the English and the Portuguese.

But Kanhoji Angrey had a new enemy now, more powerful than the English and the Portuguese: the new Maratha King, Shahu, recently crowned at Satara by the holiest of Brahmins and in accordance with the full Vedic rites. From Parasuram, Brahmendra-swami, too, sent his blessings to the new King.

For even after it was proved beyond all doubt that Shahu was not an impostor, and although he had been accepted as the King by many of the most prominent Maratha *mankaries*, even though they had sworn to support Tarabai's side, Kanhoji had continued to remain loyal to Tarabai, or, more correctly, to her son Shivaji in whose name she ruled. It was Tarabai who had given him the command of the fleet and of the Konkan. He had eaten her salt and given his word.

Besides, Shahu seemed suspiciously hand-in-glove with the Moghuls, and indeed the Moghuls were now openly announcing their support to Shahu against Tarabai. Kanhoji Angrey had grown used to Tarabai's rule for seven years, and to discard her for a stranger he had never seen went against his grain.

And so the most unswervingly loyal servant of Sambhaji was now ready to oppose Sambhaji's son with the same fierce determination and courage which had made his name a byword in the Deccan. He, Kanhoji Angrey, was not the man to 'change his turban to suit the wind', as many others had done.

26

'The Royal Terrace'

Rajmachi, a 'lantern held in the face of friend or foe, flashed upon every man' who passes.

—James Douglas

In 1711, as though to make doubly sure of keeping Kanhoji Angrey on her side, Tarabai announced that she had placed the fort of Rajmachi under his command.

Rajmachi, near Khandala, is outside the natural borders of the Konkan, but the fort was of the greatest strategic importance to the Konkan. In fact, since the ghats, the mountains which cut off the Konkan from the rest of the Deccan, had now become a frontier of the civil war, Rajmachi was one of the two key forts for the defence of north Konkan from an incursion from above the ghats. The other fort was Loh-gad, the fortress of steel. Between them, these two forts commanded the principal pass between the ghats and northern Konkan, known as the *Bor-ghat* Pass. Anyone who possessed Rajmachi could dominate the Pass and paralyse all communication between Satara and North Konkan.

Rajmachi, 'the Royal Terrace', is near Khandala, on the Bombay-Poona road. Every day, travellers going by train between Bombay and Poona can catch fleeting glimpses of its stern visage from three different angles as the trains go hurtling through the ghats. Its battlements stand black and forbidding, glistening with moisture and sunlight; a useless relic of a bygone age, no longer sought after except by adventurous picnickers. From the top, you can see an immense panorama, the hazy outline of the coast from Salsette to Colaba, including, of course, the whole smoke-filled enormity of Bombay; an unobstructed, breathtaking view of a large tract of north Konkan as far as the eye can reach, justifying the name Shivaji gave to the fort—'the Royal Terrace'.

At the base of the fort, there is an outer wall which runs for three miles. From the base, you gaze at the main fort towering above: there is a sheer block of rock, sixty feet high, and after that height, it 'bellies out in an abrupt, overhanging corporation' making the fort walls truly unscalable even by mountain climbers—they said a lizard could not find a foothold on its sides. You creep through the gateway, hewn out of live rock with an uneasy feeling of being under observation from the top, conscious that you could be fired upon through slits in the walls or mangled beneath a cascade of rolling boulders.

Rajmachi would have been a wonderful acquisition for Kanhoji Angrey. Rajmachi was also a 'prestige' fort, and its command a recognition of higher status and authority. The snag was that Rajmachi was not Tarabai's to give. Its commander was solidly on Shahu's side.

'I have placed the fort under your command,' Tarabai seemed to say to Kanhoji Angrey. 'It is up to you to go and take it.'

On Tarabai's part, the appointment was not as meaningless as it may seem at first sight. This was her attempt to frustrate the effects of an alliance between the English at Bombay and Shahu. It was known that Shahu had appealed to the Governor of the East India Company, Sir Nicholas Waite, to send him guns and ammunition. The control of Rajmachi would have gone a long way to block off the effectiveness of such an alliance.

But, however desirable it might have been to take Rajmachi and control the lifeline between Bombay and Satara, Kanhoji was reluctant to show open hostility to Shahu: in a civil war, he had no wish to be the aggressor, although, of course, he was quite prepared to oppose Shahu in the field if the need arose. Besides, Rajmachi, upon whose walls even a lizard was said not to be capable of finding a toe-hold, was not going to be easy to capture.

The overall situation in the Konkan was charged: there was an atmosphere of calmness before a storm; everyone could see that an explosion was imminent. A lot would depend on which way the English and the Portuguese would go. For Kanhoji Angrey, this was a period of waiting and watching, and holding back; not plunging into hostilities blindly. Along the coast, his relations with the English and the Portuguese were fast deteriorating, and he had no wish to commit himself to a prolonged siege far away from his bases, and expose his own forts to the danger of an attack by the Portuguese or the English.

Characteristically, he utilized the uneasy respite for strengthening the fortifications of Gheria and Colaba. At about the same time, he also struck his own coins and circulated them in the Konkan. His main effort was directed to preventing the civil strife from above the ghats seeping into the Konkan. Although in the Konkan too, public opinion was sharply divided for and against Shahu, so far there had been no open rift. In case of a conflict, Kanhoji Angrey was confident that he would carry the whole of the Konkan with him.

Above the ghats, the impending battle between Shahu and Tarabai had still not taken place. Notwithstanding the large following she commanded as compared to Shahu, Tarabai was in no position to muster a sizeable force under one command. Shahu, on the other hand, was a soft-hearted man, and in his anxiety to avoid a clash with his own kith and kin, he kept putting off the action on one pretext or another, still hoping that things would sort themselves out in some way without his having to go to war with Tarabai.

But in 1711, Shahu's fortunes suffered several unrelated setbacks, which must have made him wish that he had not delayed the crucial battle so long. The chief among his misfortunes was the death of his Commander-in-Chief, Dhanaji Jadhav, and the subsequent defection of his next Commander-in-Chief, Chandra-sen Jadhav, Dhanaji's son. Chandra-sen's appointment to the office was no more than a matter of accepted practice: Shahu made him the Commander-in-Chief merely because he was Dhanaji's son. Chandra-sen was a vain, illtempered, small-minded youth and Shahu did not trust him much both in regard to his loyalty and his military capabilities. As a check upon Chandra-sen, Shahu appointed Balaji Vishwanath as a kind of administrative commander-in-chief. This arrangement involved dual responsibilty and was bound to lead to trouble. Within a few months, Balaji Vishwanath and Chandra-sen fell out[11] and there was an open clash of arms between the two. When matters reached Shahu's ears, he sided with Balaji Vishwanath. In protest, Chandra-sen Jadhav went off and joined Tarabai. Many other Maratha chieftains, who, for some reason or the other had been discontented with Shahu, also took this opportunity to change sides.

The defection of Chandra-sen Jadhav and the other *mankaries* was a serious loss to Shahu's side, for, according to the practice of

---

11 The quarrel between Chandra-sen and Balaji Vishwanath arose over a hunted deer. Chandra-sen's army was camped near Karad, fifty miles south of Satara, when a black buck pursued by one of Balaji's servants happened to run into the tent of one of Chandra-sen's clerks. The clerk, who must have been a devout Brahmin and thus opposed to all killing (except presumably the killing of human beings) refused to permit the hunters to kill the deer. The quarrel that ensued was taken up by their respective masters so seriously that it led to a battle between their two factions. Balaji's side was trounced, and Balaji himself had to go into hiding, accompanied by his young son Bajirao, then nine years old. At this stage, Shahu intervened and offered protection to Balaji. Chandra-sen thereupon threatened Shahu that unless he delivered Balaji into his hands to be suitably punished, he would go over to Tarabai's side. When Shahu turned down this insolent demand, he went off and joined Tarabai.

the day, when a chieftain changed sides, he also took away most of the troops under his command.

At about this time, Shahu received two more rude shocks. First, the English completely ignored his appeals for help; and secondly, the Moghuls, upon whose help Shahu had pinned great hopes, bluntly told him that they would recognize him as the Maratha King only if he won his impending battle against Tarabai. This, Shahu was aware, was merely an excuse to deny him help, since if he could win his battle against Tarabai without Moghul recognition or help, he did not have much need of such recognition or help afterwards.

The one man who stood by Shahu's side, staunch as a rock in the face of many vicissitudes of fortune, was Balaji Vishwanath, who was not even a professional soldier but a Brahmin. However, what Shahu needed most at this hour of crisis was not a military leader but a capable statesman; an exceptional combination of a diplomat and administrator, and above all a financial wizard who knew not only how to make a gold mohur go a long way, but who had the ability and contacts to borrow the vast sums of money needed for the maintenance of a standing army.

Balaji was Shahu's man. He borrowed from his numerous friends in Poona and he borrowed from his spiritual master Brahmendra-swami; and with the money thus raised he organized a staff and an army whose main qualification was that of implicit loyalty to Shahu. To provide against the everpresent danger of the defection of troops whenever their leaders changed sides, he organized a special force of picked men to form a personal bodyguard for Shahu. These troops later came to be known as the *Huzarat* or 'The King's Men'.

As it happened, Tarabai was in no position to take advantage of Shahu's difficulties. If Shahu was in serious trouble, his aunt was in even worse trouble. It may be recalled that when Rajaram had died, he had left two wives and two sons, and that when Tarabai became the Regent, she had placed the other prince and his mother, Rajasbai, in confinement. During the years that followed, Tarabai's vigilance seems to have slackened, and this was the time Rajasbai chose to strike back. With a few trusted followers, she engineered a revolt. Overnight, she turned the tables. She threw Tarabai and her son into prison. Her son Sambhaji was proclaimed King and became the new contender for the Maratha throne.[12]

Thus Tarabai, a valiant woman, passes out of Maratha history and into a prison cell where she spent the rest of her life—forty-seven years of it.

A few months later, as though to make the mess even more untidy, Tarabai's son, Shivaji, in whose name she had been ruling as Regent for the past ten years, gave up the unequal battle to keep alive. He died, never knowing that from being the Maratha King he had turned into a life-term prisoner.

As Shahu had hoped, it never became necessary for him to go to war with Tarabai. His new opponent was Sambhaji, then seventeen years old. But at this time, Sambhaji was mainly preoccupied with guarding himself against a countercoup by Tarabai's faction. Sambhaji did not possess anything like the same fierceness and determination as Tarabai. The fire had gone out of Shahu's opposition. In fact, his strongest opponent amongst his own people now was Kanhoji Angrey.

---

12 Descendants of Sambhaji still live in Kolhapur and bear Shivaji's title of *Chatra-pati*, 'The Lord of the Canopy'. Until India became independent and the Princely States were integrated, they were the rulers of Kolhapur State in the Deccan which was the last remnant of Shivaji's original kingdom. Theirs was the premier Maratha Princely State in the Deccan.

27

'Insults and Robberies'

At this juncture, it would not be possible to say whether Kanhoji Angrey was still loyal to Tarabai or had acknowledged Sambhaji of Kolhapur who had ousted her. To his mind, the ousting of Tarabai as Regent, and, in particular, the death of Tarabai's Son Shivaji, must have represented a bewildering complication. It was on Shivaji's behalf that Tarabai had ruled, and with Shivaji's death, Tarabai's Regency should have automatically come to an end. Was Sambhaji, then, his new master?

But if Kanhoji Angrey was not sure who the Maratha King was at this stage, the one thing he was sure of was that it was not Shahu.

As it happened, Shahu had not proved to be the ogre that Tarabai had made him out to be. He was a pleasure-loving and somewhat indolent man, given to procrastination; but he was not vice-ridden or cruel or vindictive like his father. He had shown surprising lenience towards those who had initially opposed his return, and if anything, had gone out of his way to offer them positions of responsibility and profit in his government.

Kanhoji Angrey had taken the fullest advantage of these years of relative calm. He had completed the fortifications of his coastal stations and had strengthened his forts. 'Almost the whole coast from Bombay to Goa was in his hands, and there was scarcely a creek, harbour or river-mouth where he had not fortification and a boat station,' comments a contemporary chronicler.

He had also remodelled his fleet, making it conform, as far as possible, to the fleets of the European powers. He had established five shipyards, and had engaged hundreds of workmen under the guidance of his foreign experts to build new ships. His sailors were regularly paid, and their terms of service were better than those offered by any other power in the Konkan. Attracted by the good terms, 'there now flocked to his standard, numerous adventurers, including renegade Christians, mostly Dutch and Portuguese, Arabs, Musselmen and Negroes, a most daring and desperate band,' writes Low, the historian of the Company's navy. He had taken special trouble to try out his ships and their gunnery, and to lick their crews into shape, and considered himself prepared to take on the ships of the foreign powers along the coast in a kind of guerilla warfare of the seas. He now possessed ten *ghurabs* (frigates), mounting from sixteen to thirty guns each, some of them over 400 tons, and also fifty *gallivat*s of between 60 to 120 tons, and mounting four to ten guns.

It was not a formidable naval force by any means, but it was a well-trained and tested force, and the other powers in the Konkan had begun to resent its growing efficiency. The Portuguese had once again become his enemies. The Treaty of 1703 which had patched up their earlier differences had been set aside by both sides, and Kanhoji Angrey had begun an unrelenting campaign against Portuguese shipping. He had captured a *pal* belonging to a retiring Governor of Chaul together with the Governor himself and all his possessions acquired during a lifetime of profitable service in the East. A little later, he fought an action with two of their gunboats and sank one and captured the other. In 1712, he attacked the yearly Portuguese *armado* of merchant ships escorted by two powerful warships under the command of Luis da Costa. One of these warships, carrying 34 guns, was disabled and the other forced to flee. Most of the merchant fleet fell into Kanhoji's hands.

The loss of the merchant convoy was something of a calamity to the Portuguese, for the yearly *armado* was the most important trading enterprise of the merchants of Goa and carried many a private fortune with it.

The East India Company, too, had been steadily building up a formidable fleet of its own. 'It had now acquired one ship of 32 guns, four grab-ships mounting between twenty and twenty-eight guns, and twenty grabs and *gallivat*s carrying between five and twelve guns'.

But it must be remembered that this force was the Company's private navy, what the Company at this stage used to call the 'Bombay Marine'. The Bombay Marine, later to be absorbed into the Indian Navy, was formed around 1690, with an Admiral in command. (His pay, incidentally, was Rs. 80 per month.) Its officers and men were replenished by drafts arriving from England. One of the squadrons of the Bombay Marine was stationed at Surat and another was kept at Bombay; the remaining ships were mostly always on convoy and patrol duties. The Company used to spend annually a sum of £51,000 on the Bombay Marine and even this sum was regarded as insufficient. The Company had also made a representation to the English Government asking for 'military reinforcements and either for a supply of seamen, or power to impress them from the ships'.

In addition to the Bombay Marine, the Company often had the help of the Arabian Sea squadron of the Royal Navy, already the most powerful navy in the world. The strength of the squadron used to differ from time to time, but in the early years of the eighteenth century, the Arabian Sea squadron consisted of 'one ship of 74 guns, one of fifty, and eighteen small ships of from 32 to 12 guns each, and some trankies or rowing boats of four to eight guns each'.

Kanhoji Angrey was no longer anxious to avoid a clash with the Company's ships. At times, his ships had to retire discomfited whenever they ran into one of the bigger ships of the Company. But this was a rare occurrence, and more often than not, their attacks were successful.

The success of Kanhoji's ships against superior ships and superior arms can be ascribed largely to the special tactics devised by him. When the big European ships came close to the coast, they had to reduce sail and slow down. This was the time when Angrey's ships, hiding in some convenient cove, would emerge and swoop down upon them, chasing them in their row-boats crammed with men. In such a chase, the advantage of better armaments could be nullified by sheer weight of numbers. Unless the victim could put on a burst of speed and get away, she was doomed.

The attackers always endeavoured to keep astern of their quarry, with the double object of keeping out of the way of the broadsides and presenting as small a target as possible to their rarely-encountered stern-guns, and also to be able to straddle their rigging with their own deadly gunfire. Their aim was not so much to sink a ship as to reduce her speed so that they could board her and make a captive of her. If any of the pursuing *gallivat*s of Kanhoji Angrey were damaged or sunk, there was always another to take its place.

Closely following the *gallivat*s, came the *ghurabs*, with their bigger guns, again trying to keep dead astern and firing at the rigging of their victims. If the wind was not sufficient for the *ghurabs* to catch up with the *gallivat*s, they were actually towed behind the *gallivat*s and pulled into position by sheer manpower. As each *ghurab* fired its salvo, it wheeled off and gave place to another.

These were wolf-pack tactics, admittedly largely depending on superior manpower, but equally so, carried out with what has come to be known as the 'destroyer spirit', and they speak well of the training and discipline of Kanhoji's fighting men. Kanhoji had evolved these tactics after a good deal of trial and error, to make allowances for the disparity in the speed, seaworthiness and fire-power between his ships and those of the European powers, and also in pursuance of what he considered to be the chief aim of his navy. He kept his ships close to the coast because they could show greater speed than the European ships only in relatively calm waters, and because his commanders were far more at home in their coastal waters and knew all their hazards. As far as possible, he also tried to compensate for his inferior guns by keeping his ships within range of his coastal guns. That the gunnery of his ships was as good as it was, was a tribute to the hard training more than to the quality of the guns and the gunpowder. Kanhoji Angrey also made the fullest use of the fact that he could send into attack at least twice as many men as his victims could carry on board, and above all he relied on hand-to-hand fighting. He knew that once his men had closed in, their victim was doomed, for in hand-to-hand fighting, in the use of the sword and the shield, the Marathas were far superior to the European sailors and soldiers.

With their new ships and their new-found proficiency, the sea-captains of Kanhoji boldly took on both Portuguese and English shipping, and encouraged by their success, they began to go after ships which were faster and stronger and better armed than theirs. More often than not, they won.

In 1706, Kanhoji's men attacked and captured the Company's ship *Monsoon*, off Karwar, but as they were towing her to Gheria, their home port, a storm at sea compelled them to release her near Goa where she was avidly pounced upon by the Portuguese. In 1707, his ships attacked and sank the Company's frigate *Bombay*, and in 1710, his ships had a two-day-long gun battle with the Company's ship *Godolphin* within sight of Bombay. In 1711, the Company were complaining to the Directors that Kanhoji Angrey could 'take any ship except the largest European ships; along the coast from Surat to Dabul, he takes all private merchants he meets'.

In 1712, Kanhoji Angrey captured two more of the Company's ships: one, the Governor's own armed yacht, and the other, the ketch *Anne*, belonging to the Company's chief factor at Karwar. Both these ships were taken after a stiff fight near Vengurla, during which their armed escort, *Defiance*, had been put to flight.

But to begin the story of the capture of the ketch *Anne* at the beginning, it is necessary to go back a few years and to visit yet another of the Company's factories: that at Anjengo on the Malabar coast, in the domain of that lady of romance and legend, the 'Pepper Queen'.

28

Tryst in the Forest

In the year 1709, Captain Gerard Cooke who had taken on a job as the East India Company's engineer at Calcutta, was taking his family there from England. Their ship, *Loyall Bliss*, had had a terrible voyage out, and when she anchored off Karwar to take on fresh water and supplies, she had been on the high seas for six months and her passengers were 'barely able to stand'.

But Karwar laid out the red carpet for *Loyall Bliss*. The Company's chief factor at Karwar, Mr. John Harvey, spared no pains to make everyone's stay enjoyable. He was particularly attentive to Captain Cooke's daughter, Catherine, who was then thirteen years old. Indeed, he was so taken up by her charms that he completely forgot to report the arrival of *Loyall Bliss* to the Council at Bombay which had been anxiously waiting for news of her, and thereby earned a severe reprimand. Within a few days, Mr. Harvey asked Captain Cooke for his daughter's hand.

There were two perfectly sound reasons why Captain Cooke should have turned down Mr. Harvey's proposal, apart, of course, from the extreme youth of his daughter: first, Harvey was nearly sixty years old, and secondly, he is said to have had a 'deformity'. History mercifully refuses to divulge what the deformity was.

The one thing in Mr. Harvey's favour was money. While taking the Company's pay, he had done a lot of private trading on the side and had put away a tidy nest-egg. He entertained the Cooke family in a 'splendid manner' and offered to make 'great settlements'—

whether upon the future Mrs. Harvey or her parents, it is not clear. Anyway, when, on 22 October, 1709, exactly fifteen days after her arrival, *Loyall Bliss* pulled out of Karwar, Mr. Cooke's daughter Catherine, age thirteen, was already a bride of several days standing.

Two years later, Mr. Harvey decided to retire and settle down in England, and he and his wife went to Bombay to wait for a passage. Bombay had as many as twenty-eight Englishwomen at the time, and their taunts and their whisperings are said to have brought home to Mrs. Harvey 'the sad mistake she had made in marrying a deformed man old enough to be her grandfather'.

But perhaps what brought this realization more forcibly home to her than the sneers of the ladies of Bombay, was the attention shown to her by two dashing young men nearer to her own age: Thomas Chown and William Gyfford.

Both had romantic backgrounds. Chown, a rising young clerk in the Company's employ, had just survived a shipwreck within sight of Bombay, and consequently, must have been one of the most talked-of men amongst the Company's colony there.[13] The other young man, Mr. William Gyfford, had come to India six years earlier and, despite his youth, had already risen to a position of trust and profit under the Company. He was the Company's purchasing officer at Bombay. Incidentally, Chown and Gyfford were close friends.

But the Harveys did not stay in Bombay for long. It seems that Mr. Harvey's private trading was all mixed up with the Company's affairs, and needed a lot of straightening out; and since the Company controlled all shipping between England and India, Mr. Harvey could not leave until he had settled the Company's claims. In December 1711, Mr. and Mrs. Harvey returned to Karwar. Four months later, Mr. Harvey died, leaving his fifteen-year-old wife to straighten out his complicated business affairs.

---

13 The wrecked ship was *Godolphin*, which, a year earlier, had fought a long-drawn-out gun battle with one of Kanhoji Angrey's ships.

By all accounts, Mrs. Harvey was now a rich widow. In actual fact, however, she was quite penniless since she could not lay hands upon any of Mr. Harvey's money until the Company's claims upon his estate were paid off, and the Company was taking its own time in making up the accounts. It was just as well, therefore, that Mr. Chown, whose acquaintance she had made in Bombay, contrived to secure a posting as the Chief Factor at Karwar. Mr. Chown proposed as soon as he landed, and was accepted as soon as he proposed. Within a few days, Mrs. Harvey became Mrs. Chown.

But Karwar was hardly the place to do anything about getting Mr. Harvey's nest-egg released from the tight clutches of the East India Company. Besides, Mr. Chown had friends in Bombay, who, he was sure, would help to expedite the settlement. So the Chowns decided to go back to Bombay.

As Chief Factor of the Company at Karwar, Mr. Chown was in charge of the Company's ketch, *Anne*. Mr. Chown loaded her with a cargo of pepper and wax and timber, and provisioned her with all the necessities and luxuries he could obtain in Karwar for her journey to Bombay. He also arranged through the Governor of Bombay for an armed escort of two ships: *Defiance*, a frigate of fourteen guns, and the Governor's own personal armed yacht. There is little doubt that Mr. Chown had a lot of influence in the right quarters.

Within a day of leaving Karwar, the convoy ran into four ships belonging to Kanhoji Angrey. The odds, therefore, could not be said to have been heavily weighed against *Anne* and her escort. Unfortunately, the mainstay of Mr. Chown's convoy, the frigate *Defiance*, for all her fourteen guns, proved sadly false to her name, and made for Bombay as fast as her triple sails could carry her. The Governor's yacht fought bravely until both her masts were shot away. *Anne*, too, kept up her fire until her ammunition was spent, and then, seeing the fate of the yacht, tried to escape back to Karwar, but she was pursued by two *ghurabs* and captured. Mr. Chown had had his arm torn away by a direct hit and died in his wife's arms.

Angrey's ships towed away their two prizes to Gheria, and brought the prisoners to Colaba.

Within a few days, Kanhoji Angrey ordered the release of all the prisoners taken, except the captains and mates of the two ships and Mrs. Chown, all of whom he held for ransom. The amount demanded was Rs. 30,000. The Bombay Council readily paid the ransom, and on 22 February, 1713, barely two months after she had been made a prisoner, Mrs. Chown was back in Bombay. The ketch *Anne* and the Governor's yacht were returned, but it turned out that the yacht was too badly damaged to be of further use.

From now on, the fortunes of the young lady who, at the age of seventeen, had already lost two husbands, have nothing to do with the history of the Angreys except perhaps in an indirect way, in that a certain Commodore of the British Navy may never have come to India if he had not been specially deputed by the British Admiralty for destroying Kanhoji Angrey's power. But hers was a life of romance and danger, of peace in the most idyllic surroundings erupting in sudden violence; of courage and feminine guile; and even at the risk of digression, it would not be unprofitable to follow her career for a few more years.

When she was released from Colaba, Bombay received Mrs. Chown with open arms; for she was now a celebrity, having been captured by 'pirates'. Also, waiting for her with open arms and a proposal of marriage was Mr. William Gyfford, whom she had met in Bombay the previous year. Within a few months, Mrs. Chown became Mrs. Gyfford. She was now eighteen years old: Mr. *Gyfford* was twenty-five.

Mr. Gyfford was highly thought of by the Governor of Bombay. Soon after his marriage, he was given the job of being *supercargo* on one of the Company's merchant ships. The position of *supercargo* was an especially coveted one, since it afforded excellent opportunities for private trade, which, after all, was the chief aim and object of almost every ambitious servant of the East India Company in those days. As far as Mr. Gyfford was concerned, the new job was right down his street, for although he had been in the service of the Company, he had already begun to make a name for himself as a successful, if sharp, private trader.

Two years later, Mr. William Gyfford was given another appointment of even greater trust and responsibility, and which gave him even greater scope for private trading. He was appointed as the Chief Factor in a place called Anjengo, on the Malabar coast, a position next in importance and profit, if not in rank, to the Governor himself.

Anjengo lies on the Malabar coast, about a hundred miles from Cape Comorin, in the domain of the Rani of Attinga. Attinga was known to produce the finest pepper in the world—it still does.

There is a story that the Rani of Attinga fell in love with an Englishman and showered gifts upon him, and one of the gifts that the Englishman, with extraordinary presence of mind and almost unbelievable loyalty to the Company, asked for was the monopoly of the pepper trade desired by his Company. The facts, if less romantic, bring out the pattern of European infiltration into the East. The Portuguese, as always, were the first on the scene, until they were ousted by the Dutch. Then came the British, and for a few years, there was the bitterest rivalry between them and the Dutch. It seems that the Dutch intrigued shamelessly against the British, but that the British gave more lavish presents to the 'Queen'. In the end, the presents won, the Dutch were forced to leave, and the British were permitted to build a factory on a spit of land which, in a few years became the prosperous—and heavily-fortified—settlement of Anjengo. Over the years, the custom had grown for the Chief Factor at Anjengo to send annual presents to the 'Queen', but, in 1714, when the 'Queen' protested against the factory being converted into a fortress, the presents were stopped.

This then was Anjengo, God's gift to an unscrupulous private trader: all the factors before Mr. Gyfford had either left the Company's service in suspicious circumstances, or had ended off as wealthy men.

Mr. Gyfford went one better than his predecessors: he systematically double-crossed the pepper merchants as well as the Company. He used the Company's money to become a bigtime private buyer of pepper.

He began by beating down the price of pepper. Since the East India Company had the monopoly of the trade, the growers had to accept his price or allow their stocks to rot. The agreement made with the 'Queen', that a 'fair' price would be paid for the pepper, was openly flouted by Gyfford on the grounds that his factory had broken off diplomatic relations with the 'Pepper Queen'.

Initially, the pepper-growers held on for a whole year, but in the end they gave in. Having won his point, Mr. Gyfford began to use false weights. What he used to do was to buy the pepper of Attinga at his prices and at his weights, privately, using the Company's money for the purpose, and then send it off to the neutral markets in a ship called *Thomas* which, by a happy coincidence, belonged to Mr. Thomas Cooke, none other than the brother of Mrs. Gyfford.

Having, within a few years of his taking over, organized the trading activities of the Anjengo factory to his entire satisfaction, Mr. Gyfford began to look round for ways and means of consolidating his position. It occurred to him that if he wanted the present happy state of affairs to continue, he must win the favour of the 'Pepper Queen'. He therefore decided to revive the pleasant custom of visiting the 'Queen' with gifts every year, and as a gesture, announced that he was anxious to carry to the 'Queen' personally all the gifts that had been missed out during the previous seven years. This, he felt, was the one sure way of maintaining both 'peace and pepper' to say nothing of prosperity.

Mr. Gyfford was walking into a trap of his own making. He was assured that the 'Queen' would be delighted to receive his presents. Accordingly, on 11 April, 1721, he set out in a pleasure boat for the 'Queen's' palace which was five miles up the river. Mr. Gyfford wanted to do things in style. He was 'accompanied by all the merchants and factors of his settlement, and ... all his best men, about one hundred and twenty in number, and the same number of coolies.'

The pepper-growers were waiting at the landing. Mr. Gyfford's party was enticed into a small enclosure, and there the crowd rushed upon them and cut them to pieces, reserving 'the principal English for a more cruel death'. What form their punishment took, no one knows.

At twenty-five, Mrs. Gyfford was a widow for the third time. But she had little time to mourn. The angry mob was already said to be heading back for the English factory. She and two other Englishwomen who had just been made widows, were hastily put on board a country boat, which by the sheerest of chance happened to be anchored near the English settlement, and sent off to Madras. Mrs. Gyfford remembered to take as much ready cash with her as she could lay hands on, as well as the books of the factory, but the main portion of Mr. Gyfford's treasure, amassed as a result of four years of systematic swindling of both the East India Company and the pepper-growers, had to be left behind. She is said to have tried to 'carry away Peter Lapthorne with her', but was prevented from doing so. Lieutenant Lapthorne was the youngest of the three Englishmen still alive in the fort of Anjengo. 'I entrust all my property to your care,' she called out to Peter Lapthorne just as her boat pulled out.

Alas, the dashing young Lieutenant seems to have played her false. A letter writen by him a few weeks later laments that the only 'property' he could find belonging to her was 'two wigs and a bolster and some opium'.

Of Mrs. Gyfford's journey to Madras, the less said the better. For nearly a month, she and her companions were crowded in an inadequate boat which had set out without the slightest preparation, and the voyage was performed in the hottest time of the year. To add to the trials, there were six children on board. Upon the boat's arrival at Madras, even the hard-headed Council of the East India Company were sufficiently moved by their plight to have sanctioned to all the passengers a subsistence allowance. But Mrs. Gyfford was now an extraordinarily rich woman and had no use for the Company's charity; she haughtily turned it down.

Then, with a naiveté surprising in someone who had gone through so many changes of fortune, Mrs. Gyfford turned in the records and account books of the Anjengo factory to the Council at Madras. After that, Mrs. Gyfford went off to Calcutta, where, it will be recalled, her father had been appointed the Company's Engineer. Captain Cooke was still in Calcutta.

When the Company's accountants at Madras went through the books of the Anjengo factory which Mrs. Gyfford had so rashly handed over to them, they began to notice the discrepancies in the books, and called upon Mrs. Gyfford to make good a sum of £1,000, which she seems to have paid without a murmur. But the Company's accountants kept finding more and more discrepancies in the books and demanding payments from her, and in the end Mrs. Gyfford told the Company that 'it was a shameful thing to demand money from her, an unfortunate widow whose husband had met his death serving our Honourable Masters.'

But you could not go on living in India and flouting the East India Company; nor for that matter, could you escape from India since all ships going to England belonged to the Company. At this time, the Company played its trump card and told Mrs. Gyfford that if 'resistance was carried too far, her father might be made to suffer'.

Even her youth and beauty were of little use now against the Company's displeasure; for though Calcutta had just as many eligible bachelors as Bombay, they were all servants of the Company. But Catherine Gyfford was not the kind of woman to give up the fight even when everything seemed lost.

In September 1722, a squadron of the Royal Navy, flying the flag of Commodore Matthews, Commander-in-Chief of His Majesty's Eastern Fleet, sailed into Calcutta. One of the first persons to visit the Commodore was Mrs. Gyfford, seeking his protection. Commodore Matthews was a gallant man, always ready to help a pretty lady in distress. From then on, the Royal Navy was firmly aligned on the side of Mrs. Gyfford. Out went an order to the Governor of Bengal, telling him that she was 'now under the protection of the Crown, and was not to be molested'.

From Calcutta, Matthews brought Mrs. Gyfford back to Bombay, where she 'lived under the same roof as Matthews much to the wrath of the Council and the scandal of her former acquaintances'. The Governor at Bombay sent her a stringent order forbidding her to leave Bombay until she had settled the Company's debts, which by now had reached formidable proportions. Commodore Matthews countered by putting Mrs. Gyfford on board his flagship again, 'lest the Council should lay hands on her'.

When, at the end of 1723, the naval squadron sailed off for England, Mrs. Gyfford went as a passenger in the Commodore's flagship. On the way, the squadron paid a visit to Anjengo, bent upon recovering some of Mrs. Gyfford's property, but the Company or its servants had taken good care to see that not even the 'two wigs and a bolster' could be found. Otherwise, Mrs. Gyfford must have found that things were being carried on exactly as in her husband's days, in whose place the Company had appointed a Mr. Middleton as the Chief Factor. Mr. Middleton proved to be 'no honester than his predecessors, ... and ... monopolised the pepper trade to his own private account, making himself advances out of the Company's treasury'. A new refinement that Mr. Middleton had introduced was that he had regularly drawn pay for twenty European soldiers who did not exist.

It is best to leave off Mrs. Gyfford's story at this stage, as she returns a rich and beautiful woman, still young, in a flagship, escorted by a squadron of the Royal Navy, with a British Commodore all her own. The rest of her story is a dreary legal battle with the Company in England, and in which the Royal Navy is not likely to have been of much assistance.

But Commodore Matthews has not bowed out of this story; indeed, he has not even made his formal entrance yet. He has slipped in the wake of Mrs. Gyfford, without benefit of an introduction. We shall be meeting him again soon, at the proper place in this history, when he will make his entrance formally, insisting upon a 17-gun salute, which he considered his right.

29

'If an Englishman of Credit'

The capture of the two ships *Anne* and the Governor's armed yacht, and in particular the cowardly escape of their escort, *Defiance*, a frigate of fourteen guns, caused great commotion in Bombay. The Captain of *Defiance* was instantly dismissed from the service.

The very next month, another two ships of the Company, *Grantham* and *Somers*, coming from England, were attacked by a *ghurab* and a *gallivat* of Kanhoji Angrey. The English ships escaped, but the Council had been alarmed at the boldness of the *ghurab* and the *gallivat* in attempting to take on two ships bigger and better-armed than themselves.

The Portuguese in Goa, too, had taken serious note of the growing audacity of the Maratha ships. The time for the annual *armado* was fast approaching, and they were anxious to avoid the fate of the previous year's *armado*. The Viceroy hopefully wrote a letter to the Company's Governor at Bombay, William Aislabie, proposing a joint expedition against Angrey.

A month earlier, Governor Aislabie would have jumped at the Portuguese offer, but now he was no longer interested in it, for a few days earlier he had received a letter from Kanhoji Angrey, proposing terms of a treaty, and asking for the Company's counter-proposals to be sent to him at Colaba, 'through an Englishman of credit'.

On his part, Kanhoji had said that he would undertake not to molest English ships if the Company promised to give him military assistance in times of need, and permitted the people from amongst the sea-faring clans in Bombay to take up service with him. He also asked the Company for regular supplies of 'powder and shott' on payment, and for a place in Bombay where he could manufacture gunpowder.

Aislabie cleverly side-tracked all that Kanhoji Angrey had asked for. He called up a meeting of his Council and made the following alternative proposals:

> 'Firstly: That he deliver up all that he has taken that belonged to the Company and our people.
>
> 'Secondly: That upon no pretence whatever he meddle with any English ships or with the ships belonging to the merchants who live under the protection of the English at Madras, Bengall or any other factories or Colonys belonging to the English whatsoever.
>
> 'Thirdly: That whatever ships or vessels belong to any nation whatsoever that are coming into our harbour and in sight thereof he is not (to) meddle with them, that is between Mahim stakes and Cundry (Khanderi) and at their going out the same rule is to be observed.
>
> 'Fourthly: That he grant our merchants the free liberty of his ports they paying usuall customs being conformable to the rules thereof. If any vessels belonging to Sevagee Rana (Raza) or Sow Razah shall take or molest any vessels belonging to Bombay they have his convoy which he is obliged to give he shall be answerable for the damage.
>
> 'Fifthly: Wee on our part promise that wee will permit no ships or vessels whatever to wear English colours, but what belong to the subjects of the English nation, which shall be inserted in all their ships.
>
> 'Sixthly: Wee grant him free liberty of our port of Bombay to buy sell and merchandise he paying the

> usuall custom and observing the rules of our port, which if he complys with that wee send the *Blenheim Ann* and *Manchua* to fetch the Company's effects which he has taken and our people'.

Since the interpretation of some of these terms now proposed by Governor Aislabie, and which were later incorporated almost verbatim into the treaty made between Kanhoji Angrey and the East India Company, were the subject of sharp differences of opinion between the two, it might be useful to single out those terms which led to these differences and analyse them briefly.

According to clause two, the Company sought to bind down Kanhoji Angrey not to interfere with any ships belonging to the 'merchants ... under English protection'. This could be subjected to the widest interpretations, and the English continuously sought to take the fullest advantage of its vagueness, and even contended that any ship which carried the Company's cargo was under its protection.

But obviously clause five was provided as a safeguard for the wideness of clause two; both sides must have foreseen that clause two could cause a lot of mischief. The Company, therefore, undertook not to permit the use of English colours by ships other than those belonging to 'subjects of the English nation'. The wording of this clause seems clear enough, but it was the dispute over the interpretation of this clause that ultimately led to hostilities. Angrey interpreted it literally, to mean that the Company would give its passports only to English ships : the Company, on the other hand, took the view that any ship that bore the Company's cargo automatically became an English ship. According to the Company's interpretation, an Indian ship today, carrying iron ore to China, would be classified as a Chinese ship and thus become entitled to whatever privileges Chinese ships may be enjoying in, say, Russian waters. If it sounds absurd today, it was no less absurd two-hundred-and-fifty years ago.

Clause three sought to make Bombay a neutral port as far as the enemies of the Marathas were concerned. Under this clause, Kanhoji Angrey undertook not to molest foreign ships 'in sight of harbour'. The term 'foreign ships' is somewhat misleading. It clearly referred to the ships of the powers hostile to the Marathas, and in particular, to the ships of the Siddy. The intention seems to have been that while in Bombay, these ships should enjoy immunity; once they were out of sight of the harbour, Angrey was at liberty to deal with them as he saw fit. This interpretation was subsequently agreed to by the Company, who undertook to convoy foreign ships only 'out of sight' of Bombay, and no further.

And lastly, clause four clearly shows that the Bombay Council was fully aware that Angrey was not independent of the Marathas, but, on the other hand, answerable to the Maratha King.

In this clause, the Company had specifically sought to make Angrey responsible for any loss caused to them by ships belonging to Kanhoji Angrey's Maratha superiors. The pointed reference to two Kings, both Shivaji (Tarabai's son) and Shahu, in this clause also brings out the fact that at this time, Angrey himself was not certain who his monarch was and had offered his protection to the English ships, from molestation by both contenders.

Even though the Bombay Council had decided upon the terms that were to be offered to Kanhoji Angrey, it seems that the deputing of a 'gentleman of credit' that Kanhoji had insisted upon, presented some difficulties. The Bombay Council, it appears, 'knowing him to be a man of ill principles' did not wish to order any of its servants into such a hazardous undertaking. They were, however, prepared to pay a thousand rupees to anyone who would undertake to convey the Company's terms to Angrey, and on this understanding a Lieutenant Mackintosh undertook to act as the Company's Gentleman of Credit.

Kanhoji Angrey could not have failed to notice that the Bombay Council had totally disregarded the concessions asked for by him.

But he accepted the Company's proposals at face value. It must have become clear to him that what the East India Company wanted was not a treaty of friendship so much as a treaty of non-belligerence; only an undertaking on the part of both sides that they would not molest each other's ships, but not of mutual assistance. He had offered the hand of friendship, but the Company was not willing to meet him half-way.

But Kanhoji accepted every one of the Company's conditions. In this, he must have been guided to some extent by reasons of higher strategy. If the English were anxious to come to terms with him at this particular time, he was even more anxious to come to terms with the English. He was aware that some day soon he would have to face the forces of Shahu, and he wanted both his hands free for the major conflict. More than at any time before, he was concentrating on his land frontiers: the great danger was now from above the ghats. Before Shahu's forces came marching down into the Konkan, he wanted to make sure that he had eliminated the possibility of an attack from the sea.

Like all good military commanders, Kanhoji Angrey strove never to have more than one major enemy at a time, but if that could not be avoided, at least to avoid warfare in two different elements at the same time.

The treaty between Kanhoji Angrey and the East India Company, embodying all the terms proposed by the Bombay Council, was formally signed in April 1713.

30

Across the Land

Angria ... was a great land-shark, or magar if you will, who came out of the water and strode across the land, eating every green thing.

—James Douglas

When the issue of the succession of the Moghul line had been fought out and decided, the Moghul Army of the Deccan was once again free to exert its pressure in the affairs of the Deccan. The Moghuls had lowered their sights several notches, however. They had given up the grand design of Aurangzeb. They no longer thought in terms of conquering the whole of the Deccan and ruling it as a Moghul province. Now they would have been content merely to get the Marathas to accept their overlordship.

Oddly enough, both the factions amongst the Marathas were willing to acknowledge Moghul sovereignty. Wholly absorbed in a civil war, they too had given up their stand of retaining absolute independence. All that either side now wanted was recognition: that the Moghuls should accept their King as the Maratha ruler. In such a state of affairs, the Moghul force acquired an importance far beyond its capabilities; since, by throwing its considerable weight on the side of their choice, the Moghuls could have helped that side to win—or so it was believed by both the factions of Shahu and Sambhaji.

Thus the life-long enemies of the Marathas became the arbiters of their internal strife.

In the beginning, the Moghuls had consistently supported Shahu's claim. They regarded Shahu as being almost one of themselves. But when they found that Shahu, although desirous of Moghul support, was not willing to play the role of a Moghul stooge, they began to waver. At this time they had bluntly told him that they would recognize him as the Maratha King only if he won his battle against Tarabai. In 1713, the Moghul attitude to Shahu had further stiffened. Early in that year, as a result of the periodic upheavals in the ranks of the Moghul generals, the new Moghul Viceroy of the Deccan openly declared himself to be in favour of the new contender to the Maratha throne, Sambhaji, who had set up his capital in Kolhapur. Chandra-sen Jadhav, who, it will be recalled, had been Shahu's erstwhile military Commander-in-Chief and who had defected to Tarabai, had also aligned himself with Sambhaji's faction. He and his followers now made common cause with the Moghul Viceroy and began a march against Shahu's capital, Satara.

Shahu had no military commanders of proved calibre, but he was not altogether friendless. The organizing genius of Balaji Vishwanath was already showing results: Shahu now possessed an army which he could call his own. Balaji Vishwanath, who was now Shahu's chief military adviser, does not seem to have worried unduly about the combined threat of the Moghuls and of Sambhaji's army. He restricted his campaign to a series of planned withdrawals, forcing delays upon his opponents, knowing that if he could hold out until the onset of the monsoon, the threat to Satara would be over. Luckily for him, the rains broke early, and the Moghul Army, always terrified at the prospect of being exposed to Maratha raids while bogged down in the rains, made haste to reach its cantonment of Aurangabad. For the time being at least, the hostilities were called off.

As a result of this military success, if success it was, Shahu began to lean even more heavily on Balaji Vishwanath, and now promoted him to the command of a field army, and gave him the title of

Sena-Karte, or organizer of the forces. Balaji now became one of the three most important men in Shahu's court. The first was the *Peshwa* (Prime Minister), a man called Bahiropant Pingale; the second was his Chief Military Commander for the time being, the Pant Sachiv; the third was Balaji Vishwanath.

Admittedly, except for the successful planned withdrawal of his forces without committing them to a major battle against the Moghuls referred to above, Balaji Vishwanath had displayed no special ability as a military commander. On the contrary, his military career had been singularly mediocre: he had cut a sorry figure against Chandra-sen in the quarrel that had arisen over the wounded deer, when he had been forced to flee and seek Shahu's protection. More recently, when he had set out to reduce a rebel chieftain called Damaji Thorat, he had allowed himself to be captured by a ruse, and been forced to undergo severe indignities. Damaji Thorat had threatened him with the torture of fastening horses' feeding bags filled with ashes on to his mouth unless a heavy ransom was forthcoming for his release. And again Shahu had run to his rescue, and got him released by paying the full ransom.

The very next year, however, Balaji justified Shahu's faith in him. Shahu had chosen three special military tasks for the three most important men of his court. He sent the Pant Sachiv against the rebel chieftain Damaji Thorat who, in the previous year, had captured Balaji Vishwanath and held him for ransom. He sent Balaji Vishwanath against another rebel chieftain called Kattoakar. And he sent Bahiropant Pingale, his Prime Minister, to reduce yet another rebel chieftain, Kanhoji Angrey, and thus bring the whole of the Konkan under his rule.

Of the three expeditions, only one was successful: that commanded by Balaji Vishwanath. The Pant Sachiv, who had been sent out to deal with Damaji Thorat, failed miserably. Thorat repeated his earlier success, routed the Maratha column and threw the Pant Sachiv into captivity.

But a far worse fate was in store for the expedition against Kanhoji Angrey. Not only did it end in a shattering defeat; it backfired with astonishing force.

As has been described earlier, Kanhoji had foreseen this attack from above the ghats and had been making preparations for it. He had tied down the English with a treaty of friendship and could now devote himself entirely to land warfare. He was aware that the most likely route of the expedition would be through *Bor-ghat* (today's Bombay-Poona road) which could be dominated by whoever possessed the fort of Rajmachi.

Kanhoji Angrey had made his plans and preparations well in advance, and the King's *Peshwa*, Bahiropant Pingale, can only be said to have walked into a neatly-laid trap.

Kanhoji permitted the Maratha column to come through the Pass unopposed. He acted only after the column had penetrated deep into the Konkan. Then, instead of offering a headon battle with the *Peshwa*'s force, Kanhoji went behind him and occupied the Pass, shutting down the door of his mousetrap.

The Marathas were caught unawares; they had not expected Kanhoji's forces to attack the ghats when the Konkan itself was threatened. Indeed, they must have been so confident of themselves, or careless, that the important fort of Rajmachi was left wholly undefended. It fell into Kanhoji's hands without much opposition. However, if Kanhoji himself was surprised at this easy victory, it did not put him out of his stride. Ever quick to follow up a successful military operation, he marched straight on to Loh-gad, within thirty miles of Poona, and succeeded in capturing Loh-gad too.

Only then did he turn upon the Peshwa's column caught helplessly in the Konkan, already thoroughly shaken by the speed of Kanhoji's victories. Kanhoji routed the Peshwa's force and took the Peshwa himself prisoner.

The tables were turned. Bahiropant Pingale, Shahu's Prime Minister, was now a prisoner in the hands of Kanhoji Angrey.

Rajmachi, the fort placed under Kanhoji's command by Tarabai, he had taken by the sword. Even Loh-gad was now his.

Kanhoji's success on land must have come as a surprise to those who had always regarded him as merely a naval commander. Shahu and his *Peshwa* must have been sure that he would be hopelessly out of his element on land. If so, they could not have given sufficient thought to Kanhoji's early career. They would have discovered that Kanhoji Angrey had considerable experience of land warfare. His earliest military exploits were almost wholly confined to land: he used to organize and lead regular long-range raids into the Siddy's territory; even in the last few years he had carried out some notable operations on land. For instance, in 1703 when the Siddy had invaded his territory, Kanhoji had made a swift counter thrust into Thal.

And this action against Shahu's forces was something he had been planning for. He had also been able to pay undivided attention to it, since, for the moment, he was at peace with both the Siddy and the English.

From Loh-gad, Kanhoji Angrey sent word to Shahu himself, that he intended to march against the capital, Satara.

31

'*Surkhail* for all Times ...'

But in spite of his friendliness with the British, even at sea, the year 1713 was a busy one for Kanhoji Angrey. The Portuguese, stung by the East India Company's refusal to join hands with them in an effort to destroy Kanhoji Angrey, had turned to the Siddy for help, and though there was an uneasy peace between Kanhoji and the Siddy, in the face of such a heaven-sent opportunity to subdue his hereditary enemy, the Siddy's neutrality was fast cracking up.

The Portuguese still regarded themselves as masters of the ocean. Their military prestige was fast dwindling and they were determined to regain it. They had acquired several new ships for their feet and they were waiting for a chance to avenge the insults suffered at the hands of Kanhoji Angrey. Accordingly, when their annual *armado* sailed from Goa for the northern ports, each ship was armed to the teeth and the convoy was provided with a formidable escort of fighting ships. Kanhoji's ships, lying in wait for the *armado*, saw it pass in a tight convoy. They followed the *armado* at a safe distance, hoping to pick up the stragglers, and in the end, they pounced upon two *pals* which had lagged behind. But it is possible that the *pals* were merely a decoy, for as soon as Kanhoji's squadron came out into the open, the Portuguese warships circled back and opened fire. The battle which ensued, lasted for two days and two nights, and in the end, Kanhoji's ships must have decided that the opposition was far stronger than they had bargained for. They retired, 'with much loss.'

Again the next month, Kanhoji Angrey's ships attacked a fully-armed Portuguese warship of 34 guns which had just landed a Portuguese military force at Chaul, but the Angrey ships were hopelessly outclassed and out-gunned, and although numerically superior, had to retire after suffering heavy losses.

As a result of these two quick successes, the Portuguese Viceroy decided that it was time to finish the job even without English help. He despatched a force of six frigates with their accompanying *gallivats* under a seasoned naval commander called Antonio Cardim Froes, to Colaba; and appealed to the Siddy of Janjira to give him all possible assistance.

This was the time that Kanhoji Angrey himself was either actively engaged in his campaign against Shahu's forces, or was concentrating all his energies in preparing for his expedition against Satara. His fleet, which had received two severe maulings within a few weeks, was in no condition to give battle with the powerful Portuguese task force. Not wishing to commit his forces to an unprofitable action, Kanhoji decided to nullify the effect of the Portuguese invasion by pulling back all his ships and hauling them ashore as he used to do at the beginning of every monsoon. 'Operation Monsoon', the drill of dragging all ships on dry land to save them from the fury of the elements, was Kanhoji's answer to the Portuguese attack against Colaba. He pulled up his ships well out of the range of the Portuguese guns, and laughed in the face of the opposition.

Antonio Froes sat doggedly at the entrance of Colaba harbour, 'gnawing his own wrists with rage', his tight blockade showing absolutely no results, his powerful guns rendered ineffective by Kanhoji's absurd strategem of pulling his fleet out of the range; and above all, unwilling to risk taking his ships too close to the shore and within range of the shore guns.

The Viceroy at Goa made frantic appeals to the Siddy. But however anxious the Siddy might have been to reduce Colaba, he could see for himself that the blockade of the harbour channel was having absolutely no effect upon the normal life of the fort. He delayed his participation on one excuse or another, not wishing to violate his treaty with Angrey and commit himself to action irrevocably, unless he could see some signs that Kanhoji's strength was breaking up. Possibly he waited to see how Kanhoji's battle against the *Peshwa*'s force was going to turn out before making a decision.

In the end, the Portuguese Viceroy did succeed in enticing Siddy Rasool Yakoot Khan to join forces with him, and ultimately, the Siddy did bring his fleet to Colaba. But he had taken more than three months to make up his mind, and it was already too late. At this time the Portuguese Viceroy received news that an Arab fleet had been seen near Surat. Nearly twenty years had passed since the invasion of Portuguese territory around Salsette by the Arab pirates, but the arrival of any Arab ships was always regarded as a sign of danger. The Viceroy ordered Antonio Cardim Froes to the northern Portuguese possessions for patrolling the coast; and reluctantly, Antonio Froes gathered his ships and sailed off to the north, leaving a bewildered Siddy with his handful of ships in charge of the siege.

Thus once again, the Siddy's latent enmity with Angrey came into the open; the treaty made four years earlier, and scrupulously observed by both parties, now stood violated. The Siddy took over the blockade of the channel near Colaba without much enthusiasm. Kanhoji, on his part, ignored the Siddy altogether. After ineffectually keeping to his stations for another three months, the Siddy, too, withdrew his ships without achieving any visible results.

The naval reverses of the year 1713, or if they were not reverses, at least Kanhoji Angrey's deliberate shift from the offensive to the defensive, can be largely ascribed to the fact that Kanhoji himself was preoccupied above the ghats, far from his base, in land warfare which had reached a stage from which there was now no getting back. Following up on his earlier successes, he had taken seven other forts besides Rajmachi and Loh-gad, and he was encamped at Loh-gad, barely thirty miles from Poona, poised for his next move, gathering together his forces for the grand assault on Satara.

The shark from the seas had scrambled up the tops of mountains, and was now headed for the capital of the kingdom.

There was panic in Satara. In its shattered state of morale, the capital would have been an easy prey for Angrey's army. For its defence, the only force that Satara had was the *Huzarat*, Shahu's personal bodyguard. The only field army at Shahu's disposal was the scratch force assembled by Balaji Vishwanath for his campaign against the rebel chieftain, Kattoakar. Although this force had defeated Kattoakar, it was not half as powerful either in strength or firepower or mounted personnel as the force already routed by Kanhoji Angrey.

It was a hopeless situation; it needed desperate remedies. Shahu ordered Balaji Vishwanath to gather together what forces he could and march towards Loh-gad to give battle to Kanhoji Angrey's force. He promised Balaji Vishwanath that if he could only succeed in bringing Kanhoji Angrey to terms, he would appoint Balaji to be his Prime Minister, the *Peshwa*.

Balaji Vishwanath, riding high on the crest of the wave of his first military victory, was far from keen to stake his shining new reputation against an enemy like Kanhoji Angrey. At the same time, Balaji must have realized that this was his moment: that if he hesitated now, the opportunity knocking at his door might be gone forever. The highest position in the kingdom was now his if only he could bring Kanhoji Angrey to terms. If …

Balaji Vishwanath, they say, always thought two moves ahead; this time, he must have applied his mind to thinking out several moves in advance, and came to the astounding conclusion that every other move depended upon his being made the *Peshwa*.

He argued with Shahu that his appointment to the *Peshwa*-ship should come *before* he set out on the expedition against Angrey, and not after its successful conclusion: for, Balaji pointed out, the success of his expedition would depend largely upon whether it was led by Balaji Vishwanath in his capacity as the *Peshwa*, or as one of the military commanders; that it was of the utmost importance to make Kanhoji Angrey realize that even though he had captured the King's *Peshwa*, another had already taken his place—that the King was never without a *Peshwa*.

The reasoning may have been full of holes, but Shahu, who in any case did not have much choice in the matter, was easily convinced by it: he agreed to make Balaji Vishwanath the *Peshwa* before he went out to tackle Kanhoji Angrey. It was therefore as the Chief Minister of the Maratha King, that Balaji Vishwanath, the one-time clerk who never learnt to ride a horse, set out at the head of a hastily-assembled force to suppress the most powerful of the King's enemies: Kanhoji Angrey.

If there was something laughable about this spectacle, Balaji Vishwanath himself did not think so. For he was not thinking in terms of the relative military strengths of the opposing forces alone: he was banking on his early friendship with Kanhoji Angrey and upon the fact that he, Balaji, had helped Kanhoji to bring about his first military success, the revolt at Suvarna-durg; he was almost certainly banking on their common veneration for Brahmendra-swami. But above all, he was banking on his own powers of persuasion and diplomacy. He may not have been a redoubtable military leader, but he was certainly the most outstanding brain of his times in the Deccan, and he now went off to his mission with the easy confidence of one who held all the high cards.

He played them like a master too, timing every move to perfection, using flattery, veiled threats, appeals to loyalty, to religion, and to self-interest; he sent spies and intermediaries and the blessings and good wishes of holy men; he used every other trick known to politics and diplomacy, for Balaji Vishwanath was a man playing for the highest stakes in the Deccan.

He began by sending off a somewhat stern letter to Kanhoji Angrey, reminding him of the duties and obligations of a chieftain towards his sovereign:

> 'You are among the premier commanders in the service of the Maratha King; your father, Tukoji, served the elder Shivaji with exemplary loyalty. In spite of this, although you are aware that the Maharaja Shahu is (of the) elder (branch) and the real master of the throne; when he has come back to rule his Kingdom, you bear enmity towards him and have made common cause with the younger branch of the family, and have captured his government's districts, and have made a prisoner of the King's late Chief Minister'.

'Is this how', Balaji Vishwanath charged Kanhoji Angrey, 'you observe the obligation of a loyal retainer?'

It is interesting to note that Balaji had signed this letter in his capacity as the King's *Peshwa*, and had made a pointed reference to Bahiropant Pingale as the 'King's late Chief Minister'.

This letter, sent after a considerable amount of preliminary softening-up through intermediaries, soon brought the desired reply from Kanhoji Angrey: 'You leave your force behind and come to Loh-gad accompanied only by your personal bodyguard', Kanhoji wrote, 'so that we can meet and discuss matters …'

Balaji Vishwanath's personal courage in agreeing to go to Loh-gad deserves a word of special praise. Hardly a year earlier, Damaji Thorat, another chieftain who had refused to recognize Shahu, had enticed him to a similar meeting, after swearing what is known as the *bel-bhandar* oath guaranteeing Balaji's safety, and had captured him and held him for ransom. Kanhoji had given no such assurance, and it is unlikely that Balaji would have felt the need of any such assurance from him. The one thing Balaji did make sure of through the intermediaries was, characteristically, that Kanhoji would accord him a reception fitted to his prestige as the *Peshwa* of the Maratha King.

The historic meeting took place at Valvan, near Lonawala. The two men, who had known each other in their early youth and who, in their own spheres, had risen to be the two most powerful men in the country, now met together as close friends, and between them they gave form and pattern to the future history of the Marathas. Kanhoji, blindly loyal to the abstraction that was the Maratha Kingdom, had suffered many qualms of conscience since the death of Tarabai's son, Shivaji, and was now almost eager to make up his differences with Shahu if this could be achieved without loss of face. In any case, even if he was not already almost completely convinced that the right as well as the prudent course was to side with Shahu, he could hardly have withstood the powers of Balaji's persuasiveness and the compelling force of the arguments put forward by him.

Balaji employed every weapon in his redoubtable armoury: he brought out the great heritage of Shivaji and how every Maratha owed a debt to his memory; he brought out the military weakness of Sambhaji's faction, and even more so, the moral weakness of Sambhaji's claim to the throne; he played upon the fact that Sambhaji had now openly joined forces with the Moghuls in pursuit of his claim; he made pointed reference to the numerous enemies that Kanhoji had in the Konkan itself, and explained the advantages of the security offered by his not having to bother about the defence of the Konkan from the land side; he drew a glowing picture of the advantages of a common defence, and the help that he, Kanhoji, would always have at his beck and call to oppose his enemies in the Konkan; he extolled the many virtues of Shahu, and he played upon their earlier friendship; he brought out the whole-hearted support given by Brahmendra-swami to Shahu, and it is almost certain that he even carried a message from the Swami addressed to Kanhoji Angrey, exhorting him to make peace with Shahu. It would have been most unlike Balaji Vishwanath if he had not also emphasized 'how both their personal and national interests would be promoted by their acting jointly under Shahu's suzerainty'.

Balaji's logic was irrefutable: but would Shahu uphold whatever promises Balaji made? On this crucial point, Balaji was able to reassure his friend. He explained that he was speaking in his capacity as the King's *Peshwa*, fully empowered by the King to settle terms with Kanhoji Angrey, and that Shahu's agreement to the terms that might be agreed upon between them, was merely a matter of form.

Shahu unhesitatingly gave his approval to all that Balaji Vishwanath had promised Kanhoji in return for Kanhoji's acceptance of Shahu's suzerainty. The two men thereupon proceeded to Colaba where the treaty was formally ratified on 8 February 1714. Bahiropant Pingale, who, until his capture by Kanhoji had been the *Peshwa*, was released from captivity by the intervention of his successor in office, Balaji Vishwanath.

The Treaty of Colaba later formed a model for many a similar treaty between the Maratha King and his feudatory chieftains, 'thus gradually building up a fresh constitution for future Maratha expansion'.

Under this Treaty, Kanhoji Angrey agreed to accept the suzerainty of Shahu. The King appointed him to the permanent grant of the three districts that comprised the Konkan. Kanhoji was entrusted with the task of guarding the coast: he was to patrol the coast from Dassara to the summer festival with a view to 'reducing to dust', the *Phirangees* and the *Hubshies* (Europeans and Abyssinians). Out of the nine forts captured by Kanhoji Angrey since the beginning of hostilities five, including Loh-gad, were to be returned to Shahu, and four others, including Rajmachi, together with their surrounding territories, were to be retained by Kanhoji Angrey. It was further agreed that Kanhoji would not offer employment to those who had left Shahu's service. In case Kanhoji happened, as the result of military action, to acquire any of the forts in the area of

Thal in northern Konkan, he undertook to transfer them to Shahu, and Shahu in turn offered military assistance to Angrey whenever called upon to do so.

As a result of the Treaty of Colaba, Kanhoji Angrey obtained control of ten seaside forts and sixteen land forts; his annual income from the territory placed under his authority was thirty-six lakhs of rupees. He was confirmed as the *Surkhail* and *Vazarat Ma-aab* in hereditary perpetuity. From now on, he signed all his correspondence as 'Kanhoji, son of Tukoji, *Surkhail* by the grace of King Shahu', and his seal of office read: *Shahu-karya dhurandar Tukoji tanujanmanah Kanhoji Surkhailasya Mudrikeyam Virajate.*[14]

The whole of the Konkan, from Bombay to Goa, with the exception of three small strips, was now formally recognized as being under his command. With commendable presence of mind, Kanhoji had, by special request, obtained from Shahu the control of an island called Khanderi, at the mouth of the entrance channel to the harbour of Bombay.

---

14 The seal of Kanhoji: Son of Tukoji, *Surkhail* in the service of Shahu.

32

The Festival of Colour

The treaty of Colaba was a triumph of diplomacy, a resounding personal victory for Balaji Vishwanath. He had been sent out on a seemingly hopeless mission: to resist a fearsome enemy with a hastily-assembled and ill-equipped force. And while they watched, he had transformed that enemy into a powerful ally.

Shahu's gratitude was immense. When Balaji returned, he found the capital *en fete* in his honour. All along the way from Lonawala, there were triumphal arches in every village, decked with mango leaves and banana plants; he was escorted by a band and garlanded at every stage by pretty women; he was taken round in a procession of elephants, at the end of it all, he was ceremonially installed as the *Peshwa*, and Shahu showered him with presents.

The Marathas had turned the corner. Shahu's reign was now acquiring shape as well as substance. The new alliance with Kanhoji Angrey had added great strength to Shahu's cause. It was a moment for joy and celebration; an occasion for thanksgiving, Shahu sent a pressing invitation to Kanhaji Angrey to come to Satara for the Holi festival, the festival of colour, and ordered his officials to organize a fitting reception for the Lord of the Konkan.

But the feasting had to wait a whole year. The Treaty of Colaba may have ended one war, but it had provoked another. The Siddy of Janjira, Rasool Yakoot Khan, found that even though he was not a party either to the war or the Treaty, some territory which had been his for the past thirty years had been given away to Kanhoji

Angrey. The outraged Siddy immediately called upon his new allies, the Portuguese, for help and even without waiting for them, marched out to defend his districts which had been portioned off between the Marathas and Kanhoji Angrey without his knowledge or concurrence.

Although they had been egging on the Siddy for a whole year to attack Angrey's territory, the Portuguese now decided to remain aloof. They sat back watchfully, waiting to see how the new alliance between the Marathas and Kanhoji Angrey would work out in practice, the Siddy's challenge would put its strength and solidity to test. Kanhoji Angrey by himself had been a sufficiently formidable foe, and they had no wish to jump into the conflict, if the Marathas were going to run to Kanhoji's help.

Angrey was once again free to devote greater attention to the coast. He was sure that the Portuguese would come to the help of the Siddy and create a diversion by attacking one of his forts. He invoked his new alliance with the Marathas and called upon them to defend his territory from the Siddy's attack. The new *Peshwa*, Balaji Vishwanath, acted with speed. He came down personally leading a mounted column and boldly marched into the disputed territory and occupied it. Then, having already covered more ground than the Siddy disputed, he halted his forces and sent an invitation to the Siddy calling upon him to come and discuss peace terms.

The Siddy had no choice left. Not without serious misgivings, he decided to take advantage of Balaji's invitation. Balaji treated him with honour and offered to let him keep whatever territory he still possessed. This, since the Siddy had been pushed back several miles by Balaji's troops, was somewhat less than what had been first left to him under the Treaty of Colaba. At first, the Siddy was inclined to turn down this offer. On his part, Kanhoji Angrey too was not in a mood for yet another treaty with the Siddy which would leave him a powerful and hostile neighbour, as he described, 'a live coal in my robe'.

But Balaji Vishwanath, a man of compromise and diplomacy, of finesse rather than brute force, brought the two men together and added yet another laurel to his growing collection. The treaty of peace was formally signed between Kanhoji Angrey and Siddy Rasool Yakoot Khan, on 30 January, 1715. With it, the Siddy drops out of this history for the next ten years, for almost surprisingly, the terms of this treaty were scrupulously observed by both sides for that period in spite of considerable outside pressure. And in the end, when the Siddies and the Angreys once again took up arms against one another in what came to be called the Elephant's War, it was almost unwillingly that they did so, prodded into hostilities by others less tolerant than themselves.

The Portuguese denounced the Siddy for making peace with Angrey with all the outraged fury of a sleeping partner in a venture that fails. The Portuguese had failed to make common cause with the English, and now the Siddy too had forsaken them. Left without a single ally along the coast, they turned, inevitably, to Sambhaji of Kolhapur. Sambhaji had no territory along the coast, but he was ever willing to welcome any enemy of Shahu as an ally. He agreed to make an offensive and defensive alliance with the Portuguese, which was duly signed at Kolhapur a few months later. As it turned out, this alliance was never invoked by either side, and remained at all times only a paper friendship.

The next three months Kanhoji devoted to a job after his own heart. At his special request, Shahu had placed the island of Khanderi under his command. Kanhoji had long appreciated the strategic importance of this island to his fleet, but since the Subedar of Khanderi had been a man of Shahu's party, he had refrained from taking possession of it. Now he lost no time in visiting the island. He ordered elaborate fortifications of his own designing to be built up with all speed. He strengthened the garrison of the island, and mounted new guns on its fort. From Khanderi, he now could have a constant watch kept on all the shipping that passed in or out of Bombay, unless they took a wide detour to keep out of range.

Like the fort of Rajmachi on his land frontier, from which you could keep a check on all movement between the ghats and north Konkan, Khanderi was also a sentry-post; a sentry-post with a lantern held high upon all the shipping that passed in and out of Bombay. Kanhoji Angrey now held both these lanterns, and he was anxious to make Khanderi just as formidable and effective an outpost of the Konkan as Rajmachi.

Only after Khanderi was fortified and built up according to his specifications, only after its garrison had moved into place, only after the ships had been allotted their separate duties and the island was fully provisioned for the monsoon, did Kanhoji find time to avail himself of the pressing invitation sent to him by his monarch. He was already a year late.

But when Kanhoji Angrey relaxed, like a true sailor, he relaxed with a vengeance, working just as hard at his pleasures as at his duties as the *Surkhail.* He set out for Satara in a triumphal procession, a mile-long caravan of elephants, horses and bullocks, travelling with the utmost leisure, feasting and resting at intervals all the way. They made camp every twenty miles or so, and at each stage they were escorted into a ready built camp by a troupe of dancing girls specially chosen for their looks more than their dancing abilities, showering five-coloured *Holi* powder on their entourage. For the full moon before *Holi*, he was at Jejuri. From here onwards, he was the guest of the King. On the fifth day of the moon, he reached Satara, carrying presents for the king, whom he was going to see for the first time. A reception such as Satara had never witnessed even during the time of its occupation by the Moghuls, awaited Kanhoji Angrey.

Shahu received him formally, in a specially erected pandal, and gave him the robes of his office, together with elephants, horses, and jewellery. In the evening, he was entertained at a special banquet to which the Ministers of the Cabinet and all the highest officials and chieftains were invited. At a subsequent reception, Shahu gave Kanhoji Angrey his formal title deeds of office.

The two men must have taken to each other at first sight, and always remained the best of friends. Shahu was a magnificent host, having witnessed many of the lavish entertainments of the Moghul court. At the same time, he always remained a man of good taste and refinement. He brought to Satara only a part of the pomp and ceremony of the Moghul court, but on the whole, his inclinations were those of a country squire who liked to live graciously and comfortably, rather than those of a playboy. He had kept at his court the necessary number of dancing girls and troupes of actors, but his main pleasure in life was in outdoor pursuits, in hunting and shooting and hawking and fishing. He was a great connoisseur of horses and dogs, and of guns and swords. The ceremonial and pomp be brought to his court was only necessary after the austerity of the days of Shivaji and the chaos of the days of Sambhaji. A court had to have ritual and dignity, but the King himself was a man of simple pleasures, who spent as much time as possible in the pursuit of game, out of doors.

During the ensuing years, Kanhoji sent to his King many an English gun and sword, and watches and velvet and precious glassware. Deprived of many of the luxuries he had been accustomed to in the Moghul camp, Shahu began to rely more and more upon Kanhoji Angrey to send him regular supplies of the best scented rice, cashewnuts, mangoes, betel-nuts and other table delicacies from the Konkan, and also the pick of the goods imported by the merchants along the coast.

Shahu also began to consult Kanhoji Angrey in matters of higher policy, and although he never interfered in the affairs of the Konkan itself, he seldom made a decision of policy in regard to the English or the Portuguese without consulting his new vassal.

33

Fighting Boone

Later in the same year, 1715, Bombay too had occasion to lay down the red carpet. The East India Company had sent out a new Governor and a new set of councillors, and they were being received with the sort of fanfare that the Company had come to regard as *de rigueur* for impressing people in the East: the Company, they said, was only living up to the *nabobs*! The city was decked in finery, a public holiday was declared, and all the dignitaries of Bombay were lined up to be introduced. Guns boomed in salute as the new Governor, Charles Boone, and his party of councillors landed.

Boone, a man of extraordinary zeal and industry, is said to have differed from his predecessors in that he always placed the interests of the Company above his personal interests. He also fancied himself as something of a military genius and undertook a series of military operations against the different enemies of the Company he began to make as soon as he arrived. All these undertakings ended in resounding failure.

As such, the net result of Mr. Boone's excessive zeal and industry was that at the end of his tenure of office, the East India Company's stock had slumped far lower than it had been upon his arrival.

The first thing that the new Governor did was to order the building of a wall around the town of Bombay. The necessity of such a wall had been recognized some fifty years earlier, but since the Company's Directors had, not without reason, hesitated to entrust such a costly project to its engineers, they had been putting it off on one pretext or another. They had warned earlier Governors to discourage the project since they felt that 'it was natural for engineers to contrive curiosities that are very expensive'. But Boone got over the difficulty of finances by obtaining 'contributions' from the 'native merchants' of Bombay. If the Company's engineers made money while building a wall that had been contributed for by Indian merchants, it was perhaps just as it should be.

This might be the proper place to bring out the fact that in these early years, whenever the East India Company suffered a trading loss, it was always made up by boosting up the port dues or customs fees, or even by levying a special tax; so that, in the last analysis, such losses were paid for by the Indian merchants. Within two years of his arrival, Governor Boone offhandedly speaks of levying a 'war tax of two per cent on the people of Bombay'. Ships may be lost, either by action of the pirates or in war with the Marathas, or even due to bad seamanship, but the Company's losses were always made up. Whether all the money so collected actually reached the Company's coffers is a different matter, however—it is most unlikely that it did.

The wall around the town of Bombay with its half-a-dozen strongly fortified gates, which have given their names to so many of Bombay's streets, (e.g. Church Gate, Bazaar Gate, etc.) was meant to protect the town from Kanhoji Angrey. But Governor Boone was not the type of man to restrict himself to defensive measures. Even as the wall was going up, he launched a vigorous drive to build more 'fighting ships' for the Company's fleet. At Surat, Bombay, Karwar, where the Company had ship-building facilities, ships of war were ordered to be built with all possible speed. Within six months, three frigates, *Brittania* of eighteen guns, *Fame* of sixteen guns, and *Revenge*, also of sixteen guns, were ready, each of them carrying between 120 to 160 men. These ships were followed by others in amazingly quick succession: another frigate, *Victory* of twenty-four guns and two fire-ships and a floating gun-platform named 'the

Phram' were all already in 1718, in addition to the merchant vessels *Charles* (named after the English King) and *Boone* (named after the Governor of Bombay). Within two years of his arrival, the new Governor had built up a fleet of up-to-date vessels more powerful in fire-power, if not in actual numbers, than the fleet of the Marathas. It consisted of 'nineteen frigates, grabs, ketches, *gallivat*s, rowing galleys carrying two-hundred-and-twenty guns, besides a bomb-vessel and two fire-ships'.

But even before the Company's fleet was considered ready to take on the Marathas, the relations between the Marathas and the Company were deteriorating. Within a few months of Boone's arrival, Kanhoji Angrey had reason to complain to him that the English were not observing the terms of the treaty in good faith; that in order to escape *dastak* fees and customs dues, they had begun to permit all ships which carried their cargo to fly English colours.

It seems that the Company, too, had good reason to complain that Kanhoji Angrey, on his part, was not scrupulous in observing the terms of the 1713 Treaty. For although he had returned the two ships, *Anne* and the Governor's armed yacht which he had seized, he had not returned the cargo that these ships carried, and he had even removed the guns from the two ships before returning them. It is not possible that at the time when the Treaty was signed the precise manner of the disposal of the cargo was left ambiguous, because usually the cargo was much more valuable than the ship that carried it. What was actually agreed upon is not clear, but the fact remains that Kanhoji Angrey did not return the ships' cargo and the Company felt that he should have done so. The ketch, *Anne*, was carrying some timber in addition to other goods, and Angrey who was perpetually in need of good timber seems to have decided to hold on to the timber carried by *Anne*. Within the next two or three years, he was to get into further arguments with the East India Company over timber. As to the ships' guns, Angrey was perpetually in need of good guns and went to extremes to obtain guns of European manufacture. He always made it a point to dismantle the guns on any of the captured ships and retain them for his own use.

The fact remains that Kanhoji Angrey made no efforts to return the cargo carried by the Governor's yacht and *Anne*, and the Company on its part seems to have decided to overlook the omission. In 1716, Governor Boone wrote to his Directors that since he was not 'in a good posture to oppose him' he was not pressing his claim against Kanhoji Angrey.

But that did not end the matter. Mr. Boone was obviously only marking time until his wall around the town of Bombay was built up and his fleet was in readiness. Within a few years as soon as he felt that he was now in a 'good posture' to oppose Angrey he began to take more and more liberties with the Treaty made with Angrey by his predecessor. Trouble was inevitable, it was now only a matter of time when there would be an open clash.

As though to leave no room for doubt as to his views in the matter, in the year 1716, Angrey seized a ship within full sight of Bombay harbour, which, although it flew English colours, belonged to an Indian merchant. Early in 1717, he followed this up by making prizes of three more Indian ships which did not carry his *dastaks* and tried to pass themselves off as the Company's ships by flying the English flag.

The seizure of these ships led to an exchange of sharp letters between Govemor Boone and Kanhoji Angrey, and the same arguments were reiterated on both sides. The Company insisted that any ship which carried cargo belonging to the Council at Bombay or to any other of the Company's councils in India, was exempt from the need of taking a *dastak* from the Marathas. Angrey retorted that the only ships that were entitled to an exemption were the ships actually owned by the East India Company.

It must be emphasized that the taking of prizes of ships that did not bear the passport of an acceptable power had become the normal practice along the coast of India, and oddly enough, the English, who most denounced it in others, felt no compunction in taking ships that did not bear the Company's *dastaks*.[15] Considering that the English, who controlled no more than a minute island on the 500-mile-long coast, felt themselves entitled to deny the freedom of the coastal waters to any shipping that did not carry their papers, it is surprising that they should object to similar views being held by Kanhoji Angrey who controlled three hundred miles of coastline. Whatever grounds the Company may have put forward to deny the rights of the Marathas to seize ships without their *dastaks*, there can be no two views that the seizure of Indian ships by a foreign trading Company was nothing short of piracy.

But in India, the East India Company had always tended to regard itself as being above the laws of the land or of the sea, and Govemor Boone now considered himself to be in a position where he did not have to worry unduly about either accepted maritime practice or treaty obligations. His fleet was ready and straining at the leash. However, like a wise Commander, he did not wish to hurl it into its primary mission without trying it out on lesser targets. Before attacking any of Angrey's forts, Mr. Boone was keen to find other, somewhat lighter, tasks for his navy.

In April 1716, Mr. Boone decided that he had found the necessary light target for his fleet: he sent off his ships to attack Vengurla. The aim of this operation remains something of a mystery. Vengurla still had a small Dutch factory, and Boone may have wanted to oust the Dutch from there. What the Dutch had done to invite his displeasure is not known. Barely a dozen years earlier, the

---

15 'Like other chiefs along the coast, the Bombay authorities gave passes to traders living under their protection, and in their warfare with Angria they had adopted the practice of other chiefs of not recognizing the immunity of vessels that did not carry passes from themselves. We find at this time the Kattiawar traders complaining of two ships having been seized that held protective passes from Angria.' (John Bidulph, *The Pirate of Malabar*)

Company's Council had been rouse to indignation by the capture of a Dutch warship by Kanhoji Angrey, and now they seemed to be determined to blast the settlement at Vengurla and to drive them out. On the other hand, the expedition may have been sent out to subdue the Sawant of Wadi, but this seems unlikely. In any case, what the expedition set out to do never became clear by what it did do.

Carrying a strong detachment of infantry as a landing party, *Fame*, *Brittania* and *Revenge* sailed out for their mission of destruction. For two whole days they bombarded Vengurla from different directions. When the time for landing came however, there was a violent quarrel between Weeks, the Commander of the Navy, and Stanton, the Commander of the landing party. What the quarrel was about is not clear, but its effect was to break up the Vengurla expedition. The Company's squadron returned to Bombay without achieving any results, Stanton and Weeks throwing duelling challenges at each other.

As it turned out, the Vengurla expedition set the pattern for the succeeding ventures of the fleet that Boone built, except that at Vengurla, since there was no contact with any opposing forces, the Company's ships returned without casual ties. Its failure should have been a warning to Governor Boone that although he may have built for the Company some of the finest fighting ships in the Eastern waters, he would have to go on relying upon the Company's men to take the ships into action. But Boone was a man with a mission, dedicated to the destruction of those he had decided were the enemies of the Company, and now he had scented blood. He again launched himself into preparations for warfare with renewed vigour. He was now also a man in a hurry, for he had already discovered a fresh target for his machine of war: Karwar.

By way of showing displeasure against the Vengurla fiasco, Boone sacked the Commander of the force Weeks, and in his place, appointed a man called, Hamilton, a privateer who had shown great skill and courage in a naval action against the Muscat pirates. Hamilton was designated as the Commander-in-Chief of the Company's feet and given the rank of Commodore. Most of the other officers who had been to Vengurla, including Major Stanton, the Commander of the land forces, were, however, retained for the new venture.

In September, the squadron sailed for Karwar with the object of reducing the Raja of Karwar, who had besieged the Company's factory there. This time, Governor Boone had been careful to secure an assurance of help from the Portuguese at Goa, and while in Karwar, his force obtained its supplies from Goa which is next door to Karwar.

'The miserable display of military incompetency' that was the Karwar expedition is outside the scope of this study, except for the fact that it typifies the fighting qualities of the Company's men of those times. It was the most humiliating military setback suffered by the East India Company until that time: it was a story of colossal bungling; of indiscipline, doubledealing, and downright cowardice. The result was a resounding failure with disproportionately heavy casualties, many of them suffered even when there was no opposition. In one of the attempts at landing, *all* the Company's landing boats capsized and the men had to be fished out of the water by their enemies, the Raja of Karwar's men, as they scrambled up the beaches helplessly, having lost their arms. It was perhaps just a matter of good luck that Major Stanton, the Commander of the landing party, was too drunk at the time of this landing to have taken part in it. The Company's troops were always reluctanct to leave the safety of the ships and in this they cannot be blamed since any time the landing parties attempted to venture beyond the range of the ships' guns, they were left by their officers to their own devices. Whenever they came out into the open, the slightest sign of opposition sent them running pell-mell in all directions until the relatively insignificant and poorly-armed soldiers of the Raja of

Karwar were emboldened to come 'charging into their disordered ranks', and killing two-hundred-and-fifty men in a single encounter.

In the end, the Company sued for peace, and largely because the Company's ships had managed to seize three ships of the Raja loaded with fine Arabian horses which were now dying for want of fresh water, and also because of the increasing pressure of the Maratha forces on his northern border, the Raja of Karwar agreed to end hostilities.

The fleet slunk back into Bombay, its manpower depleted by half, carrying a large number of wounded and a whole Company of unfortunate *Topasses* (soldiers of mixed Portuguese and Indian origin) whose noses had been cut off by orders of the Raja of Karwar after their capiure when their landing boats had capsized.[16] The Commander-in-Chief, Hamilton, was so disgusted with the way the Company's officers had behaved, during the expedition, that as soon as he reached Bombay, he tendered his resignation from the Company's service and resumed business as a private trader. He seems to have been a man of rare honesty and integrity as well as courage, and reported to the Council that the whole cause of the trouble at Karwar was the Company's Chief Factor there, Mr. Taylor (the successor of Messrs. Harvey and Chown in Chapter 28) who, Hamilton asserted, had shown 'indiscretion and bad faith towards the Raja'. The Council, after investigating the charges, let off Mr. Taylor with a 'don't-do-it-again' warning. Considering that Mr. Taylor's 'indiscretions' had involved the Company in a costly expedition and had accounted for some 2,000 casualties, it must be said that he got off lightly.

Even while the Karwar expedition was going on, Governor Boone's shipbuilding programme had continued in full swing.

16 The *Topasses* were given an extra five rupees per month as compensation and formed into a new battalion called the Bombay Marine battalion. They say that this was the parent battalion of our present Bombay Grenadiers.

Another frigate, a galley and two rowing *gallivat*s, like the fast Maratha rowing boats, one of 24 oars and the other of 18 and each carrying two six-pounder guns in the prow and another ten in the waist, had been added to the Company's growing fleet.

The capture of the four Indian ships by Kanhoji Angrey in the year 1716, which the Company had been passing off as English ships, had been the subject of an exchange of angry letters between the two. Towards the end of the year, Kanhoji seized yet another ship, *Success*, which he knew belonged to the East India Company's broker at Surat, Gordhan Das. The Council insisted that she was an English ship entitled to fly English colours and, as such, exempt from Kanhoji's *dastaks*. But Governor Boone, with his fleet tied up in the Karwar expedition, was not going to risk making an issue of it. He again contented himself by sending off another stiff protest to Kanhoji Angrey at the hands of a special messenger, Captain Henry Cornwall, and privately advised Gordhan Das that he should obtain the release of his ship by negotiations.

34

Timber

Gordhan das, a shrewd Gujerati merchant, was soon able to settle the terms for the release of his ship, *Success*. The sum of money as well as the presents to be given to Kanhoji Angrey were agreed upon at the very outset, but the presence of the third man, Captain Cornwall, doggedly contributing an oar on the Company's behalf, could not have helped the negotiations. Also, Captain Cornwall was determined that Gordhan Das should make no payment until the ship was actually back in Bombay. Kanhoji, on his part, was not prepared to release the ship unless the money and the presents were forthcoming. The negotiations were still continuing, however, and Captain Cornwall was still in Colaba, when news reached Bombay that another ship, *Robert*, which carried some Englishmen as passengers, was seized by Angrey's men. A few days later, this was followed by a report that Kanhoji Angrey had forcibly taken one of the Company's boats into Colaba and had removed 'some pieces of timber' from her hold before allowing her to proceed.

Oddly enough, the removal of the timber gave the Bombay Council cause for far more anger than the capture of their ships and the English passengers. For this time, the vessel carrying the timber did in fact belong to the Company and as such, Angrey could not claim that she was an Indian ship trying to pass off as an English ship.

This altercation over some pieces of timber has a certain amount of background. Earlier, Kanhoji Angrey had sent an agent to

Bombay to select for him some suitable timber for shipbuilding. His agent had contracted for the timber with some of the Indian merchants at Bombay. There was nothing irregular or out of the way in this, and Kanhoji had informed the Governor of this transaction and had pointed out his urgent need for timber. He had also asked the Governor to permit one of the Bombay carpenters to visit Colaba and work for him. The Governor, on his part, had granted the necessary permission to the carpenter Kanhoji had chosen. Within a few days of this, however, and Angrey alleges, upon the advice of some agent of the Siddy or the Portuguese, he had not only retracted the permission he had given to the carpenter to visit Colaba without giving any reasons for his action, but had also forbidden the Bombay merchants who had contracted to make deliveries of the timber selected from their yards by Angrey's agent to deliver it. Kanhoji Angrey had protested to the Governor about this in a firm but polite letter, complaining about the 'hinderance' that some of the Governor's advisers constituted to their friendship:

> 'In this manner, things go on, demonstrating that it is not your Excellency alone that governs. Your Excellency had no intention to do anything contrary to our friendship, but you find it necessary to act according to what is told you by men who live with you.'

It was towards the end of December 1717 that Angrey took the Company's timber from its boat. At the first meeting of the Bombay Council in the new year, held on 3 January, the Council heatedly debated 'in what manner (they) should resent this insult'. At this time, the Council had received another letter sent by Angrey, and seem to have been particularly irritated by its tone of frivolity. Angrey had again explained that he had taken the timber because of his great need, but he said that he had taken it 'in a friendly manner' and offered to pay for it.

But the Bombay Council were not prepared to match their mood to that of Kanhoji and make light of the whole affair. They chose to regard it as a serious matter—a question of principle. What they wanted was the timber, not its price, and also an assurance that such a thing would not happen again.

However, wiser counsels seem to have prevailed over the frayed tempers brought on by New Year festivities. The Council decided that they were still not in a 'good condition, being so bare of ammunition, soldiers and seamen, to perform anything with our arms.' This was within a month of the return of the fleet from Karwar, and even the Council could see that they were in no position to embark on another campaign. It was further decided that Governor Boone should send a letter of protest to Angrey demanding the return of the timber as well as the return of the seized ships, *Robert* and *Success*, and in particular the release of the English passengers on *Robert*. This letter was sent off to Captain Cornwall, who, it will be remembered, was still in Colaba, having been sent there to supervise the negotiations between Kanhoji Angrey and Gordhan Das regarding the release of *Success*.

Kanhoji flatly declined to release either the ships or their passengers. He reminded the Council that since the ships seized by him were owned by Indian merchants, they could not claim the immunities granted to the Company's ships. He pointed out that even the Captains and the passengers of the ships had testified to the fact that the ships did not belong to the East India Company, but to Indian owners. This brought back a retort from Governor Boone that the confession from the Captains and others was extracted by 'attempting so barbarously to beat the Captain and other Englishmen into confession of what made for your purpose'.

Kanhoji again chose to make light of the matter of his confiscation of the timber. In a letter which is typical of the distorted logic of diplomacy, Kanhoji contrived to put the Governor into a position which left him without a graceful outlet, and made his concern over the timber appear illtempered and churlish. Angrey purported to treat the whole thing as something of a prank, implying that the Governor was showing bad taste by making an issue of such a trifle 'between friends'. It was a clever piece of logic, even if it was not altogether convincing:

> 'As I had a great necessity for timber,' wrote Angrey, 'when the boat came from Surat, I brought her in, in a friendly manner, believing that you observed the friendship without scruples; and what's a little timber? Had I wrote to you, you would have given it to mee, but as it might have happened that somebody or another would have stopt it, as they did before, and my work thereby be put to a stand, I took the timber here and wrote your Excellency to let mee know the price thereof, and had for answer you wanted timber, which I took well, expecting when mine would come to repay you. In this there is no cause for difference.'

A few days after Captain Henry Cornwall returned from Colaba with Angrey's replies, the Governor instructed his Council to seek the mediation of a prominent Bombay merchant called Rama Kamathi. Boone wanted Rama Kamathi to go to Colaba and plead the Company's cause before Kanhoji Angrey with a view to securing from him the release of the European prisoners. Realizing that Captain Cornwall's presence had not helped the negotiations undertaken by Gordhan Das, the Council this time refrained from sending their own observer to attend the talks, and in fact, entreated Rama Kamathi to represent to Angrey that he was acting absolutely on his own initiative since the Company did not wish 'to appear in it (themselves) unless a more favourable opportunity should offer'.

In the event, Rama Kamathi's mediation did not secure the release of the ships or the prisoners. But it is important to remember his name. He was later destined to be the star turn in the most infamous court trial of eighteenth century Bombay.

There is no doubt that Rama Kamathi did go to Colaba on the Company's behalf, seeking to mediate with Angrey for the release of some Englishmen he had never seen in his life. But, however influential Rama Kamathi may have been, there was no room for compromise when the opposing sides held on to their views so rigidly. His mission must have been also frustrated by the capture of yet another ship by Angrey. She was *Otter* which Governor Boone claimed belonged to the Company's Council in Bengal, on the grounds that she carried cargo for the Bengal Council.

On his part, Kanhoji Angrey again made it clear that he would not molest ships that genuinely belonged to the Company, irrespective of whether they belonged to the Company's councils at Bombay, Madras or Bengal, 'but that if the English will freight on country shipping, they must expect that (I) will make prise of them'.

> 'The English', he complained to Governor Boone, 'freight the ships of foreign (Indian) merchants and lade them with their goods, and receive no molestation they having English colours. This is gain to the owners of the ship; yet how can they carry on their trade without a pass. Today you freight the ship *Sacry*, to-morrow Your Excellency will say that you have a mind to freight fifty or a hundred ships of Surat Merchants. If so, what occasion have they to take a pass they always took of mee.'

The East India Company's attempts to pass off all ships which carried their cargo as their own ships was nothing short of sharp practice, depriving Kanhoji Angrey of his legitimate *dastak* fees and customs dues, and encouraging the shipowners to flout the Maratha domination of the coast. 'Modern practice will not uphold the contention that a ship loses its nationality when it carries foreign cargo', Mr. Surendra Nath Sen points out. But there is nothing to show that even in the eighteenth century, the Company's contention was borne out by maritime practice.

It is worth noting that as to the ships which genuinely belonged to the East India Company, Kanhoji Angrey scrupulously respected their immunity from his *dastaks*. During the Karwar expedition, while the Company's ships were lying helplessly at anchor, they were accosted by a powerful squadron of Angrey's fighting ships: 'five stout vessels, well mann'd and large guns on board.' But all they did was to check up whether the English ships did carry the Company's *dastaks*. 'They never offered to misuse us, nor do us any manner of harm', says Clement Downing. And his Captain, who was ashore at the time, was so unconcerned about the whole thing that when he was sent word that the ships were being 'rummaged', he 'neither come himself or send a pilot'. As it happened, all the ships at Karwar had only one of the Company's passports between them, but this seemed to satisfy Angrey's Commodore.

It is also worth noting that even the East India Company, with characteristic ambivalence, had themselves followed the contemporary practice of issuing *dastaks* and seizing ships which did not bear their *dastaks*. Governor Boone had himself seized a *Shibar Khanderao* belonging to a subject of Angrey, Trimbukji Meghji. 'As Trimbukji is an inhabitant of this place (Bombay) and has his warehouse here, and always takes my pass for said shybar, and this year without said pass pretended to go to sea; how could it be permitted?' the Governor had written to Angrey.

But Governor Boone was in no mood to give thought to contemporary maritime practice or to be convinced by the logic of Kanhoji Angrey's arguments. 'Let the bottom be whose it will', he retorted waspishly, 'the money lent on it is worth more than the ship, and the goods are English, you well know'.

It was in this mood that the Bombay Council met on 5 April, 1718, and decided to 'serve (Angrey) in the same kind'. The

Governor issued secret orders to his fighting ships to capture or sink Kanhoji Angrey's ships if they happened to run into them, meaning thereby, that they were not to go looking for them. As it happened, within a few days of this order, a *shibar* which belonged to Angrey's squadron at Alibag, happened to stray into Mahim. The Company's ships pounced upon the *shibar* and took her to Bombay.

At the seizure of one of his naval boats (as opposed to merchants' ships bearing his *dastaks*) in flagrant violation of the treaty between himself and the East India Company, Angrey flew into a rage. 'Our friendship is over', Angrey wrote to Boone, 'and from this day forward, what God gives, I shall take'.

Boone, never particularly known for his civility of manners, replied in a similar vein, and now ordered his ships to go out and seek Angrey's ships and to sink them or seize them. At the same time, he ordered several small parties of troops to go and plunder Angrey's territory.

35

To Sink a Fleet

Although orders had been issued to the English ships to seek out and destroy Maratha ships and to plunder Maratha territory, Governor Boone and his Council were perfectly aware that mere skirmishes with Angrey's ships and the plundering of a few coastal villages was not likely to have such an effect on him that he would immediately agree to refrain from molesting the ships which the Company were determined to pass off as their own. The Governor and his Council now transformed themselves into a Council of War, directing the moves of their not inconsiderable forces from their headquarters, and planning future operations, and in a rare moment of inspiration, decided upon sending a sea-borne expedition against Gheria, also known as Vijay-durg, which was Angrey's main depot.

The attack against Gheria was much more than an attempt at capturing the fort; it was also an attempt to destroy at a single stroke a large part of Kanhoji Angrey's fleet as it lay huddled up in its monsoon anchorage. It was Pearl Harbour two centuries before its time, miniature in size of the operation and the number of forces involved on either side, but not so in its planning and attempted execution, and least of all in its conception.

The Governor and his Council waited until the monsoon was nearly on; until it was almost too late for any kind of sea-borne operation against the coast. But their timing was perfect: they had to wait until they could be sure that every single ship in Gheria would be securely tethered in its monsoon depot. Governor Boone had also obtained the services of that itinerant soldier of fortune, Manuel de Castro, who, until the previous year, had been one of the chief naval advisers of Kanhoji Angrey. Castro was, however, only one of two trump cards held by Governor Boone; the other was the fire-ship. Castro knew everything about Angrey's fleet and could pinpoint the place where each ship was anchored or hauled up for the rains; the fire-ship would do the rest. Castro also had his own score to settle with Kanhoji Angrey, having been turned out of his navy for some misdemeanour.

Gheria was the natural target: it had the largest number of ships at anchor, crowded close together. It was too far from Colaba or Satara to receive timely assistance. It was in Gheria that the ships seized by Angrey, *Success, Otter, Robert* and others, had been held. But above all, Gheria, Boone knew, would be almost totally undefended; most of the rank-and-file having been sent on leave for the monsoon, and most of the ships' Captains and other senior officials and commanders having gathered in Colaba to attend the wedding of Kanhoji's daughter, Ladubai, which was being celebrated there just about this time.

It was a beautifully-planned operation, so far as it went; but it was planned by amateur strategists and lacked precision. It was, so Boone thought, only a matter of sneaking into Gheria and letting loose his secret weapon, the fire-ship, amidst the *ghurabs* and *gallivat*s and *shibars* and *pals*, all neatly clustered together and roofed with palm-leaves. The pre-monsoon gale would send up the lot in flames where they stood.

Everything was checked and double-checked and made as foolproof as the undoubted organizing capacity and energy of Governor Boone could make it. The Company's Chief Engineer, Major Vane, had tried out all the mortars and grenade launchers before they were fitted on to the ships and had sent up the requisite quantities of ammunition on board. He had trained the expedition's engineer, Mr. Minnim, into their use. The fire-ship was inspected

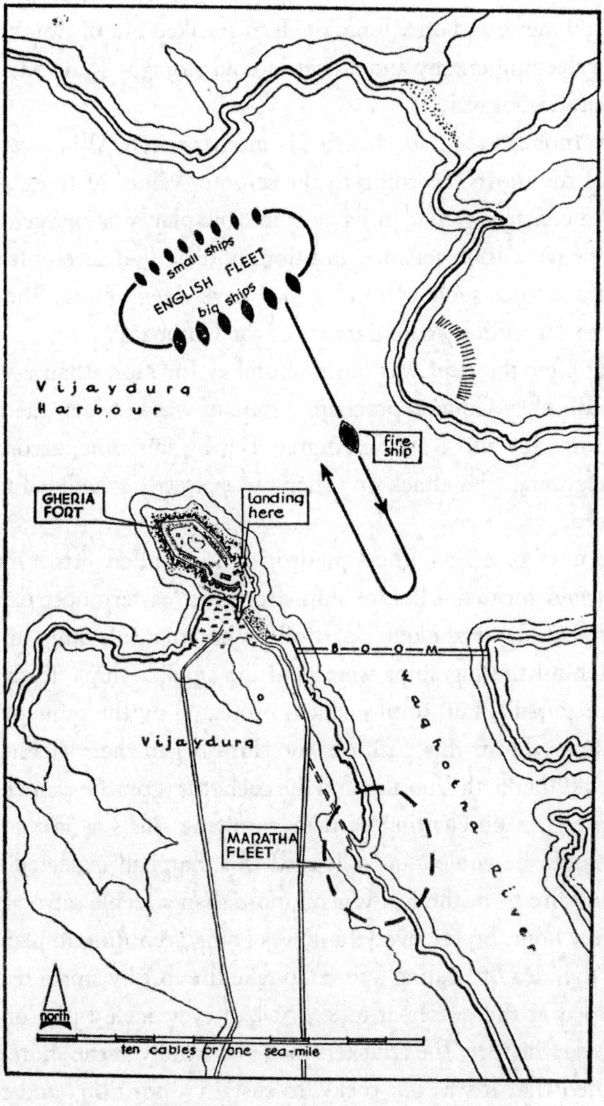

THE FIRST GHERIA EXPEDITION

and pronounced perfect. On the last day, Governor Boone risked security to carry out a review of the troops, '25 hundred well-disciplin'd men', and on 9 June, the fleet sneaked out of Bombay to attack a sleeping enemy and a fleet in cold storage. There was still no declaration of war.

Governor Boone had chosen his moment well. Whatever the ethics of the move according to the sense of values of those days, there is no denying that in its concept, his plan was perfect. His machines were in excellent condition, and he had assembled an amphibious force such as Bombay had never seen before. The rest was up to the military commanders of the Company.

Only after the fleet was out of Bombay for more than a week did the Bombay Council proclaim a state of war between the East India Company and Kanhoji Angrey. But by this time, according to the planning, the attack on Gheria was already scheduled to be concluded.

The next morning, the squadron boldly sailed into Gheria harbour and formed a line of ships from the 'easternmost part of the fortifications to the outer part of the harbour', blocking up the exits. Behind the big ships were held the smaller ships, ready for attack or pursuit, but, until needed, protected by the guns of the bigger ships. From this position, the ships began their shelling of the fort of Gheria, the mortars and the coehorns (grenade-launchers) maintaining an unrelenting barrage, throwing shells as fast as the barrels could be cooled and reloaded. As they had expected, the answering fire from the fort was no more than a feeble salvo about once every hour. So far, everything was going according to plan.

But the idea of landing a force to take the fort by storm had to be dropped at the outset, if indeed it had ever been a part of the plan to take the fort. The attackers looked wistfully at the shore and proclaimed that it was too rocky 'to sustain a position', and they looked up at the walls of the fort and decided that the walls were too high, 'so high that our scaling ladders would not reach the top of them'.

They tried to steer the fire-ship amidst the Maratha ships laid up for the rains; some hauled up, some anchored, and all of them thatched with highly inflammable matting—an ideal target for arson. But they discovered that the defenders had taken good care to pull their ships well inside the cove, and that they had erected a strong boom across the entrance channel to the cove. This elementary precaution against a surprise attack seems to have come as a total surprise, and the attempt to release the fire-ship amidst the Maratha ships was abandoned on the spot.

The merciless shelling went on for two days, however, and everyone felt sure that at any moment now, the defenders would come out with a flag of truce and surrender the fort. But at the end of two days, when part of the fort wall had been dismantled by the shelling, it was discovered that the shells falling within the fort had been doing no damage, but were being wasted amidst the rocks.

The original plan, had already misfired. Some alternative plan had to be devised in the field itself. After a great deal of hesitation, a landing was attempted with the idea of reaching the Maratha fleet by land and setting fire to the ships. Again, the plan was absolutely sound; all it needed was a reasonably determined execution.

To everyone's surprise, the landing was effected without any opposition, and there was no firing from the fort even when the landing party had to skirt its walls in order to reach the cove where the ships were gathered. It was then found that the landing party would have to cross a swamp to reach the place where the ships were kept, and again the attempt to burn the ships was abandoned. As the landing force, now made somewhat bolder by the absence of firing from the fort, were carelessly passing the walls of the fort on their way back to the ships, they encountered, for the first time, sustained small-arms fire from the fort. At this, they broke into a run, and scrambled into their landing boats and rowed for their ships as fast as they could go. On 18 June, 1718, the Gheria expedition was back in Bombay, 'to repair our frigates and to take care of our wounded of whom we had a considerable number ... ' Only the day previous to the return of the fleet to Bombay, the Council had made a proclamation that they were at war.

Here again, there were more casualties due to accidents and inefficiency than due to enemy action: a typical accident was the blowing up of the prowgun of the ship *Hunter*, 'killing three and wounding several men in a most dreadful manner'.

If the fire-ship was rendered ineffective owing to normal defensive measures, and if shelling alone was not going to bring the defenders to their knees, begging for mercy, there was nothing further that Boone's sailors and soldiers could do about it. They had done their job and subjected Gheria to the worst bombardment in the history of the Konkan. Anything that had remotely to do with the tactical exploitation of a situation or that could be ascribed to competent leadership, or even to blind courage, was not in them. If machines could not do the jobs expected of them, the answer was to build bigger and better machines. 'Returned our *gallivats*', the Bombay Council records sullenly, 'having destroyed one town of Angrias'. All the damage suffered by Gheria was the mark of cannonshots upon its rocks.

The most surprising part of the expedition, however, was not how little it was able to achieve, but how it was suffered to do what it did, and get away with it. In particular, how were the men permitted to make a landing and then suffered to get past the fort walls to make an attempt to set fire to the ships, unless it was intended to draw them in and bottle them up between the bog and the fort walls, which does not seem to have been the case? Why, when the landing party returned, defeated by the swamp, was it not subjected to a withering fire from the fort as it was attempting to slink back past the wall: why was the party not subjected to a counter-attack? Why, when an unskilled and untried opponent like the Raja of Karwar had done all these things and more, did a veteran warrior like Kanhoji Angrey fail to inflict the same kind of damage in circumstances that were far more favourable? In anyone else, it would have been a serious military blunder: in a seasoned military commander, it would be nothing short of a crime.

We have to thank Clement Downing for the answer to this puzzle. 'I question', writes Downing who was an officer on one of the expedition's ships, 'whether there were a hundred men in the castle during the time of the siege'.

Clement Downing was not the sort of person who would exaggerate the weakness of an enemy. His inclinations for distortion lay heavily on the opposite side. In all his battles, he tended to magnify the strength of the opposing forces in order to show greater bravery and military skill on the part of his own side. There is little doubt that Kanhoji Angrey was caught napping. He had no idea that the Company would go to the extent of declaring war against him, nor that the Bombay Council would send an expedition to reduce one of his forts without a formal declaration of war—it was one of those things that were just not done.

Kanhoji himself was not in Gheria, and could not have known anything about the attack until it was on. But there is little doubt that he himself must have been thoroughly surprised by the Company's handling of the expedition; for Gheria, with no more than a hundred men, had flung back a major assault by the English, inflicting more casualties upon them than the total number of fighting men in the fort.

All the same, it was a narrow escape: he was never going to be caught so much by surprise again.

36

Monsoon, 1718

The war was on. It lasted for thirty-eight years.

Undaunted by the failure of the Gheria expedition, Governor Boone, 'at once set to work to prepare for a fresh attack on Angria. This time it was determined that Kennery (Khanderi), within sight of Bombay harbour, should be the object of the attack, and all through the monsoon, preparations were made'.

If, as it seems reasonable to believe from the above extract from contemporary records, 'the object of the attack' was determined some four months in advance and feverish preparations were undertaken in Bombay to get ready for the attack, there is little doubt that almost everyone in Bombay must have known about the Council's military plans. In Colaba, barely twenty miles away, Kanhoji Angrey, too, must have come to know exactly where and when the Company's fleet was going to launch its next assault.

Meanwhile, Boone contented himself with a series of minor jabs at his enemy. In July and September, he sent two small expeditions against coastal villages with instructions to destroy the ships that might be in storage and to inflict as much damage as possible upon the land. Neither of these expeditions was able to make a landing.

Mr. Boone also wrote to Mr. Taylor, his Chief Factor at Karwar, to approach the rival Maratha King, Sambhaji of Kolhapur, and to try to enter into an offensive and defensive alliance with him. Mr. Taylor was told that he should promise Sambhaji all of Angrey's forts after they had been won. If, however, Sambhaji did not wish to join hands with the Company in its military operations against Angrey, then he was to be given an assurance that the Company had 'no design against His Highness or any of his loyal subjects'.

Than Mr. Taylor, the Company's Chief Factor at Karwar, it would be difficult to imagine a more unsuitable person for this type of high-powered diplomacy. It will be recalled that it was Mr. Taylor who had provoked the Raja of Karwar into attacking the English factory there. Diplomacy was certainly not his forte. The result of Mr. Taylor's mission was a foregone conclusion: there was no treaty with Sambhaji.

The Company also made frantic overtures to the Portuguese, but the Portuguese resolutely pretended to look the other way. The Viceroy, Conde de Ericera, made a pointed reference to the bungling of the Gheria expedition, which he called the 'sound scheme for the capturing or burning of Angria's *pals* at Gheria', and which he took credit for having suggested to Governor Boone. He unceremoniously brushed aside the English proposal for an alliance against Angrey.

Characteristically, ever since his troubles with the Company began, Kanhoji had refrained from giving the Portuguese any cause for complaint. Conde de Ericera smugly noted down that throughout his term as the Viceroy (1717-20), no Portuguese ship was molested by Angrey. Although, even at this time, there was no friendship between the Portuguese and Kanhoji Angrey, the Viceroy, on his part, was not anxious to get into the war merely to help the Company out of its troubles. Indeed, other things being equal, there is nothing that the Portuguese would have desired more than the total extinction of the English traders from India. Above all, the Viceroy was thoroughly contemptuous of the power of the Company's arms, and when he retired, warned his successor not to make an alliance with the English, who, he implied, were militarily not even as strong as the Siddy of Janjira, and of course, far less reliable.

But despite the coolness displayed by the Maratha pretender, Sambhaji, and the Portuguese, Governor Boone's preparations went on with his customary zeal brought to fever heat by the sting of two failures.

By the end of September, 300 more soldiers arrived from England, and they brought with them large quantities of warlike stores and ammunition. The first-line ships of the Bombay Council now consisted of:

Victory	24 guns	*Antelope*	8 guns
Brittania	18 guns	*Hound*	8 guns
Revenge	16 guns	*Tyger* (*gallivat*)	8 guns
Fame (galley)	16 guns	*Fly*	8 guns
Hawk (galley)	14 guns	*Swift*	8 guns
Eagle (galley)	16 guns	*Ferret*	8 guns
Princess Amelia	16 guns	*Weasel*	6 guns
Defiance	14 guns	*Squirrel*	6 guns
Drake	6 guns	*Leopard*	6 guns
Salamander	fire-ship	*Terrible Bomb*	bomb-ketch
Hunter	bomb-ketch		

Every one of these ships had two or more *gallivat*s as their permanent anxiliary vessels, and each *gallivat* held ten English sailors and from forty to fifty Indian sailors. The bigger ships held as many as 200 men, out of whom about 40 to 50 were English sailors. The total manpower of the fleet in officers and other ranks was upwards of 2,000 and this did not include the marines or the landing parties.

This might be called the 'standing Navy' of the East India Company at Bombay, but the Bombay Council always had the assistance of anything from two to six more ships which happened to be in the harbour. In the proposed expedition against Khanderi, Governor Boone had called upon the assistance of four East Indiamen, which, since the Company's merchant ships were armed just as powerfully as their fighting ships, was as good as having four more frigates.

It seems that Manuel de Castro, who had deserted to the English side from Angrey's service and who professed to know everything about the strength and dispositions of Angrey's navy and about his fortifications, had won the confidence of Governor Boone, and had been appointed as the Commander of all the Company's *gallivat*s. This appointment caused a good deal of bitterness amongst the Company's officers, and many of them bluntly told Boone that they would never serve under Manuel de Castro who was 'a fellow of a very indifferent character'. In the end, Governor Boone had to give in, and Castro's command was reduced to five *gallivat*s, the other forty-odd *gallivat*s being placed under the direct command of the Captains of the capital ships in twos and threes. Even this relatively minor position of responsibility that was given to Manuel de Castro was objected to by the Company's officials, but as it turned out, it was just as well that Manuel de Castro was taken on the Khanderi expedition—as the only non-Englishman in a position of some responsibility, he was to serve as an excellent scapegoat for many of the things that went wrong with the venture.

The bickering over the appointment of Manuel de Castro was a new symptom of an old disease: the quarrels that went on among the writers and Factors and clerks of the East India Company who had been given military ranks for the duration of hostilities. Boone's commanders had always tended to take their personal differences into battle with them regardless of the consequences. But this time, Boone was determined to prevent a repetition of such quarrels in the field. He decided to take command of the expedition himself. On 1 November, 1718, he hoisted his flag on board the *Addison*.

Addison was one of the two East Indiamen which were pressed into service by Boone; the other was *Dartmouth*. Subsequently, the expedition was joined by two more merchant ships, *Morris* and *Stanhope*. In addition to these ships, the squadron consisted of the frigate Victory; the *ghurabs Revenge* and *Defiance*; the galley *Fame*; the ketch *Hunter*; another bombketch and forty-eight *gallivat*s. 'The soldiers were put on board the said ships, with ammunition, Scaling-Ladders, & etc ... having all our Men of War, Bombs, and Fire-ship, with near 2500 men', Clement Downing writes.

The Khanderi expedition weighed anchor at two o'clock in the afternoon of 1 November, 1718.

37

D Minus Four to D Plus Nine

Khanderi, a kidney-shaped island crammed with rocks and stunted shrubs, lies three miles from the coast, ten miles from Bombay and roughly the same distance from Angrey's headquarters at Colaba. The main fortified enclosure strengthened by Angrey three years earlier, lay at the southern tip of the island, and the cove and the harbour lies to the east, in the dent of the kidney. The island is more than a mile across from north to south and about half a mile at its widest.

The English squadron arrived near Khanderi in a matter of hours. They circled around the island menacingly, and that evening and the next day were spent in doing a thorough all-round reconnaissance of the island and in getting the ships lined up for the bombardment of the fort walls to the south. Why the south wall was chosen for punishment is not known, unless it was the most prominent expanse of the fortifications visible from the sea in those days. The firing began before daylight on 3 November, but when the sun came up, it was found out that the shells were falling short. During the morning, the ships were moved closer in, and from midday onwards, an uninterrupted cannonade continued until dark.

At two in the afternoon, two of Angrey's *ghurabs* were seen to come out of the harbour and the frigates *Victory* and *Revenge* and the ketch *Hawke* were immediately ordered to engage them. What the two *ghurabs* were trying to do is not clear. They may have been trying to make a break for the safety of Colaba. But if, on the other hand, they were merely acting as decoys to draw off the fire from the fort walls, they succeeded in their object, for when *Victory, Revenge* and *Hawke* gave chase, they found that the two *ghurabs* were followed at some distance by fourteen *gallivat*s, which made them decide that the opposition was far too strong, and the three English ships beat a hasty retreat.

If, as the English later said, the Commander of Khanderi Island was desperately short of ammunition and supplies, it is almost certain that the Angrey convoy was making a break for Colaba to get reinforcement and supplies, and the English squadron should have made all possible efforts to intercept the two *ghurabs* and fourteen *gallivat*s even if it meant relaxing the bombardment of the fort for the time being. But by permitting these ships to sneak away without making any attempt to engage them, the English may be said to have already taken the first major step towards failure.

In reply to the heavy bombardment on its south face, the Khanderi fort could bring into action only three guns. The fire from the fort's guns 'did no execution', but it seems to have caused some slight damage to one of the attacking ships. By four o'clock on the very first day of the operation, however, the guns from the fort stopped firing altogether, and 'continued quiet all next day'.

The English bombardment stopped only when night fell, except that the bomb-ketch continued to fire its shells throughout the night and well into the next morning. But at this time, there was a misfire and bombardier Mule and some of his gun team were wounded, and the bomb-ketch had to stop firing. These were the first casualties of the expedition.

As a result of his all-round reconnaissance of the coast, Governor Boone had decided upon a two-pronged attack, to take place at first light on 5 November: one to the east and the other to the west of the island. The eastern landing was to be made by the English grenadiers and marines, in all numbering over 300, under cover of the guns of the frigates and the merchant ships. The western landing was to be made by a battalion of the Company's sepoys, numbering 558, commanded by Captain John Mills. The covering fire for this attack was to be provided by the *gallivat*s.

A relentless bombardment was kept up from dawn till dusk on 4 November—D-minus-one Day. As there was no answering fire from the fort's guns throughout the day, it was taken for granted that the ammunition of the defenders had run out. The Company's commanders always showed a propensity for jumping to such agreeable conclusions. If the fort's ammunition had already run out, it looked as though the fort would not be able to withstand a determined assault.

This looked a very promising situation, and to take the fullest advantage of it, the Commander of the expedition, Boone, gave orders to Manuel de Castro to blockade the entrance to the harbour of Khanderi with his five *gallivat*s and to make sure that no supplies of any kind reached the island from outside. At least this is what Governor Boone is said to have done, but the circumstances suggest that if this important mission was entrusted to Manuel de Castro at all (who was denounced by the squadron's officers as being untrustworthy), he was there only in some subordinate capacity. The log of *Addison* clearly states that on the night of the 6th, Captain John Mills was detailed to maintain the overnight blockade of the harbour with his six *gallivat*s, but makes no mention of anyone being told to guard the harbour entrance before this date. It is more than probable that before 6 November, the attackers had not thought it necessary to guard the harbour at night. In any case, the only positive evidence that Manuel de Castro was ordered to blockade the harbour channel is contained in Clement Downing's account, and the highly imaginative Mr. Downing is not be trusted in such matters.

As H-hour drew near on the morning of the 5th, the ships were moved into their allotted positions and resumed the shelling of the fort to provide covering fire for the assaulting parties. The frigates had moved to the south-east of the island to support the landing to be made by the grenadiers and the marines, and the *gallivats* had moved to the north-west to assist the landing in the west which was to be made by the Company's sepoys.

At the last minute, however, the sepoys refused to take part in the landing, and in spite of the promise of handsome rewards and the 'severest measures' which included the wounding and killing of several sepoys, they could not be made to change their minds. From the subsequent behaviour of many of the English officers under fire, it is perhaps not surprising that the sepoys refused to participate in the battle. Mercenary fighting men can only be expected to go into action with leaders who enjoy their confidence, and the Company's clerks and Factors pressed into service for the occasion were a far cry from being inspired leaders of men.

The marines and the grenadiers carried out their landing as planned, on the eastern shore of Khanderi, but they found they could not make much headway. They encountered a sustained small-arms fire from the fort, and when they crept closer, they were met with a fierce shower of stones flung at pointblank range into their ranks. When eighteen of the party had been killed and another fifty wounded—not, surprisingly enough, so much by the bullets from the small-arms as by 'ye force of stones hoven from ye rocks', as the *Addison's* log puts it—they gave up their assault and turned back for their landing boats. Just about this time, a gun from one of the *gallivats* which were giving covering fire burst, adding both to the casualties and the confusion.

Much to the astonishment of the attackers, the guns of the fort now started firing again, this time with good effect. On the eastern side alone they had twelve guns, all firing at a brisk rate and causing heavy damage to the English ships, which had been brought closer than was prudent in the conviction that the defenders had no ammunition left. This caused added distress to Governor Boone and his staff, who jumped to the conclusion that the defenders had

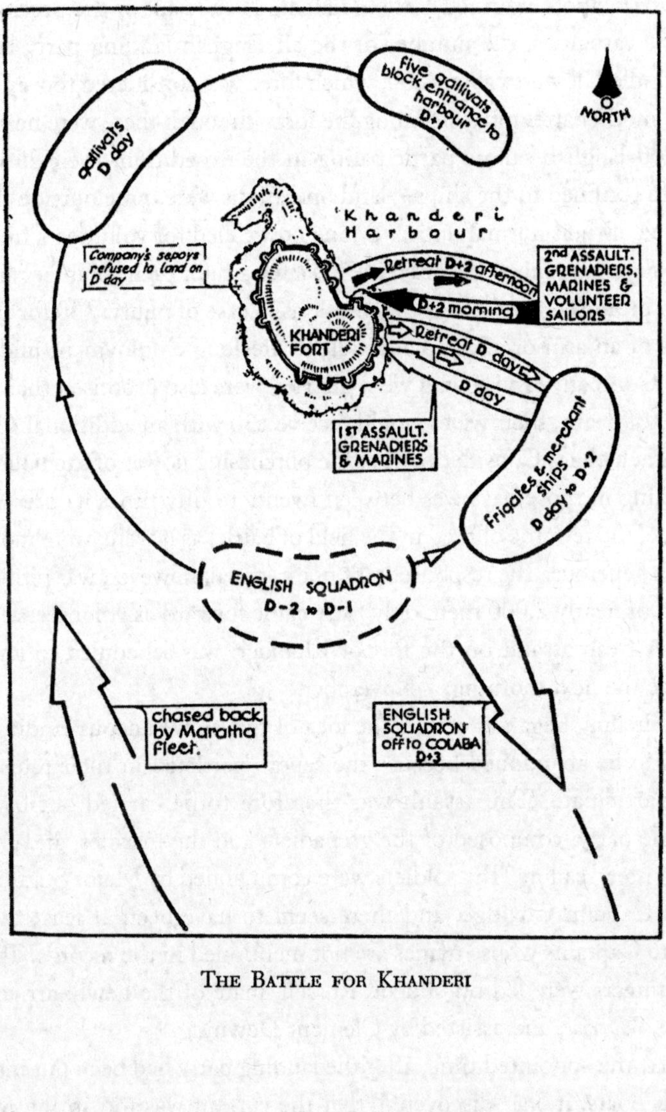

The Battle for Khanderi

obtained fresh supplies of ammunition and stores in spite of their blockade.

On 6 November, the Company's squadron was joined by *Morrice*, another armed East Indiaman. As a result of the previous day's casualties, the number of the all-English landing party had dwindled down to about 200, which force was considered too small for another attempt at storming the fort. Although there were nearly 2,000 English sailors participating in the expedition, their duties were confined to the ships—land operations were quite outside the scope of their normal duties. Boone now called for volunteers from amongst his sailors. He offered £5 as a reward for each volunteer and also promised generous compensations in case of injury: £30 for the loss of an arm or a leg in addition to life-long employment under the Company. Those who were married were also promised that in case of death, their wives would receive £30 with an additional £10 for each child. Considering that the purchasing power of the pound sterling in those days was between twenty to fifty times its present value, the rewards offered in the field of battle, as it were, were more than generous. The response to Boone's appeal, however, was pitiful. Out of nearly 2,000 men, only forty came forward as volunteers.

A fresh assault on the fort of Khanderi was scheduled to take place the next morning, 7 November.

Shelling began at dawn. The idea of two simultaneous landings had to be abandoned because the sepoys persisted in their refusal to participate. The assault was therefore to be carried out by a single party, composed of the grenadiers and the marines, and the 'volunteer' sailors. The soldiers were commanded by Major Stanton and Captain Coxidge, and there seem to have been at least two more Captains whose names are not mentioned in the records. The volunteers were led by Gideon Russell, mate of the newly-arrived ship, *Morrice*, and assisted by Clement Downing.

At the appointed time, after the landing party had been put into their boats, it was 'discovered' that the current was too strong for a landing. The men huddled together in the tossing landing boats had to wait until ten o'clock before the boats could start for the shore. They could be seen from the fort and were exposed to the fire from the fort's guns. Whatever tactical surprise was hoped for was altogether lost. 'To make matters worse, Manuel de Castro ran two of his *gallivat*s ashore under the guns of the castle, with the result that fifty or sixty men were killed or wounded', even before the assault began.

Even after ten o'clock, when the landing boats began to make for the shore, the tide was too strong and capsized some of the boats, so that many of the men who were to take part in the assault never got as far as the landing place.

But in spite of these mishaps, the assaulting party made a brave and determined bid to reach the gate of the fort. The man in the lead was Gideon Russell, heading his party of volunteer sailors. At the gate itself, they again encountered a withering shower of stones and bullets, and Mr. Russell, on whom all hopes were now pinned, fell down wounded, and the command of the party devolved upon Clement Downing and John Steele, the carpenter of *Morrice*. Mr. Russell was removed to his ship, *Morrice*. He died the next morning.

The next wave of the assault, composed of the grenadiers and the marines, also fought its way to the main entrance of the fort, and they were attempting to break open the wooden doors with axes when one of the unnamed Captains threw down his sword in a sudden fit of panic and fled. (The sword must have been retrieved by someone else in the party, for it was taken back to Governor Boone and was subsequently 'broken' at a parade specially held in Bombay.) Another of Stanton's Captains, also nameless, tried to burst open the lock on the gate by firing his pistol into it, but 'the bullet rebounded and struck him on the nose'. At this, the Captain promptly ordered the drums to beat the 'retreat' and all the soldiers, including their commander, Major Stanton, ran back to their landing boats without further ado while the defenders were 'playing very hott with putheridge (patridge) small arms and continually heaving stones'. This left the party of the volunteer sailors wholly on its own, still fighting at the gates, if Clement Downing is to be believed. But not for long, for 'seeing the hopelessness of any further attempts, (they) retreated to their boats and rowed off under heavy fire, leaving many wounded to be massacred'.

By the afternoon, the expedition had spent itself, although the ships continued a desultory bombardment of the island from a safe distance. On the eighth morning, a council of war was held and Boone and his advisers 'agreed to goe down to Calube (Colaba) with the grabs and *gallivats* leaving only the *Defiance* and four *gallivats* between the island and the main'.

Boone's squadron continued aimlessly for a few more days, shelling the coast in a leisurely manner. It is said that on the 11th an offer of truce was received from Angrey which was refused peremptorily. Whether such an offer was made, or if it was made rejected so cavalierly, without even considering its terms, is doubtful in view of the fate the expedition had suffered. What is definite, however, is that a squadron of Angrey's ships which had been sent up all the way from Gheria, put the attackers to flight. Governor Boone, on *Addison*, returned to Bombay on 14 November and the whole squadron was back in Bombay on the 24th, after, as the log of the expedition records, 'exhausting all its ammunition'.

Let us review the battle briefly from within the fort of Khanderi. Kanhoji Angrey himself was not in Khanderi. Although he was aware that the English were planning an attack and even possibly that Khanderi was their objective, he could not have been absolutely sure. He may have even felt that Khanderi was just a feint, and that the actual attack was planned for another place: the English had any of half-a-dozen places to choose from.

Khanderi, therefore, did not have more than its normal complement of troops and ships. The effective strength of the soldiers within the fort is not likely to have exceeded 500, and it is more probable that their number was only around 300, including the women. During both the assaults made on the fort, the women had to fight side by side with the men. Perhaps the greatest military asset the island possessed was its Commander, a veteran soldier enjoying Kanhoji Angrey's fullest confidence. His name was Mankoji Suryawanshi, and his main task must have been to keep up the morale of his garrison.

They could see their attackers all the time, in overwhelming strength, almost completely surrounding the island with more than fifty assorted ships, more ships than they had ever seen together; they were the target of the continuous fire from some thing like a hundred guns. In return, they could only bring three guns into action on the first day, and were forced to stop their fire soon afterwards because their ammunition had run out; or, what is more likely, in order to conserve their ammunition for the defence of the fort during the actual storming. Their chief weapon was stones; they fought off at least three determined attacks from the very gates of the fort, mainly by hurling stones at the attackers. By the 6th morning, they had either managed to bring in ammunition from outside in spite of the tight blockade of the harbour, or had conserved their ammunition so well, that they were able to keep twelve guns firing all the time. The tactical surprise achieved by these guns opening fire after their initial silence was perhaps more effective in demoralising the enemy than the actual damage caused by the guns. And in the end, when the last wave of the attack had been beaten, the men came out of the fort and launched a counter-attack and fell upon the broken ranks of their enemies as they were trying to run for their boats.

For organizing the defence of the island, for bringing up the vast quantities of stones into the fort walls and maintaining a sustained shower of stones at the attackers, for either conserving his ammunition or to have managed to bring fresh supplies in spite of the blockade; for making the best use of the meagre resources of the island; for his daring counter-attack; and, above all, for preserving his garrison's morale when they could see that they were outnumbered by at least ten to one, Mankoji Suryawanshi deserves a special tribute. By rank, he could not have been more than a *Surnobat*, and a 'subedar-of-two-hundred-and-fifty'. His coolness and determination in the face of the assault could not have failed to be rewarded by his *Surkhail*. The defence of Khanderi was nothing short of a brilliant tactical victory.

But very little is heard of the *Surnobat* of Khanderi in later years. It is more than likely that he died in the defence of the fort, or soon afterwards.

38

The Man in the 'Trunk'

Many things collapsed in the wash of the Khanderi expedition; the chief casualties being the reputation of English arms and, as will be seen, the much vaunted purity of the Company's Court of Justice at Bombay. But Governor Boone carried on just as before, his industry and zeal unimpaired. As soon as he reached Bombay, he set himself to the task of finding out what had gone wrong, and punishing those who may be found responsible for it, and, characteristically, to making preparations for yet another expedition.

When the Company's squadron got back to Bombay, Bombay held a parade. At this parade, the Captain who had thrown down his sword and bolted from the gate of Khanderi, was publicly dismissed with disgrace. In a time-honoured ritual for 'breaking' officers, his sword was broken in front of the entire garrison and his sash cut to pieces.

Boone had convinced himself that the chief cause of his failure was treachery. He pounced upon his one-time favourite, Manuel de Castro, who, Boone now declared, was secretly in league with Angrey, and had permitted the defenders of Khanderi to bring in supplies and ammunition through his blockade of the harbour. Boone had Castro put into irons and shipped off to St. Helena.

But, as though Governor Boone felt that Castro's punishment was not enough to wash out the stain of defeat, that a treachery greater than Castro the 'renegade' was capable of had to be uncovered, a treachery of a deeper dye and a bigger size, as it were, he ordered inquiries to be made amongst the citizens of Bombay.

Someone, at this stage, whispered into the willing ears of the Governor, the name of Rama Kamathi. Boone ordered some preliminary investigations and then, with his justly renowned industriousness, set about building up his case against Rama Kamathi, a man of 'prodigious influence and vast wealth', and whom the Governor himself had sent the previous year to mediate on his behalf with Kanhoji Angrey.

Rama Kamathi belonged to one of the oldest families in Bombay: his family had settled in Bombay long before the East India Company, serving first the Portuguese and then the Company with exemplary loyalty. His wealth came from enormous tobacco farms and coconut plantations, but he was more renowned as a pillar of society than for his wealth. His status as one of the leading citizens of Bombay had come to be accepted by the Company, and two years earlier, the Council had recorded with evident satisfaction that when the very first service was held in the Cathedral of Bombay on Christmas Day, 1718, Rama Kamathi was one of those who watched the service and was impressed by it. He was a religious man, and five years earlier he had built with his own money the Temple of Walukeshwar, which is still a famous landmark of Bombay. He was also the highest Indian military commander under the Company, and held an office which was somewhere between the Subedar of the Company's forces, and their overall Commander, Major Stanton. He was important enough to feel entitled to give advice to the Bombay Council on matters of strategy, and, as we have seen, be asked by the Governor to mediate on behalf of the Company.

All in all, Rama Kamathi was a big man, rich, influential, respected. As might be expected, he also had enemies, and these men now seemed to enjoy the special confidence of the Company's Governor and Council.

It took a whole year for Governor Boone's charge-sheet of treason to be assembled. It was handed over to Rama Kamathi in February 1720. Among other things it accused him of, were the following charges:

(a) That he had told Angrey that the ship, *Success*, 'belonging to Gordhan Das' (*sic*) did not belong to the English.
(b) That he had sent word in advance to Angrey, warning him of the Khanderi expedition.
(c) That he intercepted a letter from the Portuguese General of the North, which contained an offer to assist the English against Angrey, and that he had tampered with the letter and passed on its message to Angrey.
(d) That he had caused a letter to be sent to Kanhoji Angrey to invade Bombay at night with 'six or seven *gallivats*, who, landing, will gain a victory without doubt'.
(e) That when the Company's Subedar told him of an offer from Angrey's commander at Panwale to deliver his fort, he, Rama Kamathi, had 'treated him with coldness and neglect'.

The indictment stressed that the Company had witnesses to prove their charges, and also letters 'written on behalf of Rama Kamathi' and bearing his personal 'seal', sent to Angrey.

The most important exhibit, the letter said to have been sent to Kanhoji Angrey warning him about the Khanderi expedition, is worth quoting if only to show the absurd lengths to which its writer had gone to prove Rama Kamathi's alliance with Angrey. Its wholly artificial style of address was uncommon in the Konkan, and its studied superlatives, as though its author were making an effort to compose a letter rather than to write it, should have warned the Council that it was a forgery. It reeks of artifice.

> 'To the opulent and magnificent as the Sun, valorous and victorious, always courageous, the liberal, prudent and pillar of fortitude, the essence of understanding, the protector of Brahmines, defender of the faith, prosperous in all things, honoured of kings, above all councillors, Senor Canhoji Angria, Sarqueel. Ramajee Comatee, your servant, writes with all the veneration and readiness for your service, and with your favour I remain as always.
>
> 'Our general here has resolved in Council to attack and take the Fort of Condry (Khanderi) and this it is agreed to environ the said Fort the 17th of October, and the *Armado*, powder and ball, and all other necessaries for war are ready, I therefore write your Honour that you may have the said Fort well furnished. As for the side of the Rajaporee (the Siddy) I have spoken to and agreed with Allee Naiq Loucandee that they of Rajaporee shall not help either party; thus I have given this notice. I do not write more, only you will retain me in your favour.
>
> 'Dated the 12th of October 1718.'

This letter was not in the handwriting of Rama Kamathi, bore his personal seal.

Having sent off the charge-sheet to Rama Kamathi, Governor announced that the trial would be held by a tribunal and in open court, and that the tribunal was to be composed of the Governor and his Council; Boone and his commanders of the late war council, were now to act as both prosecutors and judges.

Rama Kamathi's reply to the Governor's charge-sheet, written himself, rings with honesty and impressive logic. But it is sadly lacking in tact. He wrote in effect:

(a) About *Success*: The first thing Angrey does when he captures a ship is to find out to whom she belongs. In any case, he knows every single ship from Surat. There would be no point in anyone attempting to tell him about who owned *Success*.

(b) About the Khanderi Expedition: The fact that Khanderi was wholly unprepared for the attack should prove that Angrey had no advance information; otherwise the defenders would have been better prepared. The garrison was so small that women had to assist in the fort's defence. In fact, Rama Kamathi pointed out, it was he who had told the Governor that Khanderi was poorly stocked and weakly garrisoned and had suggested attacking it, and, as the Governor saw for himself, his (Rama Kamathi's) information had been correct.

(c) About the letter said to have been sent by the Portuguese General of the North: Kamathi not only denied knowledge of any such letter said that he doubted that any such letter was ever sent. (As it happens, at the trial, the prosecution did produce a Portuguese clerk to swear that the General of the North did send such a letter. On the other hand, the General himself wrote to Boone that Boone's suspicions that the seal of any letter written by him had been tampered with, had been unfounded, and telling him unequivocally that Rama Kamathi was innocent. Boone took exception to the Portuguese General's insinuation that his proceedings against Rama Kamathi were not fair. 'You condemn an action which your Honour is a stranger to', Boone wrote in indignation. 'I had good reason to be offended with his [Rama Kamathi's] conduct.'

(d) About inviting Angrey to attack Bombay: Rama Kamathi pointed out that he had always been a loyal servant of the Company, and would not be guilty of such ingratitude. In any case, he asserted, it would be foolhardy for anyone to think of attacking Bombay 'considering how well the island is guarded by several stout frigates and forts and a number of good English officers'.

(e) About the Subedar's offer to deliver up the Panwale fort: Rama Kamathi said that if the Company's Subedar had any such offer to communicate, he would have told about it to his Commander, Major Stanton, and not to him, Rama Kamathi.

(f) Rama Kamathi also denied having caused any letters to be written to Angrey and pointed out that since he was himself able to write, he would not have trusted someone else to write a letter of such a secret nature. The letters must be forgeries, he wrote: 'those who can forge letters (can) make a false seal also.'

(g) And lastly, Rama Kamathi said that if there were any witnesses who had come forward to testify to his alleged crimes, they must have done so because they were either bribed or threatened to make them give false evidence.

As might be expected, this rejoinder touched many a raw spot on the consciences of the Governor and his Council, for intentionally or otherwise, Rama Kamathi had left a sting in the tail of each one of his replies: the fact that the Khanderi attack was repelled by an insignificant force and that even women had to assist in its defence; that it was unlikely that the Portuguese would offer to assist the English; the veiled sneer about the Company's preparations for the defence of Bombay, and the assertion that *Success* was indeed a Surat ship.

'The enemy's neglect to follow his advice is not proof that he did not send it', Boone flashed. The same empirical logic was applied to the alleged offer to surrender the Panwale fort. 'If the Subedar did not report it to Stanton, it does not mean that he did not report it to Rama Kamathi', wrote Boone.

But what must have stung the Governor more than the sarcasm in Rama Kamathi's rejoinder was the allegation that the letters were forged, and that the witnesses had been made to testify against Rama Kamathi by bribery and threats.

That the letter said to have been written by Rama Kamathi to Kanhoji Angrey, was in fact forged, may not have been known to Governor Boone at this stage, but as regards obtaining the confessions from the witnesses by bribery and by threats, that was precisely what the Governor and his Council had resorted to: only they had gone a step further; they had resorted to torture. Governor Boone himself came out with it at the trial: 'the man (principal witness) did not confess till the irons were screwed upon his thumbs, the smart whereof, brought him to confession', Boone admitted.

The trial of Rama Kamathi was a farce, and the result was a foregone conclusion. On 20 April, 1720, he was pronounced guilty of 'high crimes and misdemeanours as by trial will more fully appear', and ordered to be confined to prison for the rest of his life and his estates were forfeited to the Company. 'The offender himself thinks the (punishment) mild', Governor Boone wrote in answer to the Portuguese General's protests, 'and much less than his demerit'.

Immediately afterwards, Rama Kamathi was thrown into the 'Trunk', as Bombay's jail was then called. The Company valued his property at between sixty and seventy thousand rupees and appropriated it. Ironically, one of his large warehouses was selected as being the most suitable building to house the new Court of Justice at Bombay.

Four years later, one of the chief witnesses, Antonio, confessed to having given false evidence. Pointing this out, a Bombay citizen wrote to the Governor, 'I have also a goldsmith that falsified the seal'.

'We can never forgive Mr Boone', writes S. M. Edwardes, 'for the torture (of witnesses). Our regret ... is heightened by the knowledge, now vouchsafed to us, that Rama Kamathi was guiltless, that the incriminating letters were the merest forgeries!'

But the fact that the letters were forgeries was not permitted to ooze out until many years later. While the 'condemned man pined in prison, his family had sunk into the depths of poverty', and the new judges of the court administered the Company's justice from their courthouse which had so recently been a tobacco warehouse.

Rama Kamathi died in 1728, in Bombay's 'Trunk'.

39

Peace Talk

The trial of Rama Kamathi has taken this history somewhat ahead of the sequence of events.

After the Company's fleet returned to Bombay, it was closely pursued by a squadron of Angrey's ships. They came and took stations outside the harbour waiting to pounce upon ships going in or out. The East Indiaman *Morrice*, released from military duty, was now loaded and ready for her voyage to England. She got under way three times but was forced to come hurrying back to base when Angrey's ships gave chase. For two of the best months of sailing weather, Bombay's shipping lay bottled up in the harbour. At the end of January 1719, the Company's squadron, comprising the frigates *Defiance*, *Victory*, *Revenge*, and the galleys *Hunter* and *Hawk*, was ordered out to engage the Angrey ships. But, by this time, the Angrey ships had already gone away, and the Company's squadron collected some free credit for having put them to flight.

On the other hand, it is quite possible that the Angrey ships took to their heels after seeing the Company's squadron come out to engage them. Retreat in the face of superior force seems to have become an accepted principle of tactics. As far as possible, the Angrey ships depended on their mobility in both attack or defence. Their fire-power was seldom on a par with that of their opponents, and they often found it expedient to scuttle away into the inshore waters where the Company's bigger ships could not follow them, and where the guns from their own shore establishments could offer them protection.

At the end of January, Shahu sent a man called Shivaji Vishwanath as his envoy to the Governor of Bombay, carrying a proposal of a peace treaty, and asked the Governor that his 'servant Kanhoji Angrey' should also participate in the talks.

Upon the Governor agreeing to this, a man called Damaji Pilaji was sent by Kanhoji Angrey to Bombay to represent him in the peace talks. The terms discussed are not known, but according to a letter written by Boone to the Directors of the Company in London, the Maratha representatives seem to have agreed to restore all ships that had been taken, except *Success*, 'which was hopelessly decayed', and pay a sum of Rs. 70,000 for the goods captured as well as in payment for the damaged *Success*. This payment, Boone assured his Directors, would go to recoup the Company towards the expenditure of the Khanderi expedition. In addition, Boone also proposed a two per cent tax on the people of Bombay as a war tax.

Governor Boone seems to have been in a jubilant mood, for a treaty with the Marathas on these terms would have justified his policy and also the military expenditure incurred by the Bombay Council since his arrival. Even before the terms were finally agreed upon, he sent off Captain John Mills to Colaba to bring back the English prisoners in Angrey's hands. After reaching Colaba, Captain Mills discovered that the prisoners were actually in Gheria. It was in Colaba that he also found out that the treaty was not finalized. He returned to Bombay after getting an assurance from Kanhoji Angrey that when the terms of the treaty were finally settled, Angrey would have the prisoners sent to Bombay with his own escort.

While the talks were going on, both sides had carefully refrained from giving offence to each other. As such, the year 1719 may be said to have been a year of peace. There is little doubt, however, that on the part of the Company, the peace talks were no more than a time-saving device: 'Time was essential for perfecting their own resources ... until they were strong enough to sweep (Angrey) from their path', writes S. M. Edwardes, explaining the Bombay Council's attitude at this time. Boone had continued to foster the friendship of the Siddy, who had been permitting the Company's ships to take in supplies and water in his ports during their warfare with Angrey, and 'to keep him in the like mood', Boone periodically sent him expensive presents. Similarly, Boone had continued to make repeated overtures to the Portuguese, but the Portuguese Viceroy, Conde de Ericera, was not inclined to form an alliance with the East India Company.

Conde de Ericera had little faith in the power of the Company's arms. He openly ridiculed their soldiers as being merchants and clerks. Furthermore, he doubted the Company's *bona fides* and often said that he was sure that 'the English would quietly withdraw from the war when they saw the Portugese involved in it'.

Conde de Ericera's stubbornness provoked Boone into picking a quarrel with the Portuguese themselves. Boone complained to the Viceroy that the Portuguese friars were encouraging his slaves and soldiers to desert. Not content with a mere protest, he peremptorily banished all the Portuguese friars from Bombay, and installed in their place an Italian Bishop and Italian Brothers of his own choice. In retaliation, the Portuguese General of the North made a proclamation forbidding the Roman Catholics of Bombay from recognizing the Italian priests. He also ordered all intercourse with Bombay to be stopped and announced that those captured going in or out of Bombay would be 'whipped and put into the galleys for five years'. It is interesting to reflect that the Portuguese General of the North was the same person who, a few months earlier, is said to have addressed a letter to the Governor of Bombay, offering to make an alliance with the Company against Angrey, which letter the unfortunate Rama Kamathi was alleged to have tampered with. If he ever sent such a letter, he had certainly suffered a drastic change of heart.

It looked as though instead of making friends with the Portuguese and joining hands with them against the Marathas, Governor Boone was about to add yet another war to his record. But at about this time, Conde de Ericera retired. His successor, Don Fransisco Jose de Sampaio, seemed less suspicious of the English, and while he did not rush into an alliance with them, he kept the talks open and took advantage of the opportunity to have the Portuguese friars in Bombay reinstated.

Meanwhile, Boone was assiduously making preparations for the next season's warfare. He was building more warships, and had appealed to the Directors to send all possible help from England.

Governor Boone had also launched a programme of building new kinds of fighting ships. These were his secret weapons and he was convinced that they would bring him victory.

One of the secret weapons was described as a 'floating castle or a machine that should be almost cannon-proof'. This vessel had a flat platform for a floor, and her sides were so thick that they were guaranteed to be shot-proof. She was fitted with one mast carrying a topsail and she mounted twelve guns, each of 48 pounds. She was designed to be towed into range of her target, and her powerful guns brought into action.

This machine was called 'the Phram'. Great things were expected of it.

Another secret weapon that was being designed was so secret that no one seems to have known much about it. It was mysteriously referred to as 'Captain Johnson's machine', and 'Captain Johnson's machine' it remained.

By the beginning of 1720, the peace talks between the Marathas and the Company were finally given up, and both sides were again on the warpath. In April 1720, Angrey captured a large ship of the Company, *Charlotte*. But this time, the Governor made no protest. He was biding his time. The great 'Phram' and 'Captain Johnson's machine' were not yet ready, and the battleship promised by the Directors from England had not yet arrived. Everything was expected to be ready by the middle of the year, well in time for Governor Boone's next expedition, which had been planned to take place towards the end of the monsoon. The target, this time, was a closely-guarded secret.

While his preparations were going on, Boone received an unexpected offer of assistance. On 14 May, Kanhoji Angrey captured some Moghul ships off Surat, and the Moghul Subedar of Surat, Sheikh Ismail Khan, wrote a letter to Mr. Boone, suggesting a grandiose scheme of the Moghuls, the Portuguese and the English joining hands against Kanhoji Angrey. Boone hastened to assure the Subedar that the Company on its part was doing everything in its power to 'extirpate this pyrat', but that obviously these efforts were not enough. What was needed, Boone suggested, was a concerted effort. He advised the Subedar to raise a large force of patrol boats to guard the Surat coast, and also requested him to approach the Moghul Emperor to send an order to the Siddy of Janjira to assist the English by attacking Angrey by land at the same time as the Company attacked him by sea. It seems clear from this letter that by itself the Bombay Council had been unable to persuade the Siddy to join hands with them in their venture. Sheikh Ismail Khan thereupon sent a further letter of reassurance to Boone, and offered to pass on his request to the Emperor. But this remained the extent of Moghul interest in the matter, and nothing further came of this correspondence, although Boone must have spent many an anxious moment in the hope that some sort of assistance would be forthcoming. Charles Boone had been in India for five years and should have known Moghul ways by this time.

On his part, Kanhoji had been busy pacifying the Moghuls, in order to ensure that they would not join hands with the Company. He released the ships he had taken, unconditionally, which may be the reason why the Moghuls had no further interest in his differences with the English.

When, by the end of August, the reply from Delhi was still not received, Boone realized that he would have to do without Moghul assistance. Undeterred by the lack of response from any one of the three possible allies, Boone set himself to making the final arrangements for his new attack. The objective was still kept a secret. On 5 September, 1720, he appointed a committee for the 'management' of the expedition. Boone himself was the chairman of the committee. On 10 September, 1720, the committee announced that Mr. Walter Brown, one of the senior writers in the service of the Company, was placed in overall command of the operations.

Walter Brown had already proved his worth. It was Mr. Brown who was in charge of assembling evidence against Rama Kamathi, and the way he had handled that somewhat tricky business had won the admiration of Governor Boone. Even assuming that Governor Boone had no idea that Mr. Brown had fabricated the evidence on which Rama Kamathi was convicted, the work he had done for Boone deserved to be rewarded. That he had little or no experience of warfare of any kind did not seem to worry Mr. Boone unduly although he had been let down on two occasions by commissioned-for-the occasion officers. Boone had pinned his faith in the strength of his squadron, and even more so on the new secret weapons they were guaranteed to make the expedition something of a walkover, and since Governor Boone was due to retire at the end of the year, he was striving hard to get Mr. Brown, a worthy friend of proved loyalty, into a position from which he could easily slide into the Governorship of Bombay. Such were the rewards of unquestioning loyalty.

Balaji Vishwanath, the *Peshwa*, died on 2 April, 1720. His death was a great loss to Shahu. In his place, Shahu appointed his elder son Bajirao, then only nineteen years old. The appointment was strongly opposed by many of Shahu's Ministers. But Shahu bluntly reminded them that the kingdom owed a heavy debt to Balaji Vishwanath, and it was only fitting that his son should at least be given a chance to prove his worth. In the background, Brahmendra-swami too had used his great infuence with Shahu to urge Bajirao's cause.

Balaji's death came as a great blow to Kanhoji Angrey. Since the Treaty of Colaba, Balaji had always stood by him and come to his assistance whenever help was needed. Their friendship had grown stronger with the years. Now Kanhoji was not so sure that the King's preoccupations above the ghats would permit him to send any military help to the Konkan. That he would soon need such outside help was becoming increasingly apparent. He was aware that the English were making feverish preparations for an assault against him, and that they were trying to make common cause with the Moghuls, the Siddy and the Portuguese.

The English were now in a position to invade any one of a dozen places along the coast; if they once succeeded in capturing one of his principal forts, it would be almost impossible to dislodge them. On the other hand, it was not possible for him to maintain in all his forts a permanent garrison strong enough to repel a major English attack. His hostility with his southern neighbour, the powerful Sawant of Wadi, had also began to come into the open. The Sawant had aligned himself with Sambhaji's faction and was now in the opposite camp. He, too, was seeking to get outside help against him.

His campaign of taking English ships continued relentlessly, but, as always, he was careful to take only such ships as did not bear his *dastaks*. In the month of May, his men captured two ships carrying the Company's goods, but as soon as he found out that one of the ships did bear his *dastak*, he ordered her to be released. At this time, he also took care not to interfere with Portuguese shipping. The Siddy, too, had become friendlier than in the past, and had actually assisted Kanhoji Angrey in the negotiations for the return of the Moghul ships to the Viceroy of Surat, and no doubt, appropriated a good deal of the credit from the Moghuls for the safe return of their ships.

In 1720, Angrey fortified Hirakote, which lies across the channel from Colaba, and in the fort he built a new temple for his family goddess, Kalimbika. The goddess, shifted from place to place according to the fortunes of the roving family, was at last going to be installed in a permanent place of her own. The Angreys had come to Colaba for good, and so had their family goddess. Towards the end of the monsoon, Kalimbika was installed in the Hirakote Temple with all the ceremony and ritual that Kanhoji Angrey's heart delighted in. The goddess is still in the same temple.

40

Into Battle

In the middle of 1720, the Directors of the East India Company sent from England their own impressive contribution to Boone's war effort: a magnificent sixty-gun warship called *St. George* was intended to remain permanently in Bombay and guard the harbour while the Company's own squadrons were out punishing its enemies. The new ship was received with customary fanfare, and Governor Boone gave orders for her to be cleaned and made ready for her task before the end of the monsoon. While, however, *St. George* was being taken into dry docks for cleaning after her long voyage from England, she ran on some rocks and broke her back. The great new ship became a total wreck and was never moved out of Bombay harbour, thereby, in some manner, fulfilling her destiny of being permanently stationed in Bombay waters.

All throughout the monsoon, Bombay was in a state of mounting preparation, but the objective of the expedition was still undisclosed. Only a few days before the actual sailing date was the objective made known to those taking part in it: Gheria.

Mr. Walter Brown, now designated the Commander-in-Chief of all the forces and given the rank of Admiral, set sail for the expedition against Gheria on 13 September, 1720. His squadron consisted of *London*, 40 guns; *Chandos*, 40 guns; *Victory*, 26 guns;

Revenge, 18 guns; *Defiance*, 16 guns; and *Pelham*, 16 guns; the galley, *Hunter*; the sloop, *Prince*; and the bomb-ketch, the *Terrible Bomb*. Besides these ships, there were two *gallivat*s, a fire-ship, and an unspecified number of fishing boats for use as landing boats. 'Admiral' Brown flew his flag on *London*. The troops for the landing consisted of 350 English soldiers, and '80 chosen sepoys', and it was expected that a large majority of the 2,000-odd sailors would also take part in the landing.

At Dabhol, the Bombay ships of the expedition were to be joined by three vessels, *Chandos* , *Pelham*, and 'the Phram', and 'Captain Johnson's machine'. When the Bombay ships reached Dabhol, however, it was learnt that though these three vessels would be in a position to join the expedition within the next few days, there was no prospect of 'Captain Johnson's machine' being ready to take part in it. What 'Captain Johnson's machine' was will always remain a mystery, but the news that it would not be ready is said to have 'mightily disconcerted the soldiery'.

The squadron sailed on without the Dabhol contingent and arrived opposite Gheria on 18 September and lined up for action. Brown began the proceedings by a bombardment against the fort from a distance of a mile, but all his shots fell harmlessly into the sea. The next day, nothing much was attempted except taking the bomb-ketch close to the shore with a view to bombarding the fort at point-blank range. The bomb-ketch fired only one shell and only one fire-ball, 'neither of which went halfway'. It turned out that the barrels were so faultily constructed that they would not take a sufficient charge of powder for effective range as a result of which the shells dropped within a few yards of the guns. This misfortune is said to have 'set the people a-grumbling'. At this time, Mr. Brown confidently wrote to the Governor that he could discern the masts of only three of Angrey's ships in the harbour and that he had located a suitable landing place but that he had decided to wait for *Pelham*, *Chandos* , and 'the Phram' to join him before attempting the landing.

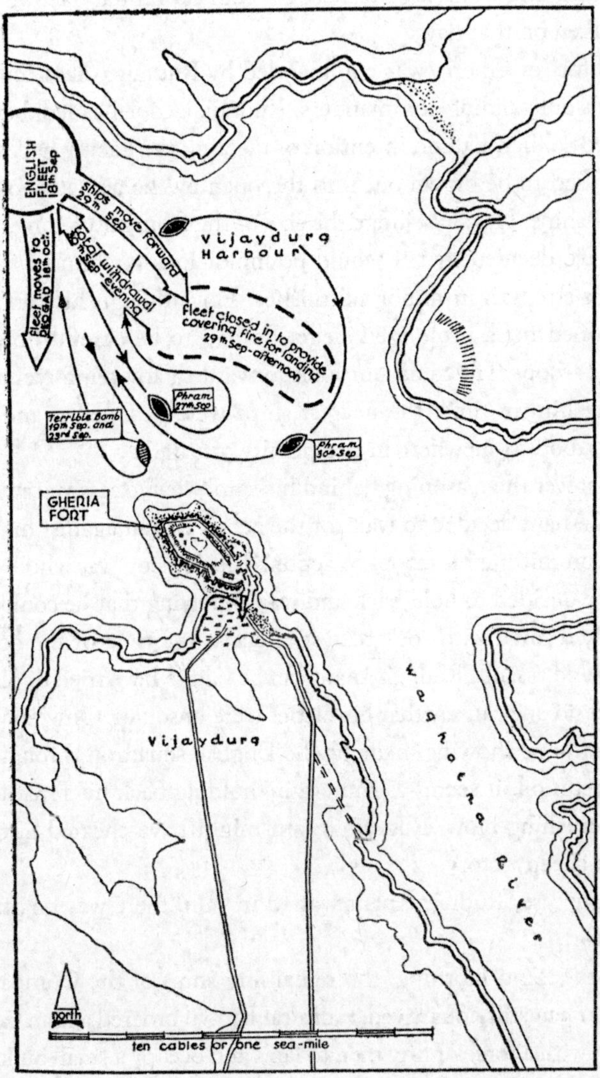

The Second Gheria Expedition

On the 21st, one of the squadron's officers, Captain Easthope, died of fever, and as a mark of respect for him no military action was undertaken on that day.

The fort of Gheria was commanded by Rudraji Anant, one of Angrey's outstanding commanders. Rudraji, a cool-headed, battle-seasoned soldier, had no intention of meeting the enemy half-way, and refused to be drawn out into the open by the activities of the English ships. He could judge the size of the Company's force, and must have decided that it would be injudicious for him to fritter away his strength in minor skirmishes. For although his fort was provisioned for a prolonged siege, he had to be careful how he used his troops. He could not look forward to any reinforcements reaching him in time: the nearest ships were in Colaba, and the nearest troops somewhere in the vicinity of Satara.

Whatever the reasoning behind his somewhat excessive caution, Rudraji Anant decided to wait for the actual assault against his fort before committing his troops to action. The decision was wholly his, and if he decided to hold back and wait, knowing that he could use his limited force with the greatest effect at the time of the actual landing and assault, Rudraji Anant can be said to have tried to play it safe, but no one can say that his tactics were unsound. Only, in view of the pathetic showing made by the English squadron throughout this expedition, it seems as though by holding back his force for a single, crushing blow, Rudraji Anant might have cheated himself out of a cheap victory.

In any case, Rudraji Anant waited in vain: there was no attack on the fort.

On the 22nd morning, the remaining ships of the Company's squadron had still not arrived. Admiral Brown ordered a man called Gordon with a force of fifty men to land and occupy a small building on top of a hill beyond the river. Gordon's force landed unopposed, but discovered that their objective, which had looked from a distance like a building, was only a natural formation of stones. This fact for some reason persuaded Gordon that it was not necessary to occupy the height. At this time, Gordon could also see that a party had been sent out from the fort to attack his position. He thereupon decided to abandon his position and get back to the ships as fast as he could. On the way back, they were caught up and attacked by the party of soldiers sent out from the fort, and suffered a number of casualties in killed and wounded. This, as it turned out, was the only contact between the two opposing forces. It seems that both the sides were far too cautious to commit their forces into a decisive battle.

On the 23rd, the bomb-ketch was again tried out, at closer range, but again none of her shells got as far as the target. On this day too, a good deal of time was taken up in punishing an unfortunate sergeant called Passmore, whom Gordon had reported to Brown for cowardice. With the fullest ritual for such offences, Passmore was sent round the whole squadron, and each ship was ordered to administer to him ten lashes of the whip in the presence of the entire ship's company.

After the ineffectual attempts to bombard the fort from an impracticable range, the Gheria expedition transformed itself into a prolonged orgy of drunkenness interspersed with rare moments of feeble military activity, and accompanied by almost unmitigated cowardice and insubordination on the part of all ranks:

> 'On board ship there was no discipline but plenty of hard drinking. In order to make the men fight well, Brown's idea was to supply them with rum: the officers kept pace with the men in their libations, and what little discipline existed, soon disappeared ... drunkenness, violence, and insubordination reigned unchecked.'

Some of his Captains warned Brown that the men's liquor should be stopped, but these were in a minority, and Brown refused to listen to them, insisting that he wanted to keep his men in the right frame of mind for the main assault, which was to be launched as soon as possible after the remaining ships of the squadron arrived.

'Let them drink as they please', Brown said.

While Brown's ships waited, the defenders used the respite well, erecting new batteries, and taking in more supplies into the fort. Boats full of armed men were constantly seen crossing the river, but no one thought of intercepting them.

'The Phram' arrived on the 27th, accompanied by the two other ships, *Chandos* and *Pelham*. Brown immediately sent off 'the Phram' to open fire against the fort. The new and still untried machine went into action amidst a hushed silence. When, however, 'the Phram' began to fire, all her shots fell into the water barely twenty yards away. It was found that her gun-slits were cut too low into her sides, and the gun-carriages were so high that no shot could be fired without depressing the barrels to the lowest level. By this time, the fort's guns too had opened fire at this strange new machine of war, and 'the Phram', considered too precious to risk being hit, was hastily withdrawn for the necessary alterations. The alterations involved the chopping down of parts of her cannon-proof walls, and all the squadron's carpenters were pressed into the task, and the whole of the next day was spent in making 'the Phram' fit for her role.

It had been originally planned that the actual assault should be carried out by a landing party composed of both soldiers and sailors, but now Brown discovered that the sailors were not willing to take part in the landing. Brown announced the by-now-established reward of Rs. 40 per head for volunteers. As a result, he was able to get 59 men from *Chandos* to agree to take part in the landing. All the other ships between them produced another 180 volunteers. The reason for the large number of volunteers from *Chandos* may be that *Chandos* had just joined the squadron, and her men could not have been affected by the general state of morale of the rest of the squadron.

But both the regular soldiers and the volunteers were convinced that duty on 'the Phram' was far more risky than taking part in the assault, and not a single man in the squadron was willing, 'upon any consideration whatsoever', to go on board her. So 'the Phram' had to carry on with whatever men had been with her when she was brought from Dabhol, although these men were presumably only a temporary crew, pressed into service for taking 'the Phram' up to Gheria.

The 29th was the day of the 'grand assault'. Two landing parties, one of 340 soldiers under Major Stanton, and the other of 239 'volunteer' sailors under Captain Woodward, were kept ready to make the assault. Soon after midday, the entire flotilla closed in to provide covering fire for the landing, while 'the Phram', now pronounced fit for action, was given the task of shelling the fort walls. The flagship *London* remained well out at sea in order to direct the operations.

An officer called Lieutenant Wise was detailed to be the commander of 'the Phram'. Either Lieutenant Wise had no idea of gunnery, or 'the Phram' was a shockingly ill-designed machine, but the majority of her shells fell into the inner harbour, all around the Company's own squadron now lined up for the final phase of the landing. It was just a matter of luck that 'the Phram's fire did not sink one of the Company's own ships. Firing from the guns of the entire squadron continued throughout the day, but 'the Marathas were quite ready' and returned the fire with equal vigour. One of the fort's shells landed right inside 'the Phram' and wounded five men.

At what stage of these proceedings the landing party was to make its assault is not known, but no landing was made on the 29th, and presumably the men already crammed into the landing boats were taken back into the ships.

The Commander-in-Chief, Brown, who had been watching the battle from his flagship, now thought fit to order 'the Phram' to sneak closer to the fort under cover of the night, and to open fire at the walls the next morning at point-blank range. He sent out the necessary orders to the commander of 'the Phram', and in order to enliven the flagging spirit of her men in the only manner he knew how to, also sent 'six dozen each of wine and arrack for the use of 'the Phram's' company. The landing was now put off for the next day.

According to Brown's orders, 'the Phram' went close up to the fort's wall under cover of the night. But when the time came for her to go into action the next morning, Lieutenant Wise was allegedly too drunk to take any part in the proceedings. The sailors, some of whom were, surprisingly enough, still sober, now took it upon themselves to fire the guns, each in his own way, to the great confusion and alarm of the expedition's officers. By now, the guns of the fort of Gheria were nicely bracketing 'the Phram' with *their* fire, and two of their shots fell inside 'the Phram' and killed fifteen men and wounded some thirty others. To add to these casualties, one of 'the Phram's' guns burst, and another, whether through carelessness or bad workmanship it will never be known, fired a shot on the opposite side, and into a boat crammed full of Negro soldiers waiting to make the landing. 'The poor wretches were terribly scorched and injured', says the logbook of *London*, which, according to the report sent by Brown to Governor Boone, meant that half the men were killed outright, and the other half suffered severe burns.

The sustained fire maintained by the ships of the Company's navy in preparation for the assault upon Gheria is said to have destroyed some of Angrey's ships anchored in the inner harbour. In all, Brown claimed, one large ship of 500 tons, one of 200 tons, and ten small vessels were destroyed. This claim, even if it is wholly true, is the sumtotal of the results achieved by Brown's expedition against Gheria. 'Burnt to ground two large ships and seven smaller ones without any loss', Brown wrote to the Governor, reporting progress. It is highly unlikely that any such destruction was caused.

'By nightfall, all hands thought they had done enough ...', and in spite of Brown's explicit orders to the contrary, ' ... took advantage of a land breeze to come out.'

This safe withdrawal of the squadron's ships seems to have given an excuse for yet another bout of unrestricted drinking, and in the middle of the night, Captain Woodward of *Revenge* appeared before Brown in panic and reported that his ship had run on the rocks close to the fort walls, and that she and her crew must be regarded as a total loss. This story, as it happened, was wholly imaginary. Half an hour later, *Revenge* was seen coming out of the inner harbour with the other ships of the squadron. The only conclusion that Brown could reach was that Captain Woodward was frightened out of his senses, so 'he was put into irons for cowardice'. That Captain Woodward may have been suffering from a perfectly well-merited attack of *delirium tremens* does not seem to have occurred to anyone on Brown's staff.

The next few days were spent in resting and in repairing the damage suffered by the ships. 'I have continuous disturbances in the ship dayly by officers' excessive drinking, and noe manner of command carryd', records Captain Upton of the flagship *London*. A few days later, he also notes how two officers, presumed to be Major Stanton and Mr. Dage, 'fought with their fists in the roundhouse', in the presence of the Commander-in-Chief, who, however, chose to take no notice of the incident.

The stocks of arrack were fast running out. Brown had sent off a special ship to Goa to bring fresh supplies, but she was not expected for another week. At this critical time, when Walter Brown was faced with the hard choice of making another attempt to storm Gheria or to wind up his expedition, an excellent excuse for abandoning the attack on Gheria without loss of face presented itself. The Sawant of Wadi had sent a special messenger to Brown offering to help the English in their war against Angrey, on condition that the English should first help him by attacking Angrey's fort Deogad, some fifteen miles further south. On the strength of this offer, Brown sent off a glowing letter to Governor Boone, pointing out the advantages of an alliance with the Sawant, and telling him that the 'Sawant was drawing out an army of 5,000 foot soldiers and 2,000 horse'. The statement regarding the size of the Sawant's force, was, of course, a transparent exaggeration. But it served Brown's purpose well. He pointed out to Boone that this offer of assistance from the Sawant was too good to turn down, and that accordingly, he had decided, in anticipation of Boone's agreement, to proceed to Deogad with all haste. On 7 October, Walter Brown detached a part of his flotilla, and sent it off to Deogad.

It was not until 16 October that 'fresh stocks of arrack, water and provisions were received from Goa', and on the strength of this, Brown seems to have mooted a proposal for another attack on Gheria. As soon, however, as the officers discovered what the Commander-in-Chief and his staff had been planning to do, they all came on board *London*, and told Brown, 'in no measured terms' that they would have nothing to do with such a proposal. One of the officers told Brown that he was mad, and that he did not know what he was doing. After hanging on around Gheria for yet another day, Brown at last decided to abandon the idea of taking Gheria and transferred his headquarters to the environs of Deogad.

The ships sent off to Deogad earlier had been lying idly in front of the fort. When Brown reached Deogad on 18 October, 1720, he discovered that there was absolutely no sign of any activity on the part of the Raja of Sawant-Wadi. Brown, however, salvaged his conscience to some extent by sending off a letter to Governor Boone with the agreeable news that 'it was confidently reported that Kempsaunt (the Sawant of Wadi), had invaded Angria's country and destroyed it as far as Rajapore which 'tis said that he has burnt and that four of Angria's grabs were sunk'.

Nothing of this happened to be true.

The Sawant of Wadi, more astute than Brown, got himself a free bombardment: for against the fort of Deogad too, 'the Phram' and the bomb-ketch and the other ships were brought into furious action. However, as in Gheria, the majority of the shells fell harmlessly into the sea, and after one or two misfires and the usual incidence of burst gun-barrels, as a result of which, 'some additional loss was suffered', the shelling was discontinued.

Brown had confidently written to the Governor that he would assault Deogad, and that the fort was not very strong. If only to make good his promises to the Governor, he suggested a landing party to storm the fort. But Brown's suggestion was met with unified opposition from all his officers. They refused to countenance the idea of yet another attempt at landing.

On 21 October, the squadron gave up the action against Deogad and set sail for Bombay. The Sawant's forces had still not showed up. In any case, even if the Sawant had got himself a free bombardment, he had not gained much by it.

From here onwards, the story of bungling and drunkenness, of incompetent officers and undisciplined men, ceases to be a military operation—it deteriorates into almost unbelievable farce.

Early the next morning, just as the squadron was passing the fort of Gheria on its journey back to Bombay, they saw four ships. Two of the ships were identified as pirate ships, and the two others were obviously the prizes taken by the pirates.

What Walter Brown thought the pirates hoped to gain by attacking warships, if indeed they were so foolhardy as to dare take on warships, is not known, but the news that his flotilla had run into two pirate ships is said to have 'struck him with terror'. He ordered his ships to make for the waters of the fort of Gheria in the hope that the pirates would not molest his ships so close to the Angrey stronghold. What the inmates of the fort thought of the strange behaviour of the Company's flotilla which, a few days earlier, had been attacking them, now huddling harmlessly close to their walls, is not known either. But Mr. Brown was not going to linger near Gheria too long. In the middle of the night, he gave orders for his ships to set sail for Bombay, making a detour so as to avoid all chance of running into the pirate ships again.

The pirate ships were *Cassandra* and *Victory* (not to be mixed up with the frigate *Victory* of Brown's squadron) and their leader was a man called England. A few weeks earlier, he had captured *Cassandra* with £75,000 on board in hard cash, and he had now appropriated *Cassandra* for his own use. On his way to the Indian coast, he had managed to make prizes of two more ships which he sailed in his squadron, and now he was more or less idling along the west coast of India, hoping to pick up some lone straggler. Glutted with booty, England certainly had no wish to come into conflict with an armed squadron. On his part, he may have mistaken the squadron as belonging to Angrey, particularly since the ships had retired towards Gheria, and he was now fast making for the high seas, hoping to get out of the squadron's path. His business was to loot merchant ships, not to take on fighting ships.

It was the strangest of coincidences, yet it was almost inevitable. The two squadrons, bent on running away from each other, almost ran into each other in the early morning dark of the 23rd morning.

To make the chain of coincidence even more fantastic, the pirate ship *Victory* began the proceedings by firing off a jittery shot across the bows of the frigate *Victory*. Thereupon the flagship *London* hailed the ship which had fired the shot and received the reply that she was the *Victory*. Relieved that she was none other than *Victory* (their own frigate) and thinking that the shot must have been fired by mistake, *London* gave an answering hail, announcing her name, and 'was replied to with a broadside'. This gave rise to an indiscriminate exchange of gunfire amongst all the ships that had now got together, but since both sides still wanted nothing better than to get away from each other, the firing soon died out. The pirates, convinced that the game was now up, hastily abandoned their prizes by chopping down their sails and throwing them overboard. They had good reason to be scared. They could see that the Company's squadron was crammed with sailors and soldiers, numbering over 3,000: their own total strength was only about 300.

But after his initial fit of panicking, the pirate chief, England was the first to recover. The anxiety of the English ships to stop firing and get away from him, encouraged England to turn back and run through the squadron with his ship *Cassandra* wildly firing off all her guns. This made Brown's squadron 'scatter in all directions like a flock of sheep when a strange dog runs through it'. At this renewed offensive on the part of his 'enemy', Captain Upton of *London* warned Brown that it would be a folly to return the pirate's fire. He argued that his ship had been allotted to the Company's squadron to assist in the attack against Gheria, and she was certainly not expected by the Directors to get involved with pirates. This reasoning seems to have been close to Brown's own views in the matter, and he instantly gave orders to put on all sail with a view to flee from the pirates. In order to leave no doubt in the minds of the pirates that he had no wish to offer opposition, Brown also gave orders for the flags to be hauled down, and this was duly accomplished amidst a howl of protests from some of the less terrified professional sailors among the crew. The man who went up the masthead to haul down the flag of *London* was so furious that he 'swore he would send flagstaff and all down with it'. Accordingly, when he went up, he hacked down the flagstaff and pushed it overboard, which, 'made the pyrats laugh in their sleeve'.

But although Brown had given orders to make all possible speed, the squadron's pace was hampered by *Chandos* since she had the ungainly 'Phram' in tow. Brown made a quick decision and decided to sacrifice excess weight for the sake of speed. And rather than endangering his whole squadron for the sake of 'the Phram', he sent off a *gallivat* to *Chandos* with orders to set fire to 'the Phram' and to abandon it.

> 'And thus that useless machine, from which so much had been expected and that had cost so much money and labour, came to an end.'

The pirate chief, whose combined fighting strength could not be equal to that of any one of Brown's major ships, now had the full measure of his opponents. He made up his mind that the best way of getting out of this predicament was to take the offensive. So he set himself to chase and harry the fighting ships, taking advantage of his better speed. Brown and his captains too devised a tactical manoeuvre to assist in their escape. Whenever the pirate ships came too close behind him, Brown detailed one of his ships to fall behind and fire into the pursuing ships in order to give the main part of his squadron a chance to make a getaway. 'In this ignominious fashion, the greater part of the fleet was shuffled along for two days by the pirates ... till at last they found refuge in Goa.'

Almost characteristically, the first thing that Brown's soldiers did as soon as they embarked in Goa was to rush into town and break open the Customs liquor warehouse. England and his pirates broke off and went further south, and in the port of Honnawar, they found what they had been looking for: a plump merchant ship fully loaded with merchandise. She was *Elizabeth*, an English ship, just getting ready to sail for home.

Governor Boone had by now come to know some of the doings of his squadron, and sent off a stern order to his 'Admiral' to go after the pirates. Reluctantly, Brown gathered his ships together and crawled out of the safety of Goa. For the next day or two, he made as if he was going after the pirates. But at this time, he received news that the pirates had taken the ship *Elizabeth*. Upon hearing this, Brown hastily altered course, and made for Bombay with all possible speed. Orders or no orders, Walter Brown had no desire for another encounter with England and his men.

The record of the Bombay Council has the following entry for 13 November, 1720:

> 'Imported the *London*, *Chandos*, *Victory*, *Revenge*, *Defiance*, *Hunter* ... from the Expedition against Gheria but last from Goa.'

It will be seen that 'the Phram' and *Pelham* had failed to return, and so had many of the *gallivat*s. Two hundred men had died, and twice that number were wounded. The only actual contact with Angrey's men had been the encounter between Gordon's party, which had been sent up to occupy a height on the other side of the river, and some men sent out by Rudraji Anant to counter-attack the party.

41

Enter the Navy

In a desperate endeavour to keep up appearances, the Government of Bombay celebrated the achievements of Walter Brown's expedition as a 'victory', and to pay for it, Governor Boone imposed a fresh tax of one rupee per ton on all goods brought into Bombay or Surat.

But Boone's despatches to the Directors in England could not have attempted to transform Brown's failure into a victory. The Court of Directors glumly noted the fact that the Council at Bombay had not had the desired success against Angrey as the 'strength of our Grabs and the courage of the people on board', warranted. They ascribed this to the fact that Angrey's ships were faster and more manoevrable, and promptly set themselves to remedy the situation by ordering the building of three fast, light ships, each of about 160 tons, for service under the Bombay Council.

The Company's Directors were solidly behind their Governor. They made repeated appeals to the English Government for assistance in their military operation in India, and succeeded in obtaining a promise from the Government that a squadron of the English Navy would be sent out to assist the East India Company.

The news from England rekindled the hopes of Governor Charles Boone. He had nearly finished his term of office as Governor, and his successor was expected to reach Bombay any day. But Boone had no wish to leave Bombay with his grand ambition still unfulfilled, an ambition which, in its intensity, could not have been less over-riding than Aurangzeb's longing to crush the Marathas. The fact that his time in India was running out drove Boone to frenzied efforts to secure Portuguese co-operation. Whatever sacrifice of principle may be involved in making an alliance with the Portuguese, it had to be made for the sake of putting down Kanhoji Angrey, before he gave up office as Governor.

Charles Boone sent a man called Robert Cowan to Goa to win over the Portuguese at any cost. He promised Robert Cowan a seat in the Governor's Council if he succeeded in his mission,

The time was ripe. Conde de Ericera, the Viceroy who had always distrusted the Company's intentions and derided their tighting abilities, had retired and gone back to Portugal.[17] His successor, Don Francisco Jose de Sampaio, seemed an easygoing man without preconceived prejudices, and Boone hoped that he might be persuaded to join hands with him on the strength of what he now had to offer in return.

Robert Cowan certainly did not have an easy task. Before leaving India, Conde de Ericera had warned his successor not to make an alliance with the East India Company. But Cowan, a pushing, unscrupulous, smooth-tongued man, stayed in Goa for five months,

---

17 On his return back to Portugal, Conde de Ericera's ship, *Nostra Senhora de Cabo* was captured by pirates sailing the same two ships, *Victory* and *Cassandra*, which had harried Walter Brown's squadron on its way back from the Gheria expedition. By this time, the chief pirate, England, had been ousted and his place taken by a man called La Buze Ericera's ship was perhaps the richest prize ever to fall to a pirate ship, for the Portuguese Viceroy was taking back with him a fabulous collection of jewels for the Portuguese Royal house, to say nothing of his own private fortune made as a result of three years of intensive private trading. The jewels alone were estimated to be worth a million pounds and the cash was five hundred thousand crowns. The pirates demanded another twenty thousand crowns from Conde de Ericera as ransom; but later on, in a fit of generosity, La Buze waived the ransom and released the Count.

wearing down the Viceroy's resistance with his persuasiveness, holding out the certainty of an easy victory, painting a brilliant picture of a Konkan divided between the Portuguese and the English, rekindling and fanning the Portuguese lust for conquest which had been lying dormant for over a hundred years.

Perhaps what finally persuaded Don Francisco Jose de Sampaio, even more than the imminent arrival of a powerful squadron of the Royal Navy, was the prospect of ruling half of the Konkan. The bearskin had been divided before the bear was killed.

The treaty between the East India Company and the Portuguese was signed on 20 August, 1721. Bitter enemies of many generations had agreed to pool their resources and share the spoils. The treaty consisted of fourteen clauses, but its two main clauses were: firstly, that the spoils of war and the territory conquered would be divided equally, Gheria going to the Company and Colaba to the Portuguese; and secondly, that neither side was to make a separate peace but that all proposals for peace were to be either jointly considered or not at all.

On his triumphant return to Bombay, Robert Cowan had two rewards waiting for him: one was the promised seat in the Governor's Council; the other was the rank of a General in command of all the land forces of the Company in the proposed campaign against Kanhoji Angrey.[18] Governor Boone was nothing if not lavish in the manner of his recognition of special services rendered to the Bombay Council.

August 1721 was an important month in the life of Bombay. The treaty with the Portuguese was concluded on the 20th. On the

---

18 Mr Robert Cowan was moving fast. Seven years later, as the Honourable Robert Cowan, he was appointed the Governor of Bombay. Alas, Mr Cowan seems to have cut one corner too sharply, for in 1734, on the eve of his retirement and an almost certain knighthood, he is said to have been 'discovered' and was dismissed from the service of the Company.

27th arrived the eagerly-awaited squadron of the British Navy. Also in August came Mr. William Phipps, sent from England to take Mr. Boone's place as Governor. But in all the excitement, no one seems to have had much time for the new Governor. In any case, Mr. Charles Boone had no intention of vacating his office so close to the hour of victory.

The whole of Bombay turned out to welcome the Royal Navy, The squadron consisted of four fine ships of war such as Bombay had rarely seen before: *Lion*, 50 guns; *Exeter*, 50 guns; *Salisbury*, 40 guns; and *Shoreham*, 20 guns. Under the orders of the Court of Directors, the Company's ship *Grantham* was also placed at the disposal of the squadron as its store-ship.

The squadron was commanded by Commodore Thomas Matthews.

Commodore Matthews has already made his appearance in this history without, however, a proper introduction. Now he comes in his rightful place, imperiously demanding all the fanfare which he considered himself entitled to. He refused to go ashore at Bombay unless the city fired a salute in his honour. Not to be outdone in rank-consciousness, Governor Boone sent a tart message to the Commodore that it was up to him to fire the first salutes since as the Company's Governor, he outranked a Commodore.

But the Commodore refused to leave his ship. He immediately assumed control of all the shipping in and near the harbour and issued orders to 'all the native vessels in the harbour belonging to the Bombay traders, to strike the English colours that they had been in the habit of displaying'.

The Commodore's orders must have shocked the Governor and his Council; for although the order was perfectly in keeping with maritime practice all over the world, the East India Company's Council at Bombay had gone to war mainly in support of the opposite view.

It will be recalled that the chief cause of the Company's war with Angrey was the difference of opinion between Governor Boone and Kanhoji Angrey on the question of Indian ships being permitted to fly English colours. Now the British Navy itself had ordered that ships belonging to Indian owners could not fly the English flag, and, as a corrollary, could not claim the privileges enjoyed by the Company's own ships.

In effect, Commodore Matthews had backed up Kanhoji Angrey's stand and had denounced Boone for endeavouring to pass off Indian ships as belonging to the Company.

While all this was going on, an order was received from the Court of Directors giving, a clear ruling that in the matter of salutes, the Commodore outranked the Governor.

The Royal Navy had won the first round, even without leaving, its ships. From then on, it reigned supreme in Bombay, its officers going about the town in an overbearing manner, throwing duelling challenges at the Company's officials at the slightest provocation.

What rankled in the minds of Governor Boone and his Council even more than the lost battle of the gun-salutes, however, was the Commodore's order forbidding Indian ships from flying the English flag.

Since this controversy went to the whole root of the dispute between Angrey and the Company, the enforcement of Commodore Matthews's order should have helped to bring about an immediate settlement. But neither Boone nor the Commodore were in a mood to think of peace. Boone and his councillors were far too confident of the impressive alignment of military power on their side, too sure of victory to think of climbing down at this stage: and Commodore Thomas Matthews, while no one could find fault with his unambiguous stand on matters of maritime practice, did not possess the necessary breadth of vision to see that the very orders he had seen fit to enforce were capable of ending the war. In any case, he was not going to be baulked of the easy war which he had been called all the way from England to assist in, and all the glory of a quick victory.

The arrival of a powerful squadron of English warships and the new alliance between the Portuguese and the English at Bombay, could not long remain a secret, nor did anyone make any special efforts to keep these matters a secret. The Portuguese, if anything, made a display of their warlike intentions and began a vigorous drive to recruit Pathan soldiers from amongst the deserters from the Moghul Army.

At the first inkling of the new alliance, Kanhoji Angrey began to make efforts to break it. Always anxious to keep his adversaries divided, he wrote to the Portuguese Viceroy pointedly drawing his attention to the series of defeats suffered by the English, and offering to enter into an alliance with them himself. The Portuguese Viceroy, however, was too sure of success this time to be dissuaded from his course of action. He curtly rejected Angrey's offers, one of the grounds for the rejection being that Angrey could not be sincere about his offers, since, as the Viceroy put it 'he was making preparations for defence'.

Again, Angrey had no idea where the blow would fall. Once the battle was joined, all that he had to do was to divert all his available resources to the scene, hoping that until he was able to send help, his commanders would be able to hold out. On the other hand, the impressive force assembled by his enemies must have made him wonder whether his forts would be able to hold out for long in the face of a determined assault.

He began to enlist fresh troops and sent off a letter to Shahu at Satara advising him of the developments in the Konkan and calling upon him for help. It is almost certain that he also sent a special messenger to Brahmendra-swami, invoking his blessings, and, at a less spiritual level, imploring him to use his influence with the King and his new *Peshwa* to send him the required military help.

For a while, Kanhoji Angrey must have wondered whether the King would be in a position to send him any substantial help. He was aware that the majority of Shahu's forces were engaged in a campaign against the Nizam under the personal command of Bajirao, the new *Peshwa*. How could Bajirao, with the best will in the world, divert a sizable force to any given spot in the Konkan at short notice?

At the same time, Angrey was confident that Brahmendra-swami would not fail him. The Swami had now become a major influence in Maratha politics: Shahu venerated him and young Bajirao, too, owed a debt of gratitude to him since it is almost certain that Bajirao would never have been made the *Peshwa* if Brahmendra-swami had not exerted his influence with Shahu.

But where would the blow fall? The finding out of the objective of the attack was Angrey's chief problem: unless he knew it, all the help he would receive from the King may not have been of much use.

Angrey solved the problem in his own, direct way. He organized a network of spies in Bombay as well as in Chaul to find out all he could about the military activities of his enemies; and to bring back the information to him without loss of time, he established a squadron of mounted scouts.

Angrey's agents served him well. He must have soon learnt about the feverish preparations that were going on in Bombay and Chaul. Well in advance of the actual date of the attack, and in any case as soon as the English force joined the Portuguese force at Chaul, Kanhoji Angrey must have discovered that what the Anglo-Portuguese force was up to, was a land operation against Colaba.

Once the objective was known, he could concentrate on its defence. By this time, he had received reassuring news from Satara. Shahu had promised to send out an army larger than he had ever hoped for: 25,000 troops. Within a few days, the advance guard of the King's force began to arrive.

The *Peshwa*, Bajirao, too, had sent word that he was personally coming to Kanhoji Angrey's help and would assume the overall command of the King's reinforcements. His Deputy Commander, Pilaji Jadhav, had already reached Colaba with Shahu's advance guard. The young *Peshwa* had already begun to make a name for himself both as a brilliant military commander and a polished diplomat, and seems to have been anxious to show his merit before so redoubtable a contemporary of his father as Kanhoji Angrey.

By the time the monsoon came to an end, Governor Boone and Commodore Matthews had patched up their initial differences and were settling down to making preparations for the campaign. A special camp was set up in Bombay for training the entire English force, and 'drilling was the the order of the day'. In addition to Robert Cowan, who had been made a General, various commissions as colonels, majors and captains were given to the officials of the Company, and even those from among the newly-arrived naval squadron who had agreed to take part in the land operations were given suitably exalted military ranks: for instance, Lieutenant Braithwaite (of the Navy) went into the attack as Lieutenent-Colonel Braithwaite.

Unlike the earlier expeditions of the Company, the Anglo-Portuguese effort was to be an overland attack, supported by the combined fleets of the Portuguese and the English from the sea. The entire land force was to be assembled at Chaul, and from there, march together to Colaba. It will be seen that Governor Boone had tried to avoid the difficulties encountered in earlier expeditions. For instance, there was now going to be no calling for volunteers: the men from the navy who were to take part in the assault were already earmarked. Similarly, there would be no question now of having to make a 'landing'. The attacking troops would be already on land. And lastly, the attacking force would not be merely a handful of marines and grenadiers as in the past, but they would be in gratifyingly large numbers; thousands instead of hundreds.

After nearly three months of hard training, the Company's force was pronounced fit for action. 'On 30th October, a seven days' fast was ordered to secure divine blessings on the undertaking, and the Chaplain was directed to preach an appropriate sermon.'

The Company's force left Bombay on 29 November, and the next afternoon, was anchored off Chaul. After this date, Kanhoji Angrey could have had no doubt in his mind that the objective would be Colaba. But he continued to keep the enemy's movements under observation, and had even instructed his scouts, that if they got the chance, they should try and kill the senior enemy commanders.

According to the terms of the treaty between the Company and the Portuguese, it had been agreed that the combined force should consist of not less than 5,000 land troops, supported by cavalry and artillery on land, and ten first-line ships accompanied by their *gallivats* providing covering fire from the sea. As it turned out, both the Portuguese and the English had taken their responsibilities so earnestly that they provided more troops than they had undertaken. As against the 2,000 men promised by Boone, the Company's land force consisted of some 2,500 men, made up as follows:

> One battalion of European and African troops: strength 655.
>
> A troop of European cavalry: strength 40.
>
> Two battalions of Sepoys; each of 750 men: strength 1,500.
>
> Volunteer seamen from the Naval Squadron: strength 200.

Artillery: two 24-pounder guns, two 18-pounder guns, four 9-pounder guns; six small field guns; two mortars; eight grenade launchers.

The entire force was commanded by 'General' Robert Cowan.

In Chaul, the Portuguese too had exceeded their promised strength, and had assembled nearly 4,000 troops as against the 3,000 they had promised. The Portuguese force was composed as follows:

One battalion of European troops: strength 1,000.

Volunteer soldiers: strength 350.

European cavalry: strength 160.

Sepoys with Portuguese officers, organized in three or four battalions: strength 2,400.

Artillery: six 24-pounder guns; six 18-pounder guns; ten field guns and eight mortars.

The Portuguese force was commanded by the Portuguese General of the North, Don Antonio de Castro e Mello, but the Viceroy Francisco Jose de Sampaio had also come in person to watch the action.

The combined force therefore consisted of more than 6,000 infantry and 200 cavalry, with eight 24-pounder guns and eight 18-pounder guns besides a number of smaller guns. In addition, the combined artillery of ten major ships, five English and five Portuguese, with nearly 300 heavy guns between them, was to provide supporting fire during the attack.

It was a magnificent concentration of troops. 'Such a force', says Bidulph, 'was sufficient ... to have destroyed all Angria's strongholds along the coast.'

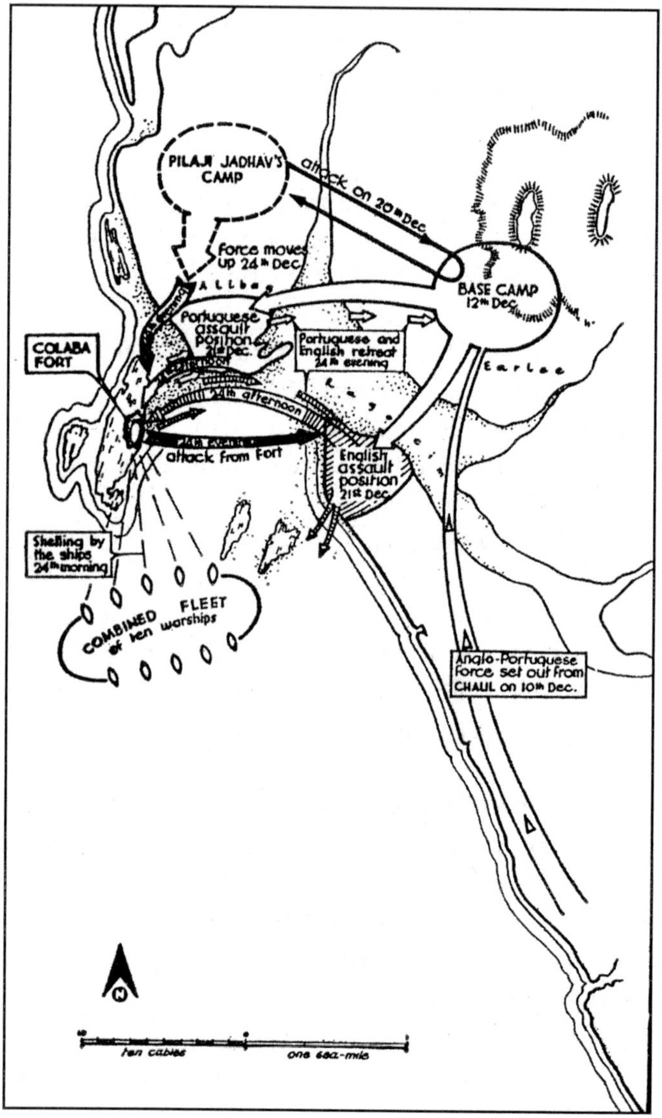
PILAJI JADHAV'S CAMP
attack on 20th Dec
Force moves up 24th Dec
Alibag
BASE CAMP 12th Dec
Portuguese assault position 21st Dec.
Portuguese and English retreat 24th evening
COLABA FORT
24th afternoon
attack from Fort
English assault position 21st Dec
Earlee
Shelling by the ships 24th morning
COMBINED FLEET of ten warships
Anglo-Portuguese force set out from CHAUL on 10th Dec.
ten cables
one sea-mile

42

… And the Guns Were Silent

Chaul, some thirty miles south of Bombay, had been Portuguese for over two hundred years. In those days, by the side of the coast battery was a bronze lion bearing the inscription, 'None passes but fights', and higher up, atop the cliff which is named the Tower of Resistance and where the Portuguese flag flew without interruption for close on three centuries, a bronze eagle threw out the same challenge: 'None passes me but flies.' Chaul, steeped in Portuguese history, was chosen for another historic role: the springboard for the Anglo-Portuguese conquest of the Konkan.

The Portuguese General of the North, Don Antonio de Castro e Mello, had already assembled his forces in Chaul, and the Viceroy had come from Goa to supervise the process of adding a great new slice to his domain.

The ill-matched allies met in Chaul, and for the first time in history, tried to live side by side. Neither side enjoyed the experience. The Portuguese considered themselves the proud inheritors of the legacy of the great conquerors and explorers of the world and clung defiantly to the dimming memory of their past glory in the East: they regarded themselves as a cut above other Europeans, and particularly the English in India whom they had always looked down upon as being clerks and merchants with uncouth habits and coarse manners. The English, on their part, had always looked upon the Portuguese with unconcealed disdain. The enforced contact as equal partners did not help to improve relations, and in particular, both the Portuguese Viceroy and the General of the North took an intense dislike to the ill-mannered and overbearing Matthews. As it happened, Commodore Matthews had few friends even among his own countrymen.

There were many difficulties inevitable in a combined military operation which a little forethought on the part of either side might have avoided. But whenever anything went wrong, each side was inclined to blame the other.

Colaba lies to the north of Chaul. The Anglo-Portuguese column set out from Chaul on 10 December, and two days later crossed the Ragocim river. The heavier guns and the other heavy equipment could not be taken across the river since neither partner had erected a bridge across it and both insisted that it was the business of the other to build a bridge. A bridge was hastily built, and a base camp was established on the heights across the river, within striking distance of Colaba. Meanwhile, the combined armada of ten warships had reached Colaba and lay menacingly close by Commodore Thomas Matthews, who considered himself to be in overall command of the operation, shuttled busily between his flagship and the base camp. It seems that Cowan, who had absolutely no idea of warfare, was glad to step aside for a professional military man like Matthews.

While on the march all the way from Chaul, the Anglo-Portuguese column had been kept under surveillance by Angrey's scouts. On one occasion, when a party consisting of the Portuguese Viceroy, the General of the North, General Cowan and Commodore Matthews, were doing a reconnaisance, one of Angrey's horsemen had come behind a cactus hedge and hurled a spear at Matthews. The spear glanced off Matthews' thigh and wounded him slightly. Matthews, a man of violent temper, cursed and flew into a rage and fired off his pistol in the air and made as if to chase his assailant, but never caught a glimpse of him again.

Every move of the enemy was closely watched. There can be no doubt that on the 12th evening itself, news reached Kanhoji Angrey that the opposing force was on the move and was camped on the heights north of the Ragocim crossing. He could read the enemy's plan like a book now and knew that their objective was Colaba; and he could not have failed to be impressed by their strength, in particular, their naval strength, for the Anglo-Portuguese flotilla was already anchored within sight of Colaba.

The greater part of the Maratha reinforcements promised by Shahu was still on the way. Only the advance guard had arrived, a force 2,500 strong, under Pilaji Jadhav, composed of 1,000 infantry and 1,500 cavalry and was now camped near Alibag. Although an enormous force was said to be due to arrive any day, this was the number Angrey could bank upon.

Colaba was ready to meet the enemy. Kanhoji Angrey had had ample notice, and had made his preparations well in advance. He had the fort stocked with ammunition, food and water. He had 1,000 infantry and 700 cavalry in the fort itself and he had no wish to clutter up the fort with more troops. This force, with the fort's powerful artillery, he seems to have decided, was sufficient for a prolonged defence.

At the same time, no one could have known better than Kanhoji Angrey that to be effective, his defence would have to be offensive; that it was just as important to attack the enemy column as it was to defend Colaba, and he had earmarked the Maratha force under Pilaji Jadhav for this purpose. It was Kanhoji's plan to use this force, if possible, to defeat the Anglo-Portuguese column while still on the march, or, after the attack against the fort was launched, to use it for a counter-attack against the enemy's flanks.

For the next ten days, the Anglo-Portuguese force was busy consolidating at the base camp near Earlee, north of the Ragocim River, gathering itself for the last lap of the offensive, assembling its guns and equipment and supplies and making final plans. It was here that Kanhoji Angrey struck his first blow. On 20 December, Pilaji Jadhav's force launched an attack at the combined base camp, and although the Marathas succeeded in penetrating the outer defences of the camp, the main body of Jadhav's column was caught out in the open by the Portuguese artillery. In the face of a heavy concentration of gunfire at point-blank range, the Maratha column was forced to retire.

On the 21st, the two allies decided to separate their forces. The Portuguese force went along the river which separates Colaba from the mainland on the north, and formed another camp to the north-east of Colaba, just outside the range of the fort's guns. Here again, a column of Angrey's cavalry attacked the Portuguese position, but the Portuguese held their ground and the attack was repelled with ease. From this advance base, the Portuguese pushed forward a column of 1,500 troops as the spearhead of their attack. This column crossed over from the mainland to Colaba on the 23rd evening, and made a camp on the beach, out in the open, ready for the final dash into the fort.

The English force moved to a point on the mainland southeast of the fort, and camped just beyond the shallow channel that separates Colaba from the mainland on the east. From here, an assault column of 1,000 troops under Colonel Braithwaite was sent across on the 24th to launch the attack against the fort.

The fort at Colaba is built on an island; but in those days, at low tide you could walk right into the island from the eastern side. It would seem that the correct place for the first line of defence would be this neck of land, submerged at high tide, so as to take advantage of a natural obstacle. But Angrey seems to have made absolutely no attempt to block the now separated forces of the English and the Portuguese from crossing this strip of land and reaching the environs of the fort itself. It is of course possible that things were vastly different two hundred and twenty years ago, and that the strip of land exposed by the tide may have presented no natural obstacle or may have been too wide to lend itself to an adequate defensive position. The fact remains that by the morning of 'D day',

24 December, both the English and the Portuguese columns had succeeded in getting into position at the foot of the Colaba fort.

To Kanhoji Angrey, distressed by the numerical superiority of the enemy, and the fact that he had already come off the loser in two preliminary skirmishes, the enemy's decision to divide their forces must have come as something of a relief. It is possible that he was even confused by this sacrifice of an obvious advantage. Unless they had overwhelming superiority in fire-power, an assaulting force against a fortified position had to be at least twice as strong, and Kanhoji Angrey could see for himself that the total of the advance groups of the enemy now camped within sight of the fort could not be more than his own forces on the island.

The Anglo-Portuguese plan seems to have been that the English force should launch the attack against the fort and that the Portuguese force should be held in reserve to deal with Pilaji Jadhav's column now camped at the north end of the island, and to prevent it from launching an attack against the English flank. It was as good a plan as any other, but it must be said that the attackers did not take the fullest advantage of their resources: their numbers were now divided, so that the fort could not be stormed with the necessary numerical superiority; the element of surprise had been totally sacrificed; and their over-riding superiority in fire-power was not used with the best effect.

Commodore Matthews and his ships cannot be said to have pulled their weight in the operation. The preliminary bombardment from the squadron's powerful guns was not sufficiently heavy, and neither was it effective. The squadron never got into position for an accurate, prolonged bombardment of the fort; indeed, from the course of events it even seems possible that such a bombardment was not even considered necessary. The main role of the immensely powerful combined fleet seems to have been the bottling up of the relatively insignificant Colaba squadron of Angrey's ships and also to prevent other Maratha ships from coming to the rescue of the fort. Even the heavy guns of the expedition itself, the 24-pounders and the 18-pounders which had been carried with so much labour all the way from Chaul, had been left behind at the final obstacle, the Channel, and could not be brought into use during the attack. The artillery support for the assault on the fort was confined to a desultory shelling by the ships in the morning. This shelling stopped long before 'H hour'. During the assault itself, the only covering fire was provided by the smaller field guns actually carried into the attack.

The timing of the attack was most unusual, but it is possible that it may have been dictated by the tide. It was not until 4 o'clock in the afternoon (of 24 December) that the first wave of the attack against the fort was mounted by the English. The assaulting force, composed of nearly one thousand soldiers and sailors led by Colonel Braithwaite, concentrated on the main gate of the fort (which is on the north-eastern side), and along the walls on either side of the gate. Despite sustained firing from the fort, the attack was pressed home with determination and the attackers succeeded in scrambling up to the fort walls, carrying their scaling ladders with them.

Those attempting to storm the fort gates were bunched up close together, and now encountered the full fury of the defenders' fire: they never succeeded in forcing the gates open. Those who were trying to gain the fort walls were more successful. Some of their ladders had fallen short of the top of the walls, but a few resolute Englishmen had managed to gain the walls of the fort. But these were cut down in hand-to-hand fighting within the fort, and those attempting to follow them were subjected to a merciless concentration of shots, stones and arrows at point-blank range, at the walls of the fort. After an hour's confused fighting at the gate, the attack lost its fury and was given up soon afterwards. The English force rushed back for the shore, leaving their field guns, ammunition and equipment behind. They also left behind over a hundred soldiers in killed or wounded.

Having repulsed the furious attack, an attack which, the defenders must have felt certain, was only the first wave of the assault, they held back, reorganizing, repairing and attending to their wounded and dead, expecting another wave any moment, and getting ready to face it. They could see down below the entire Portuguese assault force still uncommitted and poised for action.

But, as the winter sun began to dip, it became plain to Kanhoji Angrey that the Portuguese were not going to make an attempt to storm the fort; that if he wanted to engage the Portuguese force, it was he who would have to take the initiative and that this was his chance. There was hardly an hour of daylight left. Angrey made an astonishingly quick battlefield decision and ordered Pilaji Jadhav's force which had been held back in reserve, to swoop down upon the Portuguese force as it waited uncertainly on the beach.

The Marathas had always exulted in a wild cavalry charge against a stationary enemy. Pilaji's force could not have asked for a better assignment. Fifteen hundred horsemen came thundering down upon an enemy force already demoralized as the result of the English repulse from the walls of the fort. They came charging down, yelling their terrifying war-cry: 'Har har Mahadev!', their long spears held aloft.

The Portuguese force had watched the fate of the English assaulting party, and had stood transfixed; it is possible that according to the plan, their own attack was timed to take place only after the English had got into the fort. But the plan had already misfired, and now they were caught out in the open, exposed to the full fury of Pilaji Jadhav's cavalry charge, bereft of their artillery support since the guns had not been dragged across the Channel. They were beaten even before the Maratha cavalry reached their ranks, yelling hoarsely and flashing their spears and those terrible curved Maratha swords which they preferred above all weapons for hand-to-hand fighting. The Portuguese soldiers began to run, 'in wild confusion' as an eye-witness describes it; falling as they ran, breaking their ranks and dispersing in all directions.

It was now late in the evening, and by this time the English column, which had been thrown back from the walls of the fort, had begun to regroup near their original assembly point where they had crossed the Channel. Kanhoji Angrey saw them, and snatched the last few minutes of daylight to send down another party from the fort to attack the English. The men from the fort came charging down into the remnants of the English assault force before it could form itself and 'made a terrible slaughter'.

Both the advance columns had been routed but further pursuit and destruction was prevented by the darkness and also possibly by the rising tide. The Maratha troops made no attempts to pursue the Portuguese or the English, but regrouped in their original positions upon the island, holding all their forces in their original tight concentration, ready for the next move.

If the mighty joint expedition of the English and the Portuguese had already collapsed, those in the fort did not know it yet. They had over-estimated their enemy, and expected a renewal of the offensive. But by nightfall, many of the English soldiers had made for their ships, and the Portuguese on the island had straggled back to their base camp in the sands of Alibag. On the morning of Christmas Day, the beaches of Colaba were clear of the enemy, and Kanhoji Angrey must have realized that there was now no likelihood of a regrouping of enemy forces for another attack against the fort.

Commodore Thomas Matthews who had been watching the battle from his Flagship, *Lion*, flew into a rage at the way things had gone. In defeat, his mind jumped naturally to the conclusion that the East India Company had always found so convenient: the cause of all military reverses was treachery! Convinced that the failure of the attack was due to no other cause than Portuguese treachery, he rushed to the Portuguese base camp and flew at the General of the North, Antonio de Castro e Mello, in a seething rage, openly accusing him of treachery and cowardice, and thrust his cane into his mouth'. It is said that he treated the Viceroy 'not much better'.

Whatever vestige of friendliness was still left between the commanders of both the allies, must have been shattered by Commodore Matthews's rough treatment of the Portuguese dignitaries, particularly since there had been no cause to suspect treachery. It is even possible that the Portuguese had good reason to feel let down by the English for their failure in storming the fort. The relations between the European allies, straining under weeks of enforced living together, weeks during which the Portuguese Viceroy was 'disgusted at the constant drunkenness, quarrelling and want of discipline amongst the English', were now finally snapped. In a huff, the Viceroy went over to his ship and announced that he had been taken ill.

Not content with his rough treatment of the Viceroy, Matthews now ordered his ship's doctor to examine the Viceroy, and the doctor came back and reported that there was nothing wrong with the Viceroy.

As soon as Kanhoji Angrey detected the rupture between his enemies, he applied his mind to taking the fullest advantage of it. At this time, he must have been more anxious to break the alliance between the English and the Portuguese than to crush their military forces. Admittedly, those who had reached the ships were now safe, but there is little doubt that at this stage, he could have easily finished off the remnants of the beaten Portuguese force, for another strong column of Maratha troops had arrived to assist him.

Instead, Angrey sent an emissary to the Viceroy, offering him generous terms for a treaty of peace. As soon as the Viceroy received Angrey's proposal, he sent a message to the English that he thought it best to suspend hostilities at least for the time being. The English, who, in any case, had no hopes of being able to launch another attack by themselves, made a virtue out of necessity and agreed to suspend hostilities, only however, under protest.

Don Francisco Jose de Sampaio cannot be blamed for his anxiety to save whatever he could out of the wreck. He was eager to accept the terms offered by Kanhoji Angrey. At the same time, he considered himself bound by his recent treaty with the English by which both sides had undertaken not to entertain separate peace proposals. The Viceroy could not have failed to notice that even as the talks were proceeding the strength of Kanhoji's force had increased further, and now the redoubtable Bajirao himself had arrived on the scene at the head of a strong column of cavalry, making the total of Maratha reinforcements 25,000 strong. The menacing presence of these troops must have proved a far more convincing reason than the arguments put forward by Kanhoji's intermediaries, for the Viceroy could have little doubt left now that his column could be easily destroyed by the Marathas.

But honour had to be satisfied: a solemn undertaking could not be lightly brushed aside. Over this issue, however, Kanhoji Angrey was prepared to make concessions to suit the Viceroy's conscience. To save the Viceroy's face, they found a somewhat juristic solution; a solution which sought to preserve the letter of the Anglo-Portuguese treaty even though its spirit was violated. The Portuguese, it will be recalled, had undertaken not to entertain any peace proposals from Angrey. They got over the difficulty by routing Angrey's proposals through Bajirao. The Viceroy had not bound himself down to any such undertaking as far as Shahu was concerned. Accordingly, the treaty that was made was not made between the Portuguese and Angrey, but between the Portuguese and the Maratha King Shahu; and Bajirao, as the King's *Peshwa* signed the treaty on Shahu's behalf. The form was maintained, and as further proof of good faith, the Viceroy invited 'General' Cowan to remain present during the negotiations. But Cowan declined the invitation, and reiterated his accusation that the Portuguese were breaking their solemn undertaking given in the treaty made with the English.

The terms of the treaty were agreed between the Portuguese and Angrey in the Portuguese camp at Alibag within a few days of the Colaba attack, but the formal treaty was not executed until 9 January, 1722. In a sense, it was a defensive and offensive alliance: both Kanhoji Angrey and the Portuguese agreed to help one another against enemies who were not at peace with themselves. In addition, both threw their ports open to the merchant shipping of the other side. The Portuguese undertook not to convoy the ships of the enemies of the Marathas, and also agreed to supply to the *Peshwa* all the ammunition and artillery needed by him at a fair price. On their part, the Marathas undertook to restore the ships captured by Angrey's fleet. Again, to make everything conform to procedure, a copy of this treaty was delivered to Robert Cowan and the English were called upon by the *Peshwa*, (not Angrey) to accept similar terms within eight days.

But the English, safe in their powerful ships, had already left. As far as they were concerned, their alliance with the Portuguese was already shattered. They were in no mood to wait for the formalities to be completed. On 28 December they had sailed back to Bombay.

No one could have been more disappointed with the fate of the Colaba expedition than Governor Boone, for this was to have been the crowning achievement of his Governorship. His successor, William Phipps, had been cooling his heels in Bombay for five months, but Boone had clung to his office on one pretext or another,

Now Charles Boone laid down his office and sailed for England. His ship *London* which, it will be recalled, had served as his flagship during the Khanderi expedition, weighed anchor on 9 January, 1722. He is said to have been a Governor of 'outstanding merit'. Militarily, however, his record had been a monotonous succession of failures. During his last year in Bombay, one of his councillors had been so fed up with him that he was charged with having 'plotted to seize his person and uttered threats against his life'. This was a Mr. Parker, who during the trial of Rama Kamathi, had shown a streak of honesty by protesting against the manner in which the trial was being conducted.

Mr. Parker's forthrightness was also partly the cause of his downfall. Boone deprived him of his seat on the Council and later had him tried for 'clandestinely erasing his own signature from an important minute of proceedings'. For his crimes, Mr. Parker was forced to run away from Bombay. Nobody could provoke the displeasure of 'fighting Boone' and go on living in Bombay.

Whether Mr. Parker had plotted to seize Mr. Boone's person will never be conclusively proved, but it is certain that if he did, the sympathies of most of Bombay's citizens would have been solidly on the side of Mr. Parker.

'At Mr. Boone's departure', John Bidulph records, 'salutes were fired from every gun afloat, except from Matthews's squadron which did not fire a gun.'

43

The Quiet Years

The new Governor, William Phipps, was left to fish in the troubled waters of Boone's soiling. Just before his departure Boone had acquired yet another enemy: the Portuguese.

Many rude letters passed between the Bombay Council and Goa, and only succeeded in opening up all the old wounds and causing a few new ones. The Portuguese General of the North once again levied a tax on all goods taken into Bombay from his territory, and the English sent their ships to bombard the villages around Mahim and Bandra. Soon it developed into a sort of catch-as-catch-can warfare, both sides rattling their sabres and giving out war-whoops, but doing their best to avoid a major battle, and concentrating on doing as much damage as possible in each other's undefended territory.

In this indiscriminate shooting match, Captain Loader of the Company's frigate *Revenge*, took it into his head to burn down the village of Elephanta without any rhyme or reason, and is said to have been responsible for the destruction of some of the most valuable ancient relics. In an unaccustomed pang of conscience, the Bombay Council actually resolved to punish Captain Loader for wantonly destroying a village and killing its people. He was deprived of his rank for a week! During August and September, there were many skirmishes in and around Bombay between the Portuguese and the English, accompanied by the burning down of more villages.

While all this was going on, Commodore Matthews had taken his squadron and gone on an expedition, supposedly after the Madagascar pirates, but in actual fact on a mission of private trading in open rivalry with the East India Company. His squadron came back to Bombay in September, by which time the Bombay Council was willing to forgive and forget all its differences with the Royal Navy and even offered to overlook the Commodore's trading activities, in return for help against the Portuguese.

But the Council were to receive a rude shock: almost incredibly, the Commodore's sympathies seemed to be solidly on the side of the Portuguese. He refused to participate in an expedition against the Portuguese, and instead went off to Surat to try and raise money from Indian financiers for a more ambitious trading venture. But the Company, jealous of its trading monopoly, had done a lot of canvassing against the Commodore, and he had to return from Surat empty-handed, wilder than ever at the doings of the Bombay Council.

As soon as the naval squadron had left Bombay, the Company had resumed its practice of enforcing Indian ships to fly the English flag. On his return to Bombay, Commodore Matthews issued an order, 'in insulting language' forbidding all Indian ships from flying English colours, and had a copy of his order put up at the sea gate. The horrified Governor and his Council had the notice removed from the sea gate. When this came to Matthews's notice, he threatened the Governor that unless the order was replaced at the sea gate, he would have it proclaimed all over the town by beat of drum and that 'should any resistance be offered, he would not leave a house standing in the place'. The notice was promptly replaced.

It was in this atmosphere that the Council vaguely talked of a naval attack against the Portuguese, but no one seriously expected it to materialize. It must have been almost a relief when someone brought news that Kanhoji Angrey had assembled a naval force of

5,000 and was due to sail for Karwar. At this, all talk of attacking the Portuguese was dropped, and as a substitute for action the Company sent off one frigate, with orders to defend Karwar.

Angrey himself, scrupulously observed his treaty with the Portuguese. Although, from time to time, his ships ran into Portuguese ships, they did not molest them. Official Portuguese records confirm that their ships were permitted to take on supplies in Angrey's ports and that the Angrey ships did not interfere either with their merchant ships or warships.

At this time, Kanhoji Angrey was trying hard to get the Portuguese to join hands with him in a major offensive against the English. He was aware that by himself he was in no position to deal a decisive blow against the English, particularly in the face of their overwhelming naval strength. At this time, the Bombay Council had at its disposal nearly twenty major warships with 400 guns and 4,000 men. Shahu's forces had hurried back to the ghats, and were now wholly committed in warfare against the Nizam.

Almost imperceptibly, a certain degree of coolness had crept in in his relationship with Shahu. Angrey could only ascribe this to court intrigue. Shahu's mood was reflected in his repeated demands for the arrears of the tribute that Kanhoji had to pay annually for holding the Konkan for Shahu. Kanhoji had always contended that the expenditure incurred in protecting the Konkan was far more than his tribute payable to Shahu, and as such Shahu should waive the amount of the tribute.

The reluctance on the part of Angrey to pay to Shahu the agreed tribute could have been no more than a question of principle; for at this time he seems to have been well provided with funds, and offered the Portuguese all the money they might require for the conduct of the war with the English, if only they agreed to join hands with him. He had no wish for inconclusive, half-hearted jabs at the English and was desperately keen that the Portuguese should assist him.

But the Portuguese had more things wrong with them than the shortage of funds. Even though they were supposed to be in a state of a localised war with the English around Bombay, their heart was not in it. They were content to live and let live, and all they hoped for was that no single power got strong enough to drive the Portuguese out of their possessions in India. Although Angrey is said to have 'offered to swear perpetual friendship on the heads of his sons', and promised them all the money needed for the prosecution of the war, they had made up their minds that it was better to live with two more or less evenly-balanced powers than to enable one of them to become overwhelmingly strong. In effect, the Portuguese were just as much frightened of the rise of Angrey as were the British, and indeed, at the time, they were secretly doing their best to undermine Angrey's power. A Portuguese writer clarifies his Government's attitude in the following words:

> 'They secretly helped ... (the Sawant of Wadi) in his war against Angrey because they preferred to have the weaker of the two combatants as their next-door neighbour.'

At sea, Angrey had become bolder than ever, and begun to seek out the Company's fighting ships as well as merchant ships. In the very first month of Phipps's Governorship his ships attacked two English galleys *Hunter* and *Eagle*, and after a whole day's fighting during which both sides are said to have made attempts to board the ships of the other side, *Hunter* was blown up and *Eagle* was forced to flee for shelter to the Portuguese post of Sargaon, 'in a shattered condition'. Since the Portuguese, too, were hostile to the English at this time, two more ships of the Company hurried to Sargaon to bring back *Eagle*.

In April 1722, Angrey captured an East Indiaman loaded with merchandise and bullion, and in October of the same year, there was a fierce naval battle between the Company's fleet and one of Kanhoji's squadrons near Underi. The English ships, *Victory*, *Salisbury* and *Revenge* mounting between them over 80 guns, engaged one of Angrey's *ghurabs* and several *gallivats*. Angrey's Commander, a Dutchman, was killed in this battle, and after heavy fighting, the battered *ghurab* was carried to Bombay as a prize. This was regarded by the Council as a signal victory, and since it was more than Governor Boone had ever achieved, there was some justification for the resulting jubilation in Bombay.

In September, the three fast light ships specially commissioned by the Company's directors for service in Bombay, arrived from England. They were *Bengall*, *Bombay*, and *Fort St. George*, all sailing together, and on their way out, they had already made a good showing, having captured two Portuguese ships. Now the Bombay Council had the strongest and the most modern fleet on the coast.

Neither Kanhoji Angrey nor the Portuguese could, however, have had much idea of the state of the relationship between the Royal Navy (as represented by Commodore Matthews), and the East India Company. To them, all English ships represented the strength of the Company.

Commodore Matthews seems to have been thoroughly dissatisfied with the way things were going on in India. In particular, he was astounded by the political pretensions of the East India Company; for at this stage, the true state of affairs in India was not generally known in England. Matthews was the first to make it clear to the Bombay Council that if the Company considered itself to be a political power in India, the Navy had no intention of being a party to such pretensions. Also, to his mind, it was a shocking abuse of treaty privileges for the Company to encourage Indian vessels to fly the English flag if they happened to be carrying the Company's goods, and thereby avoid the payment of legitimate dues. Indeed, Matthews must have at times wondered what the war with Angrey was about, since he himself whole-heartedly agreed with Angrey's interpretations of the very terms of the treaty which had led to the differences.

No one can blame Matthews for not striving hard to back up the Company's private territorial ambitions in India with all the naval power at his disposal. He filled his pockets by private trading, defying the Company's monopoly, and was forthright in denouncing the Company for its wrongs and pretensions. Whenever possible, he went out of his way to help some of the victims of the Company's persecution, such as Mrs. Gyfford. Another protege of his was a Parsee broker named Bomanjee, who had been placed under arrest by the Company on a charge of fraud, and confined without trial, and Matthews undertook to take Bomanjee's son to England with him so that he could represent the case to the Company's Directors. Of course it is more than possible that Matthews's interest in the affairs of his protegés was not altogether altruistic. Bomanjee was reputed to be a very wealthy man, and Mrs. Gyfford was a very lovely woman.

As a parting insult to the Bombay Council, Matthews sent word to the Viceroy of Goa that he would present him with an old woman's petticoat if he did not capture every single one of the Company's ships.

The Navy's attitude compelled Governor Phipps to seek a hasty peace with the Portuguese. Both parties had no feeling of friendliness for one another, but both were anxious to avoid serious military action as well as trade losses, and the 'phoney war' between the English and the Portuguese died a natural death without a single major battle being fought.

In December 1723, Commodore Matthews sailed his squadron for home to the intense relief of the Bombay Council. Never again, they swore, were they going to seek the help of the Navy to fight the Company's wars. It was twenty years before another naval squadron came to India. The East India Company disliked home truths from its compatriots as well as from foreigners, and were not prepared to be told that they were merely traders and not a ruling power, even by its own navy.

Towards the end of 1723, things began to happen again. The Sawant of Wadi had been getting increasingly hostile towards Angrey, and had been making efforts to get the help of the European powers against him. The Sawant's territory was at the southern end of Angrey's domain without a natural boundary between the two. A state of war with the Sawant would have involved a certain degree of relaxation of his vigilance in the north, and Angrey was anxious to avoid it. At this time, a 'prize ship which Connajee Angarie laid claim to', is said to have been forcibly taken away by the Sawant. In retaliation, Angrey led an expedition into the Sawant's territory which seems to have been nothing but a mission of destruction. He is said to have captured or burnt a large portion of the Sawant's feet at Vengurla and destroyed a number of his villages.

Any such fighting in the vicinity of Vengurla was bound to cause distress to the Dutch who had a factory there, and the Sawant was quick to take the fullest advantage of it. By himself, the Sawant of Wadi was not the sort of adversary who would have caused much worry to Angrey, but if he joined forces with one of the European powers, he would become a formidable enemy. The Sawant who had drawn a blank with the Portuguese and the English, now eagerly turned to the Dutch, and after Angrey's attack so close to their factory at Vengurla, the Dutch were in the right frame of mind to form an alliance with the Sawant.

At about this time, Angrey's men happened to seize a Dutch ship, and the outbreak of hostilities with the Dutch now became only a matter of time. Strategically, this was dangerous position to be in, and it is surprising that Kanhoji Angrey had allowed himself to be drawn into it. He would now have to contend with two strong enemies on either flank: the Dutch in the south and the English in the north. It was a position he had always striven hard to avoid.

His warfare with the Sawant had brought him a new enemy, the Dutch.

Early in 1724, the Dutch attacked Gheria. But they had chosen the wrong place and the wrong time, for Gheria was now a strongly-fortified, heavily-garrisoned and well-provisioned stronghold; and what is more, having already withstood at least two such sea-borne assaults, the state of morale of its garrison was sky-high. The Dutch attacked with seven ships, each mounting between thirty to fifty guns, and two bomb-vessels. They are also said to have carried a large body of soldiers. The total number of sailors and soldiers could not have been less than 3,000.

Rudraji Anant, Angrey's battle-seasoned Subedar of Gheria, might have prayed for such an opportunity as this. He let the Dutch troops make the landing, and then swooped down upon them as they were still scrambling up the beaches, before they could get a toe-hold. Low's history dismisses the attack as having been 'repelled with great losses'.

The threat to his southern flank was broken, at least for the time being. But whatever relief the defeat of the Dutch attack on Gheria brought on must have been curdled by a somewhat routine naval skirmish which took place at this time between two of Angrey's ships and the Company's squadron. After a prolonged fight, Angrey's *ghurab* was disabled and captured by the Company's ships. The Commander of the *ghurab* was Shivaji Naik, one of Angrey's seniormost commanders. What was more, Shivaji Naik was also a close friend of Kanhoji Angrey.

The thought of his close friend, Shivaji Naik, in the captivity of the English seems to have caused great distress to Angrey at this time. By now, his heart should have hardened to such incidents inevitable in a soldier's life, but it seems that he was prepared to make astonishing sacrifices to obtain the release of his friend. He immediately began negotiations for a truce with the English.

44

'Your Excellency!'

On 24 May, 1724, Kanhoji Angrey wrote a letter to William Phipps.

'To the most Excellent, Opulant, and Renowned Senhr. William Phipps, President and Governor-General of Persia as far as Indostan, in the Port of Bombay, Conajie Angria, Sarquel, sends cordially Greetings:

'I hope your Excellency enjoys perfect health, and that you will please to favour me with that agreeable news.

'At the time we were friends without reserve sundry incidents fell out, by means of which that good understanding was at an end, war ensued whereby (according to the Devine appointment) were occasioned such losses and advantages the world is well acquainted with, and notwithstanding the ancient friendship of our predecessors continued firm on both sides, yet did the poorer sort feel the effects of this war, being almost reduced to ruin. It now appears to me as a matter incumbent on those who seem so much regarded by Devine providence to endeavour after the general good and benefit of the people, and to promote the ancient and good correspondence between us, to which end, I write to your Excellency, for where neighbours disagree the result will be loss on both sides and the public at the same time suffer,

> all which I have duly considered, and desiring to cultivate a good correspondence, I write this to your Excellency, your Excellency may likewise if you please reflect maturely thereon with regard to future consequences, and in this case, your Excellency intends an agreement, you may be pleased to send an answer to this, that according to which I may if necessary, send hither a person of credit. I am much of opinion the mutual benefit of both parties depend on an accommodation as likewise the public good. It is needless for me to write more on this head as your Excellency has good understanding'.

It was the hand of friendship, offered in all good faith and without reservation. Its over-riding motive may have been to secure the release of Shivaji Naik, but the whole tone of the letter was frank and sincere: there are no insults in the letter, no hidden barbs; no question of who was wrong and who was right; just a willingness to cultivate good relations because when 'neighbours disagree, there is loss on both sides', and that instead of working for the good of the people, they make the 'public suffer'.

Every word rings with sincerity. It is difficult to conceive of anyone who would not react favourably to such a letter from an enemy. It was the sort of letter that Rommel may have written to his opposite number, or Mountbatten; full of grace and warmth. There is not a word of abuse or of self-importance.

The reply from Governor Phipps speaks for itself. It brings out all that was petty and snivelling, all that was incapable of responding to an appeal of good fellowship. It reeks of the logic of petty tradesmen holding positions far beyond the reach of their abilities. In short, it was wholly typical of the corporate mind of the East India Company's Council at Bombay. Phipps wrote:

'To the famous Conajee Angria *Sarquel*, William Phipps, President for all the forces and affairs of the English Nation, send Greetings:

'After so long a time as two years and a half that I have had the honor to govern in these parts for the powerful English nation, I find myself at last favoured with a letter from your Honor whose contents gives me the greater satisfaction as it expresses an earnest desire in your Honor to recouncile the subsisting differences between us, in order to allow a friendship that I must assure you and yourself and all the world must allow, you (were) the sole occasion of reducing it to the footing it is at present.

'From whence produces war, but ambition in regarding the right of another, or from breech of faith, for proceeding further in taking what is another's on the high seas is termed Pyracy, and those guilty thereof are esteemed enemies to all nations, a character I therefore hope your Honor will not be fond of.

'It is observed that greatness persued after and obtained by these means is of short duration, whereas a state improving and flourishing through trade is of a much longer continuance and never decays but through corrupt Councils. Had your Honor in the beginning of your rise in the World (with which I am well acquainted) cultivated in your territories, a correspondence that is peculiarly necessary for merchants, and employed that power providence has by degree blessed you with, to protect trade, instead of quite the contrary practice you have made use of, the territories your Honor now governs might by this time have been equal in some measure to vie with the great port of Surat, your honours power estimated to be raised on justice, and yourself become revered for your virtue, whereas now your Honor is more terrible to your friends than enemies.

'War is prejudicial to that party of the public who make not the sword their profession, and whoever prosecutes the same purely for the sake thereof will find cause at one time or another to repeat is as experience has shown. But any state bordering upon a neighbour that lives on plunder and robs under colour of friendship must necessarily be careful for their defence ...

'When I acquaint your Honor that I do well remember your coming to annoy this island in the time Mr Burniston governed here under His Excellency Sir John Gayer, General then at Surat,[19] you will believe I am no stranger to your proceedings ever since, and you must therefore excuse me if I accept not entering into any Treaty with you until you give me proof of your sincerity by immediately setting at liberty the people of our nation you have with you prisoners, taken by you going on their lawful occasions without giving you any offence, when I shall be ready to receive from you any proposal towards an accomodation you shall think proper to make, as well as I shall demonstrate to your Honor you have to deal with one as knows how to return your civility.'

In short, William Phipps, English trader, had told the Maratha Admiral, firstly, what a great power he, Phipps represented; secondly, that the war was entirely due to Angrey's faults; thirdly, he had called Angrey a pirate; fourthly, he had given Angrey a long sermon how he should mend his ways; fifthly, he had told him

19 This must be a reference to Kanhoji Angrey camping with his ships at the mouth of the Pane river in 1704, in retaliation to the Company's seizure of the ship from Aden bearing his *dastak*, which act of Kanhoji's had paralysed the traffic between Bombay and the mainland.

that only after he had given proof of his future good behaviour by releasing all English prisoners, would he consider any proposal of Angrey's; and lastly, he pointed out that he could be just as civil as Angrey, but he did not choose to: that he would be equally civil only after Angrey had given positive proof of mending his ways—in short, that he, Phipps, was being deliberately rude.

And then the Company complained of the uncivil manners they encountered amongst Indians. The code of the conquerors covered up a million ugly blotches!

Kanhoji Angrey was no fool, and he did not suffer insults easily. But his desire for peace at this particular time must have overshadowed his resentment of Phipps's insulting remarks. His reply to Phipps is a model of even-tempered statesmanship. He takes full note of all the insults and aspersions, but his retorts are not venomous, as they might well have been, but full of restraint and in the best of taste. He still manages to leave the door open for negotiations; and above all, for the exchange of prisoners.

His reply was dated 23 July, 1724. Angrey wrote:

> 'I received your Excellency's letter, and have understood all your Excellency writes me, that the difference that continues even until now are through my means; that the desire of possessing what is another's is a thing very wide of reason, and that suchlike proceedings cannot continue long; that had I from my beginning cultivated trade and favoured the merchants, the port I now govern might by the Devine favour have in some measure become like the great port of Surat, and my name have become famous, all which your Excellency says is not to be brought about but by opening a fair trade; that he is least expert in war generally comes off a sufferer thereby, and that he who follows it purely through love that he hath thereto will one time or another find cause to repent; that if I had

considered this thing sooner, I might have found some benefit and convenience thereby. Your Excellency says you are very well acquainted with the manner of my government from its beginning and for that reason you would not on any term open a treaty with me until I set at liberty the people of your Nation that are prisoners here, after that you would receive any proposition made by me that were friendly or might tend to an accomodation at all which I very much admire especially when I find your Excellency persuaded that I have been the cause of the past differences and disputes, the truth of which your Excellency will soon find out when you examine both sides. For as touching the desire of possessing what is another's I do not even find the merchants exempt from this sort of ambition, for this is the way of the world, for God gives nothing immediately from himself to any, but takes from one to give to another. Whether this is right or not, who is to determine.

'It little behoves merchants, I am sure, to say our Government is supported by violence, insults, and pyraces; for as much as Maha Rajah (which is Savagee) making warr against four Kings founded and established a Kingdom, and this was our introduction and beginning and whether or no by these ways this Government hath proved durable your Excellency well knows, so likewise did your predecessor, and whether 'tis durable or no, I would have your Excellency consider; 'tis certain nothing in this world is durable, if which if your Excellency considers as such, the way of this world is well known.

'Your Excellency is pleased to say if I had any regard to the weal of the people and favoured the commerce, my power would be much augmented, and my port become like that of Surat; but I never have been wanting in favour the merchants trading according to the laws of this country, nor of chastising those transgressing the same, as your Excellency well knows. The increase of power depends on the Devine will, in which human dilligence little availeth. Until this day, I have kept up the power that was necessary; whether I shall continue it or no for the future who can tell, but that will be as God is pleased to determine.

'Your Excellency was pleased to write that war proves most fatal to those whom the use of sword is not understood, but in the Government of His Excellency Charles Boone, nobody can say there was not loss on both sides, for victory depends on the hand of God, and for this reason take little notice of such losses.

'Your Excellency is pleased to write that he who follows war purely thro' an inclination that one hath thereto, one time or another will find cause to repent, of which I suppose your Excellency hath found proof, for we are not always victorious nor always unfortunate.

'Your Excellency was pleased to write that you well understood the manner of my Government, and for that reason you could not enter upon any treaty of Peace with me, unless I would first set at liberty the people of your Nation that are prisoners here. I very well know your Excellency understood the manner of my Government from its beginning, therefore, this gives me wonder; but if your Excellency says you will admit any proposition after seeing your people released, I must then likewise say my people are prisoners under your Excellency. How can I then give liberty to yours? But if your Excellency's intent was cordially to admit any overtures of peace for ending our present disputes and do really write me for that end concerning the liberty of your people, I am to

> assure you my intent is cordially the same. It is therefore necessary that some person of character intervene and act as guarantee between us to who I will presently send your Excellency's people. Your Excellency will afterwards do the like by mine. The prisoners on both sides having by this means obtained their liberty, afterwards we shall enter on what relates to our friendship and treaty of peace for the avoidance of prejudices on both sides. For this end, I now write your Excellency, which I hope will meet with regard, and if your Excellency's intention be to treat of peace and friendship, be pleased to send an answer to this that conformable thereto I may consider on what is most proper to be done. As your Excellency is a man of understanding, I need say no more.'

Kanhoji's letter, while it merely explores the possibility of peace, and more definitely offers a proposal for the exchange of prisoners, is also a clear enunciation of his creed. He reiterates with pride that he is a vassal of the descendents of Shivaji; that he has never been 'wanting in favour' to the merchants trading according to the laws of the country; and he makes it equally clear that he has always regarded it as his duty to chastise those who transgressed these laws.

45

Silver for Peace!

The man who, in 1702, had sent word to the Company's Governor that he would make the English dread his name, had, in 1724, swallowed English insults with surprising equanimity. This was not merely the difference between thirty-two and fifty-four, or the anxiety to secure the release of Shivaji Naik. Least of all, was it a sign of military weakness, for the military strength of Kanhoji Angrey was now greater than ever before, and his forces had piled up an unbroken record of victories, or at least, of repelling the onslaughts upon his territory. Now, when Angrey spoke, he spoke from strength, a calculated awareness of his capabilities and limitations. If he wanted to avoid war, it was not because of the fear of defeat.

Many things had contributed to this mood for all-round reconciliation, and the chief among them was the genuine desire for peace for its own sake. As a youth, he had sought conflict with avidity, regarding warfare as merely an opportunity for professional advancement; in manhood, he had never turned away from the prospect of conflict if it meant the slightest unbending of principles; now he was making a deliberate effort warfare.

The desire for peace, if not at any price, at least at a price he would not have agreed to pay in his early days, is clearly evinced in the treaty he made with the Sawant of Wadi. He sought the intervention of Shahu and Bajirao to negotiate a settlement between himself and the Sawant of Wadi, and in February 1724, a treaty was duly concluded which, although Kanhoji Angrey may be said to have been the victor in all the the battles fought between him and the Sawant, brought him no special advantages. The letter written by Bajirao to Kanhoji Angrey at this time explains the main terms of the treaty:

> 'When, at the time hostilities were going on between yourself and the Sawant of Kudal, (Wadi), Raghunath Prabhu came to see the King on your behalf. With him and Naro Ram Mantri as medeiators, the King has effected a settlement between Yourself and the Sawant of Wadi; it being agreed that neither party will encroach into the territory of the other, and as to the disputed district of Salsi, it has been agreed that the revenue shall be divided equally between both ...'

This extraordinary craving for peace at a price hitherto unthinkable, was even more forcibly manifested in something which happened a whole year later. In 1725, the Siddy Rasool Yakoot Khan, egged on by the Bombay Council and the Portuguese and amply supplied with ammunition and stores and promises of tempting rewards by both, came and besieged Colaba with an assortment of naval craft which, for sheer numerical strength, Colaba had never witnessed before. It consisted of 12 *pals*, two frigates, and 100 *gallivat*s, which means that it had between 5,000 to 6,000 men.

Kanhoji Angrey knew his Siddy by this time, and made no attempt to drive him away by force. Instead, he sent emissaries to the Siddy and offered to buy him off. After a good deal of bargaining, the Siddy accepted the bribe that was finally settled upon, which seems to have been far larger than any amount the English or the Portuguese could have promised him to go on with a futile siege, and quietly withdrew his fleet.

This extraordinary expedient to avoid a siege which would, at best, have constituted a prolonged nuisance, demonstrates the lengths to which Kanhoji Angrey now went in his desire to maintain peace.

His mind now shrank from the thought of war and the resulting destruction of life and property; he saw war more as a thing of misery and poverty than a thing of glory. Altogether, he had become more of an administrator than a fighting chieftain, a man who governed rather than ruled. He had no desire for further conquest; only to look after what was his own, and to nourish it and develop it. A dedicated soldier and sailor had now turned himself wholly to the tasks of administration, and if the new mantle sat upon his shoulders awkwardly, he made a sincere attempt to adapt himself to it; and took care to see that it did not slip off altogether.

He began to improve the productivity of the rice fields and the salt pans in his domain, and made frequent grants of money to needy farmers. His timber plantations now covered large tracts, and he may be said have been the first ruler in the Konkan who thought of conserving and improving its forests. According to the practice of the day, he was also the supreme judicial authority in his domain, and he had begun to take a greater personal interest in the administration of justice. He had gathered around himself all sorts of artists and artisans with the same acquisitiveness that he had once displayed towards collecting dancing girls and bands of actors. He had done more for education than any other contemporary Indian ruler. Each group of four or five villages had a common elementary school, and the bigger villages and townships were given their own schools. In Colaba fort itself, he had established a boarding house for students and took a personal interest in its affairs. Above all, he had established an efficient postal service and had appointed mounted couriers for the speedy delivery of letters. Communications in the Konkan are still so primitive that it is doubtful whether the timings of Kanhoji Angrey's mail carriers have shown much improvement.

He had begun to make large endowments to temples and other religious institutions, and his almost blind veneration for Brahmendra-swami had grown with the years. He sent constant gifts to Brahmendra-swami, who, despite being a man who was said to have renounced all worldly pleasures, seemed to be inordinately partial to rich food. Angrey was forever sending him table delicacies from the Konkan such as fine selected rice, dates, walnuts, grapes and even perfumes and silk garments. There are some interesting letters between the Swami and Kanhoji about the selection of a set of perfectly matched pearls which was intended as a gift for Brahmendra-swami.

In 1724, Kanhoji Angrey began negotiations for the purchase of land in his ancestral village of Angarwadi, and he was particularly pleased when he was able to buy a half-share in the village revenues. The price he paid was sixty thousand rupees which, by all standards, was a stiff price, but Angrey was now an enormously wealthy man and could afford to be extravagant.

His thoughts were straying into the future even more than into the past. By buying up the land of his ancestral village, he had forged a link with the past; his religious activities and his avoidance of warfare were indications of his preoccupation with the future. He wanted to withdraw from active warfare not so much for the sake of a quiet life of ease, as for a life dedicated to the prosperity of the Konkan. But even more than this, he was anxious to leave for his sons a legacy not of war but of peace. If he could do it, he wanted to tie down all the neighbouring powers with perpetual treaties of friendliness so that he could devote himself to constructive fields during his remaining years, secure in the knowledge that his sons would go on enjoying the fruits of his labour.

He was a strict yet indulgent father, intensely fond of his children. Sekhoji, his eldest son, was also his favourite, and Kanhoji Angrey had been grooming him to take his place after him. Whenever he was called away from Colaba for any length of time, he had made it a point of installing Sekhoji with some formality to look after his affairs. This was a conscious attempt to get his other sons used to the idea of having Sekhoji as the head of the family, the King's *Surkhail* and *Wazarat Ma-aab*, with themselves working under his authority and obeying his orders.

For Kanhoji Angrey was becoming increasingly aware that his sons would never pull together as a team. Already, there was disunity and bitterness amongst them, created mostly by his second son, Sambhaji. Sambhaji was as brave as a lion, but he was ruthless and ambitious; he was not the sort of man who would be content to take a second place in any scheme of things. Sambhaji had already made it abundantly clear that he considered himself to be a better choice to be the King's *Surkhail* than his elder brother, Sekhoji.

Sekhoji was the quiet one; dignified, straightforward, the perfect gentleman, and perhaps the ideal man to rule the Konkan. On the other hand, Sambhaji must have been very much like Kanhoji himself was in his twenties. It was a problem that seemed to have no solution.

Then there was Manaji, almost equally ambitious and equally ruthless. With these two stormy petrels pulling their own ways, there was little chance for an easy-going and straightforward man like Sekhoji to rule in peace.

These were the thoughts that haunted Kanhoji Angrey's later years; the growing certainty of strife amongst his own sons. Already, he could see the tension, the constant bickering, the sudden flashes of anger; already he could visualise the agents of his many enemies making approaches to his sons, putting up one against another, dividing them and destroying their power—for in the warfare of the Konkan, no holds were barred. If they fell out, and if one or the other of them went over to his enemies, there was little chance that his domain would survive. He could see the ghastly example of disunity in the house of the Maratha King himself; there were still two Maratha Kings and two kingdoms, both intriguing and fighting against each other, and seeking the support of outsiders.

The seeds of destruction of the house that Kanhoji Angrey had built were already there. They were his own sons, and he was fond of every one of them. They were all brave men, all handsome, and any one of them could have carried on his name with power and prestige. But they would never pull together: two of them were too spirited and too ambitious to live in unison with the other.

This, then, is the possible explanation of Kanhoji Angrey's ardent desire for peace at a price which he would not have hitherto agreed to pay. He was haunted by the foreboding that his house would be divided and destroyed by the dissensions amongst his own sons. The only way to save his house, and save the Konkan was to make sure, if possible, that the powers that had a stake in the Konkan were bound by treaties of peace.

The rest was in the hands of the 'Divine Power'.

46

Elephant!

The exchange of letters between Kanhoji Angrey and William Phipps produced some desirable results in that it secured the release of prisoners on both sides. In the face of Governor Phipps's truculence, this in itself must be regarded as a major achievement.

As soon as Commodore Matthews had left India, the Company had gone back to its practice of permitting Indian ships which carried their cargo to fly the English flag: Phipps stuck to his point that nobody had any right to demand shipping dues from any ship which the East India Company chose to call 'English' by the simple expedient of flying an English flag upon her. In the end, the Company won its point, but it took another thirty years before it could do it; and the point was won only by conquest, by refusing to accept any other principles of justice except the one of brute force—that might alone was right.

But as far at the Company was concerned, it undertook no further military operations against Kanhoji Angrey; his strongholds were now regarded as invincible; his territory inviolable. The Bombay Council confined its military activities to the provision of stronger escorts to their ships. Kanhoji Angrey, on his part, never sought to molest the English on land, but continued his activities at sea with unabated vigour, taking all ships that did not bear his *dastaks*. From this duty he never deviated.

But otherwise, he scrupulously avoided friction, often going to extremes to maintain peace. And in his anxiety to maintain at least the *status quo* if he could not establish friendly relations with the other powers in the Konkan, he even went to the length of incurring the displeasure of both Brahmendra-swami and Shahu.

By this time, Brahmendra-swami had become a major institution in the Deccan. His influence transcended political frontiers and religious convictions. He had followers amongst the Muslims as well as the Hindus, and both Shahu and Sambhaji, bitter rivals for the Maratha throne, were his disciples. He had established a flourishing township around a temple that he had built near Chiplun in the Siddy's territory.

The temple was built in a place called Parasuram, and somewhat surprisingly, it was built mainly on the charity of the Siddy Rasool Yakoot Khan of Janjira, a Muslim. Rasool became the Siddy in 1707, but it seems certain that he knew the Swami many years earlier and had come under his influence, for within a year of becoming the Ruler of Janjira, Rasool made a grant to the Swami, donating the income of two villages, Ambdas and Pedhe, to enable him to build the temple. To this income, the Swami had subsequently added the revenue of several other villages in the vicinity which he had obtained from Kanhoji Angrey, Balaji Vishwanath, and King Shahu. His colony which originally began in the Siddy's domain on the border of Maratha territory, had now begun to spread out beyond the borders of Janjira, into Maratha territory. Around the original temple in Parasuram, he had built three other temples with their own auxiliary buildings, a public rest house for pilgrims, a monument which was called 'the pillar of light', and a large hall for religious functions. Many practising Brahmins had flocked to Parasuram and settled down there, as a result of which, a thriving township of devout Hindus had grown in the domain of the Muslim ruler, the Siddy of Janjira.

Every year, towards the end of the rains, the Swami would terminate what was called his period of meditation, and 'come out'. Over the years, the day of this coming out, the date of the festival of the Elephant God, (the fourth day of the moon in the month of bhadrapada), had become associated with the elaborate ceremonial with which Brahmendra-swami surrounded all his doings. The custom had grown, that on this day, the commanders from the surrounding forts of the Siddy and Angrey came to greet the Swami's annual 'coming out' with suitable gifts and to seek his blessings. Although, at such time, there was a large gathering of troops belonging to two opposite camps, there were no incidents.

After the festivities attendant upon the coming out were over, the Swami would set out on a round of visits to all his wealthier disciples and to collect donations from them for his religious and other activites of public benefit. He travelled with a large retinue, and his tour lasted several months. Usually he returned to Parasuram at the end of the winter.

The Siddy of Janjira, Rasool Yakoot Khan, was a tolerant man and a devotee of the Swami. The Siddy's chief commander, the Siddy Satt, however, was far less tolerant, and had always resented the Swami's religious activities in the midst of their Muslim kingdom. Siddy Satt had no personal regard for the Swami, and he had never concealed his contempt for the elaborate ritual attendant upon all Hindu religious festivities. Even more than his master, the Siddy Rasool, Siddy Satt had never reconciled himself to the treaty of friendship with Angrey which had been forced upon them by Balaji Vishwanath in 1713, by which treaty Janjira had lost a sizable slice of territory to Angrey. Siddy Satt was the Siddy's chief General, and was in command of the fort of Anjanwale, on the south bank of the Dabhol creek, and was in charge of the territory surrounding the fort. This command gave Siddy Satt control over the Swami's township of Parasuram, and he seldom lost an opportunity of harassing the inhabitants of Parasuram and of having frequent digs at Brahmendra-swami himself.

In 1725, the Siddy of Janjira's friend, the Muslim Nawab of Savnur, presented to him, what is described as a 'beautiful' elephant. This gift may have been something of a jest, for the Siddy was supposed to make his own arrangements for taking away the elephant from Savnur to Danda Rajapụr the Siddy's capital. Savnur lies some 400 miles to the south of Janjira, and the trouble and expense of bringing an elephant all the way would have been more than the price of the elephant, however beautiful; for between Savnur and Danda Rajapur, there were at least four different powers who ruled the land; powers who were perpetually at war amongst themselves, and who were in no case friendly with the Siddy of Janjira. In those days, there was a check-post at the interval of every few miles along the highways, and no traffic was permitted except with the *dastak* of an accepted power. As such, to bring the elephant from Savnur to Danda Rajapur was almost an impossible task.

The Siddy of Janjira, Rasool Yakoot, (not to be mixed up with the Siddy Satt who was merely the chief inilitary commander of the Siddy), brought his problem to Brahmendra-swami and asked for his intervention with the various rulers in the Deccan to grant their *dastaks* for his elephant. At least, four such *dastaks* were needed: that of the Sunda Rajah in the south, of Sambhaji of Kolhapur, of Shahu of Satara, and of Kanhoji Angrey.

But the Swami offered a simpler solution. He had just performed his 'coming-out' ceremony, and was going south on his annual tour of fund-raising which would take him as far as Savnur. He offered to bring back the elephant himself. He told the Siddy not to bother himself about *dastaks*; so long as the elephant travelled with the Swami's own party, no *dastak* would be demanded by anyone in the Deccan.

Siddy Rasool Yakoot Khan must have been highly pleased at the Swami's offer. He sent ten men as an escort for the elephant to travel with the Swami on his tour of the south.

Brahmendra-swami went on his tour and brought back the elephant. All along the way, no one attempted to demand a *dastak* from him for the elephant. He came down the ghats and into the

Konkan, and when he was only a day's march from his destination, he sent the elephant ahead of him with the Siddy's men and himself stayed back for an auspicious moment for his return to his own seat.

There was only one more check-post between the elephant and the Siddy's territory now, that of Makhjan (beyond Sangameshwar) on the frontier between the domains of the Siddy and Angrey. It was absurdly improbable, but it had to happen that way. It was at Makhjan the very last check-post in the elephant's path, that trouble cropped up.

At Makhjan, Angrey's men stopped the elephant and refused to permit it to be taken into the Siddy's territory without a *dastak*, although it is certain that if Brahmendra-swami had been on the spot, no one would have thought of demanding a *dastak*. This caused an altercation between the Siddy's men and the guards at Makhjan check-post, and when some of the Siddy's soldiers from a nearby garrison came to take the elephant away by force, Angrey's men resisted them and had the elephant sent away to their own fort at Jaigad. The Siddy's men thereupon went and reported to Siddy Satt that Brahmendra-swami had deliberately allowed this to happen; that having brought the elephant all the way from Savnur, he had made a present of it to Kanhoji Angrey.

In a fit of temper, Siddy Satt marched down upon the temples of Parasuram and razed them to the ground, inflicting unheard of cruelties upon its unfortunate inhabitants. Everything that was worth taking away, he took, and what he could not take, he destroyed.

Ironically, neither Brahmendra-swami nor Kanhoji Angrey knew anything about the cause of this outrage until much later, and nor, for that matter, did the ruler of Janjira, Siddy Rasool Yakoot Khan.

Near Makhjan, as soon as Brahmendra-swami received the news that the elephant had been taken to Jaigad by Angrey's men, he sent word to Kanhoji Angrey and had the elephant released and sent off to the Siddy. But it was already too late. Siddy Satt had wreaked his vengeance: the Swami's life-work lay smouldering because the elephant's arrival was delayed by a day or two.

Siddy Rasool himself regretted the precipitate action of his Commander of Anjanwale. He ordered Siddy Satt to return all the loot taken away by him, and Satt promptly did so. At this time, some medallions studded with precious stones, which the Swami had had made for the adornment of the temple gods on festive occasions, were actually returned by the Swami to Rasool Yakoot Khan as a personal gift. Not to be outdone in this mood of concialiation, Rasool offered Brahmendra-swami two more villages in perpetuity as a compensation for the destruction of the temples and township of Parasuram.

But the Swami's anger against Siddy Satt was not to be consoled. 'You have ravaged sacred idols and killed men of religion', he cursed Siddy Satt, 'You will yourself be subjected to the same fate!'

After pronouncing this terrible curse, Brahmendra-swami announced his intention to leave the Konkan for good. The entreaties of Kanhoji Angrey and other disciples were of no avail.

The Swami knew that he had made a powerful enemy in Siddy Satt, who had suffered further humiliation by Siddy Rasool ordering him to return all the loot taken from Parasuram. Satt was not the type of man who would forgive and forget.

Neither was Brahmendra-swami.

He spent the rest of his life in urging his disciples to destroy the Siddy. For a whole year, he hammered at Kanhoji Angrey and even offered to change his mind about leaving the Konkan if only he could make the Konkan safe for the Hindus by uprooting the Muslim power of the Siddies. But Angrey was not willing to plunge into warfare with the Siddy, even to placate the Swami. After that, Brahmendra-swami left the Konkan and settled down in a place called Dhawadshi, near Satara, and there built up a religious establishment many times the size of Parasuram. His spiritual descendents still look after the temples and other religious buildings he left behind—not that many of the structures are still standing.

From Dhawadshi, he worked unrelentingly for the downfall of the Siddies, using his great influence, shamelessly urging his disciples with threats and curses, and in the end, he achieved his object, or very nearly achieved it. The war which came to be called the Elephant's War, did not begin until 1733, and it was not until 1736 that Siddy Satt was killed in battle with a thousand of his followers to make good the curse pronounced upon him by Brahmendra-swami. But by that time, both Kanhoji Angrey and the Siddy Rasool Yakoot Khan were dead.

In the year 1727, Shahu had sent a peremptory summons to Angrey to discuss the campaign against the Siddy, and Kanhoji went to Satara and dissuaded Shahu and Bajirao from getting involved in warfare in the Konkan. Kanhoji Angrey was now too seasoned a General to be pushed into war by appeals to his emotions. He convinced Shahu that the Maratha armies were too deeply involved above the ghats in their war with the Nizam of Hyderabad to divert the requisite number of troops to the war against the Siddy. He argued that the war in the Konkan would never remain localized, and that the Siddy would be almost certainly joined by the English. At this, Brahmendra-swami countered by offering to intervene with the English at Bombay to refrain from helping the Siddy; but in the end, Kanhoji Angrey's sound military logic won the day. At this meeting, which was held in Satara in October 1727, at the time of the Dassara festival, it was decided that some sort of amicable settlement should be sought with the Siddy, and to this end, Angrey offered to do all in his power.

In the year 1728, Kanhoji Angrey captured the English ship *Derby*, an East Indiaman. *Derby* is said to have been the richest prize he ever took. Almost fittingly she was the last prize-ship captured by Angrey.

At the meeting in Satara, in addition to holding out against going to war with the Siddy, Angrey had shown open disapproval of the incessant warfare above the ghats. But he knew that although he had won the day, as soon as his back was turned, Brahmendra-swami would undo all that he had done to save the Konkan from war. His forthright criticism could not have found favour either with Shahu or Bajirao, and Angrey knew that the Swami would win them over to his views sooner or later.

It was sooner than he thought. Almost as soon as he returned to Colaba, he received another summons from Shahu to visit Satara for the sole purpose of discussing the steps to be taken against the Siddy. All throughout the year and in the early part of 1729, he received several invitations, each more pressing than the last, but he kept puiting them off on one excuse or the other. From the spring of 1729, it was no longer necessary for him to find excuses; he was taken ill.

He died on 4 July, in the year 1729, resisting until the last the incessant demands from Shahu and Brahmendra-swami to attack the Siddy. But he must have felt it in his bones that he had lost, that war could no longer be avoided. His last thoughts must have been that he was leaving for his son Sekhoji the legacy of an almost ready-made war.

For he was aware that after him, Shahu would appoint Sekhoji as the Maratha *Surkhail* and the *Wazarat Ma-aab* of the Konkan, and he was equally certain that at the time of the appointment Shahu would demand a promise from his new *Surkhail*, that he would immediately begin operations against the Siddy.

Knowing his sons, he was equally sure that Sekhoji would wholeheartedly give the necessary promise. Oddly enough, the thought must have gladdened his heart in its last moments.

About the Author

Manohar Malgonkar (1913-2010) was an eminent post-Independence writer whom R.K. Narayan once referred to as his 'favourite Indian novelist in English'. He was hailed as 'one of India's most exuberant storytellers' in an article published by *The New York Times* in 1965. Born near Belgaum, Malgonkar was the grandson of the prime minister of a former princely state of Dewas. He served in the army during World War II, was a big-game hunter, a farmer, a mine owner and an adventurer. Later, he started working as a journalist and thereafter took to book writing. His works are as diverse as his personal life and have a blend of history, romance and military life. Some of his major works include *The Princes*, *A Bend in the Ganges* and *The Devil's Wind*. Many of his works have been translated into several European languages.